The aut..... .. . .c, charismatic and flamboyant individual who relishes world travel, sport, socialising, listening to an eclectic variety of music. He has an incredible zest for life. Writing is an invaluable forum, enabling him to exhibit his personality.

Dedications

My girlfriend Kiki, who initially motivated and inspired me. Without her influence this would not have been possible. My adorable late father Sinclair, for giving me powers of articulacy, expression, individuality and self belief. My beloved mum Cheryl for her wisdom, compassion and understanding, sister Maria, angelic and precious daughter Adriana, nana Joan, late grandparents Michael, Emile and Audrey! Without forgetting my important special friends Mike C-Man, Ashilito, Fluffy Donkey, Rocca Fella, Fro Boy Wez, Nasty Nick, Mushtafa and The Nodster Jonny Boy.

Julian Wilkes

HEAT ON THE STREET

AUSTIN MACAULEY
PUBLISHERS LTD.

A CIP catalogue record for this title is available from the British Library.

ISBN 978 184963 908 8

www.austinmacauley.com

First Published (2015)
Austin Macauley Publishers Ltd.
25 Canada Square
Canary Wharf
London
E14 5LB

Printed and bound in Great Britain

Chapter 1

Daily Delight

The Heat on the street… It was fastly approaching sunrise. Steam dispersed from bathroom extraction fans, and the clink, clank, jingle, jangle of the bottles being placed in outside front door holders by the milk man, as he hummed and sang. The energising, fresh and nose tingling scent of freshly cut grass on the mounds outside garden walls and gates, curtains being opened by people ready to start their early morning wake up routine as the hot sunshine beamed down on the dry stationery car packed boulevard streets. As the light summer breeze gently blew the finely refined statuesque rows of solid oak trees, there was suddenly a bang. It was only Felix engaging in yet another cat fight with the local terrorising enemy, the proud, arrogant and antagonising Petra, the elegant Persian neighbouring pedigree. She hissed angrily at Felix. *Sssssssssssssss, miaaooooooow*, as she'd audaciously entered foreign soil, a hint to say, *I'm the Lady of the Manor around here*! Felix hissed back, let out a huge moan and strategically and meticulously paced towards Petra. This being his masculine demonstration that no cat, dog, hedgehog or human, without consent was gonna dare trespass on his territory at 33 Mysterious Street in Honeyville! The bang was the sound of Petra clumsily knocking off the unevenly fitted aluminium rugged old bin lid as she propelled herself in a not so swift and elegant manoevre, attempting to dive onto Felix. This noise awoke Jammin' Boy.

'Lord boy, what a g'waan down dere? Dem freakin' cats again. I tell Felix time n time again, leave dat pussy alone, becauuuse, she's damn trouble, like most o dem women. She reels im in, hisses n den spits im out! Better get a move on, don't wanna be late for di second day runnin'!' Jammin' Boy bleated out in his exotic Caribbean hypnotising lilt.

He pulled the quilt off him, stretched like a wild tiger waking up in the jungle and roared out,

'Yeah man, let's go get em, di day is dere for di takin'!' He said, smiling infectiously and feeling oh so proud of himself.

Meanwhile, Felix had bizarrely and miraculously began to cajole Petra after their weekly engaging fight. It was all part of their love hate relationship. So laughable, considering, they'd regularly be hissing, yelling and howling at each other as if detest, resentment and disgust were teetering on the brink of their cat lips. Amazingly they began to frolic around on the dry uneven small pebbled front of house area, licking each other, nibbling, biting and wrestling as if they were competing in a televised Sky WWF tournament.

Jammin' Boy was enjoying a warm jet spray shower, lathering his athletically toned body with Mango Foamburst, while singing, 'Buffalo Soldier, in the heart of America, stolen from Africa, to the heart of the Caribbean. I'm livin' di life of an afro don, enjoyin' every damn day, especially even more, when di Mr Yellow Man shines down so brightly... Oooooooo... I love to feel di heat o dat sunshine ray!'

As usual he wore his swimming cap to protect his large mass of afro hair from the water spray, as it wasn't due a wash, shampoo, condition and blow dry until the weekend. He loofered the hard to reach areas of his back, scrubbed his neck as if he'd been duped and pranked by someone throwing itching powder down his t-shirt. This was his ceremonious cleansing ritual.

'Right bwoy, me betta get a move on, otherwise John (Head of Year) won't be too appy bout me strollin' in late again. Come on, step on it, its time to roll.' He turned off the shower, removed his cap, opened the shower door, picked up his warm fluffy turquoise towel and began to pat himself dry. Bbbbbbbbrrrrrr Bbbbbrrrrrrrr... 'OK, I'm gonna turn you off,' he said, chatting to his iPhone alarm clock.

It was now approaching 7.30 am and Jammin' Boy had to be at work for 8.30 at the local High School, Oatmill. After drying himself and checking his striking appearance in the mirror, he picked up his electric toothbrush, clipped the cap of the Arm and Hammer toothpaste and placed the usual pea sized amount on to his brush. The vibration started, the epitome of a ladies pleasurable Rampant Rabbit, fast circular motions of the brush head, frantically cleaning the molars, incisors, pre-molars and yes of course, Jammin' Boys wisdom. The pristine white teeth, of this well educated, articulate young twenty nine year old man from St. Christopher, known commonly as St. Kitts. A tiny, beautiful, luscious green and mountainous island a few hundred miles from the coast of Antigua in the heart of the Caribbean.

JB finished brushing his teeth and self grooming, smearing cocoa butter on his exotic milk chocolate radiant skin, ensuring he massaged his dry elephant elbow and knee skin, hollering out, 'Give me some skin brudder and turn dese big mammal skin creases to silk.' He let out a huge cry of laughter. He realised it was time to move faster than a hare and delve into his extensive sartorially elegant wardrobe to don a suit exuding panache and immeasurable couture. 'Boy, it's Tuesday mornin'... No man, am I crazy or what? Its Friday mornin', I tink todays definitely a sharp dark blue suit day. Fix up look sharp. Yeah man, dats di one I'm wearin'. Bumper claaart. Now....' he let out a huge sigh. 'Which tie do I go for? Di shockin' pink, di ivory white, di deep blue or dat sterlin' silver sleek number? So many decisions man! Right, dats it, forget all dis crazy assed self fightin', it's da silver one, Yeah man!'

On went a fresh scented newly washed pair of white CKs, a figure hugging vest top that accentuated his athletically honed and sculptured muscular contours. A simple pair of plain black cotton socks. One of his many white shirts, finished off with diamond cuff links, the silver tie, elegantly secured Windsor style, his favourite heir loom passed down by his late father, Sugar! He pulled out a belt from his never ending belt rack, a very chic brown snake skin, sprayed a few projectile pulses of eau de toilette, his adorable favourite Issey Mayake, checked his afro in the bedroom mirror, smiled contently and then made his way downstairs. He put on his sharp and smooth brown slip ons and unlocked the door before opening it.

'Feeeeelix, Feeeeelix! Lord, dere you are. Sort ya tail out and relax cat. You been fightin' again wi dat Persian Princess?!

'Miaaooooow.' Felix let out a happy as larry miaow, appearing ultra pleased with his morning antics. 'Lord, better dish you out some Whiskas n biscuits, wid a l'il agua. You can stay in now till I return ome from work. Behave yaself, and don't start scalin' dem curtains, ya not on a Gulf Tour o Duty.'

He picked up his man sack, a very cool rucksack, bought for him by his mum for Christmas 2009. He threw it over his shoulder and quickly set the burglar alarm. Then he dashed out of the door, closing it behind him, then locking it.

Chapter 2

School Bus Ride Journey

He skipped from the front door step, jogging to the front gate, blown open by the wind in the night. He made his way to the bus stop for the number seven. Like clockwork, it arrived right on time. 'Ride on Time, Because ya ride on time!' He sang a verse of one of his favourite 80s songs by Black Box.

Other passengers at the bus stop smiled, chuckled. Some gazed in amazement, some in dismay. One lady bleated, 'I wish my husband rode on time!'

Jammin' Boy replied, 'Feed im ginger, salmon, dress up n role play, den you'll see a difference. Di man needs foods dem good, to stimulate his wood!'

This led to cries of uncontrollable laughter as the passengers climbed on to the bus. Jammin' Boy showed his Metro Card and walked with a sophisticated gait to the back right hand seat, where he always preferred to sit. He plugged his iPhone speakers into his ears and selected his favourite compilation of RnB big hits. As usual, he swung from side to side, clicking his fingers every now and again and smacking his thighs in time to the music as if he was playing the drums. Fifty Cent's track Just a l'il Bit boomed out of the speakers. Realising it was a little loud, as usual he proceeded to turn it down a few notches, smiling as he did this.

The journey as usual was a pleasant one, taking roughly thirty five minutes for the seven mile journey, before stopping close to Oatmill High. Jammin' Boy was a little tired this morning after a late-ish night, getting to bed around 1am, the result of watching Hangover. As he drifted in and out of consciousness on the sofa, he had to rewind the DVD on several occasions, hence rolling into bed post Cinderella time. He rubbed his hands on the bus and thought in his head, 'Dis is warm boy, di energy o di engine sends goodness to mi bones n skin. I feel like a hot water bottle widowt di top!'

He saw C Man getting on the bus. 'Yes C Man, what appenin' brudder?'

'Yes, yes, JB, I'm all good thanks. Just gettin' ready to start plainin' mi wood. I've just got a six month contract at your school, doin' the joinery work.'

'Respect, I'm delighted for ya, after all di adversity you've been tru recently, wi di recession, it's di least you deserve... Yeah man, if I ad a drink I'd toast ya. I don't mean tro you under di grill, till ya crispy bred... Ha Haaaaaa!' Replied JB with vigour in his voice.

'I don't know how you can tolerate sittin' here at the back of the bus, it's boilin'!' retorted C Man.

'When it gets cold, it warm up mi body from ead to toe, n gives a l'il extra curl to mi gigantic fro.'

'Meeeeean... Yeah, you've got a point JB,' responded C Man.They caught up on the bus, rather inadvertently, as they hadn't spoken or seen each other for months, due to different circles of friends and hectic lifestyles. Jammin' Boy was overjoyed at seeing C Man and the feeling was mutual, as they'd been good friends for well over twenty five years. They laughed and joked as if they were doing a double act live on stage at the London Apollo Theatre or the more intimate 99 Club in London's Leicester Square.

The bus was full of school kids, white collar workers, unemployed travelling to get their giro cheques, college and university Students and a wide plethora of other workers. Eventually after the standard thirty five minute journey the number seven pulled up about half a mile from the school, where Jammin' Boy, C Man and other school pupils hopped off, ready to walk to their educational haven. The heavens began to open and down came a mini torrential downpour.

'No man, blast dat. C Man, you got a brolly to tro up, otherwise wi gonna be soakin' wet?'

'Yes, don't worry, you know me, like the Last Boy Scout, always prepared!'

Jammin' Boy started to sing in his sweet voice, 'It's rainin' men, halleluyah, it's rainin' women everywhere… An we're not gonna get absolutely soakin' weeeeeeeet.' He chuckled and grinned as he sang and improvised his own lyrics.

It was so funny, because they looked like a loving couple, C Man holding the umbrella with Jammin' Boy walking close by his side trying to avoid the splish n splash from the ever increasing puddles, a result of the water deluge from this passing storm.

'Damn…Mi suit trouser legs lettin' in water, mind dem puddles, Mike.' Mike was C Man's real name. ' I don't wanna be sittin' on di radiator all day teachin' di kids dem,' quivered JB.

'That's why you should always expect the unexpected and like me, prepare for every eventuality,' C Man pulled out the sun block and wide rimmed cricket hat he had bought during his year out Down Under in didgeridoo land, Australia.

'Gidday Mate, gi ding, gi donga, how ya doin' blue?' C Man said, impersonating Aussie dialect.

'Ha Haaaaaaa. You always know ow to make light of any situation, touch mi brudder… aye,' replied JB, laughing and touching knuckles with Mike.

This being a mark of respect, brotherhood, love and harmony the pair regularly displayed. They reached the school gates and parted company, 'Laters Mike, see ya real soon, prob tomorrow morn at same time!'

'Yeah, I hope so, have a great day and stay dry. In fact Jammin', unlikely, because today's Friday,' said Mike, sniggering to JB.

'True dat. Soon I ope den. I'll be warm like a sizzlin' steak in dem classrooms. You protect ya wood, n don't be droppin' any tools on it. You have to treasure it n keep it strong!' shouted JB.

Chapter 3

School Daze

It was Friday morning which excited JB, as he was ready to celebrate a friend's 30th birthday bash tomorrrow. JB only had four lessons of English to teach to Year Ten pupils, aged fourteen to fifteen, which would take him up to lunchtime, giving him a lesson free afternoon. This made it his favourite day of the week. He gracefully strolled in through the school main entrance, greeting fellow teachers as he made his way to the staff room. Just enough time for a quick herbal tea before class starts, he thought. 'Mornin' Jennifer, mornin' Jasper, mornin' Bethany, mornin' Tom, mornin' Jamie, in fact mornin' all would o been simpler, but den again, dat just aint me, peeps,' he laughed.

'Are you ready for the party weekend, JB?' said Bethany.

'Damn right, it's gonna be one hell of a fiesta n we're gonna celebrate in traditional 30th year style! Tom, has everything been sorted out, bar hire, festivities, food?'

'We're ready to roll, just waitin' for a few guys to get back to me, confirming that they're hookin' up,' replied Tom.

'Most importantly, di ones dat confirm dare presence are di most important ones, di rest o dem who don't confirm or make false promises, kick em into touch like Kevin Sinfield kickin' a 40/20 fa di Leeds Rhinos.'

The kettle boiled, while JB placed his camomile and spearmint tea bag and freshly sliced ginger into his big white mug with Cool Man artistically written on the side under a smiling Rasta Man. 'Would anyone else like a pot o tea?'

Everyone agreed, with Bethany saying, 'Ooooooo, JB, how can anyone decline the temptation of one of your trademark aromatic herbal teas, they're legendary.'

'You know dat,' he responded with aplomb.

He poured the hot water into each cup followed by a teaspoon full of honey.

'No honey for me thanks Jammin', as you know I'm as sweet as cotton candy,' responded Jennifer.

'I wouldn't know, coz I've never tasted ya,' answered JB. He thought, uuuuuum... What a pleasure that would be!

He knew that Jennifer had been single for a few months now and was looking for a bit of companionship. She was a statuesque, shapely and strikingly attractive brunette with long flowing hair. Her olive complexion hinted at Latina heritage. 'Right den, you never know Jen, one day I may be lucky. Have a great mornin' all, see you at lunch,' he said with a chuckle.

Ding-a-ling-a-ling, Ding-a-ling-a-ling sounded the school bell, indicating it was half past eight and time for register and the first lesson of the day. He picked up his tea and rucksack and walked down the corridor to classroom six.

When he opened the door, it creaked, reminiscent of a haunted house floor board in Halloween the movie.

'Sir, ya need to drink some more milk to provide calcium for ya bones, that ain't healthy!' bellowed Ama Retto.

'Ha Haaaaaa. Dats quite sharp for you. Why don't ya do me a jungle size favour n buy mi some? I'll make sure you pass dis mock exam. Favour for a favour,' joked JB.

'Oooooooooooh… Are you tryin' to bribe me Sir?'

'Just teasin' ya, but if you continue to write poetry n stories like you have recently, you'll fly tru it like Mary Poppins!' replied JB.

He started to sing, 'Just a spoonful of glucosamine helps di bones dem not frown!' Instead of a spoonful of sugar helps the medicine go down. JB as usual improvised his own lyrics, entertaining his captive audience in classroom six.

BAAAAAAANG!!

'Geeeeeez, Lord!' shrieked JB, as a deafening roll of thunder reverberated round the sky.

'Haaaaaaaaa Haaaaaaaaa Haaaaaaaaaa Haaaaaa!' A crescendo of laughter injected the room with immense warmth and energy, as the class were high fiving each other, knuckle touching and giggling uncontrollably as Sir (JB) almost fell off his chair at the front of the class. 'Let's settle down now n get ready for the day ahead, it's TGIF… It's time for that daily ritual, the register… Jonny Basnett!'

'Here.'
'Rebecca Button.'
'Here.'
'Jessica Stropsville.'
'Here.'
'Alessandro Romeo.'
'Here.'
'Aspen Colorado.'
'Here.'
'Sally Worsnop.'
'Here.'
'Jameel Taylor.'
'Sir.'
'Frankie Arpegio.'
'Sir.'
'Peaches Longley.'
'Here.'
'Leonardo Caprio.'
'Here.'
'Jemima Saltfish.'
'Sir.'

'Jack Fulton.' Followed by the customary shriek of laughter. 'Touch me, touch me… OUCH… Ya ice cold Jackie bwoy,' chuckled JB.

'Yes Sir. But today I'm scorchin', as mi Mum turned the freezer off. She's defrostin' it! laughed Jack.

'You should be a stand up Jack!' blurted out Peaches.

'Yeah ya right, I prefer to be sat down though!' responded Jack.

Followed by giggles from around the classroom. 'Order, Order... Court is about to start!' JB banged on the desk to restore control and sensibility in the classroom.

'After all that mornin' hilarity, we're gonna continue wi di stories about our most memorable experiences. I will speak in my proper English heritage tongue, not the one that my Mother taught me in the Caribbean. I do sincerely hope that this concisely spoken language is perfect for you all! Come on then, let's get to work, less chat and more cultured creativity. Liberate your minds, write with fluency and imagination, match and enjoy seeing what the ball point pen finds.' JB spoke in his exaggerated improvised English dialect.

'Come on then, chop chop chop, let's produce the satirical magic!' He smiled to himself. He enjoyed inspiring his faithful English class troops, as if they were about to go into battle with the enemy. Writing combat a pure educational pleasure, armoury in mind entwined with a fully loaded weapon, the pen about to explode with clinical potency, as endless thoughts crossed frantically through every child's grey matter. Take Aim... and... Click, Pull and... Fire... The ammunition was now in full flow. It was the epitome of an army strategically, meticulously and cunningly plotting their attack in a synchronised, slick and calculated manner. Fingers placed on lips, hair being swished from side to side, scratching of faces, contortions, grimaces, transfixed stares of displaying deep concentration, table tapping, pen shaking, arm stretching, torrential downpour outside World gazing, what a wondrous collaboration, enchantment, enterprise, great splendour, How amazing! Jammin' Boy had a chance now to contemplate his wardrobe for tomorrow evening's 30th birthday party for Tom. He started conjuring up various *combinations from his extensive collection. Hhhhhhhhmmmmm, he thought. Shall I go for a pristine, distinguished, sleek n chic virginal white n emulate Richard Gere in Officer and a Gentleman, or cultured, couture n mysterious black? So many decisions, but thankfully so much precious time. Whistle n Flute or smart casual fused with a cravat, vest n ankle cut boot? Oooooooo... I could do with a make-over, he surmised. Gok Wan, come n find me, transform me, revitalise me, where are you when I need you, supplyin' me wi the essential garment shabang.*

'Sir, How d'ya spell rhythmical?' asked Peaches.

'R H Y T H M I C A L!' said JB.

'Thanks.'

JB's mind started to wander, as the sensuous, harmonious prospect of dirty dancing proportions titillated his pre weekend excitable mind.

Hhhhhmmmmmmmmm... Jennifer dancing with elegance n grace, what a prospect!! He also needed to buy a gift for Tom and sort these clothes out. He smiled and had the James Brown classic, 'Get Up Off That Thing', circling round beneath the dense head of softly textured bouncy hair mayonnaise scented fro, but not the edible salad type.

There may be trouble ahead, let's face the music and dance*., get up off that thing...* JB hummed to himself, a collaboration of various tracks from many genres. 'Would anyone care for any assistance, or are we all fine, refine and dandy writing troops?'

'Yeah, OK, cool as a cucumber, running tings, rolling, swingin' in lyrical time, bossing it,' Came back a crescendo of responses, in other words a pleasant harmonious positive answer.

'Shall I take dat as an N.O. den peeps?' retorted JB in his too cool for school street twang.

'Weeeeell, Sir, Would you care to use me for a little more melodic musical accompaniment?' said Frankie.

'I think we'll leave the arpeggios to the music lesson with Mrs A Sharp... I feel good dunno dunno dunno uh!' replied JB with a smooth swagger as he stood up off his chair and glided down the classroom aisle, epitomising a half jerking robot and graceful swan.

He gazed out of the window, transfixed by the deluge of water running down the windowpanes, splashing on the external sills and rebounding in projectile fashion into the air. It was like someone below blowing the rain drops up through a straw. Booooooooom... Another deafening roll of huge bass drum reverberating thunder shook the school and the world outside, forcing shivers, shakes and jumping momentarily off seats of pupils in the classroom. JB thought to himself, Hhhhhmmmm... Is that an analogy for my heart palpitating profusely if I'm so fortunate to dance intimately and sensuously with Jennifer on Saturday night? *I'll have to contain my excitement at the prospect of this unadulterated gracious pleasure,*he thought.

He walked over to the window at the back of the classroom and propped himself up against the hot authentically styled radiator, staring out into the dark, gloomy and unendearing sky. He was willing the morning on so he could prepare a herbal tea and engage in delightful conversation at lunch with the very appealing Jennifer, his prey for the weekend. 'Like a vulture, snaring his prey with strategic and sinister style, dats the wild jungle culling culture, he moves, he circles, waits for dem lions to disappears, pounces and feasts on di carcas, yeah di man, he like a martyr!' he swung his shoulders side to side as he sung in a low tone, immersed in his own fantasy world.

'Sir, you've just inspired me there with those lyrics. Thank you, what a Godsend. My Safari Adventure has been uplifted and enhanced with that poetic song,' whispered Aspen.

'It's my pleasure captivating Master Colorado. I'm always contriving to assist and cultivate one's imagination!' he responded in his imitated aristocratically English heritage speak.

As the horrendous weather conditions had dampened the spirits of this Friday morning, the Headteacher had decided to cancel morning break, at the discretion of the pupils. An announcement was made over the Public Address System asking the pupils if they wanted to work through to lunch? Woeful sighs, boos, foot stamping and tuts reverberated around the class and no doubt throughout the entire school. The consensus was to work through to lunch. After the momentarily interruptions, the class soon settled down. The morning flew by and suddenly, twenty minutes to go peeps and then its lunchtime.

'Keep the ink flowin', reminiscent of Redgrave, Pinsent n crew Olympic rowin,' encouraged JB.

After three hours of Monsoon like weather, the storm gradually began to subside to the delight of most in the classroom. JB returned to his seat at the front of house after giving his legs a brief exercise, as his bottom had began to feel a l'il numb. Probably a result of cycling and rowing at the gym last night for a good hour. He returned his mind to contemplating his wardrobe for the birthday party. His phone began to vibrate in his pocket. He pulled it out and saw that it was one of his closest friends, Joe. Obviously being in class, it wasn't protocol and etiquette to answer, so he decided to respectfully leave it and then text, just to say he'd phone later in the day. Lifting his head, he turned to look out of the window, amazingly and quite astoundingly, the rain ceased, as if the Fairy Godmother from Sleeping Beauty had waved her magical wand. The sky in moments became a beautiful unpolluted sea blue with white clouds, the epitome of cotton wool being gently broken from the pack and providing a more alluring and attractive image. A spectrum of colour beautifully glimmered, this being apparent as a rainbow arced quite elegantly, as if it were an Olympic Gymnast preparing to perform a walk over from a back bend position. *I think I'll invite Joe to Saturday night's birthday bash, well at least if Tom will let me. I don't wanna cause any conflict encouragin' friends to gate crash like a rampant bull in an amphitheatre,* he thought to himself. *Right, I've decided… That's my couture n cuth outfit for the party. A pair of navy blue tailored trousers with a satin black pinstripe up the side, a conservative sky blue shirt, but that's where the similarity ends. I certainly ain't an Aristocratical Elitist voter of that bureaucratic, mercenary, callous n devious political party, on the contrary. For me, I'm wi da Monster Ravin' Loonies, Ha Haaaaaaa,'* he muttered to himself. Not being materialistic but being a real 21st century fashionista, he decided that he'd also wear the diamond cuff links, a precious sentimental eternal gift bought for him by his mum and late father Sugar. I'm gonna design my hair into big Phat clumps, so I look like a cabbage patch, dats di look. I tink too, I'll wear dat sleek silk tie dat Mum bought me last Christmas, di dark blue number. A stylish light blue cardigan n dem chic dark tan Cuban Heels. Yeah Man, dats di Booooomb!' Spoke JB a l'il too loudly. Instantaneously, several chuckles sounded around the classroom.

'Sir, have you got a date this weekend?' said Gemma.

'No, Miss Saltfish, but I'll be havin' a whale of a time celebratin' Mr Chrysler's 30th Birthday!' responded JB.

A rapturous applause transcended from the class, ripples of hand clapping entwined with a few wolf whistles.

'You're the Man.'

'Stand Up.'

'Sit Down.'

'Hoo Hoo Hoo Hoo.'

'Comedy Caper.'

'Yes Sir.'

'Uuuuuum… Sir's going out with a lady!' Were comments that were flying round the classrooms, from intrigued pupils wanting to invade JB's private life.

'Hush now please children. Come on, we've five minutes left, keep thinkin' n writin'. Those pens should still be producin' black stuff on to paper. Get up, stand Up, don't give up the fight!' replied JB, singing a famous Bob Marley song.

The wind started to blow a little and a plastic bag brushed against one of the windows, causing JB to raise his head and catch sight. He thought, 'That'll be me at the weekend, floatin' through the air like a bubble being blown by a Mother, showing her young child how to force washing up liquid and water through a tiny hand held hoop.'

Ding-a-ling Ding-a-ling Ding-a-ling, the school bell made a piercing shrill at exactly twelve pm to alert the kids it was lunchtime.

'OK, Finish ya last sentence, put ya pens away, be respectful, not too much noise and let's get ready for lunch. Well done everybody, we'll continue next week with these appetisin' stories. Go n enjoy ya dinner everyone,' he shouted, raising his voice above the droning noise of all the kids excitedly dashing around the school.

As soon as everyone had left the classroom, he made his way to the staff room, ready to enjoy his usual mouth-watering lunch. His stomach was empty and mouth dry after the standard three and a half hour morning. Most of the teachers converged, ready to tuck into their array of lunches.

'Anyone for a brew?' asked JB.

'Please.'

'No thanks.'

'A herbal for me.'

'Milky coffee please.'

'Yep, just tea and one sugar please.'

'Heeeell yeah. Make it strong, dark n flavoursome, how I like my men, please,' joked Jennifer.

'No probs all, I'll play Mother again shall I,' he said and laughed.

Wouch, Jennifer likes her men dark, strong n flavoursome... hhhhmmmm. Was that a flirtatious hint that I have a chance?? I'm just gonna play it ice cool, without givin' her any inclination, Ha Haaaaaaa, thought JB. 'When you say you like em dark, strong n flavoursome, d'ya prefer em short or tall, you know what I mean. What kinda mug?' he laughed.

'Weeeell, Jammin', As long as it's tasty, smells good and has an air of class, I'm happy!' said Jennifer.

'Interesting! I prefer her to be sweet scented, hot with a l'il hint of spice. The herbal tea I mean.' he chuckled.

They were constantly teasing and flirting as if they were two horses frolicking and chasing each other in a luscious gay meadow. The drinks were served and everyone occupied themselves, Surfing their smart phones, reading the newspaper, eating their lunches, slurping their drinks. They were amusing and entertaining themselves, savouring the hour break. JB had made himself and Tom a soothing, revitalising and detoxing Pukka Herbal Tea containing aniseed, liquorice root, fennel and cardamom. After five minutes of letting all the ingredients infuse, Tom tasted it.

'Geeeeez, no wonder you're always tired J, this must strengthen the blood in ya wood. I keep tellin' ya to share a few of ya ladies, as opposed to being greedy.' He pulled a face, becoming accustomed to the unconventional taste, as he was used to drinking typical English tea.

'On the contrary Tom. I'm rejuvenated, also, it's an illusion I have a harem of honeys, most of them are platonic,' responded JB.

'Platonic? How about the other six?!' laughed Tom.

'One for the weekend, one for the movies, one for dinner, one for the theatre, one as an agony aunt and the other's my mum!' answered JB.

'You joker! You disguise it so well,' replied Tom.

'Whaaaat! D'ya mean how I hide my penchant for Jennifer?' JB retorted.

'Penchant? Isn't that one of those things that sports captains exchange before international matches?' questioned Jennifer.

'That's a pendant! Thank God ya not a blondie, otherwise you'd be the brunt of many jokes. Thankfully ya blue rinse has saved you.' said Tom.

A cry of laughter lit up the staff room.

'Anyway, so are you confessing your love for me J?' asked Jennifer.

'Oh my darling, I am just making a fleeting impudent pass at thee!' JB spoke in a Thespian dialect.

'I thought Tom hinted that you must have strong blood in ya wood from all those detox herbal teas, so how can you be impudent?' said Jennifer.

Again another ripple of laughter electrified the room like a 25000 volt current!

'Hhhhmmmmmm. Thankfully ya not an English Teacher Jen. You stick to ya artistically alluring portraits, Dali-ing! I think you'll find, the word you're looking for is, IMPOTENCE! It's when a man's drill runs out of batteries and he needs some more!' bellowed Stuart.

'Blue pills! Thankfully I've never had to use em,' stated John.

'D'ya mind.' Jen bit into her hot dog, releasing brown sauce into the napkin, running between her fingers.

'Sorry Jen. No one asked you to eat hot dogs today. Speakin' of which... Oooooooooooooow,' howled John, emulating a dogs mating calling.

'Can we leave the smut until after the watershed please n interact in a more civilised n respectable manner. We're slightly underminin' the words decorum n etiquette, especially durin' eatin' times!' JB smiled and pretended to act in a serious fashion, then blurted out a laugh.

The humour and rapport was evident amongst a very closely knit group of teachers. Laughter, joy, sincerity, understanding and reciprocation in abundance. After a crescendo of noise pollution for at least ten minutes featuring howls, laughter, high fives, knuckle touches and cries of joy a sudden calm spread across the staff room. Everyone became engrossed in their smart phones, some checking their diaries while others who weren't so fortunate to have them, had to contend with flicking through the tabloid and broad sheet daily papers. Suddenly a spray of projectile saliva flew across the room. 'Uuuuuurgh, that's absolutely revolting! Can't you use a handkerchief John?' asked Jennifer, with a look of disgust and disdain on her face.

'Ha Haaaaaaaaaa. Stop panicking woman, that's my pet snake,' responded John.

'Aaaaaaaargh. What d'ya mean PET SNAKE,' said Jen.

'Exactly what I said. My pet snake. It's a Spitting Cobra!' answered John.

'Jen, don't look so petrified. Spitting Cobras are in safe sanctuaries, like Tropical World Complexes or in the jungle.' said JB.

'And some o them in Oatmill Highs staff room,' chuckled Tom.

'No way! John, Stop it, don't play ridiculously dangerous games. Leave me alone!' shouted Jen, feeling extremely vulnerable to that potent serpent.

'Relax, Jen. It's synthetic. I bought it from a joke store, it's totally harmless. You fill the pouch under its neck with a sticky gunge substance and then press the back of its head, then… Like that. Hey Presto!' John replied, re-assuring Jen.

'Uuuurgh! You're disgusting. Keep that dirty stinkin' slimy scaly snake away from me!' Jen spoke in a forthright manner.

'Which one d'ya mean Jen? Sssssssssssss… The one on display?' hissed John, reminiscent of the serpent.'

'Hhmmmmm… You aren't funny John, you repel me!' laughed Jen, teasing him.

'Well, at least I know I won't be your date Saturday night!' he responded, winking at JB.

'Anyone care for another drink?' asked JB.

'No thanks,' answered everyone in synchronisation, as if they were sets of identical twins.

JB was delighted as he had a lesson free afternoon. This gave him plenty of time to prepare for the weekend's exploits and organise his lesson plan for next week. So many things crossed his mind. Hoping Felix had managed to stay out of trouble after the escapade occurring this morning with Petra, a fusion of love and hate. His plans for this evening, should he stay in, should he go out for a meal with Joe and Ashillito.

Somewhere cultured, sophisticated and contemporary, or is it party time and a prelude venture into the city before Tom's 30th tomorrow? What exciting language challenges should he set for the pupils next week? Should he go to his Friday evening yoga class to alleviate any mental and physical fatigue, a result of endless hours of stimulating children's minds, or rest and recuperate after another exhausting yet enjoyable week at Oatmill?

'Wake up Jammin', It's time to start the afternoon final session.' said John assertively.

'Eh! Pardon? Oooooooooh! Hmmmmm, was I dozin', J?' replied JB in a tired dreamy manner.

'Yeeeeees Boy!' said John.

'Did you say something about an afternoon session?' answered JB.

'Correctamundo, it's time to get to class!' John responded.

'Lord, di way ya dressed, anyone wud tink u were playin' at di Crucible Teatre in di Snooker World Championships. Check out ya waist coat. Chiselled n sharp ya kno! Also, I'm alright, because, I don't ave any afternoon lessons. Dats what I call an away win on di Pools Coupon!' JB replied humorously.

Dat dream was nice boy. But now I've woken up, I can't remember what it was? Hmmmmmmm... Yeah man, dat was it. Summer holidays to somewhere Hot, Exotic wi Paradisical scenery, JB thought below his mass of sweet scented afro hair. 'Take care John n enjoy ya afternoon of double Maths you statistical guru!' JB said, wishing farewell.

'Yeah, take care too, enjoy ya free afternoon period and get yourself ready to party tomorrow night!' responded John.

'Don't worry bout a ting, I'm gonna relish my afternoon of pure freedom. I've got marking to catch up on. Take care too and let's live la vida loco manana!' replied JB.

John was the Head of Year and also a maths teacher.

Chapter 4

Afternoon Delight

The week thankfully was almost over, well, the working one at least. The closely knit group of teachers were relishing the enjoyable prospect of partying tomorrow night for Tom's 30th birthday shenanigans. He'd booked a cool, chic, couture and classy bar in the centre of Marlborough, a sizeable vibrant town on the outskirts of the city of Lillyford. Lillyford was a large metropolitan city in the north of England with just over a million population. Popular for its modern comercial shopping district, it was an epicentre of entertainment, hosting a plethora of amenities ranging from restaurants, theatres, cinema complexes, sport arenas, bars, clubs, galleries, Conservation Sanctuaries etc. JB decided to stay in the staff room, as it was the perfect retreat away from the noise of the classrooms and corridors of pupils dashing to and from their lessons.

'It's time to immerse miself in dese books, as I wanna leave on time today at three twenty pm,' he thought in his mind.

He was feeling extremely tired and decided to have another ten minutes of relaxation after lunch. He had all the poems to mark from last week. He'd promised to award a prize to the two best poems. The poem had to start with, 'The floral scented bouquet, was so elegant, with its silky soft petals, not at all risqué…'

JB's eyes began to slowly close, with a little flicker, reminiscent of a candles yellow flame blowing side to side, gently, as a light breeze drifted in through an open window. Bright flashing strobe lights, Hip Hop music supported with a heavy deep bass sound reverberating around the bar, people dancing, drinking an assortment of drinks, guys at the bar knocking back the shots, the fresh fragrant scent of eau de cologne and perfume, the strong smell of blown out candles placed on tables in intimate coves around the venue, people hugging, high fiving, kissing, laughing, while others are slumped on couches struggling to deal with chronic alcohol inebriation and suddenly bang…

JB woke up after a docile one legged pigeon collided with the staff room window. He checked his state of the art iPhone…

'No man! Where's the blasted time gone. I've been snoozin' for a good forty five minutes and its now one forty five pm. Booooy, I better get a move on wi dis marking! Poetry in motion!' He started to sing in a way to inspire and motivate him to begin looking through the poetic delights skillfully written by this morning's class, last week.

He had thirty books to browse through, wanting to at least get through ten before the end of day school bell sounded at three twenty pm.

He went to the staff toilet down the corridor to freshen himself up, as the extended cat nap had made him feel incredibly tired and lethargic. The toilets were in immaculate condition. Compliments to the cleaners for their immeasurable attention to common hygiene. Compared to the old school before it was demolished, the two year old, three-storey modern structure was regal. Self closing fire doors, new extinguishers, lifts, reliable central heating, smooth tiled floors, classrooms with soft textured carpet, high tech gymnasium, indoor tennis courts, 3G football pitches, a record club for break time use for the pupils along with many other modern conveniences. Jammin' Boy gave his face a good wash, after a brief toilet stop, a blow of the hand dryer after washing his hands, then returned to the staff room to begin his chores. To be honest, a chore was probably slightly inappropriate, as he loved his job, but his mind was set on weekend partying shenanigans. 'Right den, let's get to work n mark dis poetry,' he said aloud.

He picked up the first book and started to read, nodding his head, smiling and becoming engrossed in the wonders of the ink written architecture. He was flicking through books as if he were shovelling coal in a mine with confidence and ease, possessing super powered strength. Before, he even realised, six poems had been marked, every one different in style. Some with flair and flamboyance, others with fluidity, conciseness and conventionality. This made it even more pleasurable with the expansive enigmatic nature.

Ding-a-ling-aling... The piercing shrill of the hometime bell, it was 3.20 o'clock already. Where had the afternoon disappeared to?!

'Yeah Man, it's time to rock n roll, step foot on di floor, avoid dem pot hole n cruise for di bus wi style n soul,' he yelled out.

Magically, he'd managed to mark his target of ten books. 'Dats what I call hittin' di Jackpot man, boyakasha, I'm di dawg. Ha Haaaaaaaaaa,' he screeched and chuckled.

He was too tired to go to yoga class tonight, so he was going to go home, watch TV, relax and put his tired aching feet up.

Chapter 5

30th Birthday Morning

After a relatively early night by JB's expectations, he awoke with a loud lion style Rooooooar. He had a relaxing night watching one of his all time classic Box Office smashing movies, Pulp Fiction.

'Tonight Man, Jennifer di gal'll be no Pulp Fiction, she di real McCoy! I feel like a new revitalised man after that fabulous *zzzzz* stretch. Tonight I'm gonna be di don n king o di dance floor, runnin' tings widowt a doubt... Aye!' he said half chuckling.

'Weeeell, I suppose I might be di Prince in waitin', as its Tom's special milestone n his day... Respect boss,' stated JB.

He was so relieved that today wasn't a working one, after a really intense week had prevailed. JB was always cool, but the early mornings weren't the perfect tonic for him, as he was more of a nocturnal being, coming alive at night. Reminiscent of a fruit bat, but with 20/20 vision. That was quite an apt analogy for him, as his personality was rather infectious and charismatic with a fruitful coating. Wherever he went he had an uncanny knack of making friends. Last night after work, he returned home by bus and decided to buy some hot pepper sauce, milk, eggs and other essential provisions from the local supermarket, along with Tom's birthday card and present. He bought the 6th season of Entourage as it was his and Tom's favourite drama series. JB wasn't being frugal though, by expecting to share with Tom. That would've been extremely audacious. JB had the entire series to date anyway. After he reached home he had plenty of time to entertain Felix, who was appearing quite subdued, but after thirty minutes he quickly changed his mood and was wagging his tail, purring and fussing over JB, obviously immensely happy at being re-united with his King. Felix was fed his favourite Whiskas mix of tuna and sardines washed down with a bowl of fresh corporation pop, otherwise known as tap water. JB changed his clothes and relaxed into a pair of light jogging bottoms and vest top, as the weather was warmer now, thankfully with summer on the horizon. It was almost the Summer Solstice, which meant the longest day of the year. JB had enjoyed a palatable tea of a light chicken salad draped in balsamic vinegar dressing, followed by a freshly sliced juicy and lip lickingly scrumptious exotic mango. He rested for the night watching Pulp Fiction, while Felix slept on his chest nuzzling his face and nose under JB's chin. He had decided to climb the steps to his sacred sleeping haven at just after eleven o'clock, which was very unusual, as Cinderella time or just past midnight was his regular sleep time.

It was now June 18th 2010, Saturday morning, Tom's special day. It was nine thirty am, time for JB to get up, but Felix had other ideas, jumping on the bed and cuddling up to JB's right arm.

'OK den, I suppose ya tryin' to tell me I've earnt di right of avin' an extra alf an our sleep in after a hectic week?' he stated.

'Miiiiiiiiaaaaaooooooooooow,' yelped Felix in acknowledgement.

JB responded by stroking his silky smooth orange stripey coat. Felix was part of the Siamese breed, an Oriental Red with striking emerald green eyes. Outside the cars passed by and he could hear the occasional squeak of the breaks as vehicles slowed down and stopped at the side road junctions. He flicked the TV on and scrolled down to MTV Music, which was a purrrrrrrrrfect tonic to kick start his day, with a few uplifting hip hop tracks. He sent Joe a text just to confirm that he was going to hook up tonight. Even though Tom didn't really know Joe, he had said that it was OK for guests to bring one or two friends. There were several couples going, but as JB was an eligible bachelor he thought a little bro-mance was ideal for a Saturday night birthday shindig. He also checked the weather on his smart iPhone. Thankfully it was going to be a very warm twenty four degrees, which meant short sleeved t-shirt conditions. Eventually JB managed to drag himself out of bed, giving Felix a nudge, enabling him to move, as it appeared Felix was preparing to settle down to a long snooze long after JB had left the cosy sacred haven of comfort. JB opened the curtains to allow a stunningly powerful ray of light shine brightly through the window. This was comforting to Felix, forcing him to roll over onto his back, stretch out, rub his head on the quilt, squint his eyes, as the sun was so strong and roll over again, giving out a contented miaow.

JB had thrown on his jogging pants and t-shirt and trotted downstairs to prepare his breakfast. He opened all the curtains in the hallway, living room and kitchen and decided to make an omelette. His favourite Latvian special which had been recommended by an absolutely adorable and gorgeous woman who had brought in some traditional delicacies for Latvia Day. This was for the Historical Cultural Project that was being used in the National Curriculum to educate, diversify and unify pupils/students across the ethnic spectrum. All JB could remember was being mesmerised and dumbfounded by this unbelievably, infinitely beautiful woman who he passed in the corridor several weeks ago. She was one of the most beautiful women he had ever set sight on. Their eyes were transfixed on each other as if in slow motion, as if it was all a lucid dream. He remembers a twinkle in her eye as his jaw dropped and heart was palpitating as frantically as a World Record Breaking Bongo Drum attempt in thirty seconds. He asked the Home Economics Teacher who she was and Mrs Jerk said she was returning home to Riga that weekend. This chance meeting occurred several weeks ago and it still gave him goose bumps on his skin and sent a shiver down his spine. He thought he'd never get the chance to ask her out on a date. That was his only recent regret, to have been daring and trying to acquire her details. The consolation is that Mrs Jerk had given JB the recipe, hoping that this would somehow, with the art of spiritualism lure this Baltic Buxom Beauty back to the UK and Lillyford in the future. 'Baby, Baby, Baby, Please may I have ya number, Baby, Baby, Baby, Give me a chance to dance with you to Rumba!' he sang.

In went the oil, along with three eggs, semi skimmed milk, a dash of ground pepper, fresh red and yellow vegetable peppers, diced carrots, mushrooms, finely sliced bacon and a l'il helping of paprika. The pan sizzled, the aroma hypnotic, especially with the special addition of spicy paprika. JB's taste buds were beginning to water as he inhaled the herbs and spices sprinkled on top of this most wonderful kick start breakfast of the day. The cat flapped as Felix had also sprung into life, serenely glided down the staircase, giving a loud miaow as he came into the kitchen, before, brushing his body and tail against JB, then walked into the flap. He didn't want to go out, as he was distracted by the ingredients on the hob. 'Felix, go for a play outside and then come back in when brekkie's ready!' he advised.

'Pprrrrrrrrrr… Miaooooooooow. Ha-chuuuuuu,' Felix made a concoction of noises, ranging from prrrrr-ing to sneezing.

As he could smell the eggs and milk, nothing JB said could encourage and convince him to go out to play for ten minutes. Felix knew that breakfast was on the horizon and this was his ritual Saturday morning treat.

The mobile phone rings and vibrates, Don't Woooorry, about a thing, because every little thing is gonna be alright… JB picked up. 'Yeeeeah Man, what's appenin' Fluffy Donkey?' answered JB.

Fluffy Donkey was one of the names he used for his close friend Joe. They spoke about the plans for tonight. Joe agreed to get a lift over to JB's for six thirty pm, so they could have a few drinks before catching a taxi into Marlborough. 'Ash is coming over a little earlier, because he's staying tonight. If you wish, Fluffy one, you can also crash in the spare room?' promised JB.

Joe agreed to stay over too, so there was gonna be a house full. "Hhhhhhhhmmmm, possibly, but I don't tink we'll ave time to go for erbals earlier. Weeeeeell, unless we go shopping in Lillyford dis avo, say… 1ish?' asked JB.

Joe thought it would be a grand idea, so that was the arranged plan. JB agreed to pick up Joe from his place at one pm, which gave them plenty of time to buy any cool and couture garments for tonight's shindig. 'Better get back to mi brekkie den. Lord, I'm so ravenous man n need a mornin' belly full feed.'

He opened the door, just to let a little fresh air in and to clear the smoke that had developed as a result of the scrumptious Latvian omelette he had just made. The smell was jaw dropping and mouth dribblingly delicious. Felix was trying to jump up onto the worktop near the sink, but JB had to gently nudge him away. 'Relax cat, brekkie'll be served in a mo. Get down boy. Ya gonna enjoy dis special dish, courtesy o dat Latvian lovely who left di recipe at Oatmill. Boooooy, she was damn hot… bbbbbrrrrrrr!'

Felix responded as if in acknowledgement, 'Miiiiiiaaaaooooow!'

JB served the omelette with some freshly baked sweet smelling granary bread, with a small helping of traditional butter, to give it a creamier taste. They both enjoyed their breakfast, Felix licking and slurping every last drop and swilling it down with water, then gazing at JB, expecting to have a little more. 'You've ad ya portion. I don't wanna feed ya like a king, otherwise you'll ave a bloomin' midriff resemblin' a mini beach ball. Di rest is for me. I gotta long day n night, so need all mi energy resources n to absorb di drink!'

JB ate up every drop and then placed the cutlery and crockery in the dishwasher. He dashed upstairs as it was fastly approaching twelve pm and he had to drive over to pick up Joe in an hour. As his time keeping was distinctly terrible, for example, the time he arrived at Airport check in just as it was about to close, pre flying out to New York several years ago. Let's just say, he functioned on the Caribbean concept of time. When he gets there, everything begins, or so he liked to believe! He dashed upstairs to get himself cleaned and freshened up for the shopping expedition.

JB threw on a pair of light blue skinny jeans, a casual white long sleeved buttoned fronted top, a dark blue contemporary cardigan with a pair of white slip-on canvas plimsolls. Teeth brushed, flossed, afro groomed, milk chocolate skin replenished with Palmers cocoa butter, he was ready for City Centre going wild in the shopping aisles action. He decided to wear his stocking cap today, as he was gonna unleash the wild and crazy jungle style afro tonight. He only displayed it on special occasions, with it being Tom's 30th birthday bash, there was no excuse needed. He picked up his car keys to his beloved black Audi A3 1.8l Sports coupé, skipped down the stairs, not literally with a rope in hand, set the burglar alarm, picked up Felix and gave him a kiss goodbye, saying, 'Behave yourself boy! No mischief please, like climbin' curtains and destroyin' di leather sofa. Best behaviour please. May be a good idea to go out n spend time wid Petra!'

Beep Beep Beep... sounded the burglar alarm as it set itself. 'Right, I'm gone. 21 seconds to go, 21 seconds to go, did you see me on di video oh no, did you see me on di video oh no, aaaaaah, aaaaaaah, aaaaaaah. Yeah man, dats me, So Solid, like di rap group. Better get out before di alarm kicks in!'

For once Jammin' Boy was ahead of schedule? Surely not. Joe would probably pass out in amazement, as he had never been on time for the Fluffy Donkey. So as usual, if he had time to spare, he'd kill a little time. He decided to go the local supermarket to buy some liquor for tonight. Himself, Joe and Ash were gonna have a few drinks before heading into Marlborough to meet Tom and crew at the bar he'd hired called Starstruck. The bar was two floors, so Tom had hired the upstairs area, which was quite spacious, holding approximately three hundred and fifty people. It was a very trendy, cuth and popular venue, which was arguably the best in the town. Therefore, the intention was to stay there all night. Not quite dusk till dawn as it closed at three am, but depending on how busy it was, they occasionally gave it an hour extension! JB had reached Morrisons and started to gracefully parade down the aisles, looking for a few bottles of spirit. He plucked out a bottle of Appletons dark rum and Joe and Ash's favourite, Woods dark rum. He also decided to pick up a few munchies too. Doritos, Twiglets, an array of nuts, sparkling water, milk thistle tablets to minimise the risk of a head zumming hangover and a few dips. He went through the self service checkout, as it was now twelve forty pm and he was picking Joe up from home at 1pm. He needed some fuel, so went to the Petrol Station to juice up the car. As he was rushing, no surprise there then, he decided to pay at the pump after pouring in £30 worth. With the time fastly approaching one pm, JB sat back in his car, revved the engine, as a demonstration of bravado in his very sleek, classy and alluring sports edition. It was only a ten minute drive, but he wanted to get there on time for once, just to put a smile on Joe's face, to alleviate the usual head shaking, tutting and frowning reception he recieved from most of his family and friends. The traffic appeared to be very quiet for a Saturday. Probably with a lot of people deciding to head to the coast or the Yorkshire Dales, with the weather being a stunningly beautiful twenty five degrees. JB let out a sweet vocal sound, 'Suuuummer breeze, makes me feel fine, drivin' thru di streets in mi hard top motor, lookin' sweet n refine. Summer breeze, makes me feel cool, you know Lord above I am definitely a jewel. Feelin' Hot Hot Hot, Feelin' Hot Hot Hot, ole ole ole ole, ole ole ole ole, so me want rum bum rum bum! Yeah Bwoy, Its time to party, comin' at ch-ya, comin' at ch-ya wi style n grace, Mr Yellow Man, puttin' a big cheeky smiii-iiiiile upon mi face!' Jiving in his comfortable bucket style sports seat as he as usual, invented his own lyrics.

He arrived at Joe's at just turned five past one pm, rang the intercom system to his appartment... Joe answered, 'What time d'ya call this Hedgehog?'

'Jammin' time, let's hit it...' Following on in harmony, they both sang, Na na na na naaaah, na na na naaaaah, na na na na naaaaah, Here come di hotstepper, Murderer... and then comically, both let out a big chuckle telepathically. Ha Ha Haaaaaaaaa! Come in then!' Joe inviting JB in.

'D'ya still wanna go town, or shall we drive back to your place, have a l'il dinner and start the party early?' asked Joe.

'Let's get this party started on a Saturday day, everybody's waiting for us to arrive!' JB sang while simulating swinging a hammer in the Olympic Event.

'We can just go back to your place n get on it. We rarely drink, so let's enjoy this special treat!' persuaded Joe.

'OK den! Lord, u kno ow to twist mi arm wi dem shovel like ands o yours. If u started eatin' Ready Brek, u'd cause untold damage? Ha Haaaaaaa.'

'Listen Hedgehog, do you want to feel one o my big flyin' right hooks to ya lamb chops?!' responded Joe.

Joe locked up the apartment and then followed JB to his place. JB phoned Ash from his hands free set and endeavoured to encourage him to come over earlier. Ash was busy as per usual working on his Business Project, so declined. He compromised and agreed to come over for four pm instead. 'Don't forget ya hibiscus for Sunday morning Sabbath day drinks. We'll need to rehydrate n detox our body, mind n souls after no doubt copious amounts o drinkin' tonight,' reminded JB.

'Yeah, don't worry, I'll bring all the essential ingredients as long as you let me spoon you when we get back,' said Ash.

'You dutty bwoy. U tink me is a batty boy? I'll go top n tail n nibble ya toe nails,' laughed Jammin'.

'Deal!' chuckled Ash.

This was just their usual daft camp, flirtatious behaviour, even though they were both strictly heterosexual. They enjoyed teasing each other, as they were both alpha male metro-sexual specimens with a very trustworthy, treasured and special friendship. Joe decided to follow JB in his car, so he could drive home on Sunday afternoon, as opposed to JB having to drop him off. JB put the top of his Audi down, so he could cruise and pose back to his place. As he pulled away, he gestured to Joe with a click of the fingers, as he slid his Police shades onto his face. Joe, shook his head and smiled, as if to say, 'Typical, you think you're the untouchable Don Juan!'

The drive back to JB's was a little over five mins as they drove through the busy buoyant suburb of Fruitville. An aptly named district, as it was populated with ethnic diversity, with a strong Latin and Eastern European population. It was similar to Marlborough with a plethora of amenities, hosting a young business professional segment. JB and Joe's heads turned from side to side as if they were in the arena of a tennis Grand Slam Tournament. They were both admiring the array of beautiful scenery on show, dressing down to hot pants, micro mini-skirts, boob tubes, bikini tops, halter necks, tight figure hugging vest tops, heels etc. The boys' temperatures appeared to be hotter than the weather, searing with testosterone. It was inevitable the party was gonna be in full swing tonight at Starstruck, with many people revelling in the late spring/early summer weather.

They arrived at JB's for just after one thirty pm, reversing their cars into the driveway, JB electronically returning his Coupé top back into situ. JB unlocked the door and de-activated the burglar alarm, then pulled out a chair for the Fluffy one to sit on. Joe suggested they sit outside on the decking, enabling them to bask in the wondrous baking sunshine. JB agreed, asking Joe what he wanted to drink. He poured them both a sizeable Appletons Rum with Ginger Ale, dropping in a few cubes of crispy cold ice. Felix and Petra were both bathing on the patio savouring a relaxing siesta side by side. Felix sprawling out on his back, eyes closed with his tail wagging now and then. Petra resting leisurely on her side, eyes closed and nose twitching as a circling blue bottle fly was playing a game of Cat Attack. JB put some cool summer uplifting tunes on his iPhone, plugging it into his docking port. Annual Summer Anthems XI mixed by the Legendary Radio 1 DJ Pete Tong. Joe had put a pair of soft cotton shorts, khaki t-shirt and sandals on, as it was now the prelude to Tom's 30th birthday party night. 'Suddenly, life has new meaning to me-eeeeeeee, There's beauty up above, and things we never take notice o-ooooof, wake up, suddenly you're in love!' JB's phone rang out the calming, serene and beautiful harmonic lyrics and melody of Billy Ocean's classic. It was Ash, phoning to say that he'd be over earlier than expected, as he'd managed to get ahead of schedule and finish his work for the day. 'Woooooooooo-ah Yeah, Come on, brother. Ash is gonna be here in 30 mins. It's time for the three amigos to take control, aaaaye!' JB screamed out.

Ash was going to catch a cab over, when he'd finished preening himself, putting together his man bag full of toiletries, clothes and other essentials. The tunes started to pump up once again, as JB shouted out, 'Pump up di volume, puma up di volume, dis dis.'

Him and Joe started bouncing about from side to side, throwing their hands in the air and spinning around. All they needed now were a few honeys to entertain them. Joe said, 'We need a few waitresses now, to serve us on hand n foot!'

'Dat'd be a dream, but to be onest, they'd get in da way, dis is Bro-Mance avo!' JB spoke, smiling, rather pleased with himself.

Chapter 6

BBQ Loving and Living

Joe and JB were waiting intently for Ash's imminent arrival, he was the epitome of the track by the musical artist in the 80s, Black Box. He was always Ride on time. The spirits were flowing now as the afternoon sun shone high and brightly, infecting the boys with such vibrancy and positivity. 'Heeeeeeeello My Brothers, Uuuuuum Uuuuuuuum, Give me some sweet lovin'… Ya bloody love it, ya bloody love it! Saaaargent!' he gave the Fluffy One a large friendly hug.

'Alphaaaaaaaaaaaa. Jaaaaay Beeeee, what's happenin' my brother?!' Ash squeezing him tightly as if it was a cold winter's day.

'Yes, Yes, Yes Ashilito, you've arrived just in time, get some more drinks in for the boys. urry up, shake dat skinny tush, wiggle dem ips n trow di cubes in. Get me another Appletons n ginger beer please. Joe, U avin' di same?'

'Yes please Ashinaldo!' answered Joe.

Ash poured another round of drinks for the boys. He'd certainly made an effort, although, conversely, for him it was just traditional no effort attire. As he was so cool, he never made a concerted effort to impress, just exuded pure elegance entwined with panache. 'Yes brothers, these are drinks skilfully and expertly concocted by the indisputable Alpha. Exquisite claaaaarse in a tumbler glaaaaaarse! This rum will taste a l'il better than the average kind, because it's been prepared by moi, huuuuurgh!' he pronounced with aplomb.

Ash was wearing a rugged, slightly worn pair of boot cut navy blue jeans, brown leather Cuban heel boots. A linen naked fawn loose fitting shirt with a Burkina Faso necklace, a gift from his Granny. His hair had just been pulled around with his bare hands. No need to groom with a delicate touch, as it was the kind of texture that automatically sat in place. A similar effect to sculpturing putty, little effort needed. 'So JB, what's the news on the ladies front, any recent developments with Jennifer?' questioned Ash.

'Jenny's got the Wow X-factor, but a woman came into Oatmill several weeks ago, OMG! She was absolutely devastatin' boy. Believe me, when I say jaw droppin', dats exactly what I mean! W-OUCH. She's dis Latvian chef, oo came into di school to supply some Eastern European delicacies for Latvia Day. Mrs Jerk our Ed teacher ad a consultation wid er, n I was gutted, as I didn't av di chance to chat to er man. Once again, mi ed couldn't Adam n Eve it, she was drop dead! Di Ed sed she now return to Latvia, so I better try n unt er down like a Bounty Killer or M.I.5. covert operation… bbbbbbzzzzzzzzzzzzz!' JB was astounded and dumbfounded.

'Well brother, I hope you get the chance to be re-united. They'll have her name in the School Visitors book!'

'Yeah man, good thinkin', I'll check it.'

'Boys, you n ya hareem of honey's! I'm just usin' those datin' sights to capture mi dream soul mate,' stated Joe.

'If you wanna use dem, it aint a problem. In fact, it's an easy way to av a l'il fun, till dat sensational stunnin' beauty materialises in front o ya eye!' JB applauded.

'Why don't we… Get the barbie started on a Saturday day, that's a great idea to sizzle this way,' Joe suggested in a dulcet tone Pink-esque style.

'Yeah man, dats a super idea. Seein' as u suggested it, d'ya wanna ead to di local Tesco Express to get some succulent meat in?' proposed JB.

'Here!' taunted Ash.

'You two are so damn lazy!' jibed Fluffy Donkey.

'It's a new Millennium and the slave trade ended centuries ago, plus we're not livin' under President Boata apartheid rule in Jo'Berg!' responded JB.

Him and Ash high fived each other and then did their African War dance. 'Get ya ass into gear Fluffy!' demanded Ash.

That comment was received with a ripple of laughter. 'Ass! Yeah Man. Get ya big ass to di shop Donkey Man!' shouted JB.

'Eeeeeeeeee-aaaaaaaaaaaaaaaaaw!' mimicked Ash, sounded like a fractious four legged friend.

'Right. Sausages, Chicken Breasts, Legs and Burgers?' asked Joe.

'Just get to di shop n use ya vivid imagination man. Kick ya legs, shake a hoof n move boy. We're ungry n need some finger lickin' BBQ cuisine,' joked JB.

'Jammin', what did ya last slave die of?' said Joe.

'E's still alive makin' a big Ass outta imself. Eeeeeeeee-aaaaaaaw! Come on man, move it n go for a trot. Us boys are sick o your cheap vegetarian grass food! We want some tasty carcass!' laughed Jammin'.

Joe gave JB a look of disdain as if to say, don't you worry, I'm gonna get my own back! Ash and JB tucked into the Twiglets, Doritos and other snacks. JB threw some fire lighters onto the BBQ and lit it. 'Dats how scorchin' we're gonna b tonight. On proverbial fire n admirin' dem scorchin' honeys!'

'Uuuuuum Uuuuuum, You bloody love it, you bloody love it!' chuckled Ash while takin' a sip of the strong but yet tasty and sweet Rum and Ginger Ale.

JB and Ash relaxed in the garden on the decking, slightly elevated from the immaculately laid patio below, gazing at the horizon and the picturesque valley below. JB's house was perfectly located, as the rolling, undulating luscious green fields and River Frantic were about 200 feet below. Obviously not directly, but strategically placed, as if they'd been placed there on a jigsaw. The sky was a glorious sapphire blue, with whispy cotton wool like clouds slowly drifting along, as if they were relaxing, enjoying a lazy river at a water park. The sun shone powerfully, beaming down rays onto the garden, as if the boys were in the spotlight on TV. The boys were relishing the weekend pleasures of this stunning virtual summer day. Petra and Felix were still cooling out on the patio, when clink, clonk, clank… Their ears suddenly pricked up and they both flinched as Joe came walking along the drive with a few bags in his hands. 'Don't say I never do anything. and you JB, if you aren't careful, are gonna be on the recieving end of one of my Wurlitzers!'

'Why man, u gonna hit me wid a piano?' asked JB.

'Bbb, brrr-er, brrr, brrr-brrr, bbbrrr-er, bbb-er, bbb-er bbbb-er…!' responded JB and Ash in perfect harmony, taunting Joe.

'I think ya goin' piano loco Joe!' hinted Ash.

As they both suddenly jumped off their chairs and started to simulate playing a piano at rapid speed. 'OK, OK, Just relax boys. I meant a humdinger, not a Wurlitzer!' answered Joe.

'Dats a Major Key point Joe!' said JB.

'I'd just say it's only a minor Freudian slip. Slightly outta tune though!' followed Ash.

'Weeeeeell, is this outta tune?. Lovely juicy meat, pork sausages, beef burgers, chicken kebabs, a leafy salad, vinaigrette dressing and another bottle of liquor. Get ya teeth n jaws into those bad boys, fellas! It might keep you quiet for a while Jammin'!' remarked Joe.

Joe started unpacking the edible delicious essentials, then placed the meats on the BBQ, which was now increasing in temperature and crackling away. Ash had gone inside to prepare the soufflé salad, JB peeling the potatoes, ready to provide the salad with a creamier texture. Felix and Petra began to frolic around on the patio, wrestling each other. Typically, Felix started to antagonise her, biting her tail and side, followed by licking her. Terms of endearment in the animal kingdom, although Petra wasn't best pleased. She started hissing, opening her sharpened claws in the process, staring at Felix, encouraging him to leave her alone.

'You two, Stop irritatin' each other n show a l'il affection. You've been chillin' like two peas in a pod for di last hour, n now u start fightin' like angry wild cats? Relax now maaan!' JB endeavoured to display a bit of unity for the frustrated creatures.

They were getting restless because they could smell the sweet scented odour of the meat gently grilling on the BBQ. 'Lord, those sausages smell sweet. What flavour did ya buy Fluffy one?' asked Ash.

'For you my brother, as special concoction of aromatic apple and sage, basil and tomato and leek and herb. I don't think Jammin' deserves any of those, he should go n suck on another sausage!' laughed Joe.

'Yo, why di need for dat behaviour? I amt been tree months widowt sex like you, just eleven weeks n six days Bachelor Boy. U should run to di Monastery, grab old o ya broom handle n stick it where di sun don't shine!! Ha Haaaaaaaaa,' responded JB in fits of laughter.

He walked to the door, with potato peeler in hand, threw a slice of potato at Joe, who manager to duck, but still caught the flying vegetable on the side of the head. 'Justice Man. Tank ya, tank ya. Dere is a God! You better improve ya reflexes, you big giant statue, di Statue o Liberty as more movement dan you!'

JB, stuck his middle finger up at Joe and said, 'In fact, forget a trip to di Monastery, sit on dis!' he chuckled.

'D'ya want some big whopping sixteen stone Wurlitzer, oops I mean Humdinger like I promised?!' Joe responded, desperately trying not to laugh.

JB eventually peeled, sliced the potatoes and put them on a low heat with boiling water in a pan, sprinkling a l'il salt to add flavour. Ash conjured up the salad, lacing it with vinaigrette dressing, mixing sea salt croutons in with the spectrum of vegetable colour, with celery, beetroot, capers, olives with pimientos, feta cheese, cucumber, tomatoes and a leafy lettuce. It just needed the potatoes, which would be done in thirty five minutes. The boys sat down again, resuming where they left off, enjoying their delicious Rum with Ginger Ale. Their mini party was certainly now in full flow like a water fountain in a marble paved opulent city square.

JB glided over to the BBQ to check on the fastly browning meats. The aroma was absolutely divine, lingering and drifting in the gentle breeze, blowing over the inquisitive noses of the alpha male harem. He flicked them over to ensure they were darkening on all sides, also turning over the firelighters smouldering and glowing brightly. 'We're almost dere wi dis delicious, scrumptious n mouth-watering meat feast. Oo wants to christen it?!'

'What ya gonna do, bathe it in water n strike a cross on their meat foreheads?' joked Joe.

'Church doesn't open till seven, so maybe we should skip the ceremonious ritual n enjoy the delights, by simple saying grace before we eat!' Ash humoured.

'Who's Grace, Ashilito?'

'You joker. It's what you say before you eat, sayin' thanks n praise to the Lord for providing the Bovine n Swines... Oink Oink... Moooooo, n luscious organic vegetables supplied on our plates this avo!' emphasised Ash.

'Switch on Jammin'. Considerin' you have several Church going relatives, I'm surprised you haven't heard of Grace?' chuckled Fluffy one.

'Weeeeell, djaaaamn fool. If you'd av introduced me earlier, I may av ad di chance to meet er??! Get it?! Meat er. You know, spelt di edible savoury food way n not di double ee one, were ya acquainted for di first time!' joked JB.

'Boy, mi soul on fire, party people, feelin' HOT HOT HOT, All around me, party people feelin' HOT HOT HOT!'

'Olé, olé, olé, olé...' the three of them sang in harmony.

Joe went inside to check on the potatoes bubbling away in the pan on the large statuesque Aga stove. It was spitting like a rabid dog, wetting the surrounding neighbouring hob surfaces. If they were living siblings, I don't think they'd have been too happy by being subjected to hot potato water projectile saliva! He took them off the scorching hot hob, turned off the heat n pricked one to make sure they were done. It stuck to the knife for a few seconds and then nonchalantly slid off, back into the pan to float along side its family. The potatoes were then poured into a colander to drain the water off. Joe then threw them into the vinaigrette salad soufflé that Ash had skillfully and creatively prepared earlier. Tomatoes sculptured into stars, floral shaped cucumber etc. Certainly a very picturesque display of fine salad couture. He then proceeded to sprinkle rosemary and thyme over the potatoes, mixing them into the appetising salad, compliments to Ash.

'Saturdaaaay-aaaaaay, let's celebraa-aaaate, if we lived for Saturdaaaaaay-ay, we'd bring back all of those happy days, All around the World...!' JB's phone rung, playing a doctored tune sang by Madonna.

'Yes Lady, what's appenin'? Come round to my place if ya like, we're avin' a Barbie, Me, Joe n Ash, so ya more dan welcome to join us!'

JB shook his fist in the air and smiled like an excitable Cheshire cat. 'Di girls r comin' ere in forty five mins. Jennifer, Stacey, Annabelle and Jasmine. Wooooohoooooo, I tink its time to rock. Look no fuuuurtheeeeer! Booooy, di gentleman r gonna b entertained dis avo, n di temperatures just about to get even otter, because, dem ladies r crisp, like Thai Chilli Pringles!'

The three of them started high fiving, Excited at the mouthwatering prospect of savouring the juicy, flavoursome BBQ food along with the imminent arrival of the harem of four honeys, all teachers from Oatmill High. The sun was still shining brightly as three thirty pm approached. JB placed the potato salad, a champagne bucket of crunchy ice, a few bottles of wine, Appletons, Bacardi, Amaretto, cutlery, herbs, spices and an array of sauces on the table, which was was covered with a floral paper table cloth. Joe checked the sizzling meats and placed a dozen sausages in a glass caserole dish. The burgers and chicken vegetable kebabs weren't quite ready, so he left them, after turning them over and checking the consistency. The drinks were slowly sunk down the oral hatches, as the boys engaged in conversations ranging from world peace to agricultural farming during the Jethro Tull era of centuries past: comedy, serious and thought provoking discussions of an entertaining nature.

'We can't start a fire, because the wood won't burn, n the flame won't turn, we can't start a fire...!' Ash, spinning a few lyrics wanting the BBQ to hurry up, as he was extremely hungry. He thought he was Billy Joel for a moment.

'Yeah man. Come on, di boys are ravenous n in need of some sustenance o whole meaty goodness. In fact Fluffy, dats what you're lookin' for after almost a century in di Monastety! Ha Haaaaaaaa!'

'You're cruizin' for a big bruisin' hedgehog. Anybody would think you were the ultimate Don Juan God's gift?'

'Noooo man, I just av a gift. Di gift from God!' JB shrieked with laughter and high fived Ash.

'I'm gonna slap you right up!' answered Joe.

'Oooooooooooooooo... You aren't a Prodigy, so you can't smack me up, I aint ya bitch!'

'I think someone's feeling a l'il restless. Who needs a woman for cosy, intimate nights in!' responded Ash.

The sound of heels were clicking and clonking down the driveway. The boys were amazingly suddenly distracted at the prospect of seeing the Charlie's Angels arriving at JB's. As Joe and Ash hadn't seen the girls before, they looked at each other, smiled, knuckle touched with an inquisitive look in their eyes. Ash then said, 'Let's get the show on the road, Brothers n Sisters... Wooohooooooo!'

'Ouch!! OMG,' Joe sighing in virtual disbelief at the sight of four eye catching heavenly honeys.

He was finding it rather difficult to contain himself, while trying to remain as cool as the ice in the champagne bucket. The girls were certainly an attractive sight, providing more energy and cosmic colour to the afternoon BBQ proceedings.

Jennifer – twenty eight, a Spanish Teacher, was very boisterous, charismatic and the queen of cool, possessing a little Latin feistiness – Olive skinned, long flowing brunette hair, and a curvaceous size ten with well endowed assets. She was wearing a pair of brown leather four inch heels, a chic pair of brown denim shorts with a figure hugging white vest top, which caught the boys' attention, certainly capturing the imagination. The heels definitely enhanced her athletic figure making her as tall as JB at five foot eleven inches.

Annabelle - was a petite five foot four inches buxom blonde, very demure; decorous and dainty; size eight; twenty five year old history teacher. A very witty and entertaining young woman when she grew in confidence in good company, but initially very pensive and shy. A good description would be, a little fire cracker who would explode into an energetic personality when the appropriate moment arose. She was also tanned, a gene passed on from her Italian grandfather. She had very striking emerald green eyes. She was wearing a flowing yellow floral summer dress that certainly accentuated her figure. It was tapered off just above the knee. Her hair was long, but she'd tied it up with a very decorative angel brooch. Her nails were brightly painted with a shocking pink varnish, smoothly pedicured feet fitted with a pair of three inch toe pointing sunshine yellow shoes.

Stacey - was mixed race, dynamically extrovert with short bobbed black hair, just above shoulder length. She was one of the PE teachers who excelled at heptathlon, still competing to this day, with aspirations of competing at the World Championships in years to come. She was a young rookie at twenty one years of age, having recently graduated from University. She was in her final stages of her PGCE, hoping to be offered a permanent position at Oatmill. Her golden brown skin was rippling with toned muscle. She wore brown leather two inch shoes that were ornately decorated with a raised pattern of butterflies. She wore mint green hot pants, a light lilac short sleeved blouse of silk cotton texture, bright red lipstick, a soft ruby red blusher, mascara and golden hooped earrings that a baby dolphin could almost leap through.

Jasmine - was a thirty four year old vivacious and flirtatious redhead; prominent dark brown eyes; hair flowing half way down her back; legs to die for; a very statuesque figure with a pert B cup chest. She was head of the Art department and specialized in conceptual elements. Quite apt as she was evidently a concept of beauty, by no stretch of the imagination. Originally from Cheshire, the epitome of bubbly. If she was a Champagne, she'd be far too fizzy for the bottle… five foot nine inch woman of pure dynamite who knew what she wanted and would go out to get it, whether that being a new car, job, exclusive designer shoes, house or man, on the contrary to late musical RnB songstress Alliyah, she was forth (coming) without any backward step. A highly intellectual woman with a philosophical mantra, she was devoutly loyal to her principles. Her friends perceived her as the archetypal Good Time Girl. She wore a virtual belt skirt in beige, a halter neck pale orange top without a bra, which left very little to the imagination, an exhibitionist to the last. She adored the attention, although thankfully had the decency to wear a pair of knickers, well, a skimpy little G-string at that. Her outfit was complete with a petite orange bag with golden handle and bright orange five inch heels.

The boys couldn't take their eyes off her. She had a distinct resemblance to the actress Julianne Moore although with a darker complexion, as she worshipped the sun and tropical climbs. 'Man alive! Look what the cat dragged in!' bellowed JB.

'Are you taking the mickey Jammin?' responded Jasmine.

'I was just commenting on the pedigree feline, Felix, he's just brought a bird inside!'

'That'll be his date, JB,' joked Jennifer.

JB ran inside to find Felix, so he could prize the defenceless little sparrow and spare it its mercy. 'Come ere Boy!' he shouted, displeased that Felix had attacked the fragile little creature.

Thankfully, on being distracted by JB, whose jaws had loosened, allowing the tiny bird to fly from his grasp in pure panic. It'd rested on the top of the bedroom blinds in the spare room. JB climbed on the futon and rescued it cupping it in his hands, stroking it to re-assure, as its heart was beating faster than a drum roll. It let out a powerful chirp, as if to thank JB for his animal welfare heroics. Felix went to hide under the bed, as he expected a tirade of abuse from his owner. 'Don't worry Felix, you ide under dere boy. I'll summon ya later. Wait till I sink my teeth into ya!'

Really he had visions of enjoying an interlude with Jennifer. He came downstairs, through the kitchen and out on to the decking. 'Look at you Jammin'!'

'When a Hero comes along, with the strength to carry on, you gotta toss your fears aside, because you know you can survive!' The group had decided to sing a harmonious acapella rendition of Mariah Carey's Hero to applaud JB's rescuing skills.

'Come on, Stop it. Duty calls a l'il like Ace Ventura di Sleuth Pet Detective! To di rescuuuue… Here I am, want ya to know, l'il birdie in distress, if ya understand, I'm a rainbow too, I'm a rainbow too!' His own inimitable rendition of Bob Marley's 'I'm a Rainbow Too!'

Shrieks of laughter circulated the group. 'Right den peeps, elp yourselves to di beautiful sunshine and savoury delights o di breathtakin' BBQ Jammin' style!'

Jammin' decided to liven up proceedings to lift everyone furthermore so, into party spirits. He scrolled down his iTtunes play list and selected a House-tastic Pete Tong Essential Selection Anthem Album 2002 Classic. Joe was engrossed in conversation with Stacey and Jasmine, while Ash engaged and magnetised Annabelle with his wondrous charm. The drinks were flowing below the powerful sunshine, still radiantly glowing, while a gentle summer breeze was South Easterly blowing. The pre-party was in full flow with everyone thoroughly enjoying themselves. Laughs, jokes, ambient allure, food being savoured, drinks being consumed, conversation riveting from pastimes, dreams, hot topical to beyond the realms of reality, a proportion of it absurd. Jammin' was flirting subtly with Jennifer, whispering things in her ear, comments witty, smutty to sincere. She was at times laughing uncontrollably, otherwise smiling and smirking with a sparkling glint in her eyes. 'Is anyone ready for a game of twister or a game of kiss ya preferred Mister?' JB proposed.

'Just chill, enjoy the fabulous weather, we can get a lil closer on the dance floor tonight,' Jasmine joked, although with her reputation, a certain seriousness and ulterior motive in her voice.

'How about a game of Poker then?' asked Ash.

'Weeeeell, we could play Strip?' responded Jasmine in a sexy and husky tone.

'Let's leave that till after the watershed, and in fact, if JB invites us back for an After Party, let's wait and see what sensuous entrapments occur. It could be a sight for even the sorest eye?' retorted Joe.

It was certainly raising temperatures as the boys glanced at one another with a coded covert, literally under (the) cover (s) look. Joe was hoping to escape the clutches of the Monastery as he'd been celibate for several months. He was certainly enamoured by the asthetics of both Stacey and Jasmine, and would be too glad to cavort with one of those beauties. Ash was endeavouring to lure Annabelle out of her proverbial shell, reminiscent of a deep sea fisherman anticipating relishing the scrumptious meat from his prized catch. She was evidently consumed by his irreplaceable chivalrous silver tongued demeanour. She was virtually hanging on to his every word as if her lips were locking on to his in a sensually highly charged erotic clinch. He was always immaculately dressed with not a crease in sight or a mini dreadlock roughly and rebelliously out of place. His hair was emitting a hypnotising sweet scented fragrance. A product he would never reveal, as it was a secret special concoction that his Granny prepared in her home of Burkina Faso, a tiny country on the border of African Senegal. Annabelle's chest, just above the low plunging line of her yellow floral dress, was beginning to change to a pinky red, but not quite as vibrant as her nail varnish. 'Are you feeling a l'il flush and flustered Belle? Is it the warm glow of the sunshine or is Ash making ya tingle, because ya nippies are like bullets?' said Jasmine in her husky Cheshire accent. Everyone burst out laughing in a crescendo of noise.

'Ooooo yeah, I never even realised. Ya not jealous are ya, Mina?' answered Belle.

'Don't worry, we can share him!'

It appeared the pair of them were in awe of Ash. He was definitely humbled and excited at the mouth-watering prospect on the horizon. He chuckled and winked at JB. As the hours passed by, the drinks continued to flow along with the conversation entwined with the deliciously juicy and phenomenally flavoursome BBQ grilled food. It started to get a l'il cooler as a few white cotton woollen fluffy clouds slowly drifted in front of the early evening sun. Hands began stroking hair, fingers softly and flirtatiously being run along naked bare flesh, flickering of eye lashes, pouting of lips, conversation becoming a l'il more risqué. If it had been a TV show pre watershed, the plug would've been pulled as occasionally it was certainly of a more gratuitous nature, although, none of the group were phased and embarrassed by comments rather close to the proverbial bone! Thankfully it was exclusively an alfresco summer BBQ at JB's house, so ethics and morals were still high, however, thankfully no cameras were rolling, just a few eyeballs and they were predominantly the cat Petras as Felix continued to antagonise and irritate her at any possible opportunity. A couple of flashes were seen, they were the occasional unintentional displays of knickers or thongs, as the girls changed their positions in the chairs, or when they had to get up to either go to the toilet, suppress their food appetite, quench their alcohol drinking thirst, or probably on the contrary knowing Jasmine, as she was a serial flirt and Lady Godiva, on purpose! She was an extremely attractive redhead, always craving attention, bordering on the realms of exhibitionism. When she didn't have to conform with codes of conduct in the Educational System, she was a pure rebel and adored to parade her evident beauty whenever she could! Ash and Joe were certainly becoming rather hot at the sight of the four Charlie's Angels and hoping for a little action tonight, whether that was dirty dancing at the club called Starstruck, hired for Tom's birthday, a kiss or more. Who knows what the boys were going to indulge in? It was approaching six thirty pm, the original time JB had asked Joe to come to his place for, but as per usual the proceedings had been as predictable as a Football Pools Coupon accumulator. In otherwise, a rollercoaster experience, excitement personified.

'Well then boys and girls, how about we make a fish bowl, just to spice up the proceedings, entwined with a game of truth or dare?' suggested Jasmine.

I'd say, this was certainly a way of Jasmine being able to kick start her seductive mantra, on hypnotising Ash, Joe or JB with her alluring beauty. 'Yeah, fish bowl man! Or should I say woman too, Ooops, I mean women. Dats a great idea. But we need a l'il more liquor, as we only ave Appletons, Amaretto and Bacardi! Does anyone wanna ead to di local shop to buy some more contributions, because, we don't want slippery nipples yet, we can save dem till later Jaz,' laughed JB.

'What ya tryin' to say Jammin', are you a little shy of torpedoes?' asked Jasmine.

'No woman, I can already see Annabelle's nipples are ready for take off, so I don't wanna be taken out yet, by dem lethal weapons! My apologies Belle, I don't mean to embarrass ya, but dem tings pokin' tru ya top are certainly eye catchin'. OUCH, I just felt like I'd been poked by one?!' joked JB.

'You never know Jammin', tonight could be your lucky night?!' Annabelle chuckled.

'Come on people, let's leave the risqué talk till later on. We need more alcohol for this bizarre fish bowl. To be honest, I'd be a l'il concerned to be swimmin' in that contaminated water?! Do you want to dash to the shop Joe?' responded Stacey.

'Yeah, let's leave these fish bowl slurpers alone for five minutes. We need essential fish food!' answered Fluffy Donkey.

Chapter 7

Off Licence to Thrill

Joe and Stacey left and made their way to the local off licence to buy additional liquor to add to the rather mouth-watering fishbowl. To be honest, they could have used the spirits they already had at JB's, but decided that a few more flavours would enhance the quality of this popular holiday resort international drink. Stacey glided elegantly alongside Joe and was dwarfed by his gigantic six foot four inch sculptured frame. 'Are you a little cold Stace?'

'No, I'm all good, although it is coming across slightly cooler now the powerful yellow spot has disappeared behind the clouds. Would you care to put ya arm round me, just to warm me up a bit?' asked Stacey.

'I wondered when you were gonna ask?' Joe replied, smirking, as he was longing for her to ask the question, but never expected it.

'Don't get ya hopes up though, only a loose arm is what I need. Just to feel a powerful physical presence transmitting some body heat. I've heard on the proverbial grapevine, you've allegedly defected to the monastery?'

'I can't believe it! Hedgehog, by any chance at School?'

'No! Ash whispered it to me earlier on. Don't worry, I adore a man who has self respect and isn't one of those usual player types. Meeting girls for fun, sleepin' with em n then just desertin' them, as if they were a cheap piece of KFC chicken meat!' remarked Stacey.

'Weeeeell... I've been known to like my KFC, but I normally munch on a good piece of succulent medium rare steak, laced with an aromatic mushroom sauce. They don't call me the Average Joe for nothin'!' Laughingly he responded, giving Stacey a good squeeze.

She liked his banter. Her skin started to tingle as his large, but gentle hand lightly brushed against her shoulder. 'Ooooooooo... I just felt a cold shiver run all the way down mi spine.'

'It's probably the presence of the Fluffy Donkey, makin' you go all gooey!'

As he was considerably older than her and had a vast amount of life experience, he exuded immense confidence, however, being a very humble man, suppressed many of his resonating qualities. 'Don't flatter yaself. I know ya hot, but I'd only give you an average seven outta 10,' she blurted.

I'm quite impressed with that, as mi heads a six, feet are a 10 and mi inside leg...'

'Hmmmmmmm... Behave yaself, n don't get too carried away!'

'I was only gonna say forty five inches... But, speakin' of which, I'd give you one!' he coolly stated.

'Ha Ha Ha Haaaaaaaaaaaaaaa. I'll give you one for humour,' she responded trying ever so hard to control her laughter.

It was a laugh reminiscent of a hyena/wild coyote cry. It certainly made Joe laugh, anyway. 'I thought we could wait at least till later…' Joe said.

'Take it easy Fluffy one. I only meant one as in a kiss on the cheek. Bend over then. I think I'm gonna need a pair o step ladders.'

'Geeeez… Thank God for that, I thought you were gonna publicly violate, seduce and terrorise me in the middle o the street for a moment?'

'Don't be daft, you don't call me Jasmine. That girl's hungry like the wolf. I'd certainly be terrified if I played Little Red Riding Hood in her vicinity,' joked Stacey.

'Why? Surely her bark's worse than her bite?'

'No, believe me.'

'Go on…!' Joe encouraged Stacey to continue.

'She's like a Portuguese Man o War.'

'How does that work when she's a Cheshire Cat?' queried the Fluffy one.

'Just metaphorically speaking. She's a proverbial alpha female man eating lady. She knows what she wants n goes out to get it.'

'So I've got a chance then?' he asked.

'Possibly, but it depends on whether I get my hands on ya first?!' Stacey said flirtatiously.

'Would you catch me though? I know you're a Heptathlete, but I've heard sprinting's ya weakness?!' he teased laughing hysterically.

'I've always got a javelin n also sharp talons!'

'Uuuuuuum… I can feel that… OOOOOW!' he winced.

Stacey dug her nails into his side to demonstrate her dominance. She was definitely a feisty young woman, who was explicitly extrovert, never afraid to express herself. They eventually reached the nearby shop, after a five minute walk. So many choices. They decided to buy a bottle of Blue Curacao, Brandy, a bottle of Port for a more musky spicy flavour, three cartoons of assorted Fruit Juice, Lemonade and some more Ginger Ale. Joe threw several packets of Kettle Chips into the basket that Stacey was elegantly carrying. She swaggered and swayed, the epitome of a catwalk model, obviously traits she'd acquired through honing her athletics skills from a very young age. Posture was an essential trait, as it would definitely help to minimise the risk of injury, especially to the back. Athletes trained extremely rigorously, immersing all their vital energy resources, in order to reach their summit. Stacey still had visions of competing at European, World and Olympic level. She was currently ranked in the top five in England and was ranked second in her age group under twenty one level. She rarely drank, but as this was a special occasion, being Tom's 30th birthday shindig, she felt she deserved a celebratory treat.

Joe paid for the drinks, then the two of them walked back to JB's, laughing, joking and revelling in conversation as they moved.

Chapter 8

Hot Stuff

'What time d'ya call this?' asked Ash.

'Interesting! It's taking you all of twenty five mins, to go to a shop, only two mins walk away?' Jasmine inquisitively queried.

'Love is in the air, Everywhere you look around,' Bella sang while clicking her fingers and swaying on her chair.

'Maaaaan, you two boy. Leave ya fa five minutes n ya take an hour. I hope ya got er digits Donkey?' sniggered JB.

'Yeeeeeah. Thirty four, twenty three, thirty two.'

'Ha Haaaaaa. Dats quite funny fa you!' chuckled JB.

'Anyway peeps, most importantly we bought the liquor,' announced Stacey.

'And a few bags o crisps,' followed Joe.

'Come on then Jaz, here are the ingredients, get to work Man-eater!' teased Stacey.

'Easy. I aint no Portuguese Woman o War,' she responded, with a hint of humour in her voice.

'JB, have you got a blanket I could use?' asked Jennifer. It had now started to cool down, with a mass of extensive cloud cover over the sunshine.

'I could jus put me arms round ya n transfer some radiatin' energy lady?' he proposed.

He went inside to get a handful of blankets for the ladies, as they were all highlighting how cool it was becoming. Jaz was busy preparing the large concoction of fish bowl mix, shaking her ass as she poured and stirred. She'd pulled out a large glass bowl from JB's cupboard, which was certainly big enough to use at the fairground at one of those Hook-a-duck stalls. Although, you couldn't see a goldfish surviving five seconds in a mini ocean full of knockout alcohol. JB collected a handful of blankets from the airing cupboard and brought them downstairs. 'Ere you are peeps, just what the Love Doctor ordered. Warmth, energy and colour, to elp brighten up n kick start ya evenin'!'

He gave one each to the girls, as the guys were quite content with the temperature, even though it had cooled quite significantly. Jaz eventually magically and skilfully finished conjuring up the highly toxic fishbowl. She put enough alcohol in there to feed a dependant vagrant with a year's supply of liquor, or so it seemed. She used one and a half litres of strong alcohol, port, Appletons dark Rum, Blue Curacao, brandy, an exotic array of tropical fresh fruit juices, cranberry, ginger ale with a l'il hint of fresh citrus juices, lemon and lime. It exuded a sweet, yet super strong aroma and the group couldn't wait to dip their curly wurly straws into the alcoholic ocean. Everyone appeared to be thoroughly enjoying themselves, the company, the weather, the cuisine, albeit, probably better being known as quite simply, BBQ middle spreading junk, although the salad gave it a healthier element. The drink and entertainment were harmoniously uplifting, comparable to an 80 year old female high rolling Movie A-Lister post breast augmentation. As the frivolity becoming increasingly more evident, it was approaching time to leave for Starstruck to celebrate Tom's 30th birthday bash. 'Shall I phone a cab now, because times movin' on and we don't wanna get there close to Pumpkin Time?' asked Bella.

'Are you sure you wanna so soon Belle, especially when you n Ash seem to be cosier than a caterpillar cocooned in a chrysalis?!' tormented Jaz.

Ash decided to interrupt the conversation, as he thought before it became too gratuitous, especially when the hormones of Jaz were racing, probably faster than a Formula One Grand Prix car. 'I think it'd be a good idea to go shortly, because, we don't want you jumpin' in to bed with me before we've hit the Club do we?' Ash said, flirting ferociously.

'Weeeeeell, Adonis, you'd be a lucky man. I don't work that quickly, but then again, like a werewolf, I'm nocturnal so come alive at night. I can never control myself come twilight!' teased Jaz.

'Ha Haaaaaaaaa. Please don't take advantage of me then under the flashin' strobe lights of Starstruck. I don't wanna blow ya cover, just fumble under the duvet!' he remarked with vigour extreme outrageousness.

'I never plan my nights, I'm an educated confident female seductress, so impulsion controls my inner mind!' Flirted Jaz.

'I think ya even more than that Jaz. You're one hell of a woman. But of course, not a woman from hell! Just one saucy sexy Devil,' chuckled Jen.

Stacey nudged Annabelle, winked and whispered, 'Let's sing a few lyrics of Nelly Furtado's Man-eater, as it's the perfect track that best describes Jaz! Ready?'

'1, 2, 3… You're a Man-eater, make him work hard, make him spend hard, make him want all your love! Ha Ha Ha Ha Ha Ha Ha.' The two of them high fived, laughing uncontrollably.

'That's a l'il harsh ladies. Considerin' I prefer toy boys, you could hardly call me a Man Eater?! All the guys I've been involved with have been the right side of 27.' remarked Jaz.

'The right side? *No verdad porque mayoria chicos eran jóvenes de veintisiete!*' questioned Jen.

In Spanish, she said. '*It's not true, because most of the guys were younger than twenty seven.*'

'*Perdon. No entiendo,*' responded Jaz, demonstrating her basic Spanish language.

'Not bad Jaz. I said, most of the guys you've been with were younger than twenty seven. So that means, if my maths is correct, n that's not mi strong point, they were the left side of twenty seven n not the right? *Si or no?*' Jennifer replied.

'OK. You smart sexy ass, you're right, ooooooops, I mean left!'

'*Claro!*' Jen once again faded into her Spanish language.

This word meant clear in Spanish. They all slurped away through their curly wurly straws relishing the exotic delights of the glorious aquatic fish bowl. The BBQ food was also going down very smoothly and was incredibly tasty. A quite delicious, spicy and aromatic odour was seducing the nostrils of all party revellers in JB's garden. It was a most wonderful scented aphrodisiac that was hypnotising the minds of all, reminiscent of a Veuve Cliquot champagne with the finest caviar. Belle decided to phone the cab, twenty minutes later than first planned. There had been a large amount of digression, with conversations about seduction, surrounding predominantly Jasmine as she had been flirting rather outrageously with Ash. Also Stacey went to the shop accompanied by Fluffy Donkey, so these factors had slightly delayed their intent to get across to Lillyford to meet Tom and the birthday entourage. The fish bowl was nearly almost finished. It was obvious that the group were thoroughly enjoying the exotic, fruitful and incredibly strong alcoholic concoction, compliments to Jasmine for a most delicious and tasty delight. Belle eventually managed to call the local taxi company Lucky Star, organising for the group to be picked up at seven thirty pm. She asked for a mini bus, as there were seven in the entourage. The early eve was already in full swing, but surely the night was gonna be even better. It was a perfect prelude having a BBQ, just to get people in the mood for an exciting shindig of supreme shenanigans. 'Right all, I've booked a taxi for seven thirty, so we've got an hour left before it's proverbial show time,' confirmed Annabelle.

'Why, are we goin' to a boxin' event tonight Belle?' Tormented Stacey, fastening up the top button of her light lilac silk blouse, as she was certainly feeling the cool breeze whistling by.

'Well Stace, I'm sure there'll be a few knock out guys tonight, so just make sure you keep ya guard up! We don't want you bein' too drunk and throwin' the towel in before the night's out. You better pace yourself, because ya an athlete n not used to drinkin'!' warned Annabelle.

'Don't worry, I had a pint o milk to line mi stomach before I came n Jammin' kindly gave me a milk thistle tablet. I know I'm a young rookie, but I don't drink like a thirsty hippo. Thanks for ya sisterly love and concern tho. I'm sure if I'm strugglin', Big Joe can look after me n wrap me up in his muscular arms?' remarked Stacey giving a cheeky flirtatious nod, smile and wink in Fluffy Donkey's direction.

'You'll be in safe hands Stace. If I have enough strength, I may even throw you over my shoulder Fireman style!' said Joe, grinning like a Cheshire Cat.

'Oooooooo... Yes please! If I get too hot, would you hose me down?!' said Stacey.

'If we come back for an after party here, I can use JB's garden hose, but I promise I won't squirt it in ya eye!' said Fluffy.

'Oh My God! Watch the smut and sexual vulgarity please. Can't believe ya chattin' about the money shot already. You've been to the local shop together, shared a BBQ sausage and now ya makin' porn star threats?!' said Jaz, licking her lips in a teasing sensuous suggestive manner.

'Jaz! Why d'ya need to lower the tone? I only said I wanted hosin' down. It wasn't supposed to be a sexual innuendo! Only you could have those thoughts on the tips of ya lips.' Stacey replying with a tantalising look on her face.

'Please, Please, Please! Could we ave a l'il more order n respect in da place. I know di sun's disappeared behind di clouds, but deres no need to be chattin' as if ya rehearsin' a script for an adult movie! Surely di flavoursome meat cre should spice up proceedins!' piped up Jammin', Trying hard to contain his evident laughter.

'Come oooon JB. What d'ya expect? You have to prepare for every eventuality. If you didn't want this chat, you should o bought a space heater to provide us with artificial heat. I must admit tho, I luuuuuurve the real thing!' Jaz said, stroking her erect left nipple.

'Right. Let's have some more fish bowl. Take our minds into an Aquatic tropical adventurous underworld. It's all about what lies beneath. Leavin' a l'il to the imagination, if ya get mi drift Jaz?' Jennifer said, trying to divert the group's attention to a more respectful act.

'Oooooo… That sounds interestin' Jen!' replied Jaz, raising herself up from the chair, bending over to pick up her earing that had just fallen out.

Ash, Joe and JB got an eyeful, receiving a beautiful glimpse of Jasmine's fabulously shaped bottom and a skimpy brown G-string. The boys didn't know where to look, as they'd just seen a full moon underneath a picturesque Cheshire sunset strip. 'You aren't commando are ya Jaz?' asked Stacey.

'Noooooooo! I'd never display my ass-ets in public, apart from behind a bike shed or in a gazebo. My mum always taught me to be sophisticated n refined,' said Jaz.

'Are you being serious? We just saw the full moon, n if I'm not mistaken, a werewolf too!' Jen said, questioning Jazmine's decorum.

'I've got a shaven haven, so there's no chance o that!' confirmed Jaz.

The boys once again looked at each other, smirking, smiling and wondering whose lucky night it was going to be. At this rate, it appeared that Jasmine might not even get to the party in Marlborough. She was such a red hot blooded woman, who when she knew what she wanted, was never held back, reminiscent of a spoilt single child in a very privileged loving environment. She ALWAYS got what she wanted. Jammin' started singing a song by Starship, 'And we can build this dream together, standing strong forever, nothing's gonna stop us now…! Ooooooooo, All that I need is youuuuuuuuuuuuuuuuuuu!'

JB along with Ash and Joe ended with playing a vocal rendition of an electric guitar ensemble, gurning and jumping off their chairs, dancing around the decking.

'What are you boys doin'?! asked Jaz enquiringly.

'Don't worry Jaz, it's just a private joke with no pun intended,' laughed Joe.

'Are you teasin' n makin' fun outta me?!' she quizzed.

'Come on Jaz. Just a private joke. We occasionally like to go into song rendition mode when the mood takes us!' Joe smoothly responded, re-assuring Jasmine.

She was still rather unconvinced and said, 'Is it my tits, my ass, my horses hair mane, my legs, the way I speak?!'

'Absolutely not. You're an attractive female specimen, who's a sculptured Cheshire Pedigree,' Ash stated, while digesting a granary seeded bun with beef burger, salsa relish, Dijon mustard and leafy salad inside.

'Oooooooo…Thank you Ash. That's a wonderful compliment. Look at me I'm Sandra Dee, Lousy with virgini-teeeeeee, won't go to bed till I'm legally wed, look out, I'm Sandra Dee-eeeeeeeee!' Jasmine went into her own rendition to compete with the boys.

Seven ten was fastly approaching and the long awaited party for Tom was emerging on the horizon. There were a few pieces of BBQ food left, chicken kebabs, beef burgers and potato salad, but all the sizzling sausages had been devoured. JB started clearing crockery and cutlery up, placing it in the dishwasher. Jasmine, Belle and Jen kindly assisted with sweeping and mopping the decking. Joe, Ash and Stacey chatted away whilst drinking their liquor. The fishbowl had all but gone, so JB and Jen finished the remaining half a pint amount. It was like a visit to Noah's Ark, as everyone desperately needed the toilet to empty their virtually imploding bladders, a result of a considerable quantity of alcohol consumption. JB had a toilet downstairs too, which made it easier, as Jasmine and Stacey were finding it difficult to contain their urinary relief.

'At last, we're gonna be catchin' that cab n headin' to Marlborough. Thank the Lord n his Prodigal Son... JESUS!' Ash gasped, relieved to say the least, knuckle touching Fluffy Donkey.

'Yeah, it's about time. Just a l'il concerned temporarily Jasmine was gonna try to escort me upstairs to heaven sent passionate paradise?' Joe responded, with a sense of relief in his voice.

He was certainly enamoured by Jasmine, although he appeared to be more attracted to Stacey, as she was his preferred athletically sculptured aesthetic type. To be honest, Joe had been doing a lot of international jet-setting, as he was held in high esteem by the English Football Association, as he was a rapidly emerging precocious coaching talent. His current role was to evaluate philosophies and methodologies used in Central Europe, Latin America and Africa, with the intention of being able to export those traits, therefore, introducing them to the British Academy system. He hadn't had any time for interludes of a sensuous nature really, as his time had been saturated by this exciting mouth-watering project. Fundamentally, that's why JB was always taunting him, implying he'd been assigned to the Monastery. Joe wasn't really the archetypal monk, as he didn't have a fallow field on his scalp with a mass of harvested hair around the periphery. Effectively meaning he wasn't bald or didn't have a distinctive receding hair line. On the contrary, he had a refined, soft and silky mound of follicle, swept to the right epitomising the Special Agent 007 James Bond!

'Are we all just bout ready den? We need to ook up wid Tom n di crew n continue to live la vida loco!' JB asked, as it was seven twenty five pm.

La vida loco meant the crazy life in English, but it sounded so much more attractive in the Spanish language.

'We just need to go to the restroom to re-apply our make up!' Belle indicated to the guys, meaning they had to make themselves look pretty.

'You don't need to wear that much, you've all got rich golden sun tans, n as for you, Ash n Jennifer, ya lucky. Where did you buy yours from?' asked Joe.

'Mine came from the heart of Burkina Faso, Fluffy,' responded Ash in an artificial pompous voice.

'Mine was made in Valencia, Spain *amigo*!' quoted Jennifer rather proudly.

'I got mine from mi Momma's oven, she said I popped out at just di right time. She said tho, she was a l'il concerned when I was pulled out, because I got stuck in di door momentarily. Den, di juice n gunge came flowin' out! Mum ad to call di engineer, but tankfully di midwife came to di rescue! Ha Ha Ha Haaaaaaaaaaa,' joked JB.

The BBQ had virtually burnt itself out now, so one fire was certainly out, now the boys wondered who else would be flaming hot tonight.

'Miiiiiaaaaaaoooooow!' Felix suddenly appeared, being chased by Petra. They were friends once more after their usually earlier temperamental tantrum. JB ushered them both inside, following as he needed to go to the toilet too. Joe and Ash took the bottles of liquor and put them back in the drinks cabinet. Jasmine came downstairs, as Ash caught a bird's eye view up her beige skirt, which was impossible to miss as it displayed her modesty. He puffed his cheeks out and said,

'It seems even hotter in here, Wooooooow.'

'Open a window then, or use somethin' to cool yourself down with. Do you want to waft this hanky in front o ya face?' asked Jaz.

'I could do with a cold shower really, but it's too late, maybe tomorrow mornin'?!' he responded winking at Jasmine.

'Who knows, it could be ya lucky night?!' Jasmine flirting once more outrageously, inserting her finger into her mouth and sucking it suggestively.

'Come on peeps, the taxi's here. Get ya asses into gear, it's time to hit di road,' shouted Jammin'.

'Yeeeeeep, just puttin' on some lippy!' answered Annabelle.

'Won't be a min Jammin'. Just freshenin' myself up. Bit of perfume sprinkled n then I'm ready!' shouted Stacey.

Seven thirty had arrived. The afternoon had flown by. All the crazy, comical, cultured, captivating and cool shenanigans faded into a distant memory, or so they thought. The party was only just getting started.

Eventually everyone, after preening, cleaning, mirror screening, were ready to leave 33 Mysterious Street. JB went upstairs and closed the windows, blinds, curtains, doors and came downstairs to do the same. He put the light switches on timer, which was always a useful method, to give people in the outside world the impression that there was human life inside, besides feline. The group made their way down the driveway and climbed into the mini bus. JB programmed the burglar alarm, waited for the beeps and then left the house saying bye to Felix and Petra, who were now cosily snuggled up in the cat basket. He locked the door, walked to the minibus and jumped in.

Chapter 9

Tom's 30th Birthday Pre-Shindig Antics

The silver minibus left 33 Mysterious Street and headed to the bright buoyant shining lights of Marlborough town centre. The group were extremely excitable, as they'd consumed a large quantity of alcohol throughout the afternoon at Jammin' Boy's BBQ. They were all quite controlled though considering the amount they'd had. It's probably unlikely though towards the end of the night/early hours of the morning, that the party group would be compos mentis. No-one wanted to sit in the front of the taxi, however, Jasmine was trying to DJ from the back of the bus, bellowing instructions for the driver to change the station and put on some livelier music. The driver was playing some Bhangra musical beats, which most of the group were jiving and grooving to in their seats. 'Driiiiver! Can you change the station please, koz, this is doin' mi ed in?' requested Jasmine.

'Yes Yes, There's absolutely no problem wi that. I was just listening' n enjoying' it after dropping off the last passengers. Dis is some of India's finest music. But just for you young lady, I change it!' answered the driver in his Indian dialect.

'Jaz, I think we should have a vote, as most of us are likin' these tunes. It's nice for once to savour a l'il culture!' suggested Stacey.

'I think that's a perfectly legitimate solution. What's your name young lady? I like you already. Also, you have a beautiful exotic kinda skin!' he responded, smiling while looking through his rear view mirror.

'I'm Stacey. Ooooooooooo, thank you very much, that's so kind. I'm grateful for my milk chocolate skin, thanks to my Mum and Dad.'

'Where are you from Stacey?' he asked.

'I'm from the UK, but my Mum and Dad both come from the Caribbean.'

'Which islands are they from? I long to visit there, it's so exotic!' he answered with a soft and gentle manner.

'Ands up for a radio station change!' JB spoke, reminding the group of Stacey's suggestion.

'Just change it please Mr Taxi driver,' demanded Jasmine.

'Noooooooo Jaz. Stop being so stubborn n selfish, it ain't all about your world!' Annabelle emphasised.

'Leave it as it is!' asked Jammin'.

'Yep, agreed!' said Jennifer.

'Keep pumpin' out the bhangra driver. It's rockin' n a perfect tonic to get us even more in the mood,' requested Ash.

'I think that's a resounding NO Jaz. Right, perfect, leave it as it is please driver,' confirmed Joe.

'Yes. No problem. Your wishes are my command. I always aim to please my customers, as their needs come first. If you wanted to hire me for the day n sight see, I'd look after you. If you want RnB, Hip Hop n any of that bouncin' n jumpin' music, I provide. But if you want to fly abroad, I'm not a pilot, but can take you to the airport!' he chuckled.

'You're hilarious Mr Taxi man, my sides are splittin' in two. If I can't get my own way with my choice of music, you can stimulate me with ya comedy!' laughed Jasmine.

'Thank you!' The driver was extremely happy with Jasmine's glowing comments.

After the ten minute journey they arrived at their party stop, just outside Starstruck. The street was bubbling hot with vibrant human existence. With it being such a hot day, lots of people had been savouring the unusually pleasant, pleasurable and glorious British weather. It was as if some kind person, being or element had graciously transported the sunshine from Central Europe to the West and dropped it on the tiny English isle. 'Thanks Mr Taxi driver, you've been absolutely amazin'! Despite ya Bangin', or was it Bangalore musical taste, you were terrific! Can we request you personally next tiiiime?' commented Jasmine.

'Weeeell, young lady, you can call for me anytime you like. If I'm working, I'd be very grateful to assist and chauffeur you!' he answered in his lovely soft endearing Indian lilt.

'Yeah, please. Be our personal exclusive chauffeur!' re-emphasised Jaz.

'It could be a lucky experience for all parties!' Mr Taxi man replied.

'Before we go, just two questions. One how much do we owe ya and two, what's ya name?' asked Jasmine.

'Firstly, as you've been a fabulously entertaining group, it's a special Lucky Star discount of £10. Secondly, my name is the same as your friend. Joe. But reeeally in the Punjab region of my Indian home, its Jaleem,' he said.

'Jaleem, or Joe, Many thanks for being the best Mr Taxi driver I've ever had!' said Jennifer.

'I'd be careful wi that phrase Jen. You mean, ever had the pleasure of havin'!'

'Jaz, that's even worse. You would think you'd had an interlude with Jaleem!' joked Jennifer.

'Weeeell… Whatever, or however you say it. Jaleeeeeeeem… You're the best Taxi man in the whole world. For that, I wanna kiss ya!' said Jasmine.

Jasmine, climbed out of the mini bus and shuffled quickly to the driver's door, opened it, climbed up the step and planted a huge kiss on Jaleem's right cheek. Jaleem was so overwhelmed, even his dark brown smooth skinned face couldn't disguise the embarrassment.

'Thank you, thank you. I could marry you, ya lovely.' Jasmine stated, smiling like one of her namesake Cheshire Cats.

'There you go Jaleem. We'll give you a l'il bonus payment for such a thoroughly enjoyable journey. You're the maaaaaan Jaleem.' Ash thanked Jaleem, by paying him £15 for the addictive banter.

They all climbed out of the taxi, closed the doors and stepped on to the pavement, walking to the door of Starstruck. Jaleem pipped his horn, which sounded like a huge ferry cruise liner floating in to the docks of a resort, welcoming the waving soon to board excited tourists. He'd obviously had it customised, to be a little different, and of course unique, so everyone new Jaleem was around. He was a gentle five foot seven inch slender built man, with a shining smile on his face, lighting up the environment around him. He must have been in his late forties. He had silky slicked back and side swept hair, exuding immense style and panache. It looked freshly washed and groomed, neatly combed. His eau de toilette was a sweet scented fragrance, that stimulated the noses that came into contact. It had a light aquatic ocean allure. He drove away, giving the group a graceful royal wave, smiling and displaying perfectly shaped and gleaming pearly white teeth. This accentuated his glowing soft brown skin complexion.

Chapter 10

Starstuck, Flashlights and Starry Eyed

The doorman outside Starstruck were quite relaxed, engaging in pleasant conversations with party revellers. Marlborough was a very cool and ambient suburb, that thankfully wasn't known for too much public order, so the door staff never really had many unsavoury incidents to deal with. The queue was quite large already, as this was arguably the most popular bar/club on the strip. There were about fifteen bars in the vicinity, but this was by far the liveliest. It stayed open usually until at least four in the morning, occasionally till five, depending on how busy it was. Thankfully as Tom had reserved the upstairs for a private 30th birthday function, all those invited were on the guest list.

'That driver was lush. 'I've never known such a charmin' n wonderful gentleman. Maybe I should get a flight out to India! Shall we go girls?' asked Jasmine to the ladies.

'I'd love to go Jaz, but I'd probably get a belly as turbulent as a cyclone!' said Annabelle.

'Ooooooooooo… We should get it booked for the summer time. It's better than goin' to our usual European holiday resorts, like Napa, Magaluf, Kavos, Kos etc. I think it's about time we embarked on a l'il culture, a more refined n exotic location,' suggested Jennifer.

'Geeeeeez… that's a big word for you Jen. Embarked. Woof Woof! Could you bite off more than you could chew? I'd like to have a good gnaw at them Asian chaps!' teased Jasmine.

'Jaz, ya never restin' are ya. Always on the hunt for men of mystery! That driver, Jaleem, is almost old enough to be ya Father!' stated Jennifer.

'Men of mystery?? Don't you just mean men Jen? I'd say that Jaz ain't fussy, she's like a hyena, feastin' on scraps! Ooooooooooow-hoooooooo.' Stacey tormented Jaz, laughing uncontrollably while imitating a howling hyena cry.

'HYENA! Charmin' Stace. I'd describe miself as more of a golden eagle. I bide mi time, stalk mi prey, n then swoop n pounce with graceful serenity. I've got more class than one o those wild dogs!' emphasised Jasmine.

'Yeah, maybe I was being a bit too harsh with hyena. Sorry Jaz. Don't take it offensively!' replied Stacey.

'Don't worry Stace, I won't. Just remember it's a long night. Be on ya guard, because, I might just av to scavenge the man ya tryin' to make a hit on?! Ooooooooooooow-hoooooo. It's all about payback.' Jasmine was quite pleased with her riposte.

'Come on ladies, let's not fight, we've got too much partyin' to do,' Annabelle said, trying to restore some calm.

The girls were only teasing each other, as it was their usual banter. They had great camaraderie and were forever playing pranks and testing the proverbial waters. It wasn't too hot tonight, just luke warm. Inside no doubt was gonna be smoooooookin'!

'Anyway girls. I think a holiday to India's defo on the horizon, we'll just have to muzzle Jaz,' ssaid Annabelle joking with the group.

'Ooooooooo… That sounds so sexy and allurin' Belle. Nuzzlin' up to me?!'

'I said muzzle and not nuzzle Jaz.'

'Belle, just do it all to me. I may even start tippin' the velvet!'

'What does tippin' the velvet mean?!' Joe asked inquisitively.

Considering he was a very well educated and articulate man, it was quite surprising that he'd never heard the terminology.

'Fluuuuuuffy, come on. Get with it. It means, when another woman wants to drink from di furry cup, in other words, savour some juicylicious goodness!' Jammin' explained to Joe.

'W-OUCH! There's gonna be a party on someone's vegetable patch,' Joe answered rather startled.

'Isn't it organic, don't you think, a l'il organic…!' sang JB.

'Don't you mean orgasmic Jammin'?' asked Ash.

'Aaaaash, Brudder. Of course I do. It's just a play on words, hence, vegetable patch, meanin' di cuffs down below. Den again, sayin' dat, dependin' on di woman, it could be a fallow field. No grass down dere, bare like di Serengeti! Ha Haaaaaaaa,' Jammin' replied chuckling.

They eventually managed to walk through the door after the doormen had body searched them all and the V.I.P. Guest List girl had checked their names off. Starstruck was a two storey bar/club that held three hundred and fifty people. As they walked through the inward opening door, the music consumed the party as it reverberated around the entire place. The doors shook with the heavy bass sound. It had high rise ceilings, so the acoustic effect was accentuated even more. If it was an earthquake, it would have surpassed the World record Richter Scale score of 9.5. This occurred in the cities of Valdivia and Puerto Montt in 1960 and was famously known as the Great Chilean Earthquake. The final death toll was unknown, although it's rumoured to have been in excess of one thousand six hundred and fifty people, having such a decimating tragic effect.

As soon as they all passed through the entrance door, they all started to twist, move and shake their bodies to the beat, in their own inimitable way. The song that bellowed out was Notorious B.I.G.s Nasty Girl. Jammin' Boy slid his body to the left, to the right, spun around and as if by magic, Fluffy Donkey and Ash started bouncing back and forth as they were at the BBQ earlier. The atmosphere was absolutely electric with what appeared to be an ocean of people. The girls were magnetised by the boys, therefore, started to shake their booties, wiggle their waists and rock their heads from side to side. It was as if they'd had a choreographed dance routine for a concert performance, but consequently something had gone a little wrong, as they weren't synchronised. Not that this was a problem, because they all had rhythm, or at least thought they had.

'This is wicked peeps, let's live it up like there's no tomorrow!' shouted Jasmine.

As the music was so loud, no-one could hear themselves speak, let alone think. There was a chill-out room upstairs, so if people wanted to relax and chat, they could spend time in there, to allow themselves to breathe easily, take the weight off their feet and engage in stimulating, educating or drunken conversation.

'Yes Tommy, what's appenin'?! Appy Birthday to ya. Di big tree zero, yeah man. Give me a big squeeze my man!' shouted JB, as he caught sight of Tom busting a few moves at the top of the staircase.

Tom was ecstatic to see everyone from Oatmill High School, along with additional members of Jammin' Boy's entourage. 'Yeeeeeeeees JB, come on, let's party! Ooooooooow-hoooooooo!' Tom replied with a beaming smile upon his face.

They wrapped their arms around each other, squeezing tightly, conveying their sentiments of good friendship. Tom was holding a glass tumbler of jaeger bomb in his hand, which was a red bull with a Jägermeister shot dropped into the glass. He was wearing a pair of yellow Allstars Converse, skinny black jeans, a pale blue v-neck t-shirt with a yellow buttoned cardigan. He was looking slick, chic and exuding the refinest panache. His hair was styled with a left to right James bond sweep, not shaken or stirred. It was dark brown in colour. JB introduced Joe and Ash to Tom, as he'd never met them before. They exchanged handshakes and congratulated Tom on reaching thirty. The girls all individually gave Tom hugs and wished him a happy birthday. To the bar they all went, to ply themselves with even more alcohol. The day had been a revelation and hopefully the night would be the crowning glory. As there were seven people in JB's entourage, they decided to split into a four and three for drinks in rounds. Jammin' Boy, Ash, Fluffy Donkey and Jennifer were a quartet with JB pulling the strings, quite apt as they were in n music forum. Stacey, Jasmine and Annabelle were a trio, good friends, although, very much like sisters in harmony.

'What are we drinkin' peeps?' asked Jammin'.

'Ooooooo… I'll have a bottle of Modelo Negro please!' said Ash.

'Uuuuuuum… Make that two!' Fluffy Donkey confirmed.

'*Para mi, un ron con cerveza jengibre por favor*!' Jennifer charmed JB with her Spanish fluency.

'*Fabulosa. No problema amiga sensual*!' replied Jammin'.

He'd learnt a bit of Spanish at school many years ago. He could get by, although wanted to be fluent as he adored the language. Jennifer was impressed by his accent, pronunciation and sexy recital of the language of love. Jennifer gave him a flirtatious glance, following his confident response. Jammin' winked, nodded, then gave Jennifer a knuckle touch of appreciation. The queue for drinks was big, at least 3 deep. There were three bars upstairs, so Jammin' decided to move away from the main one and head to the quieter, more intimate one that was in the chill-out room. There were several large and extremely comfortable three, four and five seater sofas in there along with two double beds with cushions on. They weren't for sleeping on, just for relaxing. It was a popular room as nights progressed, catering for those who were desperate to take the weight off their feet, drunken heads and those that wanted to escape to a more intimate and relaxing haven. There weren't any quilts on the beds, just wholesome mattresses, surrounded in satin retardant sheets. Both beds were four poster, so gave a light regal mantra. JB maybe had visions of taking Jennifer in there later on, unless he had other plans. Maybe Fluffy Donkey had a few magical tricks up his sleeve, however, for sure he didn't have a rabbit in his hat, as that had been left at the monastery, the name Jammin' used for Joe's sacred apartment haven. It was certainly a distinct possibility that Ash would be escorting either Jasmine or Annabelle there, as it was obvious, both were rather keen on him. Jammin' ordered the drinks, also deciding to get shots in for the four of them. Tequila was his penchant, he just hoped the crew would be as inclined. Ash had gone into the chill-out room to see how JB was getting on, also wanting to give him a hand with the drinks.

'Could you ask Jen and Fluffy to come in ere please, because I've ordered some shots too?' said Jammin'.

'Who's gonna have a sore head in the morn?' Ash hinted.

'All of us. Tonight's a special night, so no excuses. We're gonna drink till we drop or dance till we stop or crackle till we pop!' laughed JB.

'Booooooy.....We're alphas, so we aren't gonna drink till we drop, we're just gonna party till we stop.' re-assured Ash.

Ash smiled, patting Jammin' on the back, then left, making his way to call Jennifer and Joe into the chill-out room to knock back the Tequila Gold shots.

'JB, the man's a buffoon and crazy. He'll be on his back if he ain't careful?' Joe shouted out in a concerning manner.

'Ooooooo-hooooooo. I certainly like the sound of that. Uuuuuuum Uuuuuuuuum!' purred Jennifer in a rather sexual tone.

Jennifer, Fluffy Donkey and Ash walked into the chill-out room joining JB at the bar. 'Come on guys, I've got us a shot man. Put salt on ya and n get ready fa di finest Tequila Gold. Dere's lemon dere too, to give it a kick.'

'Jammin', ya crazy man. All the drinks we've polished off today, Appleton's n ginger beer, Jasmine's fish bowl n now these?' said Joe, rather bemused.

'Let's live it up, it's party time. Stop bein' so prudish, ya spoil sport!' bellowed Jammin'.

'Just the one then,' answered Joe.

'Ready?' asked Jammin'.

They all looked at one another smiling and high fived. 'Three... two... one... Goooo,' counted down Jammin'.

They all poured salt on the top of their hands, licked it, picked up the tequila shot and threw it down the hatch. Followed by frantically gnawing at a quarter piece of lemon to take away the potent strength of the Mexican spirit. 'Wooooooooooooooooo-hoooooooooooooo!' shouted out JB.

Jammin' then handed the Modelo Negros to Fluffy Donkey and Ash, a rum and ginger beer to Jennifer, picking up the remaining drink for himself, which was the same as Jennifer's. An Appletons with ginger beer.

They clinked and clonked their glasses against each other's, said cheers, then proceeded to drink. They left the chill-out room, which was gradually beginning to fill up with party revellers, all of which were V.I.P. guests invited out for Tom's birthday. After finding Tom, they stood on the balcony, overlooking the dance floor below, watching people dancing, kissing, hugging, jumping up and down, intrigued at their behaviour. Tom was in an effervescent mood, relishing his birthday delights. Upstairs held a hundred and seventy five people. Tom had invited a hundred and twenty, but did encourage people to bring a friend or partner. JB danced around with Fluffy Donkey and Jennifer, who inadvertently smacked his bottom in a visible display of cheeky chivalry. Jammin' smiled and responded by smacking her pert backside, then squeezed it with his left hand.

'Hhhhhhhhhmmmmm… Who has pert l'il cheeks den!' he whispered in her ear, craftily nibbling on her lobe as he withdrew his face.

A shiver vibrated all the way down her spine, forcing her body to shake from side to side. Her eyes closed momentarily, dreamily imagining what fun and frolics they might potentially get up to later on that evening. Her exotic tanned olive skin started to display tiny goose bumps, as if it were a raw chicken before it was going to be placed in the oven to slowly roast at two hundred and twenty degrees for two and a half hours. Her nipples also became torpedo erect as her nerve endings were the epitome of a rollercoaster, frantically swaying to the right, then suddenly to the left. It were as if they were dancing on the edge of her curvaceous C-cup mountains. Jennifer turned round to JB, swishing her long flowing brunette locks like a pedigree racehorse in the paddock, brushing them sexily against his face. JB was rather aroused by this display of sensuous attraction, but nonchalantly stepped back, playing it cool, then proceeding to talk to Tom. This tormented Jennifer, but made her even more wanton.

'Are you enjoyin' di birthday exploits den Tommy?' he asked.

'Yeah! It's been a fab day n night so far. We have so much partyin' to do. Let's get some more drinks in!' he suggested.

'I'll get you a birthday special!' JB promised, with a glint in his eye.

'Come on then, let's hit the bar.'

'We're better goin' to di chill-out room, because it's far quieter in dere.' proposed Jammin', having to speak loudly, as the music was reverberating around the place with the heavy bass sound.

It appeared that the speakers were going to explode like a semtex bomb, as they were vibrating quite violently. That was rather apt, Jammin' thought. He'd had a brain wave! TING… The light switch in his heavily thought provoked mind had signalled and shone like a thirty watt bulb. 'Marzipan man!' he cried out.

'JB, are you OK? I ain't a marzipan man, although as you know I do have a likin' for the colour yellow!' Tom replied.

'No man. I was just tinkin', marzipan. I've got a l'il secret surprise for ya! You stay ere n I'll be back before you can say boo tree undred times!' JB said.

Tom thought to himself purely out of curiosity. 'I wonder if I could say boo three hundred times before he gets back from the bar? To be honest, it's the last thing on my mind. OMG! Who? Damn! She's drop dead boy! OUCH!' His mouth drooled, his legs began to tremble and the hairs on the back of his neck stood up reminiscent of three meerkats peering out of their burrow at the sight of momma coming home with an evening feed.

Ironically, as Tom had had a fair bit to drink, he couldn't remember that it was actually Jasmine who was walking up the stairs towards him, with her pert B-cupped chest bouncing up and down as she approached him. She looked so different out of the confines of Oatmill High. He'd actually never seen her in all her glory. To his defence, she did look rather ravishing and the man-eater knew it herself.

'Hiya Tom, how ya doin'?' she asked.

'I'm great thanks. All the better for seein' you!' he responded, smiling from almost ear to ear.

Her orange halter neck top certainly accentuated her assets, as she was bra-less, but thankfully she had, out of decency and respect to the ogling masses, donned a skimpy little G-string, which left barely anything to one's vivid imagination. Her micro mini beige belt skirt fractionally covered her modesty. She absolutely adored the attention. An artiste was definitely her ideal profession, although judging by her attire, despite being almost summer, she could have been on the stage working as a Stripper! She was a respectable and respectful young woman, although loved to be risqué by exhibiting her alluring and attractive assets. She gave him a big hug, along with a continental kiss to each cheek.

'Jaaaaaaaz... I didn't recognise you. Wowzers! You look entirely different to how you are at school. When ya hair's tied up and ya teaching, you just blend in. Now ya dressin' down literally, it's a transformation. I almost thought it was a Film Star glidin' up the steps, attendin' the Golden Globes ceremony?' he said rather teasingly.

'So, ya tryin' to say, I'm average at school n just blend in to the background like a plain Jane?' she responded frowning.

'Noooo, weeeell... Noooo!'

'Spit it out then!'

'Spit what out?' answered Tom quite flustered.

'Ya words Tom, you aren't usually this overwhelmed! What's wrong, has the cat got ya tongue?' asked Jasmine.

'I aint gonna spit in public, especially on a carpeted floor. I'm, I'm... I'mmmmm...!'

'Come on then, I'm waitin'. Shall I choose ya words for ya?' Jasmine said forcefully.

She grabbed hold of his right hand and ran it down her thigh. Licking her lips in the process.

'Would you like a birthday treat?' she asked.

'Weeeeeeell... Before that, I was gonna say, I swallow. Oooops, I mean I swallowed what I had in my mouth. It was just a mint. I'd love a treat. Can I have a drink of my choice?'

'You can, but also, how about this!'

She bent over to re-adjust the strap on her shoe, exposing her deliciously shaped tanned bottom, also displaying her modest thong. Tom was totally astounded and didn't know where to look. He could see the moist patch on her thong along with the outline of her throbbing vaginal lips. He almost fainted, managing, as he stumbled to grab on to the balcony rail as he almost fell to the floor. Jasmine gave him a hand up after she'd fastened her shoe strap.

'Are you OK Tom? What happened?' asked Jasmine.

'I, I, I, I, Iiiiiii, just saw the total eclipse! I think I'm dreaming!' he answered in a rather woozy state of mind.

The effects of the alcohol and the ambience entwined with the panoramic sight of Jasmine's posterior. As Tom endeavoured to restore his sane mind, overcoming the incredible gift that Jasmine had kindly provided for him, he decided to head to the toilet for some light bladder relief, to also mop his brow and wash his face to cool himself down. His temperature had been raised to what would seem, scorching heat wave proportions of an impossible human one hundred degrees plus.

Chapter 11

Eyes Glowing, Drink Flowing

Meanwhile, Jammin' Boy had circulated the BBQ harem and managed to get five pounds from them, amounting to thirty five pounds. They decided after having a conflab, what delights to treat Tom to. Hopefully the additional celebratory drinks wouldn't tip him over the edge? Especially after he'd been bamboozled by the picturesque sight of Jasmine's bottom flashing escapade.

'Sex on the beach pitcher,' suggested Annabelle.

'Let's get him a bottle of Moet n a few shots wi the change!' remarked Fluffy Donkey.

'I reckon, a few jaeger bombs n a twenty five pound bar tab,' Stacey proposed.

'Let's jus get im drunk man. A few Courvoisiers, slippery nipples n pussy galore,' JB retorted.

'Hasn't he already had that when Jaz bent over a few minutes ago?' laughed Jen.

'Jen, I'm wearin' a thong, you can hardly see anythin'!' stated Jasmine.

'Hhhhhhhmmm... I thought I saw the black hole of Calcutta? If it wasn't that, it must av been the Sahara Desert, because it was bare, bronzed n a l'il sandy!' blurted out Jen.

'Charmin' Jen,' responded Jasmine.

'You should leave a l'il more to the imagination Jaz. In future get a room, or do some moonlightin' at one o the lapdancin' clubs in Lillyford?' Jen suggested.

'Weren't we supposed to be discussin' what drinks to buy for Tom?' Ash interjected.

'Yeeeeeah... You got that right Ash,' said Stacey.

After an amount of calm was restored, they thankfully managed to decide on the drinks. They opted for two double Courvoisiers with coke and ice, two jaeger bombs and a Starstruck cocktail special, which was a mass concoction of spirits, liqueurs and soft beverages. It contained blue curacao, grenadine, dark rum, vodka, Bacardi, amaretto, a dash of lemon and lime cordial, angostura with lemonade and banana smoothie, decorated with an umbrella and a slice of melon straddling the rim of the cocktail glass. Jammin' Boy decided it would be a sensible idea to get three pints of iced water too, as they didn't want Tom collapsing like a Grand National racehorse at Bechers Brook, bringing down his rider, whoever, that was going to be, if success prevailed. Ash and Fluffy Donkey gave JB a hand with the drinks, as they took them away from the bar after paying, taking them to Tom who was engaging in conversation with an eye catching brunette. Conversation wasn't the only action he was engaging in, as when they got closer, he was quite visibly engrossed in a game of tongue wrestling, in other words, kissing her like there was no tomorrow. To his defence, it was a good excuse for a partying celebration with it being his welcome to his thirty first year.

'Toooooom! Give ya tongue a rest and enjoy deze spiritual delights from di crew.' Jammin' Boy placing a hand on his shoulder, encouraging Tom to savour the mammoth drinking treats.

Tom introduced the brunette to JB and the group, 'This is Jade.'

'Hiii,' Jade acknowledged the group of Jammin' Boy, Fluffy Donkey, Ash, Jasmine and Jennifer.

They responded with their various Hi', Hello's, Y'alright etc. All the drinks were placed on a table close by where Tom's brother and other friends were sitting. Thankfully with the upstairs area exclusive party V.I.P. there was no way anyone else could get their hands on Tom's drinks, unless obviously he was struggling to finish them. Tom's brother Ethan was a little older, hopefully sensible and protective, making sure Tom was in safe hands, just in case he started swinging, swaying, leaning and dropping to the floor as the night progressed. This probably wouldn't be a trademark choreographed dance routine either, likely the result of more than slight inebriation. Tom thanked everyone for the kind gesture of buying drinks for him, knocked back the first jaeger bomb down the hatch saying, 'BOOM! There goes the first one. BOOM BOOM! One more. Two down, three to go!'

He put the empty glasses down, slamming them on the table, causing other empty glasses along with those full of alcohol to move. There was a mini alcoholic river flowing on and over the edge of the round table, as glasses wobbled, others leaned fractionally, held up by the level of liquid inside them and a few fell over. People sitting at that table, had to take evasive action as if they were avoiding bullets on a war torn battlefield. 'Tooooooom! Just calm down n take it easy boy! It's not a race!' shouted Ethan in an agitated, bemused manner.

'Woooh, Wooooh, Woooooh! OK bro, chill out man. Just enjoy the party,' responded Tom in a patronising manner.

'LISTEN, I'm not playin' games with ya. I could still drop you right here and now in front of ya friends n embarass ya!' emphasised Ethan quite angrily.

'Wooooh, Wooooh! Just calm down man. There's no need to start gettin' angry. Anyway, if ya gonna start gettin' confrontational, COME ON. I'LL DROP YOU! Those days are gone now. I'm not ya baby bro anymore!' Tom reacted irritated that his brother was making a scene at his special bash.

Tom walked over to Ethan, put his arm around him. Ethan pushed him off in a temperamental display of machoism. He then swung for Tom, but Tom just manager to avoid the punch to the side of his face, by somehow in a drunken manner ducking, like a cricketing opening batsman eluding a viciously rising bouncer from a fast bowler. Tom was really incensed by his brother's actions, which provoked a situation that could have been resolved quite easily. In one smooth movement, he punched Ethan to the stomach, causing him to wince and drop to his knees.

'That'll teach you. Why you gettin' so aggressive? It's my birthday party, I've spilt a few drinks accidentally, then you wanna start a sibling war? Why! Why! Why Ethe?' asked Tom.

Ethan managed to after twenty odd seconds rise to his feet and say,

'Bro, don't you dare belittle me again.'

'What's ya problem? Relax. Everyone's enjoyin' themselves apart from you,' stated Tom.

Ethan then unexpectedly swung at Tom again, this time with an open palm, slapping him hard across the right hand side of his cheek.

'THWACK.' The noise was loud enough to be heard, despite the music being quite deafening with the heavy bass sound. Jammin' Boy intervened and held Ethan back, wrestling with him as he was frantically trying to throw a few cheap shots at his brother.

'ETHAN! Enough's enough now, just cut it out! If you wanna box, hit di local gym boy!' recommended Jammin'.

'He shouldn't have slammed the glasses down on the table!' bellowed Ethan.

'I'm sorry to everyone. I've had a bit to drink man. Cut me some slack n stop wantin' to knock my head off!' responded Tom in a composed manner.

Stacey, Jasmine and Jennifer pulled Tom away, re-assuring him, reminding him why they were here. Jasmine gave Ethan a look of disgust.

'Ya pathetic Ethe! Can't you see what scene you've made, just over a few spilt drinks. Go outside n cool off. If I'd ave been Tom, I'd ave dropped ya there n then! Go n take a chill pill!' Jasmine advised.

'It's OK Tom. Go n wash ya face n cool down in the toilet. Ya OK luvvy!' said Jennifer.

His right cheek was red raw, as Ethan had given him a good old fashioned slap. Ethan had decided to go outside for a few minutes to calm his temper right down. Ash went to the bar to get a cloth to wipe down the table. Jammin' went with Tom to the toilet, to re-assure him. Tom was visibly upset, as he never expected to engage in crossfire with his brother, at least not at his Birthday party. Ethan had recently separated from his long-time girlfriend, so that was probably one of the fundamental reasons why he flew off the proverbial broom handle.

'Don't worry Tom. E's just a l'il worked up tonight. Mus be di effects o di relationship breakdown. Maybe e needs sum terapy or sumting?' Jammin' Boy suggested.

'He just needs to relax n open his heart more. He's always been so insular with his emotions! Probably ya right too, he needs to take up a martial art at the gym for stress release!' said Tom.

'It'd do im di world o good!' highlighted JB.

Peace was thankfully restored, Tom and JB returned to the group, resumed drinking their drinks, groovin' and movin' to the music and indulging in friendly banter. Jade wondered back across to Tom and planted a big kiss on his right cheek. 'OUCH! Be careful Jade. It's a l'il sore.'

'Sorry. Just wanted to give you some TLC,' she said smiling and whispering into his ear.

'It's fine. Many thanks for ya concern,' replied Tom, turning to face her, giving her a sensuous kiss to the lips.

Jade was dressed like a real true fashionista, a petite lady with a blonde mass of hair, sprayed with thick hold, styled to one side,with the other side shaven to a grade three length. It looked couture and chic. The shaven area was coloured dark brown, making her look a little like a human racoon. She wore white slip on pumps, tight figure hugging gold sparkling leggings, a white vest top with shiny sequins on the front spelling the words 'Dunk the Funk', an exclusive fashion label. Her left wrist was jangling with cream and silver coloured bangles of different shapes and sizes. Jade was one of Tom's casual dates. He'd known her for a while, their feelings for one another were definitely mutual. She was certainly an attractive young lady, who Tom was enamoured by. Thankfully after the unnecessary altercation shenanigans involving the two siblings Tom and Ethan, the atmosphere had gradually cooled and become more relaxed.

After having the back of his hand stamped by the lady in the paying kiosk, Ethan wandered outside. He took a packet of Silk Cut cigarettes out of his pocket. He opened the box, pulling one out between his middle and forefinger and started to twiddle it around. He was still very uptight after the spat. He had been trying so hard recently to give up this horrible anti-social habit, although the breakdown of his relationship had consequently affected him, he started smoking like there was no tomorrow. This really annoyed his brother Tom, as he'd been helping him gradually kick the habit. Ethan had heeded his brother's advice by resorting to meditation to soothe his mind. It had been a huge success, as Ethan had cut down drastically from twenty per day to five. This really impressed and pleased Tom. Unfortunately, the breakdown of Ethan's relationship to Alexandra had knocked him for six. They'd been together for ten years, planning to marry next year. They both desperately wanted children, however, after several years of trying, they still couldn't conceive. This had put an enormous strain on their relationship, resulting in the recent separation. Ethan was still meddling with the cigarette, deciding whether to smoke it or not. A cigarette would surely help to relax his mind state, but he didn't want to damage the good work he'd done recently. He stared at the unlit cigarette, rolled it back and forth between his fingers, justifying in his mind,

'Shall I, should I not, shall I, should I not!'

He placed it between his lips, slid a transparent yellow lighter from his dark brown cotton three quarter length trousers, pressing the button of it profusely. He then wiped off a stream of sweat, as it flowed down from his forehead, jumping on to his nose, proceeding to run down the contours of his upper lip. He took out a white silk cotton handkerchief and mopped down his face. There were still a lot of people milling around on the streets, horns beeping at drunken people ambling obliviously across the street, Wolf whistles at women wearing the shortest of clothing, some not even covering their modesty, people shouting, screaming with excitement. It was a real hub of entertainment. Ethan felt sorry for himself and regretted the fracas with Tom. Emotions had been running high after the accidental glass slamming, however, the ensuing incident could so easily have been avoided. Despite the drama, Ethan was fighting with his urge to resist the temptation to smoke. 'Have you got a light mate?' asked a fellow party reveller.

'Yeah.' Ethan acknowledged, handing his lighter to the guy.

'Cheers mate.'

Off he walked puffing his cigarette with pleasure. Ethan's mind tormented with the complexed saga of should I, shouldn't I, decided to put the cigarette back in the box. This could potentially be a revelation, as the compelling personal circumstances enhanced with inebriation, couldn't force him to smoke. It was an impressive moment, that could transform his fortunes. In life these experiences can be the making or breaking of mankind. He smiled, popped the box back into his pocket and walked back inside the bar, showing the lady the stamp, before re-uniting himself with his brother's birthday entourage. He tapped Tom on the shoulder, who was immersed in lip sucking with Jade.

'Bro! Bro! Bro!' he said a little louder.

'What d'ya want man?' replied Tom, rather bemused at being interrupted from his passionate clinch.

'I just wanna… I just wanna say… I'm so sorry Tom! I shouldn't have done, acted the way I did. It was inexcusable. It's ya birthday, but even without that, there's just no defendin' my behaviour!' apologised Ethan.

He thrust his arms around his brother, giving him a kiss on the cheek.

'It's OK Ethe. I know you've been experiencing a difficult time of late. I shouldn't have slammed the glasses down on the table, but sometimes, these things happen! I forgive you. Now get to the bar and get us both a drink of something special,' responded Tom, winking at his brother.

Ethan smiled, then swaggered his way towards the downstairs bar, shaking his waist as he moved, as Shakira's track of Hips Don't Lie was being played by the DJ. Jasmine was relishing the music. She dragged Ash to the dancefloor, gyrating her bottom, shaking her hips and shuffling her shoulders, with her back to Ash, so he could admire her alluring contours. His eyes almost popped out of their sockets when her barely there belt skirt once again paraded her rear cheeks. She looked one ravishing specimen, Ash thought. He smoothly followed her and pretended to spank her bottom, which she saw and suggestively bent over pushing her pert cheeks into his groin area. He pulled her close, spun her around, grabbed hold of her waist and danced a little salsa with her to the beat. 'Oh, I'm on tonight, and my hips don't lie and I'm startin' to feel ya boy,' Jasmine sang to the lyrics while wiggling and jiggling every part of her anatomy in Ash's vicinity. He was savouring the passionate dance she provided. Purely sublime!

While they were strutting their sexy stuff, Fluffy Donkey was engrossed in conversation with Stacey. They both stretched out on one of the cosy beds in the chill-out room discussing her prospects at becoming a potential Olympian in the next eight years. She was currently one of the Team GBs emerging starlets, excelling at heptathlon. Her dream was to win World and Olympic golds. She definitely had a chance as she was in the top five in England and ranked second in her age group at under twenty one level. Fluffy was entertaining her with his comical chatter, which she was drawn towards magnetically. He thought the odds were quite high, after months of celibacy, that the Monastery might finally allow him out, after righteous loyalty. He didn't intend to sleep with Stacey necessarily on the first night, but he definitely wanted to give himself a chance within the week. He had a high level of self respect and wasn't a person that would exploit the vulnerability of an attractive young woman. Stacey was extremely respectable, so realistically, Joe probably wouldn't get his wicked way as soon as he'd hoped. He ran his hands up and down her thigh, feeling how tightly toned and muscular her athletic legs were. Goose bumps quite quickly appeared, as he was certainly exciting her with his gentle touch. They were enjoying a rum punch, although spent more time gazing into one another's eyes, as opposed to drinking. Fluffy Donkey was hooked, like a fish caught on the end of a line.

Jennifer and Jammin' Boy were also busting moves of a rather sensuous nature, sporadically locked in steamy brief kisses. He wasn't too sure whether or not to take things further though, as he didn't want to jeopardise a very sound working professional relationship with Jennifer. It didn't mean it would stop him though, he was just playing it cool and cautiously. Anabelle waved to Jennifer, gleaming brightly with her ivory white teeth accentuated even more with the dazzle of the flashing strobe lights. Annabelle had plucked up enough Dutch courage to engage now in a game of chance with Jasmine. They both desperately wanted to get their hands on Ash, whether or not he would be inclined to partake in their game, only he knew. Annabelle spun around on the dance floor, shaking her body and shimmying. She decided now was the time to unveil her beautiful mass of long flowing blonde locks, as it had been tied up with an attractive angel brooch. Ash caught sight of her as he was being entertained by Jasmine. It enthralled him, the image of this buxom petite fire cracker of a woman. He had to blink, aghast and then shouted, 'Bella, is that you?!'

'No, it's mi sister. Which d'ya prefer? The quiet, demure and shy one with shorter hair or the supremely confident and gregarious alter ego?!' replied Annabelle, licking her lips.

'I like both. The tame one by day and the wild one by night!' he stated with aplomb.

'Well tonight mister, it's your lucky night!' she answered, kissing the nape of his neck and brushing her ample sized breasts against his back.

Jasmine had briefly turned away, so Annabelle acted very briskly and discreetly, reminiscent of a clinical assassin. A strategic, meticulous and silent entry, a potent execution followed by a rapid graceful exit. Ash then quickly followed behind Annabelle, tapping her on the shoulder, 'What did you mean, by it's your lucky night?' he asked.

'Exactly what I said!' she replied.

'Isn't it Tom's lucky night? Surely, with him being the birthday boy!' he said.

'Don't ask so many questions. Jasmine's gone to the bar, so let's go somewhere a l'il more private!' she suggested.

Annabelle grabbed his hand and escorted him up the staircase to a quieter corner of the V.I.P. area. There was a comfortable looking brown leather rugged two seater sofa. They sat down, Annabelle flung her arms round his neck and began a very passionate long lingering kiss. Ash was totally taken aback by her actions, as from the BBQ earlier, she was very pensive, conservative and quite shy. Suddenly, alcohol consumed, music blasting out from the speakers, hair unleashed, she had becoming a wild female with hunting intent.

'Are you stayin' at JB's?' she asked.

'Yeah, probably!' Ash said.

'I may just have to join ya, that's if JB agrees?!'

'I'm sure he won't mind. He has a cat basket downstairs, so maybe you could crash out in that with Felix?' he jokingly proposed.

'That's not what I had in mind!' she stated rather firmly.

Ash was getting a little hot under the collar with Annabelle's proposition. He was usually extremely cool and relaxed, but for some unknown reason, he had slightly lost momentary control. Annabelle's evident wow factor, was doing the trick.

'Let's go downstairs, because Jaz has bought me a drink, so I don't want her knowin' I've been tryin' to seduce ya!' she hurriedly said.

She rose to her feet, giving Ash's hand a little tug, just encouraging him to follow, but not in close proximity. She scurried down to meet Jasmine, who was chatting to Jammin' Boy and Jennifer. 'Where'v you been? You dirty l'il rascal! Have you been tryin' to snare my man?' teased Jasmine.

'I've been upstairs to the toilet, to freshen up,' Annabelle responded fervently.

'You look all flush to me Bella. I see ya chest's gone that shockin' pink colour again, almost as bright as ya nails.' Jasmine frowned, speaking with vigour.

'Anyway Jaz. Did you get me that sex on the beach?' asked Annabelle.

'By the state of you, it looks like you've just had sex runnin' outta ya knickers!' laughed Jasmine.

'I'm not the one who was barin' mi ass virtually in his face. Bendin' over n leavin' l'il to the imagination. I'm sure I saw a spider's leg crawlin' outta ya thong?' chuckled Annabelle.

'That'l o been mi dental floss for mi you know what. I've got teeth down there, dint you know?!' responded Jasmine with even more illicit humour.

'HA HA HAAAAAAAA…' Jennifer, Jammin' Boy and Annabelle cried with laughter.

'Ya drink's here Bella. Don't cum too quick will ya. Don't want you stainin' ya dress! Ya drink's here,' Jasmine taunted, while passing Annabelle her cocktail.

Ethan joined the group and apologised for his earlier antics. Jasmine was quite critical and cynical of his behaviour with his brother Tom, although did have an affinity for him.

'I just wanna say sorry to y'all for my earlier behaviour. I've already spoken to Tom to reconcile our differences. So just wanted to say, I hope it dint spoil ya night n ya can all forget about it!' he said rather embarrassedly.

'Don't cha worry. It's all water under the bridge now. Peace yeah?' Jasmine accepted the truce.

'Yeah man. I know you've ad ya problems Ethe. You jus need to talk wi ya bro a l'il more. Peace man!' Jammin' Boy touched his knuckle and also accepted the apology.

'No worries Ethe. I didn't know guys slapped tho? I thought it was a girl thang. It's nice to know you can show ya feminine side! I forgive ya,' Jennifer said, tormenting but in a jovial manner.

'I think ya need a l'il relaxation after the recent exploits. So now you've cooled down, how about hottin' things up a l'il?' Jasmine insinuated.

'Phhhhhew! Could you may beeeee, a l'il more explanatory? I'm possibly being slightly naive, but… what d'ya mean?' Ethan queried.

'If you take my hand, we can go somewhere a l'il quiet!' she suggested, whispering into his ear.

This instantaneously excited him, as her soft and tender lips gently brushed against the edge of his left earlobe. Jasmine escorted Ethan to a corner at the back of the club, carrying her Sex on the Beach cocktail with her spare hand. There were several high tables accompanied by similar height stools, which were stainless steel from seat to base. The seats had a small lip at the back to give a little more comfort to those resting on them. A guy who appeared to be sleeping, obviously due to drunkenness, was slumped over a stool, as if it was his comfort blanket. His legs were draped on the floor, with his hands and face resting on the seat. He was letting out quite a loud snore. Jasmine nudged him.

'Sorry to disturb ya, but are ya gonna sit on that or just slouch? I think ya need to go home!' she said.

He let off a large sigh and then slurred, 'I wuv you!'

'That's such a lovely gesture. Are ya confessin' ya love for me, the stool or somethin' else close to ya heart?' she quizzed.

'Ooooh… Soo… soo… sorry. I was dreamin' bout mi wife!' he responded once again stuttering and slurring his words.

'It's probably time you did one. Ya wife's probably at home waiting for ya to snuggle up to.'

At hearing this, the drunken man, slowly clambered to his feet, almost stumbling over, smiled, waved and then staggered off towards the exit. Jasmine climbed onto the stool and pulled the other stool closer, which Ethan hopped on to. She threw her arms around him and kissed him passionately. She'd certainly had an entertaining day and night frivolously making plays for Ash, Tom and now his brother Ethan. That was definitely her trademark though, the man-eater. As she locked her lips on his, she placed his hand on to her pert breasts and stroked them gently with his fingers. The time was fast approaching two in the morning. She was definitely wanting to go home with a guest and not Han Solo. Ethan, was a little cautious, as he'd recently come out of a long term relationship, however, thought this may be the perfect tonic to soften the blow. He hadn't been out for quite a while since the breakup. It was the first time anyone had made a concerted effort to elope with him for a long time. When he was in a relationship, he emitted pheromonal allure, therefore, many a lady would endeavour to entice him. He was the archetypal monogamous partner, never being tempted by the hypnotic charms of attractive females. He was a thirty three year old muscular man of medium build with dark brown hair. He stood tall at touching six foot. He was a real gentleman normally and a typical ladies man. Wherever he went, women's heads turned with amazement at his statuesque appearance. Jasmine had known of Ethan for quite some time and always fancied him, but previously he'd been in a relationship, so she for once maintained her hands off policy. Despite her man-eating traits, she did retain a high level of self respect, whereby she would never indulge with a taken man, knowing he was off limits. She had never really spoken to Ethan, just greeted him in passing, apart from her criticism earlier for his behaviour, fighting with his own brother. In fact she had only met him on a few occasions, one when he picked Tom up at the end of a school day well over a year ago and out and about in the community, of course also this evening. For some reason, he seemed to overwhelm her, because she was reluctant to initiate conversation with him. This was so on the contrary for her, when in ninety nine percent of cases, she would never take a back seat and be speechless, she would be the proverbial protagonist in initiating chat. With her being rather merry this evening, her temperature had risen, giving her hot flushes, strongly encouraging her to target her prey.

She nibbled his upper lip, which encouraged even more fornication, as he discreetly cupped his free hand over her other breast, squeezing it gently with his fingers.

'Ooooooooh Oooooooooh!' Jasmine squealed and moaned with pure excitement.

She ran her hand in between the buttons on his shirt, feeling the smooth honed texture of his tough skin. He removed his hand from her breast, cheekily squeezing her left buttock. What a beautiful, erotic and highly sexual sensation. She once again squealed with excitement.

'Noooot here. Shall we leave?' she asked.

'Where do you want to go Jaz?' he asked.

'We can go to mine if ya like? It'll be coffee, biscuits and then separate beds tho!' she said rather flustered and unconvincing.

'We better say bye to Tom first though,' replied Ethan.

They lowered themselves off their high stools, heading upstairs to find Tom, who was in a passionate embrace with Jade. 'Sorry to disturb ya bro. Jaz n I are gonna go elsewhere for a drink.'

'Back to mine for a coffee Tom. But don't worry, I won't corrupt im, just volcanically erupt with im! If ya catch mi drift,' Jasmine said smirking.

He squeezed in between Jade, giving his brother a massive hug and kiss on the swollen cheek. 'Take care, enjoy the rest of ya night n make sure Jade looks after ya!' he chuckled.

'I'll be OK bruv, just as long as I don' walk into any wild swingin' hands!' Tom responded, laughing to Ethan.

'I'll protect him Ethe,' re-assured Jade.

'I'm sure you'll do a great job Jade. You may even get a few more birthday treats Tom,' Jasmine said, hugging and kissing him goodbye.

As she walked away, she hitched up her skirt, well, to be honest, she didn't really have to do that, as it was so ridiculously short. She smacked her bottom and wandered off arm in arm with Ethan, for what was no doubt going to be a spicy hot encounter.

On the dance floor Jammin' Boy and Jennifer were strutting their sexy stuff, relishing the 'old skool' 1990s funk soul hip rocking beats. There was a great deal of chemistry between them. Jennifer tantalised Jammin' by flicking her long flowing silky brown hair from side to side and spinning around shaking her bottom which was as ripe as a peach, contours visible through her brown denim shorts. Jammin' was in a trance as her athletically olive skinned naked legs rippled with tone as she glided around so gracefully. They were even more accentuated with her four inch heels. 'Ooooo, what a jaw droppin' figure she as, wo-ouch.' he thought to himself.

They were the epitome of Jennifer Lopez and Usher as they virtually mimicked each other's fluent dance moves. A pure joy to watch. Poetry in perpetual motion. Jammin' moved close to Jennifer.

'D'ya want another drink, or ya wantin' to go fa food?' he asked, hoping that he could encourage her to go for a bite to eat.

'I'm OK thanks JB, just lovin' the music n wish we could dance all night!' she acknowledged with extreme happiness and joy in her voice.

'All right. I'm gonna get another one.'

'What ya gettin?'

'It don't concern you, because ya don't want one!'

'Hmmmm... If ya gonna get n Appletons n ginger beer, I'll jump on that wagon!' she hinted.

'If ya on di wagon, it means you aint drinkin'!' he responded.

'Ya know what I mean Jammin'!'

'OK den. I guess we both fallin' off di cart den. Appletons n ginger ale it is!'

He walked away with a swing in his step. As he danced and weaved his way across the crowded dance floor like a rugby player serenely evading tackles, he bumped into Tom and Jade, who had now made their way downstairs to the edge of the floor. They couldn't take their hands and eyes off each other, just like newlyweds enjoying their first dance.

'Looooord, look at you two. Arms all over like octopuses' catchin' dere prey! D'ya waaant a drink?' he asked.

'Please Jammin', if ya offering,' said Jade in her quietly spoken soft southern accent.

'Yeah, no probs. What ya waaant?'

'A white wine n soda please.'

'Tooom, what ya sayin'?'

'For me, whatever your havin' please.'

'Word up.'

Jammin' Boy made his way to the bar, thankfully it was now approaching two thirty five am, so the queue wasn't three deep like it had been several hours earlier. The evening had appeared to fly by. With all the antics that had occurred from BBQ enchantment, taxi driver sentiment, sibling squabbling, anger and confrontation, followed by Ethan's repentance, drinking incessantly, pheromonal allure mixed with sweet perfumed scent, Tom's birthday party celebrations had slowly arrived, no sooner they went. As the place was still lively, it was likely it would stay open till four o'clock. Jammin' only had to wait a couple of minutes before being served. He rested his left foot on the gold plated rail that ran about six inches off the floor. A perfect place to take the weight off tired, aching dancing feet. He rested his left elbow on the dark brown veneered bar, avoiding the tiny puddles of alcohol that hadn't been mopped up yet, then reached into his pocket for his wallet. He opened it and pulled out a crisp twenty pound note that looked fresh from the banking press.

'Can I help you?' asked the slender, mousey haired, rock chick looking bar girl.

'Yeah, if ya please. Can I get tree Appletons wi ginger ale, a white wine n soda n a pint of iced soda water!' he ordered.

'Yep, coming right up. Any particular white wine?'

'Just a dry white please.'

Away she went, pulling off a bottle of German Riesling, pouring it into a large tumbler, mixing it with soda water. Then she picked up three fresh glasses from the drying clean cluster, pouring in a generous continental measure of Appletons into each glass. Starstruck bar staff were never tight with the ridiculous British government recommended point two five stringent measure. They always gave you a healthy portion, of what could be described as being a quadruple at least. Of course physically not healthy, but good value for money never the less. She ring pulled open three cans of ginger ale, multi-tasking topping up the three glasses and then squirted soda water into a pint glass, before dropping a handful of ice cubes in with a piece of freshly sliced lime.

'That'l be sixteen pounds n eighty five pence,' she said smiling to JB.

'Dere ya go. Take a pound tip too.' He handed over the twenty pound note.

'Thanks, that's very kind of ya,' she answered with gratitude.

He looked over his shoulder.

'Tanks Tom. The soda waters fa you too.' he said, grateful that he had come over to give him a hand with the drinks.

'No probs, many thanks Jammin',' he responded, picking up the glass of white wine soda for Jade, his own drink with can of ginger beer.

'Tanks.' Jammin' Boy acknowledged the bar girl giving him his change.

He opened his wallet, put his loose change in the coin compartment, closed it, popping it back in his pocket, picked up the two cans of ginger beer and tumblers of Appletons, making his way back to Jennifer. Fluffy Donkey, Stacey, Ash and Annabelle had all now congregated around Jennifer, as she continuously busted her Latina style funky dance moves. The group had all circled, drinks in hand, slapping their thighs, applauding her refined rhythmical ability. The way she moved affirmed that she was one hundred percent of Latin American heritage. Jennifer eventually made her way to the edge of the circle, to be replaced by Fluffy Donkey, performing his funky chicken/pendulum trademarked dance. Jammin' Boy and Ash started howling like Wiley Coyote's sending out a forest mating call. Everyone else joined in. It was incredible how other party revellers were curious as to what was going on, so several dozen wandered over to have a look. The atmosphere was lively, energetic and very infectious, encompassing hypnotic electrifying beats, heavy base, shrieks, yells, hand claps and foot stamping. Very joyous indeed. It had been a thoroughly enjoyable Saturday, which had certainly been enhanced with the gloriously warm weather pre summer solstice. A few of the group were a little tired after copious amounts of alcohol, dancing and other shenanigans.

'Do you want to go fa a bite to eat, or book to my yard fa drinks?' he whispered into Jennifer's ear.

'I'm enjoyin' the music, but mi feet are a l'll sleepy. Shall we get a pizza n then head back to yours?' she suggested.

'Yeah, we can if ya like?! Let's see what di rest o da crew wanna do?' he said.

They collectively asked the group what their plans were. Ash, Fluffy Donkey, Annabelle and Stacey were keen on the idea of an after party at JB's. Tom wanted to go home. It was evident that he was looking forward to some extra-curricular activity with Jade. It was guaranteed to be a birthday treat of the highest quality, as she was a very attractive young lady. She had turned several heads throughout the course of the evening. In fact, Tom's head hadn't turned at all, apart from when he took a whopping left handed humdinging slap to his right cheek, causing a little bit of swelling.

'I just wanna say thanks for an amazin' evening. It's been out of this World. I'm so grateful for the turn out, quality company, tasty drinks n... n... n... n... Eeeerrrm... n yeah... Just everything!' Tom slurred his thank you's to all present.

'It's been fab Tom. Many thanks,' responded Jennifer.

'Extra special Tom. Thanks for the invite!' replied Ash, with a big beaming white teethed gleaming smile.

'That was the dogs Tom. Cheers mate,' answered Fluffy Donkey.

'Boooooy... Dat was one white knuckle rollercoaster event maaaan. You n Jade hookin' up, you n ya brudder wid a l'il slap n tickle, Jasmine's tong t-tong, tong tong flash. Close to di bone fa me. Dat gal's got one fine piece o tasty ass, day cud sell it at KFC!' Jammin' said, shaking his head and grinning in total amazement.

The group finished their drinks. As Jammin' Boy had just been to the bar, himself, Jade, Jennifer and Tom decided to throw their newly bought drinks down the hatch. 'Ready, Steady, Goooooooo.' Jammin' announced.

The four of them finished them like there was no tomorrow. The girls all hugged Tom, thanking him for a spectacular night. They picked up their belongings and all made their way to the exit. It was reminiscent of a Noah's Ark expedition, two by two, four by four.

Chapter 12

After 'Shock' Party

As they got out outside the bar... *WooWooWooWoo*... An ambulance whizzed by at frantic speed, with pedestrians literally jumping out of the way. Tom and Jade walked off arm in arm, kissing every now and then as they went in search of a taxi. Jammin' Boy phoned Lucky Star for two taxis to take them back to his. The entourage of Jammin' Boy, Fluffy Donkey, Ash, Jennifer, Stacey and Annabelle were ready to enjoy some late night/early morning fast food to take back to JB's for an after party. 'Shall we order food from a take-away when we get back to mine, or do you want to get sumting ere?' JB asked.

'Ooooo....I'd love a piece of that rare dark meat. Sweet and flavoursome Jammin'! teased Jennifer.

'Is dat a racist jibe Latina? You can't associate me wi meat, I'm far more juicier dan dat, if I may say so miself. I don't need grillin', roastin' or fryin' either, I'm salted n pre-cooked! Oooow oooooo,' he responded with aplomb, in a sensuous manner.

'Uuuuuuum, just how I like it. Cooked to prrrrrrrrrrr-fection. Yum yum,' Jennifer replied.

Jammin' Boy's heart started to palpitate rather quickly as Jennifer's hands began to wander to the base of his back, and her finger slipped down between his boxer shorts and his skin, into the crevice of his bottom. He'd never been intimate with Jennifer, although they'd always been highly flirtatious at school, predominantly in the staff room. It had never progressed to anything more than tantalising torment with a stroke of the leg or slap of the thigh or cheeky smack on the bottom. Tonight they'd exceded any expectation by engaging in soft teasing gentle kisses on the dance floor. The chemistry was there for all to see.

'Uuuuf... Mind where ya hands wander, dere are snakes down dere n dey might jus bite?' Jammin' Boy responded in a forced high pitched voice.

This act sent shivers right down his spine like a cold breeze passing through an open window on anautumn day.

'I'm sure I could charm the reptile and make it happy,' she said.

Jennifer had never been so forward in all the time she'd known him, however, the effects of the alcohol were just re-affirming what Jammin' always knew.

'Let's go back to yours Jammin' n have some late night drinks n food,' suggested Fluffy Donkey.

'Yeah, I'm down wi dat!' he replied.

'Good call,' said Ash.

'Di taxis shud be here in two mins, so prob di best idea.' Jammin' proposed.

'Yep, let's do it,' agreed Stacey.

'I'm so excited, n I just can't hide it… I'm about to lose control n I think I like it…!' sang Annabelle running her fingers sensually through Ash's coarse but yet refined twisted afro hair.

'Are you OK there Bella? Have you seen something you like?!' Ash said jokingly.

'I can feel something soft, warm and furry in my hand,' responded Annabelle.

'I can feel something warm, soft and furry too,' he said.

'What's that?' asked Annabelle inquisitively.

Ash put his hand on her pert bottom and enjoyed the sensation of smooth textured material against his palm. 'It moves! Is it alive?' he teased.

'Stop it. Keep ya hands off, you can't afford this piece of ass,' she joked.

'Shall we start the auction now Jammin'?' Ash tormented Annabelle.

'Mi bed, mi couch or mi cat basket?!' Jammin' propositioned.

'Good idea. How about ya spare room Jammin'?' Ash asked.

'That's where we're… Oops, I mean I'm sleepin'. Sorry Stace, I almost thought we were together,' Fluffy Donkey said chuckling.

'I've only let you put ya big strappin' arms round me tonight, don't get too presumptious. I might tuck you in though?' she said laughing.

'You have to read me a Jackanory though.'

'What's one o them?' asked Stacey.

'Come on Stace. Get wi the programme.'

'Why what's on? Wonkey Donkey by any chance?' Stacey said cheekily.

'If you wanna see a wonkey donkey, you're at the right place. Jackanory for you and in fact to anybody, rhymes with story!' Fluffy Donkey emphasised with a rather smug look on his face.

Beep, Beep. Two taxis pulled up. Lucky Star were a popular reliable local company who nearly always delivered punctually. They were so accommodating, that if ever they were late for a customer, they'd provide a noble discount. In today's society that was indeed a rare gracious trait. Jammin' Boy walked over to the first taxi and asked as the driver wound down his electronic front passenger window. 'Are these two for Jammin'?'

'Yeees. Are there six of you?' the driver asked.

'Yeah man, dat's right. Can we op in den?' Jammin' Boy asked.

'Jump in to both. They're for you,' responded the driver.

Jammin' Boy, Fluffy Donkey and Jennifer climbed into the first taxi. Jammin' Boy sat in the front passenger seat, intending on playing it cool, as he still wasn't sure whether or not he should indulge in any more frivolity with Jennifer. He didn't want to jeopardise their professional educational relationship. Basically, make things a little awkward at Oatmill High. The doors were slammed shut with slightly too much power. 'Be careful boys, I don't want mi doors dropping off their hinges,' stated the driver.

'Oops. Sorry driver, I don't know di power of mi own strength,' replied Jammin' Boy.

'My apologies driver. That was a little too powerful wasn't it. I slam dunk when I play basketball, but I'm off court now,' Fluffy Donkey said.

Fluffy Donkey decided to open the door and then close it again. 'Is that more to ya likin' driver?' he asked.

'That was easy wasn't it? Well, thank you kind sir.' The driver congratulated Joe on his gentler door closing method.

The driver was being sarcastic and this rather aggravated Joe. 'Driver, there's no need for the sarcasm. I've already apologised, so why are you provokin' me?' asked Fluffy Donkey.

'I didn't mean to. Sorry. I've had a bad night, that's all. So, am really frustrated, but don't mean to take it out on you,' the driver replied, with a genuine apology.

Thankfully peace was restored and this was just a momentary blip. The group had been partying all day, so understandably they weren't in a state of sobriety. Joe was normally a placid, easy going and affable young man, so for him to lose his temper, it required some serious provocation. 'Can you take us to 33 Mysterious Street please?' asked Jammin' Boy.

'Yeah, no probs,' replied the driver.

In the car behind were Ash, Stacey and Annabelle. Ash sat in the front and the girls made themselves comfortable in the back. The taxi they were in just followed the first one. The journey was very quick as it was only a few miles from Jammin' Boy's house in Honeyville. When they reached JB's house, both taxis pulled up outside. The drivers turned on their reading lights and checked the fares. 'That'l be five pounds fifty please.'

The group delved into their wallets, purses and bags to find loose change. 'I'll pay fa dis guys,' said Jammin' Boy assertively.

'Are you sure?' asked Fluffy Donkey.

'Of course I'm sure. To be sure, to be sure, to be sure.' Jammin' Boy blurted out in his imitation Southern Irish accent.

He gave the driver a five pound note and pound coin. 'Keep di change boss,' said Jammin' Boy.

'Thank you man,' replied the driver.

They got out of the car, making sure to close the door less forcefully. In the taxi behind, Stacey, Annabelle and Ash were charged the same fare. Ash nobly paid for the ride, as he wanted to make a concerted effort to exhibit his gentlemanly traits to Annabelle, as he was hoping for success back at JB's. The taxi drivers altered their mile meters, put their money into nylon bags, flicked off their reading lights and then drove off simultaneously. It was if they were identical twins, being cloned into the same behaviour at precisely the same time. The group were in jovial, atmospheric and lively spirits as they'd been drinking from pre dusk. They were in different states of inebriation, but thankfully no-one was paralytic. Jammin' was rather relieved as the last thing he wanted to do, was to have to clean up a horrible mosaic of stomach gunge. In other words, human sickness. There were cries of laughter, burps, clonking of shoes on the stone paved driveway, jangling of Jammin' Boys keys, jingling of bracelets and the zoom sound of fast passing cars as they walked to the front door.

'Shhhhhh… Don't make too much noise, we don't wanna wake di neighbours man.' whispered Jammin' Boy.

Giggles spurted out from Annabelle.

'Hehehehehehe… It's the weekend. They should understand that people drink n come home happy.' She was hiccupping as she spoke.

'You have to respect the restn'. It's after three In the morn, so we need to tone down the volume. It's way past pumpkin time,' said Ash.

'You spoil sport,' said Annabelle, stroking her hair and placing her hand on Ash's posterior.

'Ooooooo… Who's a l'il saucy devil,' said Ash.

As they all reached the door, Jammin' Boy took his house keys out of his jeans pocket and opened the door. The burglar alarm started beeping, to warn him that it needed de-activating. BEEP BEEP BEEP BEEP, it continued to sound. As he was a little inebriated, he tripped over the lip at the bottom of the door frame as he walked through it. The effects of alcohol distorted his awareness.Everyone burst out laughing as if they'd witnessed a comical gag at a stand up comedy night. Jammin' Boy was a little embarrassed, although it was hard to tell, with his complexion. He stumbled as he picked himself up from the oak wooded floor, eventually managing to stand up straight with the assistance of Jennifer, who had gone to his rescue. Consequently the alarm had been activated, as it only had a ten second warning. It let out a most ear piercing shrill, as the deafening noise caused all to put their hands to the ears to minimise the drone. After three attempts, thankfully he managed to de-activate it. Everyone started cheering with Annabelle letting out a high pitched wolf whistle.

'Ssssshhhhhhhhhhhh… It's bad enough, di sound o di alarm, never mind di encore to follow Bella,' reminded Jammin' Boy.

'Alright JB, keep ya woollen fro on. Ya lucky they're ain't a large gust of wind, koz, it'd have it right off!' joked and taunted Annabelle.

'OK Bella, take it easy girl. I don't want di neighbours fallin' out wi me over makin' too much late night noise!'

'If Jen has a wicked way with ya, it might just happen.'

'Shut up Bell, he's only gonna get a lip smackin' good night!' highlighted Jennifer.

'Daaaamn… I tought it was my lucky night Jen?' teased Jammin' Boy.

Jennifer gave him a flirtatious glance, swishing her hair like a pedigree race horse in the dress circle pre-race, winked, licked her lips and said,

'If ya a bad boy, I may just have to summon ya?'

'Will dis be useful?' he asked, taking a ladle out of the cutlery drawer.

'Just these soft gentle Latin hands will suffice,' she replied.

'Take ya shoes off please.' Jammin' Boy asked, as he had a light beige fluffy expensive axminster carpet.

They all took off their shoes and proceeded to the living room. It was decorated with a light lemon pastille feature wall, with the remaining three a naked beige. In the corner near the curtains was a statuesque yucca plant standing four feet high. The light brown horizontal style blinds covered the bay window, from top to sill. On the feature wall hung a forty two inch Wide screen LCD Sony TV with two speakers bracketed at opposing corners of the room, just below the ceiling. It was a very spacious room, which created space to have two three seater sofas and an armchair sitting in front of the window. On the wall as you walked in was a stunning panoramic canvas photograph of the Manhattan New York skyline made even more attractive with the North and South Tower World Trade Centres dwarfing skyscrapers besides. The fire place was a vintage wood burner with real character, which Felix adored, especially in winter. At either side of the fire place stood two scented candles in glass holders. The sweet scent was hypnotic, luring you into a state of pure relaxation. Lavender, ylang ylang and vanilla.

'What do y'all want to drink?' asked Jammin' Boy.

'Appletons n ginger beer for me please,' answered Fluffy Donkey.

'Same for me please,' replied Ash.

'Have you any wine, Jammin'?' asked Annabelle.

'Yeah, several bottles o red n a few o white. What d'ya want?' he asked.

'Myself, Stacey n Jen would like red please,' she answered.

Jammin' put his iPhone in his docking port in the kitchen and chose Bob Marley's Legend album. He thought it was an appropriate genre at that time in the morning. Easy listening, relaxing and joyous.

'Are we gonna order any food?' asked Jammin' Boy.

'Let's get a few pizzas!' suggested Ash.

'Oooo... An Indian would be great,' said Jennifer.

'Jasmine was hoping for that earlier on when we caught the cab with Jaleem,' chuckled Annabelle.

'Pizzas are gonna be easier, we can just split em Candy Five Ways, or even six,' advised Jennifer.

'Right den, I'll order dem tru di local takeaway. Exotic Island,' Jammin' Boy decided.

'They sound rather tropically delicious,' answered Stacey.

'Dere di best around ere in Honeyville!' assured Jammin'.

Jennifer went into the kitchen to give Jammin' Boy a hand with the drinks, as he had to phone to order the pizzas.

'What flavour do you all want?' asked Jennifer.

'Pepperoni,' shouted Fluffy Donkey.

'Meat Feast,' bellowed Ash.

'Ham n Pineapple please,' said Stacey.

'I don't mind. I've got an expansive palate,' responded Annabelle.

'I didn't know ya worked at a warehouse Bella?' joked Ash.

'What d'ya mean?' she quizzed.

'Well... Warehouses store items stacked on pallets, so forklift truck drivers can move them easily,' explained Ash.

'I don't understand?' queried Annabelle.

'Don't worry Bella, it's a joke. I know you mean ya a non fussy eater!' said Ash.

'Shall I order a special selection den?' shouted through Jammin' Boy.

A crescendo of yeses were blurted back from the living room.

Jennifer pulled out three wine glasses from the cupboard along with three tumblers for the spirits. Jammin' Boy phoned Exotic Island Take-away on his mobile. Stacey slid a little closer to Fluffy Donkey on the sofa, which certainly pleased and enthralled him. She ran her fingers down his strong and muscular legs. 'Uuuum, you remind me of a powerfully built sprinter, they should call you Mercedes!' purred Stacey.

'Mercedes? Why? I'd say, I'm more the epitome of a four Wheel drive Range Rover. Built for all conditions and designed to last!' Fluffy Donkey responded with vigour and aplomb.

'Ooooo…Tell me more. I meant like a Mercedes Sprinter van, but ppprrrrr… I love the sound of a Range Rover! Bruuuum, bruuuuum. Durable, reliable and full of ooomph and ooo la laaaaaa!'

The music from Jammin' Boy's iPhone started playing sweet Bob Marley songs from his twenty eight million plus selling Album called Legend. Jammin' Boy and Jennifer rocked from side to side in the kitchen as they prepared the drinks for the guys in the living room. Jennifer poured three glasses of Shiraz for the girls and Jammin' took the boys' side and prepared theirs: Appletons with ginger beer. He took a bag of ice out of the freezer, pulled cubes out from the individual bag segments and gently dropped them into the tumblers. He phoned Exotic Island pizzas from Jennifer's phone. He ordered a Meat Feast, Pepperoni, Ham and Pineapple and Chilli pizza with two fries. As their order exceeded ten pounds, a garlic bread with cheese was thrown into the fast food mix. Exotic Island was the only take away in close proximity that stayed open late, till four am, so thankfully there was just enough time to make and deliver the pizzas.

'Drinks are ready peeps. It's time to rock it up n savour dis after party. Does anyone want pre pizza munchies? We've got an array of savoury delights rangin' from chicken kebabs n sausages from di BBQ to Twiglets, carrot n cucumber sticks!' Jammin' Boy offered in his usual hospitable manner.

'I'll have a sausage JB, especially one of those fat, nutritious n fillin' ones. Uuuuum, they look bigger than the ones we had at the BBQ earlier? Have they grown, or is Jen just one lucky lady?' she licked her lips suggestively, while running her fingers through Jammin' Boy's large jungle style afro.

'Bring in the goodness JB!' Fluffy Donkey said encouragingly.

'Sounds like a great idea. Can we have some hummus for the carrot n cucumber sticks please?' asked Ash.

'Hermano Especial, seguro. For you, anyting.' Jammin' Boy shouted in a promising fashion, half Spanish, half English.

In other words, Spanglish. Jennifer carried the drinks into the living room very carefully, on a shiny aluminium tray that was so mirrored, you could see your face in it.

'Jen, you're a gem. Many thanks,' said Annabelle appreciating.

'Yes Jen. About time. What took you lovebirds so long? Next time, can you be a little quicker and leave ya caressing to the bedroom!' remarked Stacey, jokingly.

'Di pizzas should be ere in about tirty mins. Deze are di best n tastiest ones for miles around ere! Purely irresistible! Not di usual junk layered fatty ones. Ya gonna be satiated n lickin' ya lips, beggin' for Julianne Moore… pppprrrrrrrr!' Jammin' Boy stated with conviction.

Ooooo… I see you've got Jasmine on the tips of ya lips!' teased Jennifer.

'What gives you dat impression?' asked Jammin' Boy.

'She's a Julianne Moore look-a-like!'

'Shall I give her a late night call n invite her round?' Jammin' Boy proposed.

'I think you'll find she'll be all tangled up, frolicking between Ethan's bed sheets now, enjoying some ooo la laaaa!' said Jennifer.

They all chatted about various issues while enjoying their late night snacks.
BANG BANG BANG!

'Geez man, relax wi dat knock. No need to put di door tru!' Jammin' Boy jumped off the sofa, shouting loudly as he was irritated by the door being beaten.

The bang was so deafeningly loud, Felix had been awoken upstairs, dashed downstairs following an elongated stretch and agitated ear twitch. 'Miaow, Miaow, Miaow,' he frantically cried out.

'It's alright Felix, go in di room n stay cosy wi di crew. I'll deal wi dis,' Jammin' Boy re-assured Felix.

Jammin' Boy hurried to the front door, ready to give a big piece of his mind to the pizza delivery driver. He unlocked it, pushed the handle down and opened it. To his amazement, a Police Officer stood.

'Hello, hello, hello and Good Morning to you. I'm really sorry to disturb you at this unsociable hour. A car was broken into, just down the road about an hour ago, so we just wanted to inform all local residents to be vigilant.'

'Damn boy. Dis area's as safe as di zoo. Di crime rates as igh as mi cat from di floor,' Jammin' Boy replied.

'Yes sir, you're right. We think it's the operation of a migrant gang, who are selling high tech gadgets on the black market,' the officer highlighted.

'I tell you what really infuriates me, officer. It's when people use black as a bad association. Why don't dey use white occasionally too? Black n white are both good, but sometimes tings in black n white just don't make sense. Jus like di Guinness commercial.' he questioned the negative use of shades.

The officer laughed. 'Unfortunately the human race act in mysterious ways. You sometimes see people eating fire? Now, that doesn't make any sense!' the Officer commented.

Jammin' Boy chuckled, 'I tell you what, dat guy oo broke into di car needs is ass settin' on fire. Now, dat's what I call sense n sensibility.'

'Hhhhmmmmm… That would be a little extreme, but I agree that the punishment in these modern day times, never seems to fit the crime. We worked so hard to catch these rascal perpetrators, only for the courts to give them lenient sentences. What a movie though, by the way. Was that the one with a young Emma Thompson?' the officer said.

'Yeah. Dat's di one. Di justice system should become arsher boy. Bring back burchin' n lashin' I say, n also capital punishment.'

'You're a well educated man, sir,' the officer replied.

'Well officer, I thank you deeply and graciously for such an affirmatory comment of such exquisite prudence. I suppose my teaching disposition of the Universal language enables me that special privilege.' he taunted and teased the Officer, speaking in his most bespoke Queen's eloquent and articulate English.

The Officer was hysterical.

'You should be performing stand up!'

'Well, thank you officer.'

The officer shook Jammin' Boy's hand, thanked him for his co-operation, wished him a good night and good morning and walked towards the front gate, proceeding with door to door enquiries. No sooner had he closed the door, it was knocked on again. Thankfully this time, far more gently, albeit still forceful enough. Jammin' Boy opened it. 'Hi, your pizzas sir!'

'Ow much please?' Jammin' Boy asked.

'That'll be ten pounds and eighty pence please!' confirmed the delivery guy.

Jammin' Boy picked up eleven pounds from the work top and gave it to the guy. He gave him twenty pence change.

'No man, dat's an insult. Take di change n put it towards a lottery ticket on Wednesday night. It might bring ya a l'il piece o precious lady luck!' Jammin' Boy hinted.

'Many thanks. Take care and good night,' said the delivery guy in his Asian English accent.

'Yeah, good night. Tanks for ya usual rapid Express delivery service. You guys are di bomb, just like semtex, but not as sweet smellin'!' Jammin' Boy heckled.

'Hurry, we're hungry. If you don't get a move on, we're gonna have to start nibblin' human meat! Aaaaaaaargh.' Annabelle shouted from the living room.

'Come n get deze delicious pieces of extravagantly decorated breads... Yow, wouch, deze are ot property, just like you Jen!' Jammin' Boy yelled into the room.

Jammin' Boy took a pizza cutter out of the drawer, flipped open the boxes one by one and cut the nine inch thin crust pizzas into six segments. 'In fact, stay in di room, I'll bring em tru.'

'Thanks.'

'You legend.'

'You saint.'

'Cheers governor.'

Thank yous and acknowledgements were echoed over the iPhone music from all the crew. It was cowabunga time. The smell was so alluring and aromatically divine.

'What did the copper want?' asked Fluffy Donkey.

'Dere was a car break in earlier, so e's lettin' all residents know.' replied Jammin' Boy.

'Isn't it a bit too late to be doing door to door enquiries, disturbing the peace?' remarked Fluffy Donkey.

'Yeah man, but forget about dat, mi Audi's alright. Let's tuck in n disturb dis piece-o bread,' joked Jammin' Boy.

Jammin' Boy went to get some salt and vinegar from the cupboard to give the fries a more flavoursome taste. Conversation miraculously ceased as everyone fed themselves on the wonderful array of Exotic Island pizzas. But then,

'Leave dat alone n get outta ere!' JB shouted frantically.

Felix had hidden behind the sofa, waiting to pounce on the pepperoni pizza. No sooner had the box been opened, he'd wrestled a piece of pepperoni with his claws.

'Uuuurgh! I don't want any of that now!' shrieked Annabelle.

'Don't worry!' said Fluffy Donkey, as he picked up the Felix tampered slice and took a bite out of it.

'That's disgusting!' yelled Annabelle.

'He's had all his jabs hasn't he JB?' asked Fluffy Donkey.

'Yes Fluffy, apart from cat flu!' confirmed Jammin' Boy.

'Aichoooo!' Fluffy Donkey placed a handkerchief to his mouth and sneezed.

'You see, Fluffy's already caught it!' squirmed Annabelle.

'Miaow!' Mimicked Fluffy in cat language, sneezing a further twice.

'Don't worry Bella, I just get a l'il sneezy sometimes, around pussies. When their fur's short, I'm OK, but I prefer a Brazilian to be honest!' he teased while stroking Stacey's thigh.

'Ppppprrrrrr… Uuuuuuum, make sure ya silky paws are clean, before you touch this pedigree pussy cat!' Stacey taunted Fluffy Donkey.

She lifted his hand up and pushed it away from her leg, as it started to go all goose bumpy. They relished the late night post pumpkin fast food delights, washed down with their strong cultured beverages.

'Shall we play poker?' asked Jammin' Boy.

'To be honest, I'm feeling rather sleepy n wanna go to bed!' hinted Jennifer.

'Well, you'll ave to crash on di floor in a sleepin' bag, or maybe jus top n tail, as long as ya keep ya clothes on,' emphasised Jammin' Boy.

'I've brought my birthday suit, will that be OK?'

'As long as it ain't skin coloured!' remarked Jammin' Boy.

'I'm shattered n ready for shut eye. Do you want to come n tuck me in Mr Luvva Luvva?' Annabelle said to Ash, smiling sexily.

'Hmmmmm… That could be an offer just too good to resist!' Ash responded.

'Sorry, I gave Fluffy Donkey di privilege o di spare room tonight, so ya gonna ave to crash down ere. Don't worry, I've got a big duvet for ya!' JB confirmed.

Fluffy Donkey glanced at Stacey smiling and asked,

'Are you catchin' a cab home, or do you want to keep me company?'

'It's such a mouth-watering gesture n proposition, but being a good girl, I'm gonna go home,' she responded.

'You can sleep on di sofa, you couch potato!' JB offered.

'Oh thanks. At least I know my knight kn… kn… kn… aichoo… aichoo… aichoo,' Stacey graciously retorted, while sneezing.

'Oh oh oh oh oh, ya goin' crazy, my baby,' Jammin' Boy sang out Beyonce's lyrics.

'Have you caught cat flu already Stace?' asked Fluffy Donkey.

Annabelle looked horrified. 'Don't worry Bella, I just had a tickly nose for a moment!' re-assured Stacey.

'Phew. Thank God. I was about to run outta the house then!' said Annabelle, rather relieved.

The pizzas, fries and garlic bread had virtually been eaten, apart from a few crusts and well done fries. Jammin' Boy finished his drink and then went upstairs to get the duvet and blanket for Ash and Annabelle.

Chapter 13

Post Pumpkin Pleasures

By the time he came downstairs, Jennifer had finished her glass of red wine and was hugging and kissing each member goodnight. Jammin' Boy put the bed linen on the floor near the window and high fived all, saying night night. He apologised for having to take his iPhone out of the docking port, therefore, cutting off the music.

'If you want some music, feel free to dock ya fone, but keep it on di 'down low' please, like R Kelly!'

'I'll use mine, if needed Jammin'!' said Ash.

'I thought we were gonna get some precious beauty sleep Mister Alpha Male?' queried Annabelle.

'I'll massage you first, before gently layin' you to sleep,' promised Ash.

'You can take the spare room, as Stace n I 'll crash down here!' Fluffy Donkey encouraged Ash and Annabelle to go upstairs.

Ash and Annabelle stayed up for another fifteen minutes chatting to Fluffy Donkey and Stacey until they'd finished their drinks. By this time Jammin' Boy had brushed his teeth, washed his face and climbed into bed. He had taken his clothes off and put a pair of sports shorts on. Jennifer was taking off the make up she barely had on and cleansed her face, after brushing her teeth by putting a pea sized amount on her substitute tooth brush finger. She turned the bathroom light off and went to join Jammin' in the bedroom.

'Where am I gonna sleep?' she asked.

'Dere's a duvet in di airing cupboard next door, along wid a pillow case!'

'Next door? At ya neighbours house? I can't believe I have to go to ya neighbour's, to wake them up at almost four thirty am, to come back here n crash on the floor?' Jennifer questioned rather disconsolately.

'Jen, we're good friends, n I don't want ya wrigglin' in beside me wi wanderin' hands, sendin' shivers down mi olive tree vine!'

'I promise you, my hands won't wander! They'll just rest on a few special spots.'

'I don't ave any spots, just muscular lumps!' he responded.

'Anyway, I promise to behave. What's ya olive tree vine?' asked Jennifer.

'Dats mi spine. It's makeshift cockney rhymin' slang! OK, OK, on one condition, you massage mi back, legs n ead, but leave mi ego alone!' he laughed.

'Scout's honour!' Jennifer promised.

Jennifer peeled off her brown denim shorts, leaving on her beige transparent thong and white vest top. Jammin' Boy couldn't see a thing, as he'd turned over onto his front, ready for a soothing massage. 'Di coco butters over dere, on di chest o drawers. Just shine ya phone n you'll find it.'

She picked it up off the top, pulled the duvet to the side and slid in beside him, kissing his back from the base to the nape of his neck. 'Didn't I say, quite explicitly... No wanderin'?'

'My lips aren't my hands, but just wait till I get my paws on ya!' Jennifer cackled like a delighted witch.

'Ouch! Que pasa mujer.'

This meant, what happened woman in Spanish. 'Nada. Ese crema solo. Te gusta?' she asked.

It's cream only, you like it. His eye brows frowned as it was cold. Jennifer thought she'd irritate him by dropping large splodges of cream onto his toned naked back. Her soft petite hands were a soothing sensation. Groans, moans, ooooo's and rrr's were muttered. A gentle banging sounded from the spare room. 'Did you hear dat Jen?'

'It could be water from the boiler?' she proposed.

'Nooooo. Go on boy, go on boy!' Jammin' Boy shouted.

It appeared Ash and Annabelle were having their own private party in the spare room. A faint laugh could be heard along with the occasional moan from Bella as the two of them engaged in some naked gymnastic frivolity. Jennifer's nipples had become rather erect and were poking through her white vest top. She leant over to kiss Jammin' Boy on the nape of his neck, while her ample sized D-cup chest brushed against the middle of his back. He certainly started to feel rather excited, causing an explosion of life at the front of his shorts. As they were good friends and had been for several years, they were very compatible in the relationship stakes, however, Jammin' had always been reluctant to pursue her. He was very strong minded and there were numerous reasons why he didn't want to indulge in a dalliance with her;

i) He valued her friendship so highly,
ii) It could create problems professionally, as they both worked at the same school and
iii) Becoming intimate ie. longer term relationship could jeopardise their friendship, if they broke up.

Currently though, he thought, *as we're both single, it could be difficult to resist her sexually arousing urges and surely a one off wouldn't do any harm?* Jennifer continued kissing, caressing and nibbling Jammin's back and began to run her chocolate smelling fingers through his hair. Twenty or so minutes later,

'Oooooh, ooooo, aaaaaaargh, oh yeah, uuuuuum,' sounded from the bedroom next door, along with frequent banging of the headboard against Jammin' Boy's bedroom wall. It appeared Annabelle couldn't contain her emotional shrieks and cries, as Ash fornicated and frolicked in the double bed.

'Turn round JB n I'll masage ya front now!' she said rather dominantly with her latin twang.

As he rolled over, momentarily re-adjusting the monster in his pocket, so to speak, Jennifer nonchalantly slipped her vest top up and over off her shoulders.

'Oh my God! What d'ya tink ya doin'? Didn't we agree to purely a-a-a-a-a-...!' he stuttered.

'Just relax and enjoy what you see. You can let your hands do the wandering!' Jennifer purred, smiling with excitement.

'Dis wasn't part o di script!' he replied, rather flustered.

Totally out of character for Jammin' Boy, as he was usually composed and in control. Her breasts were absolutely amazing and astounding. They sat so pertly and perfectly. Jammin' Boy was overwhelmed and salivating, reminiscent of a wounded rabid dog. She picked up the bottle of coco butter, flicked open the lid after shaking the cream to the top and then squirted two big splodges onto her breasts. She encouraged Jammin' Boy to massage it into her beautifully shaped curvaceous assets. They were so picturesque, the epitome of a breathtaking mountain range at daybreak or sunset. Such a rich dark olive Latina complexion. Jammin' Boys eyes were quite literally popping out of the sockets. His mind was in such a quandary,

'Do I, do I not, what if, will it damage the friendship?' he decided to make a decision on a whim. She had decided to get virtually naked in his bedroom, in his double bed. She had decided to squirt cream onto her breasts, encouraging him to massage it in and feel the wondrous contours of her naked skin. He thought,

'Am I sane, am I stupid?'

No sex, just harmless, innocent, pleasurable hands on experience without any of that business evidently occurring next door, with Ash and Annabelle. 'Whatever happens,' he thought, it's all about destiny, or like the song Richie Dan sang in the early noughties, garage style, 'Call it fate or what you want.' His head started bobbing from side to side and he thought... Showtime! A big wide smile appeared on his face, and to be perfectly honest, who could blame him. An astounding aesthetically pleasing insanely stunning Latin woman in his bed.

'Wouch, let's get to work.'

'We're not working till tomorrow morning.'

'Weeeell... Let's just call dis overtime or time in lieu.' Jammin' Boy emphasised.

He took both his hands and gently started to massage the coco butter into her prized sizeable assets. Even though it was dark, a little ray of moonlight shone through the curtains, so you could see the distinct reddish tint on Jennifer's neckline and upper torso. He moved his hands in slow circular motions as she straddled his waist. It was now impossible to disguise the prominent bulge in his shorts, as she whimpered,

'Someone's rather happy. Have you got a friend down there? Would he like to join us?'

Her breath now far quicker than at any time in the last thirty minutes. She closed her eyes and gasped as Jammin' Boy responded,

'Mi pepperami's a bit of an animal, but e's feelin' quite lonely at di mo. Open up di cage n let im come out.'

She sucked her right index finger and inserted it down the front of her skimpy thong. She fondled herself for a few moments, withdrew her finger, sucking it once more. 'Uuuuuum, my cage tastes very juicy, would you like some?' she said in a deep husky and sensuous voice, slightly slurring.

Jammin' Boy tormented and teased her replying,

'I wanna feast on deze succulent breasts and nipples first. Dere so fruity and ripe!'

He raised his upper body, as if performing a sit up, eyes virtually popping out of their sockets at this enriching refined sight. He kissed, nibbled, licked and caressed every inch of her from the lips to the abdomen. He then skilfully and masterfully part lifted and spun her round so she was on her back, seizing control of this erotic interlude. He worked his way even further down to her skimpy thong, tugging it and stroking her loins and inner thighs. She was purring like a pedigree feline, although Felix was in the house, he was out of sight in the kitchen fast asleep.

'Are you gonna have your wicked way with me?' Jennifer asked.. Dat's appenin' right ere n now. It's like a Latin banquet, so many mouthwaterin' portion on offer, tapas ere n tapas dere!' he responded with vigour and aplomb.

All the permutations crossed his mind about his platonic relationship with Jennifer. His head was like a rollercoaster inside, spinning around, flipping upside down, stopping and starting. For all her beauty, was it really worth it? A night/morning of pure blissful heaven, the moral conscience, impact, accomplishment, guilt, frustration, elation, ego tripping? Despite the conundrum, he decided to go with his instincts, a massage, kissing, mild fornication with nothing more. He picked up the bottle of coco butter, giving it a violent shake, flipped open the lid and squirted droplets all over her torso and stomach. This is the limit he thought. She oooo'd and aaaaargh'd, as her body appeared to be paralysed momentarily with the sheer excitement of the experience. As Jammin' Boy placed his hands once more on to her breasts to massage the cream thoroughly in, he could feel her heart palpitating at such a frantic pace. Obviously she thought copulation was going to occur, yet unbeknown to her, Jammin' Boy had other ideas. He had a high level of respect, ethics, moral values and integrity, instilled by his mother and late father. He continued to massage moving in a circular and then downward motion. Jennifer's toned skin was goose bumped all over, her eyes closed, lips dribbling and body trembling as Jammin' Boy occasionally, gently moved his hands and fingers glancing over it, activating her many erogenous zones.

All was quiet next door in the bedroom Ash and Annabelle were frolicking in. It appeared their rampant behaviour had now ceased, the alcohol fatigue had kicked in and they'd eventually gone to sleep. 'Are you gonna pull my knickers to the side or take them off JB?' Jennifer asked in a very sensuous manner.

'I'm enjoyin' mi tapas too much at di mo!'

'My pussy cat needs feeding, you can't let her starve, or she'll have no strength or energy!' she said enticingly.

'Don't worry, I don't let any pussy starve in dis house, Felix and Petra always get a full dish, as for yours, surely it can't be dat hungry?' he remarked.

'She's not hungry, she's ravenous!' Jennifer said rather restlessly, lifting her right hand up and cupping Jammin' Boy's private parts.

It was becoming ever so tempting as Jennifer was literally there for the taking. He placed his left hand on top of her thong and slowly rubbed his fingers up against her. It was saturated with her bodily fluids. She squealed with pleasure. After returning the compliment he laid down next to her and started to feel all tired. As if by divine intervention, he fell asleep in the blink of an eye. He'd rolled over on to his back and started sounding out a medium sized roar.

'JB, wake up, wake up!' she pushed, pulled and even put her hands on his shorts, sighing desperately.

To no avail, there was no way he'd wake up for several hours. When he slept, he slept like a baby, very deeply, albeit at times, incredibly noisily. Jennifer had been captivated by his charisma, comical and vibrant personality for a long time. The feeling was evidently mutual, although Jammin' Boy had more reservations than Jennifer. She was more happy go lucky and was prepared to take a plunging chance and deal with any potential consequences, She stroked his chest, rested her head under his musky smelling armpit and kissed his cheek, before falling asleep herself.

Chapter Fourteen

The Morning After the Night Before

The hours drifted by and at almost eight am, Jennifer was awoken by a wet sensation on her leg. Initially, she wasn't sure whether or not it was a lucid dream or reality, until she felt something else against the side of her other leg. To her shock, as she peered under the duvet, she saw two sparkling emerald green eyes flickering and glistening straight at her. Felix had sneaked under the covers in the middle of the night and rested himself rather comfortably between Jennifer's legs. The other sensation she felt, was Felix purring rather happily and contently against her skin. Thankfully she wasn't allergic or feline phobic, rather similar to Jammin' Boy. She smiled at him and gestured for him to join her and Jammin' Boy at the head of the bed. He let out a miaow, excited at the prospect of being stroked and fussed over.

Jennifer was also wanting him to stay below, as animals have a fascination of sniffing and licking human or other creature's genitalia. This would have been a little embarrassing. Felix appeared to be extremely comfortable, so had no motivation to move further up the bed. He started licking her leg, which made her squirm and giggle. It was a ticklish sensation that she was hoping Jammin' Boy would be inclined to emulate, when he eventually awoke from his soothing deep sleep. Felix was intent on emphasising to Jennifer, that this was his and Jammin' Boy's kingdom, a sacred territory that he wasn't intending to relinquish easily. Jennifer began to stroke Jammin' Boy's back, as he'd rolled on to his side in the night. She moved her nose towards his toned skin so she could inhale the sweet scented odour of the coco butter. Jammin' Boy was smiling widely while sleeping, as he was experiencing an extremely powerful lucid dream. His body was occasionally shuddering and spasming. He was immersed in an erotic dream interlude with Jennifer. His dream was far more intimate than the Real McCoy, could this be a premonition? He'd been reluctant to engage in any cunnilingus or sexual shenanigans apart from fondling, licking, kissing and caressing her breasts and nipples and gently running his fingers down below and smacking her ass. They were making mad passionate love in positions even the Kama Sutra hadn't demonstrated and they were plentiful in there. Jennifer rode him like a jockey on a racehorse in the queen of the castle position, while whipping him with a long piece of bamboo cane. He entered her from behind, spanking her powerfully with his bare hand, enjoying hearing the thwacking noise of palm to buttock flesh. They copulated in spoons position, him standing behind her while she was bent over the kitchen table, the chair stance where he held her in a virtual squat, while she rocked up and down on his sizeable member.

'Ooooooh, ooooooh, yeeeees, yeeeeeees, ooooooh my god,' he screamed out as they both explosively climaxed together. Jammin' Boy screamed out loudly, which suddenly woke him up. A stream of saliva started to trickle down his cheek, his eyes barely open, face screwed up, he stretched his arms above his head and rolled over to face Jennifer, who was lying on her back with her ample sized breasts resting just over the duvet.

'Good morning prince charming, how are you doin'?' Jennifer asked in an imitation Italian accent.

'Mornin' Jen, I'm good tanks, but feelin' a l'il sore. Mi ed feels like a balloon. I tink I need a few ibuprofen n some fizzy water to rehydrate,' he replied in a wearily voice.

'Ya body was spasming a few minutes ago, were you having a vivid dream?'

'Eeeeeer, it's so strange ya know, di ting is, like most dreams, I can't remember!' he responded, being rather economical with the truth.

His dreams had been a no holds barred epic, but he couldn't reveal the truth to Jennifer, because he knew she was so incredibly desperate to seduce and dominate him sexually.

'I've got a l'il present for ya,' she said.

'What may dat delightful gift be?' responded Jammin' Boy.

'Look under the covers.'

'Geez, two pedigree pussies.' he laughed.

'Yeah, n I think they both need feeding, one of thems already been neglected.'

'They've both been treated wid precious unequivocal TLC, plus I can only ear one o dem purrin',' he joked.

'Are you gonna give me a morning kiss then?' Jennifer asked. He leant across to give her a gentle kiss on her right cheek.

'No, I said a kiss, not a fairy flick!'

He began to move towards her again, after pulling away following the first kiss, Felix miaowed and then wriggled from beneath Jennifer's legs and the covers and let out a frustrated cry, 'Miaoooow.'

His tail was all splayed and puffed, which meant he wasn't at all happy. Not only had he been ignored, he'd also been inadvertently ejected from the bed, thanks to Jennifer's efforts to once more entice him into a fraternising interlude. Eventually Jammin' Boy planted a kiss on to her lips, they were both rather moist with saliva and excitement. Jammin' Boy shuffled himself into the missionary position, on top and thrusted his pelvis into hers. She nibbled his lips and proceeded to insert her tongue into his mouth, which he willingly reciprocated. He could taste the stale stench of alcohol from the night before, which was hardly the most appealing. He withdrew.

'I need di loo.'

He lifted himself up. His prominent bulge in the private area of his shorts was endeavouring to force its way out reminiscent of a Concorde plane's nose, poking out of its aircraft hangar. Jennifer brushed her fingers against the bulging object with one hand and with the other slid inside to feel the silky smooth specimen. He managed to wriggle away, clambering out of bed.

'He's definitely ready to feast on his Latin banquet after falling asleep in the tapas several hours ago!' Jennifer said, purring with pleasure.

'E's ready to squirt out di poisonous toxins from io bladder.'

'Hurry up, I need some lovin',' she said sensuously.

Jammin' Boy shuffled to the bathroom rather quickly as he didn't want to have an unfortunate accident and be caught up the proverbial creek without a paddle, mid flow in other words. What a relief, the bathroom was empty. Up with the lid and down with the bottom, he decided to have a she wee by sitting down on the seat.

'Phew,' he let out a huge sigh of fulfilment as he emptied copious amounts of alcohol toxins from his super sized bladder. The door was pushed open,

'Oops, sorry, I didn't mean to disturb you.' said Annabelle extremely embarrassed as she came in to the bathroom, naked.

'OMG! Dats enough to give a man a cardiac, wi doze bouncin' fruits n ya orchard below. D'ya normally go to di toilet naked?' he questioned in a state of shock. His heart in his stomach, his eyes popping out of their sockets, his tongue dropping out and middle leg suddenly flicking at the rim of the toilet seat. He puffed his cheeks out in pure astonishment.

'I thought I was at home, sorry, I'm still really drunk!'

She turned round and walked back towards the spare bedroom, embarrassed at the unexpected toilet rendezvous. Jammin' Boy couldn't help but notice a large red hand print on her left buttock, obviously a symbol left by Ash. It certainly left Annabelle bewildered and wondering how she'd manage to look Jammin' Boy in the eye, after he'd seen her starkers and full frontal.

'What a hot honey she is,' he thought to himself.

He was still trying to come to terms with the mind blowing experience. Let alone had he seen Jennifer up close and personal, now Bella. He needed a few minutes to re-gather his thoughts, so he closed the bathroom door, flushed the toilet and sat on the lid, reflecting on an enlightening start to the day. Jammin' Boy started to droop his head and doze, suddenly, a knock at the bathroom door. KNOCK, KNOCK...

'Jammin', It's me, let me in.'

Jennifer had risen from the bed and was unrelenting. 'Can you hear that?' she asked.

'Boooy, it sounds like wolf cries.'

Ash and Annabelle were having sex again. It was incredibly loud, as Bella was screaming with pleasure, as they enjoyed themselves.

'Jammin', I'm so horny, take me, take me!' she demanded.

He was becoming so restless and frustrated at her lack of reluctance, he thought, 'Riiight, dis is it, I'm gonna give er what she wants n opefully dat'll be di end of it! Dere are some condoms in dat cabinet, pull out a featherlite ribbed one!'

He just wanted her to go, to be honest, but he didn't want to become irate, although he was a little agitated. She bit open the wrapper with her teeth, put her tongue inside the condom, outside in and then knelt down in front of him and moved her mouth towards his crown jewels. Her hands tugged at his shorts, unfastening the draw string and smoothly sliding them down to the floor, where he managed to lift his feet out of the leg holes, then flicked them towards the radiator with his left foot.

She stroked his penis with her fingers, which encouraged it to stand even higher to attention. She placed her lips around the summit and then gently rolled the condom onto it, all the way down to the base, where she began to lick and suck his glory. She was filled with immense excitement as this was exactly the situation she was dreaming of being in, however, this was the real deal. Their hearts raced ten to the dozen, as they were so immersed in this act of terrific titillation. Jammin' Boys toes curled upwards, his knees began to shake, sweat started to secrete from his armpits, his skin turned goose pimply and slightly red in colour. Jennifer stood up, rapidly whisked off her thong displaying her neatly trimmed modesty. She gazed deep into his glistening brown eyes, lifted her right leg, climbing on to him. She lowered herself towards his prominent member just so her moist lips were touching his middle man, gyrating backwards and forwards leaving him groaning with pleasure. The sensation was absolutely electric as she teased and tormented him, until he couldn't take any more. He pulled her down on to the shaft of his penis.

'Oooh, oooh,' he squealed with pure ecstasy. He never expected this moment, as he'd been so reluctant throughout the night and early hours of the morning, but was succumbed by Jennifer's rampant mood. She had accosted him in the toilet, virtually forcing him to have sex with her, which proved eventually, an irresistible proposition. She rode him like a wild cowgirl, closing her eyes, frantically swishing her body to the left, to the right, backwards and forwards. In the adjacent room, Ash and Annabelle were engaging in a sexual marathon. Their groans and moans could be heard throughout the entire house. Jennifer and Jammin' Boy were a little quieter, but still making plenty of noise. The bathroom frosted glass window had steamed up, it was no longer translucent. Jammin' Boy's bottom was beginning to feel a little uncomfortable as she rocked up and down on him. He decided to lift her off, as he didn't want to break the ceramic toilet seat, which had started to slide as the screws had become quite loose. 'Lean over di sink n I'll take ya from behind!' he ordered.

Jennifer relished his dominant Alpha Male mantra. She willingly obliged,

'Yeeees, ooooh please.' she cajoled.

What a phenomenal sight! Her backside was unbelievably perfect, shaped like a ripe horse chestnut that had fallen off the tree in the middle of autumn. It was firm, toned and so spankable. He couldn't restrain himself, so smacked her right cheek quite firmly. THWACK, was the loud sound. She pushed her backside towards him, holding on to the window sill and fondling her breasts as he entered her. The sex was earth shattering, the tempo was unrelenting, the sensation was mind blowing and the temperature was scorching. Thirty minutes later their bodies were still entwined, sliding against one another as they were saturated with perspiration. Occasionally kissing, caressing and stroking, no wham bam thank you Mam.! It was approaching ten am, they'd been indulging in frivolity for an hour and a half. By this time Fluffy Donkey and Stacey had drank a cup of herbal tea and were watching a wildlife documentary on Sky TV's Discovery channel. Jennifer and Jammin' Boy had hopped into the shower cubicle and turned on the water, as they copulated with her wrapping her legs around his waist. He was a strong athletic male at five foot eleven inches, so it was no problem holding her, it was just a great substitute for a gym workout.

She swished her hair so it brushed him in the face, enabling him to smell the sweet scent of conditioner that was emitting from the silky strands. He squeezed her bottom as she writhed up and down on him, squashing her beautiful breasts into his muscular chest. Her eyes were closed as she savoured the breathtaking experience with the guy she'd been desperate to snare for many months now. Her mind was totally transfixed and her body paralysed by her fantasy encounter. The warm water was jet propelled over their heads and bodies which provided a therapeutic massage, heightening the mood. Jennifer's body shuddered repeatedly as she came to an electrifying tingling climax. The spasm induced Jammin' Boy into reaching the same euphoric high moments later. Jennifer puffed out her cheeks, gazed into his eyes like a satiated puppy dog in awe of its owner. Jammin' Boy picked up a bottle of vanilla and ylang ylang foamburst, squirted it over Jennifer's firm chest and stomach, proceeding to massage it around her body. She continued to moan and gasp with pure excitement, in total ecstasy, savouring every moment. He gently eased her back against the light grey tiles, lifted her right leg and soothingly rubbed in some more shower cream, massaging it into a frothy lather. She was thoroughly enjoying being pampered with exfoliating beauty treatment. In her eyes it was far better than any health spa day she could have paid for. Jammin' Boy slipped on his white mesh glove, dipped his hand into a hard plastic container that had sugar and honey already mixed in. This was his home made exfoliating potion. Cheaper than buying from a store and considerable cheap too. The tough grain of the sugar entwined with the smooth texture of the honey had an extremely soothing effect on the skin. After massaging both legs, he turned her around so her front was facing the wall and gently began to massage her neck, shoulders and back. She shuddered every now and then as his warm and sensuous gentle touch sent shivers racing down her spine. He was in a state of astonishment, as he never intended to indulge in a highly explosive and passionate interlude with Jennifer, despite it being her fundamental objective for the past, for so many months. He slid off his condom holding onto the teat, tied it in a knot at the base and dropped it in the corner of the shower. After rinsing her body with a cool invigorating shower head jet spray, she returned the compliment to Jammin' Boy. He was wanting to quickly conclude this breathtaking encounter, as he had an inclination that Jennifer would probably want to savour these trysts far too frequently and no doubt be more than willing to embark on a relationship. This was definitely not on his agenda, as he was blissfully happy with his desirable status of eligibility.

They stepped out of the shower basin, each drying the other with a warm fluffy turquoise towel that had been hanging over the chic gleaming stainless steel radiator. Jammin' Boy had somehow managed to keep his funky fro virtually dry, apart from a few droplets of water that gave it a silky shimmer. He gazed briefly at himself in the mirror on the opposite wall and asked, 'Mirror, mirror on the wall, who is the king of this house in summer and fall?'

'Miaow, Miaow,' came a strong cry from Felix outside the bathroom door, as if to question his owners thought process, by answering at an opportune moment!

'Ha, haaa, I think that's ya answer. Felix runs this house twenty four seven.' chuckled Jennifer.

'Yeeaah, you got dat right. No-one's a superior being to legendary Felix di House Cat.' said Jammin' Boy rather smugly.

'Not even the well known DJing namesake rivals that pussy cat.' responded Jennifer.

After drying themselves, they made their way to the bedroom, where Jennifer dropped her towel displaying her breathtaking body once again. It was a subliminal sign that she wanted him to ravish her, however, he had other ideas, such as getting dressed and making breakfast for everyone. He quickly creamed his body with Palmers coco butter, ensuring to pay special attention to his wrinkled elephant elbows and knees. Those parts of the anatomy had a tendency to dry out ridiculously quickly on skin of the afro Caribbean race. He threw on a pair of baggy dark blue nylon above the knee Nike shorts and a plain white loosely fitting t-shirt, before slipping into his favourite light brown moccasins. He opened the bedroom curtains, the weather was stunningly beautiful, with barely a cotton wool cloud in sight. It appeared Jennifer had resigned herself to the fact that there wasn't going to be a part deux today. She put on her brown micro denim shorts over her skimpy thong and pulled on her vest top.

'Come on Jen, let's get di brekkie angover party on di road n into di kitchen.'

Chapter 14

Hangover Cure

They went downstairs to join Fluffy Donkey and Stacey who were snuggled on the sofa in the living room, still watching the wildlife documentary. 'Mornin' you two. Did ya sleep well, or were di noises from di spare room keepin' y'all awake?' asked Jammin' Boy.

'I slept like a seven month old baby.' replied Fluffy Donkey.

'I probably managed to get three hours. The grunting walrus over there n those two wild creatures upstairs, bangin', screamin', yellin' n groanin'. Geeeez! I felt like I'd taken refuge in the jungle,' answered Stacey rather wearily.

'Sorry about di noise, normally it's a ghost town wi just me n Felix.'

'Yeeeeaaah. But you roar like a lion JB!' Jennifer said feistily.

'Dat's because I'm a manimal! Owooooooo!' bellowed Jammin' Boy.

Upstairs Ash and Annabelle were making themselves look presentable, getting ready to come down for breakfast. Ash opened the curtains, while Annabelle turned her back to him and put her clothes on. A little surprising after being a rampant wild tigress in the middle of the night. Contrasting behaviour to say the least.

'Thanks for a super special night Ash. It was wicked n I enjoyed every single moment, n Tom's birthday bash wasn't bad either!'

'I like to give my guests V.I.P. exclusive status treatment.'

'That was five star deluxe with extras included,' she responded chuckling.

Ash gazed into the full length mirror placed between the pine walk in wardrobes and curtains. He softly caressed his tightly twisted curls, making sure he looked immaculate as usual. Annabelle went to the bathroom to wash her face and empty some more of her toxic bladder content. Jammin' Boy could hear movement upstairs, so shouted up as he danced through to the kitchen to prepare Sabbath day delights.

'What d'you two want for brekkie? Omelette, cereal, scrambled egg on toast or toad in di hole?' he broke out with a wicked laugh.

'Toad in the hole for breakfast Jammin', are you sure?' shouted down Ash in a forced aristocratically English accent.

'Nooo… Just jokin' wi dat. I just tought you two might wanna stay upstairs for a mornin' banquet?' he teased.

'Only if you're gonna provide the entertainment,' retorted Ash.

'Why is Bella willin' to…?'

Annabelle interjected, 'We'll have the omelette thanks Jammin'. No need for the regal banquet, and no I don't share my mouth-waterin' cuisine. I'm a selfish girl.'

'OK. Distinguished amazin' omelette comin' up. Oooops… I mean, make sure ya come down fa it!' said Jammin' Boy.

'Give us five mins.' she responded as she returned to the bedroom to give Ash a juicy morning kiss.

Jennifer became enthralled in the wildlife documentary that Stacey and Fluffy Donkey were watching on Sky TVs Discovery channel. It was a two hour long epic about the relationship of the female lion and her cubs.

'That's the perfect animal epitome of Jasmine, always on the lookout and huntin' for a good source of meat!' stated Jennifer.

Fluffy Donkey and Stacey burst out laughing at Jennifer's analogy.

'Difference is, the lioness is a l'il more meticulous n strategic. Jasmine's direct n potent n goes straight for the jugular!' replied Stacey.

The living room door opened.

'Are you three feeling a bit broody, watchin' wildlife programmes about female lion nurturin'?' asked Annabelle.

'It just seemed really interesting. Ideal n easy like a Sunday mornin', aka Lionel Ritchie,' commented Fluffy Donkey.

'I'm just analysin' graceful stride patterns for mi long jump technique. If I could sprint half as quickly as her, I'd be the World Record Holder.'

'For killin' wildebeests?' teased Fluffy Donkey.

'Yeeeeah. I'll start with you first shall I? Oops, sorry, you're a Fluffy Donkey, Joe, not really a beast!' answered Stacey in her usual wit.

'Uuuuuum. Something smells reaaaaaal good! D'ya need a hand JB?' asked Ash.

The smoke alarm started beeping in the hallway. BEEP BEEP BEEP BEEP.

'Can you jus close di kitchen door please Ashilito, so dat blasted alarm stops?' pleaded Jammin' Boy.

The aroma was divinely delicious, circulating through the entire house. It was no surprise that Felix suddenly emerged, licking his lips and waltzing around Jammin' Boy swishing his tail and purring loudly. Jammin' Boy poured a small amount of milk into his bowl.

'I'll give ya some omelette when it's done.'

'Miaooooow, miaoooooow,' was the cry from Felix, telepathically acknowledging his owners promises, as if Jammin' Boy was the equivalent of Doctor Doolittle.

It was nearly midday, so they were about to munch on some brunch. Everyone was extremely hungry, desperate to absorb the excessive alcohol consumed last night. Apart from Jammin' Boy everyone was struggling with a hangover, as the party had been a massive celebration for Tom's 30th.

'So what did you two love birds get up to this mornin, while we were all sleepin' soundly?' said Annabelle poking fun at Fluffy Donkey and Stacey.

'We slept like new born lion cubs, not like you gruntin' n groanin' wild creatures upstairs. I heard screamin' n bangin' from upstairs. Were you n Ash sleep talkin' or just re-enactin' a scene from Nine and a Half Weeks?'

'We were just kissing n caressing. You should know I don't engage in naughtiness with total strangers Stace!'

'Well...You'd known each other for at least eight hours, so that's virtually a boyfriend for you ain't it?' Stacey jibed.

'Give me a small amount o credit. I'm almost as righteous n as respectable as the Virgin Mary!'

'You mean by keepin' ya clothes on in public?' laughed Stacey.

'Yeah, maybe next time, be a l'il quieter n gag each other, or at least provide some guest invites for ya huntin' ritual!' said Fluffy Donkey.

'Are y'all ready fa di most delicious omelette in Honeyville? Deze are di most aromatic n flavoursome ones around, not to be missed.' shouted Jammin' Boy into the living room.

The group were still watching the wildlife documentary, although it was nearing a close. They all made their way through to the kitchen where Ash had kindly set the table with cutlery and condiments. They sat themselves down at the pine wood table which was oval shaped accompanied by simple matching chairs that were of a conventional design with a rustic touch, but not too extravagant. They were of course four legged like the average quadruped animal. They had two solid wooden horizontal panels forming the back, complimented by a wooden base. Thankfully Jammin' Boy had bought six chairs, as he regularly had guests round, family and friends, so he required adequate supply. Stacey and Ash had opted for a bowl of muesli with fresh yogurt and sliced banana, topped off with a sprinkling of juicy blueberries and fresh honey. Jammin' Boy and Ash served the breakfasts out. Jammin' Boy had used egg, bacon, sliced chorizo, a drizzle of hot pepper sauce to provide a spicy kung fu style kick, with dill on top, finished with a sprinkling of black pepper. A helping of sliced organic plum tomatoes was provided with a tasty enhancement of sea salt and black pepper. Lips were licked, aromas inhaled through excited nasal cavities, with a few pairs of eyes closed as this heightened the scent of assorted spices. They all tucked in to their breakfasts, relishing the contentment of being one step closer to healing their hungover heads. It was certainly a less jovial and vibrant sanctuary, compared to the shenanigans of the previous day/evening, as the noise level had reached a high octane mixed with temperatures rising meteorologically as well as physically.

'It appears that me and Stace are the odd ones out around here doesn't it!' piped up Fluffy Donkey.

'Only because you didn't share a bed and decided to crash on the sofa or floor!' answered Annabelle.

'I'd say I'm the odd one out guys.'

'Why's that Jen?' asked Annabelle.

'Weeell, I'm Latin, I'm under dressed for brekkie and I feel full of energy compared to the rest of ya!'

'Di less said di better Jen, don't cha tink?' advised Jammin' Boy.

'Que paso JB? I've nothin' to hide. I had an absolutely love-tastic mornin'! Uuuum uuuum uuuuuum. This omelette tastes almost as good as you!' stated Jennifer.

She licked her lips, swished her hair and stroked his thigh. Jammin' Boy cheekily slapped her thigh.

'D'ya mind woman. Let's possess some decorum at di table. It's Sabbath day n brekkie time. No frivolity ere please, udderwise you'll be evicted, just like di Big Brother household!' Jammin' Boy pretended to act seriously, before bursting into a crazy fit of laughter.

'Who got outta the wrong side of bed this mornin'!' remarked Annabelle in a disapproving tone.

'Bella, believe you me, if dat's di wrong side o di bed, I can't wait fa di right side. Wouch. It'l be a volcanic earthquake explosive fusion. Oooooh.'

'Are you OK Jen?' asked Annabelle.

Jennifer's eyes were closed momentarily. 'OMG. Sorry peeps, I'm just fantasisin' abouuuuut…!'

'Go on,' encouraged Ash.

'Leave it out brudder. Let's just enjoy di delights o dis beautiful afternoon. It's post nine o'clock, but no watershed.' Jammin' Boy pleaded.

Civilised behaviour was restored as they were thankfully all eventually engrossed in a feeding frenzy. Jammin' Boy stood up and went to get the ice cold water container from the fridge. He opened the freezer door and pulled out a drawer which had a tray full of ice bags. He plopped half a dozen or so cubes into the container and took it to the table. 'Would anyone like some fresh juice to mix? I've got passion fruit, mango and OJ, cranberry, peach and guava. So what you waaant peeps?' he asked.

'The OJ one please.' said Ash.

'Same for me please.' said Jennifer.

'Give me one of JB's speciality mixes please.' asked Fluffy Donkey.

'I'll have H2O please. I need to rehydrate to flush out those toxic liquors,' said Annabelle.

'Snap,' answered Stacey.

'Right den, some special concoctions of an exotic fruit juicy delight comin' right at ya!'

Jammin' Boy poured all the drinks and brought them all to the table. They were graciously received by all breakfast diners.

'Oh JB, you're good to marry!' said Ash.

'If you want Ashilito, dere's a spare room, so ya always welcome to move in n be my right hand wo-man.' he openly invited, laughing at the prospect.

'Hmmm. Would you like me dressed in my typical debonair n suave attire, or to don on some sexy slinky camp numbers?' asked Ash in a prominent forced camp tone.

'Honey, I'd love to see ya dressed to impress, wid a l'il halter neck top n a micro mini, displayin' ya refined modesty!' Jammin' Boy responded.

'Speaking of which boys. Why don't we grace the Rocky Horror show with our presence?' proposed Fluffy Donkey.

'Oooh. Is it man rule only then? Ya not gonna invite a few sexy ladies to accompany you to the spectacular?' asked Jennifer, rather displeased by the exclusively men only suggestion.

'Noooooooo Jen. I was gonna also add, the ladies are also welcome. How could I invite the girls n not the boys?' joked Fluffy Donkey.

'What d'ya mean? You just invited the boys!'

'If ya get my drift. I invited the shims firstly, followed by the man-she's!'

'What's a shim Fluffy?' asked Jennifer.

'A shims, half man half woman, or just a man in drag,' said Fluffy.

'So ya tryin' to say that the ladies are man-she's?'

'Relax Jen. It's only a figure of speech. I don't mean you all look masculine, but then again, that ain't a five o'clock shadow on ya top lip is it?' Teased Fluffy.

'Ya not too big to slap Joe,' Jennifer said disconsolately.

'Ooooooooooo, ya don't mind JB do ya, if Jen puts me over her knee?'

'No. But dis is gettin' too kinky. Can we enjoy brekkie before the convo gets even dirtier! I don't like eatin' eggs n sausage while all dese double entendre's n smut coments are bein' made! You know I'm a good righteous Christian boy!' Jammin' Boy said.

'Righteous? Christian? Practice what ya preach Jammin'. Annabelle said.

'You didn't see me walkin' into di bathroom stark naked dis mornin' did ya? Knowin' dat somebody may be in dare. Talk about gettin' a Sabbath day eyeful.' he responded, embarassing Annabelle.

'It was an accident. I thought I was sleep walkin' and savourin' a lucid dream, walkin' into the arms of my hero?!' she replied.

'Ha Haaaa. Are you tryin' to say, I'm ya hero?!'

'Hhmmmm… Noooooo. After spendin' the night with Ashilito, I couldn't call you my hero today. At school, definitely. I aspire to everything you are. You're a legend at Oatmill High. I see the effect you have on the kids. They're in pure awe of you. It must be that jungle you carry on ya head?!' said Annabelle, tormenting Jammin' Boy.

'Woooow Bella. I'm totally flattered. Dats such a glowin' tribute. I'm still in my infancy, havin' only been teachin' for a handful of years at Oatmill.'

'It's true! You should see how excited they are when they see you. They treat you like a friend n also respect you as their teacher. Ya like a Tzar of education. You inspire, instill trust and elevate self esteem in people, givin' them a sense of self belief, enablin' them to reach dizzier heights!' Annabelle raved about the resonating attributes JB possessed.

'Many thanks Bella. I extend my gratitude n appreciation to ya lady! Would anyone like some more food or drink? If so, help yaself. Any guest at my yard is virtually part o di furniture. Jus treat it as an eat all ya want buffet!'

'I'm totally full up after this mouthwatering caribbean style omelette. It was totally luscious. Just like your lips JB!' said Jennifer licking her lips and winking at him.

'Yeah boy. Almost as good as my Swedish meatball delicacy. Next time, make it a l'il spicier, just like Bella.' responded Ash.

Annabelle was starting to blush with all the antagonising comments about her sensuously erotic behaviour during the early morning hours. The grunts, the groans, the arousing display of landing nudity etc.

'OK gentleman. I think I've been embarrassed enough now and deserve some anonymity.' Annabelle pleaded.

'In dis house, everythin's discussed in an open forum. It's a liberatin' sanctuary n dare's no place to hide. Ya get swamped by di paparazzi cultures ere.' laughed JB.

Jammin' Boy wasn't a devout Christian, certainly by no stretch of the imagination, however, he had high moral values and dignity and didn't feel it really appropriate to engage in gratuitous sexual conversation at the dining table.

JB had managed to restore some decorum at the dining table with the potential of it becoming a little uncuth with a montagé of sexual connotations.

'Right den, anyone for extras?' asked JB.

'D'ya fancy giving the group the pleasurable delight of a private dance Bella? JB was quite close to receivin' one this mornin'!' teased Jennifer.

'Didn't we say the saucy smut was a l'il inappropriate pre watershed on a Sunday?' said Stacey.

'Damn right. I don't mind it in di room, in di bathroom, in di shower, in di bed, al fresco, but not at di table. Tank you peeps, let dis be ya final warnin', udderwise you'll face a forfeit. You know what I'm sayin' Jen!' said JB while given Jennifer a prominent stare of semi disdain and flirtation.

'I aint gonna embarass myself again, so ya can get those crazy ideas right outta ya filthy thinkin' head! I'm a respectable teacher of the finest history, not a charitable lap dancer. I thought you'd have more respect, unless you wanna headline a dynamic duo show Jen?' Annabelle was momentarily disconsolate, but then threw it back in Jennifer's face.

'Meeeeee? A good n honourable Catholic Latina! No chance. I leave my birthday suit explicitly for the bedroom, or behind closed doors Bella. I know you love the door open, aint that right, Jammin'?' Jennifer making a jibe at Annabelle.

'Come on Jen, give me a break. You have to make allowances for a foolish slip.'

'You slipped alright. Without a towel, bra, knickers or at the very least a dressing gown, oops, sorry… I mean a dressing down! Ha Haaaaaaaa.' Jennifer continued to goad Annabelle.

Annabelle decided to humour Jennifer as she couldn't be bothered with continuing a prolongad sledging match. They had a very good relationship both in and out of school, but this was about to bubble over. Annabelle treated Jennifer with the contempt some of her antagonising comments deserved, diffusing them with a smile, a playful response without becoming confrontational and endeavouring to belittle her. Also, Annabelle was feeling extremely light headed after the indulgence of alcohol in the last sixteen hours or so.

'D'ya have any ibuprofen JB, please?' asked Annabelle.

'You lightweight Bella,' said Jennifer.

'We're not all hardcore drinkers like you. Ya putting ya Spanish heritage to shame, by convertin' to a typical embarrasin' drinkin' drunken brit!' responded Annabelle, laughing.

'I'm still a lady on the street n a freak in the bedroom, as opposed to being a freak on the street and a lady in the bedroom!' said Jennifer.

'That's questionable, considering you were virtually physically seducin' n violatin' JB on the dancefloor last night n rubbin' your slippery nipples! Ooooow ooooooooo. Take that, I've got the formula, I've got the formula, take that!' Annabelle hit right back with a vengeance.

'Come on you two ladies. There are two fluffy pedigree pussy cats in this house, we don't want a human cat fight,' said Fluffy Donkey.

'Miiiiiaaaaaaaoooooooow,' mimmicked Ash.

At that precise moment, comically, as if the scene had been sketched and choreographed, Felix nonchantly glided back into the kitchen, curious to what the comotion was all about. To be honest, it was only a bit of playful banter between friends.

'Miiiiiaaaaaaoow.' said Felix.

'I think we should all go n make ourselves cosy in the front room.' suggested Ash.

'Yeeeeah. Otherwise, dem fireworks are gonna be explosive! BOOOM!' said JB.

Fluffy Donkey and Stacey volunteered to wash up and dry, while Annabelle put the crockery and cutlery away, Jennifer, Ash and JB went into the room to chill out. They sat down and started to look through the sky tv film listings. A romcom would be the perfect tonic, being light hearted and not too thought provoking, such as a chiller thriller, sci fi, action or suspense epic. As it was the weekend, the final day of it albeit, thankfully none of them had any plans. Even if they had, they'd probably be too exhausted after a manic, action packed and wild last twenty four hours.

'Let's watch Dumb and Dumber, it starts at two n 'll be the ideal cure for sleepy heads n wilting eyes,' saidAsh.

'Yeah, dats a classic movie. It's a laugh a minute wi Jim 'scary' Carey n dat other guy. What's e called again?' asked JB.

'Jeeeff. I can't remember his surname.' said Jennifer.

'Nathaniel, is it?' asked Ash.

'No, it aint dat. It sounds similar tho. Jeff, Jeff, Jeeeff Emmanuel. Dat's it, Jeff Emmanuel!' replied JB with conviction.

'Noooo. It definitely aint that,' stated Ash.

'Right den, I'll check mi iPhone for di film cast.' said JB.

'Why d'ya need to do that Jammin'? Just simply click on the info button on the sky remote!' suggested Jennifer.

'OMG. How drunk am I. I can't even tink straight. Mi eds splittin' like a pair o tight trousers on a twenty five stone klump!'

A ripple of laughter sounded from Ash and Jennifer.

'I think ya drunk n hypnotised by the J factor,' Ash said.

'Di J factor, what's dat?!' said JB.

'Come on Jammin'. She's sittin' right next to ya'

'Stop it Ashilito! I'm drunk on him, if the truth be known!' Jennifer responded with a humourous lilt.

Fluffy Donkey, Annabelle and Stacey had eventually fiinished their kitchen post brekkie chores, clinking and clanking pot washing and drying with immense eye catching precision. That was only because Annabelle had lost her contact lenses, so couldn't really see how dry the crockery and cutlery were. Although, surely running a trusting sensitive hand across would have been an easier option. 'All the work's done, are we welcome now to come n gatecrash this humble sanctuary?' asked Annabelle.

'Take a seat, relax n enjoy dis movie classic. Does anyone want popcorn, ice cream or sweeties? If so, you better ead to di shop, because, I'm fresh outta dem delights!'

'Loooord JB, thought this was a mini cinema with a tuck shop?' stated Stacey.

'You thought wrong, it's a room to Vue, but not a candy shop. What more d'ya want? BBQ food, alcohol, bed, brekkie, music n movies. Dis is di supreme B n B, better dan any otel, but like I said, if you want any more refreshments, move ya ass quick time!' JB heckled.

They were all sat cosily, eyes blinking, minds relaxed, stomachs satiated after a late brekkie, looking forward to the hysterical and incredibly crazy slapstick comedy of Dumb and Dumber. The horizontal blinds were closed, volume turned up with stereo sound on, to give the mini cinema style feel to the front room. As they'd all eaten breakfast, no-one had any desire to munch any snacks, just soft drinks of water and fruit juice to continually rehydrate their water depleted bodies. All parties had seen the movie before, but on the day before the start of the following week, what an ideal choice to stimulate minds and tickle the humour. The intimate couples from earlier sat side by side, with Fluffy Donkey and Stacey making up the numbers, but choosing to sit seperately. It looked inevitable though, that the two of them would organise to rendezvous at a later date. There were definitely a few flickering sparks between them.

Chapter 16

Farewell Party Poopers

After an atmospheric, enjoyable, eventful and wild weekend of partying, fornicating, drinking, eating nutritious and junk trunk food, movie watching and chilling, it was time for everyone to say farewell to JB's sanctuary. Felix appeared disappointed, as he could detect the party poopers were about to head off to their homely abodes.

'We should do this again quite soon. An absolute classic rollercoaster white knuckle ride of a weekend.'

'Yeah man. Dats a perfect description of dis extra-ordinary experience Ash. I couldn't a put it better miself.'

'I think next time we should have a movie night, what d'ya think Jammin'?' suggested Annabelle.

'Yeah, good idea Bella, but dat doesn't mean makin' x-rated ones after di shenanigans in dis place within di las twenty four hours. Purely mind blowin'!'

'You can say that again. Phenomenally explosively incredible. I can't wait for part deux.' said Jennifer.

'Part deux will appen, but widowt di extra desert dream toppin' elpin's. Dat wasn't on di menú, but I suppose, sometimes, when a dish o di day is magically appears, it's too good to resist.'

'Jammin', thanks for exceptional hospitality, apart from the wild cat roars in the middle of the night. I know Felix is a heavy sleeper, but I didn't know you reared lions upstairs? Stace n I managed to squeeze in a few hours sleep, but felt like we were campin' out in the jungle.' Fluffy Donkey congratulated JB in a tongue in cheek manner.

Felix was circling, brushing himself up against Jennifer and Annabelle.

'Don't ya like me Felix? There are more than two girls in this house!' asked Stacey.

Virtually immediately, he gracefully walked across to Stacey.

'Thanks Felix. At least I know ya not neglecting me. Just a l'il magic toooouch, just a l'il magic, I know it's not tragic, just a l'il maaagic tooouch!' she sang.

'Stace, please don't put the windows through,' said Fluffy Donkey.

'I'll try not to.'

'With a voice like that, you should be buskin' at London Underground stations. Wouch, amazin'!' Fluffy Donkey totally astounded by the arppegio sung by Stacey purely effortlessly.

Can I take him with me JB?' asked Stacey.

'Could ya deal wid, cleanin' up poo poo, moppin' up pee pee n dealin' wid sick when he's ill?'

'Yeah. I love cats. Don't wanna deprive you of the luxury of a regal cat though.'

'E aint regal, e's just a simple lovin' pedigree tiger. I'd give im to ya, but e's priceless, n it'd break mi eart to let im go, even dough e can be a handful now n den!' responded JB.

The clock had struck four fifteen in the afternoon and JB's abode was about to become a ghost town, after a lively last twenty four hours. 'Does anyone need a lift home, or are you makin' ya own way?' asked Fluffy Donkey.

'You can drop me off Joe, if you don't mind.' answered Stacey.

'If you can squeeze me in, I'd be grateful.' said Ash.

'I'll get a taxi with Annabelle, unless I stay here tonight Jammin'?' replied Jennifer.

'You could, but it'd be in di spare bedroom.'

'Uuuurgh. I don't really fancy sleepin' in stained bed sheets Jammin'! Surely I could keep you company in your bed?'

'Don't you worry, I'd change em for ya, n wouldn't expect you to sleep in di dirt left by dose two roarin' wildcats. Plus, mi bed was only a Saturday night special birthday celebratory treat.' responded JB, referring to Ash and Annabelle, also refuting the possibility of Jennifer staying in his bed.

'You spoil sport.'

'I need mi precious beauty sleep on a school night. Also, wouldn't want any rumours spreadin' about di two of us.'

'Whatever happened last night n this mornin' will be kept securely locked behind these close doors,' said Jennifer.

'Dat's a l'il tough, because di front doors now open. So dem experiences may start floatin' out into di public eye n make dere way to Oatmill High School staff room?'

'Jammin', don't you worry, we're not gonna circulate our dirty weekend sexploits. I think the secret's definitely safe with us, aint that right Stace?' Annabelle commented.

'I agree Bella, but one slight problem. How about if Victoria gets hold of these revelations?' answered Stacey.

'I don't get it?' replied Jennifer rather puzzled.

'Come on Jen. I know you're virtually commando under those skimpy denim hot pants aren't ya?' said Stacey.

'I know who ya mean Stace. That underwear guru, Victoria's Secrets,' said Ash.

'Well done. You don't cross dress d'ya Ashilito?' asked Stacey.

'Uuuuuuuum. Wouldn't you like to know. Sometimes I like to be in touch with my feminine side daaaarling,' joked Ash.

'I bet you look quite sexy in a pair of cheekies and foxy bra!' Annabelle said, smiling widely like a cheshire cat.

'I might give you a sight one of these days. Just outta curiosity, what are cheekies?'

'Oooooo please. I'd love that, what a lucky girl I'd be. You don't know what cheekies are?'

'No, I've never heard o them. Tell me.'

'They're slinky mini knickers n are really hot n sexy. I'll return the compliment and throw a pair of those on for ya, if we experience deja-vu!' stated Annabelle, giving Ash some underwear advice.

'Are you peeps ready, it's time to go?' said Fluffy Donkey.

Ash and Stacey answered in harmony. 'Yeeeah.'

They all hugged and said their goodbyes. Joe, Ash and Stacey walked out of the door and along the driveway to his car.

'Jammin', next time I'll make sure I remember the hibiscus.' shouted Ash.

'You bedder. You promised to bring it when we spoke on di phone yesterday.' JB replied.

'Don't you worry. Trust me, I won't make the same mistake twice.'

Ash's response was just about heard by JB as he climbed into Fluffy Donkey's car. Annabelle phoned a taxi for her and Jennifer. They lived a few miles away, in the other direction to Joe, so they were insistant they'd be OK catching a cab. Annabelle had ordered a taxi through Lucky Star for quarter to five. JB had put the kettle on, ready to make the girls a drink, as they had half an hour to wait for their ride. JB pulled out three bags of detox tea, as this would help to cleanse and revitalise them even more.

'Would you like oney and fresh ginger wi di erbal number?' he asked.

'Please Jammin'!' Confirmed Annabelle.

'Yeah, that'd be great please. Do you peel the skin off the ginger or have it raw?' asked Jennifer.

'I wash it n leave it fresh n raw, just like I like my girls!' JB laughed winking at Jennifer.

'Fresh n raw, what are you tryin' to say? Puto madre.' Jennifer answered a little disgruntled.

'Ya fresh Jen, but raw in terms o di ocasionally arsh Mudder Spanish tongue. Comprendas, si? Puto madre's a bit arsh dough, aint it? I've never done dat in mi life.' he jibed at Jennifer.

'Never? I doubt that, with all your ladies in proverbial tow!'

'I've probably ad an encounter wid a few, but I've never seen dere kids!' responded JB.

'I didn't know you fornicated with goats? Isn't that classed as bestiality?'

'Not dem kinda kids. Children! D'ya tink a man o my esteem would be indulgin' in repulsive n depraved animals? You're disgustin' Jen!'

'It's only tongue in cheek. I don't mean it literally.'

'So you mean, physically?'

'Noooo, but I'd like some more physical education with you!' said Jennifer.

'No chance. I'm gonna put mi chastity belt back on n join di Monastery. I need to repent for mi sexual pre-marital sins! Ha Haaaaaaaaa!'

'You spoilsport. I can't believe it! After an absolutely amazin' weekend, concluded with pure unadulterated explosive fireworks, I thought you'd wanna savour some more of the Jen factor?'

'It was all good ya know, but I don't wanna create problems at work for us both. Ya a great girl, n I really value our relationship, but don't want any friction.'

Jennifer appeared extremely dissapointed with JB's emphasis on a strictly platonic relationship. Knowing her though, she'd be continually insistant on probing and endeavouring to entice him into, at the very least a casual no strings attached relationship.

'Is that herbal tea ready yet JB?' asked Annabelle.

'Relax lady, it'll be wid ya in two.'

The taxi 'l be here soon n I wanna drink before it comes.'

'Alright. Don't worry, be happy, don't worry be happy. Ooooooooooo, oooooooooo, oooooooooo-ooooooooo hoo-hoooooo.' JB said breaking into his rendition of Bobby McFerrin's Don't Worry, Be Happy classic musical track from the eighties.

Jennifer and Annabelle started to sing along. 'Here's a l'il song I wrote, got to sing it note for note, oh don't worry, be happy,' sang Jennifer.

'Don't worry, be happy.' Annabelle reached a high octave note.

'When your lover can make it trouble, it can get even worse n double, don't worry, be happy,' JB sang in a deep lyrical husky tone.

Their own Sunday jam had just started. They were swinging and swaying side to side in the kitchen, enjoying their good quality rendition. The time was approaching half past four and it appeared the girls were enjoying themselves so much, beginning to feel gradually better as the day had progressed, with copious amounts of water and juice for re-hydration. Jammin' Boy had sliced the ginger, washed it and dropped it in the mugs. He poured the freshly boiled hot water into the mugs and then added pure sweet honey to enhance the flavour. 'Let it infuse. You ave to leave it about five mins, n den di true rich flavour starts to eminate. Dis is a total delight. Do you wanna go back in di room, or wait ere for ya taxi?'

'Yeah, we can if you like.'

'We can JB, but, maybe it's a good idea if I cancel that cab?' Annabelle suggested.

'Do you want to stay for a little longer Bella?'

'It's up to you Jen. What d'ya think?'

'Would you mind Jammin', or are we overstayin' our welcome?' responded Jennifer.

'You kno dat, where ever you lay your hat, dat's your ome. It's A OK, but if ya wantin' to snare a wiltin', non wanton wiley cat, it aint appenin'. Also, if you've got udder ideas, ya sleepin' in di spare room.'

'Uuuuurgh. I don't wanna sleep in there, unless you change the sheets. It'l have all the gunge from you n Ash, Bella.' said Jennifer rather bewildered.

'I'll change di sheets, dat's if you decide to stay. Don't forget it's a school night, so you'll ave to go ome in di mornin' for ya new wardrobe.'

'What d'ya mean by wardrobe, Jammin'?' said Jennifer.

'It's just a way o sayin', you'll need some more clothes!'

They decided to return to the living room. Felix and Petra had made their way in there and were frolicking around on the floor. They all sat down side by side on the the three seater sofa facing the featured wall, which had the wide screen TV erected on brackets. Jammin' Boy had an extensive movie collection in his pine wooden bookcase. They discussed different movie genrés, trying to decide on what kind to watch. It was probably appropriate to zoom in to another romcom or maybe a chick flick for the ladies. The girls were enjoying their herbal teas.

'OMG, this is lush.' said Annabelle.

'It's aromatically astoundin' Bella. You made a good choice Jammin'!'

'Dis is mi favourite. An ideal tonic widowt gin. It as licorice extract, cardamom, aniseed n a special udder secret ingredient.'

'What's that Jammin'?' asked Annabelle.

'It's di most precious n priceless one o dem all. Di exclusive touch of JB's TLC.'

'Money can't buy that. You're right, truly priceless. Just like the Crown Jewels in the Tower of London.' retorted Jennifer, licking her lips suggestively.

The girls stood up simultaneously and walked over to the DVD library, to browse through the essential selection.

'This is far better than Blockbusters. There are too many to choose from, where shall I start?' Annabelle said in a state of contemplation.

'Eeeeerm… Why don't ya just try di beginnin', unless you wanna go pure random.'

'What a sensible idea Jammin'. Oh, how I so love your strategic common sense n sensibility!' said Jennifer.

'Isn't that a movie?'

'Yeah, it is Bella n someone said di same ting earlier.' JB answered.

'Is it, is it the one with our very own English rose. It's… Wait a minute. Let me think… Emma Thompson isn't it, with possibily Kenneth Branagh?' Annabelle replied half stuttering, appearing part convinced, partly puzzled.

'Sir Kenneth Branagh was married to Emma Thompson fa several years, but e weren't in dis movie.'

'He's an actor though, right?' said Annabelle.

'Yeah. He's, also a Film n Play director too. Ya right about im starrin' in a movie dough, wid is ex wife Emma Thompson. It was Much a do about nottin', just like di siblin' domestic at Starstruck las nite wi Tom n Ethan.'

'Does anyone want a glass o wine?' asked Jennifer, hoping she could get Jammin' drunk and have her wicked way again.

She was unrelenting. Staggering, when JB was strongly implying that absolutely nothing else would occur. Women appear to always have that je ne sais quoi X factor when it comes to seducing men. 'Deres several bottles o red in di kitchen wine rack, so elp yaself, if you want some.'

'Go on then Jen, I'll have a glass please. It makes sense, as it's still the weekend, although I've got a full schedule tomorrow, six lessons. It's my worst day of the week. I'll be OK though, as I'm just gonna give em an assignment tomorrow. I've got year eight, so it'll take care of itself.' said Annabelle.

'I'm OK tanks Jen. Could you make me anudder erbal tea dough, please. Just di same as dis one.'

Annabelle continued to look through the DVD collection while Jennifer went into the kitchen to prepare the drinks. JB was still feeling fragile after the weekend's exploits and had no desire to enjoy a glass of wine. Especially with returning to work tomorrow, he was under no illusion that a sore head would be counter productive. After making the drinks, Jennifer brought them in on a tray into the room, where JB placed them all down one by one on to coasters. Annabelle had pulled out her choice, hoping that Jennifer and JB agreed.

'Da-aaaaaaa. I've managed to pull out, not quite a box of tricks, a rabbit in a hat, a genie in a bottle or a wizard, buuuut...' A silent pause.

'Come on then Bella, reveal all!'

'Keep ya dress on please,' said JB.

'Ooooooo-K! But will this do?' she said turning around, lifting up her dress to show her damn hot ass.

'Pheeeeeeeew, at least ya wearin' knickers, or someting barely resemblin' dat.' JB almost fainted at another performance of Annabelle's cheeky flash baring antics.

'Cheeky, cheeky!' Jennifer remarked, trying hard to contain her laughter.

'There you are. One of my favourite movies of all time.'

'Great choice Bella. What d'ya think Jen?'

'It's a tímeless classic. En español, fabuloso absolutamente.' answered Jennifer.

This meant Absolutely Fabulous, reminiscent of the comedy TV show with Joanna Lumley, Jennifer Saunders and crew. It had a star studded cast with Bill Murray and Andie MacDowell. JB stood up and walked across to the blinds, gazing out of the window admiring the beautiful early evening sky. White clouds gently drifted south westerly leaving sporadic glimpses of wondrous blue sky. He leant over to the right hand corner window and closed it, as it had been left ajar during the night to ventilate, as it was extremely humid approaching the Summer solstice. 'Shall I close di blinds, just to give it a more homely cinema style feel to di place?'

'Yeah, good idea Jammin'. Pump up the stereo sound too if you would,' Annabelle suggested.

'And this time, can we have that ice cream that was suggested earlier, prettty pretty please JB?' asked Jennifer.

'Geeeeeez girls, any more requests? Why don't ya both jus move in n take over di place? I could do wid a cook, laundry lady n general ouse maid. What qualities can ya both bring to di table?'

'I can bring charm, elegance, domestication, sincerity, understandin', humour, class, sexiness, libido and more!' stated Jennifer.

'I know dat. Where you gonna buy dem traits from den? Di pawnbrokers?' JB teased and laughed at her traits.

'If you wanna go to the pawn shop, I don't think you'll be bringing anything away with ya, apart from depleted bank account, lipstick on ya collar n a mornin' glory! Ha Haaaaaaaaaa.' Jennifer comically responded to JB's original cheekyness.

'After you too have linguistically copulated, d'ya know what I'd bring to the table?!'

'Go on.' Jennifer and JB said in harmony.

Talk about a telepathic notion. They both stared at one and other in pure amazement after their impromptu synchronised comment.

'I'd bring sweet scented flowers, cultured cuisine, broadsheet papers at the weekend, intelligent convo, finesse, fun, laughter, Roman history and occasional displays of nudity combined with joie de vivre! Take that.' Annabelle provided a quite sublime answer to JB's question.

'Pppprrrrrrrrrrr-fect. Dat's sorted den. When ya movin' in?' asked JB purring with delight, reminiscent of Felix.

'Next week, if that's OK with you?'

'I could make it next month, as I have to give my landlord a months notice.'

'Bella, ya jokin' aren't ya?' asked Jennifer in a startled and envious manner.

'Noooo. I told you the other day I was lookin' for another place to rent.'

'Why can't I move in Jammin'?'

'D'ya genuinely tink it'd be a good idea after we've taken di oney to di bee?'

'What d'ya mean?' Jennifer appearing slightly puzzled.

'I can't believe ya confused? It's literally a way of sayin', we kissed, caressed n undressed dis morn, so I wouldn't want monthly payments in kind. It ain't a hotel ya know.'

'Oh, I get it. I'm not worth it? You could call me Laurie Al.' Jennifer responded managing to restore her humour.

'Di French, dey say, L'Oreal, va va voooom ma petite amie.' JB answered in his finest attempt at a Parisian accent.

He closed the blinds, took the DVD off Annabelle and slid it into the DVD player. 'Would you ladies care for some Haagen Dazs? You've got a choice of Raspberry Sorbet, Strawberry Cheesecake, Rum n Raisin' or Vanilla.'

'I'll go for Strawberry Cheesecake please Jammin'!' said Jennifer.

'Rum n Raisin' por moi sil vous plait!' followed Annabelle.

'Comin' right at cha!'

JB went into the kitchen to scoop out dessert, while Annabelle and Jennifer sat cosily in front of the TV. Annabelle pressed play on the DVD remote control to start the trailers while JB was occupied in the kitchen. Annabelle re-assured Jennifer by telling her that she was joking about lodging here at JB's house. Jennifer would be incredibly jealous if JB were to let Annabelle house share, as she fancied him like crazy. He was genuinely looking for a house mate though, therefore this would be the perfect tonic, providing him with a greater disposable income. In the neighbourhood of Honeyville the average rental tariff would be in the region of four hundred pounds, as it was very affluent. Certainly affordable to a person on the national average of thirty grand a year. It was a highly attractive leafy suberb, with boulevards evident down several streets, expensive high performance cars, long winding driveways, albeit JB's was only a quaint size of approximately twenty five feet.

He was planning on a boys' holiday with Ash, Fluffy Donkey, C-Man and his close cousin Jay Mie. They weren't too sure where to travel as of yet, but he had to save a little more spending money. JB opened the freezer compartment door, pulled out the drawer where the ice creams were and took out two flavoured ice creams. He'd already taken three bowls out of the cupboard and a stainless steel ice cream scoop. He gouged out four scoops per person and placed the half tennis ball size pieces into the dessert dishes. Rum n Raisin for himself and Annabelle and Strawberry Cheesecake for Jennifer. He worked with precise accuracy, scooping virtually identical size balls, not that it was difficult, but he acted in a clinical manner, paying great attention to detail. He placed the lid back on the tubs of Haagan Dazs, proceeding to put them back in their freezing home, third drawer down. He was very meticulous when it came to food, always wanting to make it look as attractive as possible, even for a simple dish such as beans on toast. He would provide a touch of class, even if it meant decorating the meal with a sauce and intricately designing the recipient's initials. He took out a container of chocolate sprinkles, some guey strawberry dessert sauce and a cadbury's flake each, to make his very own ice cream man's ninety nine. It looked so yummy.

They were now all set for an evening of pure comical entertainment, ready to be enthralled by the movie Groundhog Day, an early nineties classic.

'Get ready fa a taste o movie mercurial magic, washed down wid refined Haagan Dazs creamy rich goodness peeps. Savour di unadulterated sexed up scintillatin' flavour.' he said while bringing in the desserts to the room.

Chapter Seventeen

Crash, Bank, Wallop

The trailers had now just about finished, the three of them, JB, Jennifer and Annabelle were comfortably sat back resting on the sumptuously welcoming chocolate brown three seater sofa facing the forty two inch, wide screen TV. Lights turned off, blinds closed, it was a warmly home cinema, with nicam stereo sound pumped up to provide better acoustics. They were all relishing their ice cream with JB's special home made ninety nine touch. The movie was now beginning, which seduced them into captivating comedy. Thankfully Groundhog Day for JB and friends was only a fictitious nightmare. What a frustrating, nail biting, teeth pulling, hair ripping, head vrooming experience that would surely be. Nothing ever changing, monotony, monotony, monotony and even more surprising experiences of, you guessed it… monotony. It would drive any sane human being to contemplate their existence, consequently, most probably resulting in comprehensive pain afflicting destruction. Thankfully, this was attributed to the movie and not adversely affecting JB and entourage. JB's phone started ringing. He apologised to Jennifer and Annabelle, because he'd forgotten to put it on silent. He eventually silenced it, while fumbling around in his sports shorts pocket. It was Fluffy Donkey phoning him. He decided to leave it, as it could probably wait until tomorrow, especially when he, Ash and Stacey had left only about forty five minutes ago.

'Oh my god, I almost forgot, that reminds me, I forgot to cancel that cab for us Jen.'

'Give em a call now, you said quarter to five dint ya?' Jennifer checked.

'It's gone five o'clock now, so it appears to have blobbed! They're normally really reliable too. Can you pause the movie JB please, while I cancel the cab?' Annabelle asked.

'Yeah, no probs Bella.'

She took her phone out of her bag, scrolled through her directory and called Lucky Star taxis. 'Hi, I booked a cab for quarter to five, over forty minutes ago, d'ya know where it is?' she asked.

The telephone operator was checking to find out where it was. You could here her voice faintly in the background, 'I spoke to the driver fifteen minutes ago n he said he was headin' to his next pick up, which is you. For some reason, I can't get through. His mic appears to be distorted. I'll call you back in five mins.'

'I just wanna cancel the cab that's all. Apologies for that, I almost forgot.' responded Annabelle.

'It's OK, thanks. Bye.' replied the operator.

'Thanks. Sorry to be a nuisance. Bye.'

JB's phone started ringing again, well, vibrating because he had put it on silent, so it wouldn't disturb their movie watching, 'Dat's strange, it's Fluffy again.'

'He's probably hit the call button accidentally. If he'd forgotten somethin', he'd just drive back here. He doesn't live far does he?' said Jennifer.

'About five miles o so.'

'It'll be nothin' Jammin'.' said Jennifer.

'Don't ya tink it's a l'il bizarre dough? Why would e phone me twice in di space of a couple of mins?' JB responding rather baffled.

JB was normally the archetypal of proverbial ice cool, very few situations phased him, or as some people would say, ruffled his feathers. He was curious as to why Fluffy would be so desperate to get hold of him. Had his car broken down? Had he forgotten something? Was he just wanting to thank JB for his weekend hospitality? Had he been in an accident? JB eventually dismissed that it can't have really been anything too important, he had just dialled him accidentally by pressing the last number called button. 'Are we ready to watch the movie again now people?' asked Annabelle.

'Yeah, I'll play it again.'

JB pressed play, they were all settled once again after discussions with the taxi company Lucky Star and Fluffy Donkey's motives for calling JB. Hopefully there would be no more distractions, therefore, they could enjoy the shenanigans of Groundhog Day. No more than five more minutes had passed and Annabelle's phone started to vibrate. She picked it up and answered it, it was a private number.

'Hello, who is it please?'

'It's Lucky Star taxis. I just wanna tell you, a courtesy call really. The taxi you ordered has been involved in an accident.'

'Is the driver OK?' she asked.

'I don't know, another driver came across the accident and contacted our base.'

'I really hope he's OK! Just outta curiosity, it wasn't Jaleem was it?' asked Annabelle, hoping that the lovely Indian driver from last night who Jasmine was flirting with, wasn't involved.

'No, he doesn't work on Sundays.'

'Many thanks for the call. I sincerely hope the driver's not seriously hurt. Take care n thanks once again.'

'It's OK. Bye.' replied the taxi company telephone operator.

'Our taxi's been involved in an accident Bella.'

'Yeah, they don't know how serious it is though. Thankfully it ain't Jaleem from last night!'

'At least dey at di decency to call ya. Dats why Lucky Star are di best company around. Dere was a legitimate explanation n dey've called you back. Ultimate respect ya know.'

'Let's hope that's the last interruption now. Anyone would think we were working at a customer service call centre. Press play again JB.' asked Jennifer.

All they wanted was an enjoyable, relaxing and entertaining peaceful evening, eating Haagan Dazs ice cream, drinking herbal tea and wine, of course not together though. That would be a concoction of the weirdest proportions. Probably the kind of mix an Alzheimer's sufferer would indulge in, totally forgetting that he/she was alternating between soft and hard beverages. JB's phone once again started vibrating. He pulled it out of his pocket once more, looked at the screen. 'Girls, ya not gonna believe dis.'

They both spoke out in synchronised fashion. 'It's Fluffy Donkey?'

'I better answer it. Someting ain't quite right. Tree calls in di last ten minutes. E's certainly desperate for someting.' JB looking puzzled and slightly agigated, responded.

'This is amazin'. The power of technology. Sometimes I wish mobile phones hadn't been invented, they can be a pain in di ass.' said Annabelle.

'Is that where you normally keep ya phone Bella. In a warm place where the sun don't shine? Pooooooooooooooo. That'd be a dirty reception.' replied Jennifer.

'Talk about a bad ass signal. At least it'd be protected from di elements n would have a furry cover.'

'Yeah Jammin'. I think Bella needs to go for a back n crack wax,' said Jennifer.

'Answer the phone JB. Otherwise Fluffy won't be too happy. Three strikes n he's out treatment. Ha haaaaaaaa,' said Annabelle.

He eventually picked the phone up at the third time of asking. 'Yes Fluffy, what's appenin'?'

'Why d-d-d-d-d-don't you p-p-p-p-pick the pho-pho-pho-phone up?'

'Are you OK?' asked JB.

'We-we-we-we've been involved in an ac-ac-ac-accident. This stupid taxi driver was on his ph-ph-ph-phone n pulled out on me.'

'How are Stacey n Ash?'

'Ash managed to get out… Aaaaaaargh, aaaaaaargh. My knee, my back, my foot, my head. I feel so dizzy. Stacey's slumped in the back.'

Chapter 18

The Golden Hour

Woo-woo-woo-woo, nee-naw, nee-naw.

'Oh, thank god, the ambulance n fire Service have just arrived. I must go. I'll phone you la-la-later… Aaaaaaargh.'

'Is dere anyting I can do fa you?'

'It's OK thanks. I'll phone you later n let you know which hospital we've gone to.'

'Big phat love to you, Ash n Stace. Tinkin' about y'all, n opin' ya gonna be fine brudder! See ya very soon. Take care please n don't be draggin' ya foot like a seal.'

'Ha Haaaaaa. I'll tr-tr-try n be careful. Take care too.' Fluffy Donkey winced out in a great degree of pain.

'Bye Donkey soldier.'

'Yeah, bye Jammin'.'

'How are they all?' asked Jennifer.

'Are they OK?' asked Annabelle.

'Fluffy has a few injuries, Ash managed to climb out, wid probably a l'il Ms whiplash n Stacey was slumped in di back seat. Di Firemen n Ambulance ave just arrived, so let's pray dere all gonna be OK. Lord ave mercy.'

'Shall we drive down to see them?'

'It ain't worth it Bella, because we'll get in the way. Leave it to the Emergency Service professionals.'

'Fluffy's gonna call me when dey've got to di hospital. We'll know a bit more later.'

'I'm so concerned Jammin'. I hope Stace is gonna be fine. When you say slumped, was she breathing?' asked Jennifer.

'I don't know Jen. Joe was agitated, annoyed n in alot of pain. She may just be concussed. Hopefully conscious n breathin'.' replied JB.

The three of them were so anxious and awaiting further news on the health state of Fluffy Donkey, Ash and Stacey. Unbeknown to the crew at 33 Mysterious Street, Honeyville, the accident had been quite a bad one. Joe had been driving down a main road at the correct speed limit, as he was always cautious and sensible. A taxi had pulled out from a side street on the left and crashed into the passenger side of the car. The taxi driver who was heading to pick up Annabelle and Jennifer had been talking on his mobile phone, but not hands free. Consequently he had been breaking the law, holding the handset to his ear. This gross negligence could have quite easily wiped out the three of them. Thankfully they had all survived but their injuries were unknown yet. The Fire Service had arrived very quickly, this being paramount as the Golden Hour was the period from the accident occuring to arrival at hospital to receiving emergency medical care. The fire engines had arrived within five minutes, followed minutes later by three ambulances. Fluffy had managed to phone 999 virtually immediately and the response was instaneous. As it was a crime scene, the Police were also on scene. As a matter of course with the circumstances, they decided to breatherlise the taxi driver who was in the black Toyota Avensis, as it appeared he was at fault. Ash had managed to climb through the passenger side front window, but he couldn't get into the rear nearside door to attend to Stacey. He had walked around to the driver side rear door and tried to open the door, but it was jammed. Stacey was slumped in the back seat, but thankfully had her seat belt on, which had probably saved her and minimised the risk of catastrophic injuries. Fluffy Donkey had managed to communicate with Stacey, she muttered a response, but appeared to be concussed. He could see her chest moving outwards, which re-assured him, knowing she was breathing, albeit probably unconscious. Fluffy Donkey was trapped in the driver's seat, probably because of his large muscular build, his legs were jammed under the steering column, although he had movement of his upper body, which meant that his spine was possibly jarred, but not seriously injured.

He was complaining of head, back, knee and foot pain. Probably severe brusing, with the impact causing trauma. They'd all definitely suffered from whiplash, as it was a side impact with a forty miles per hour force. The car was chronically damaged, certainly a right off. Fluffy Donkey had always had a penchant for German cars, so it was no surprise that when he bought his first car, it was a Volkswagen Golf. This car was a Volkswagen Scirocco, which had a fantastic robust reinforced safety cage, as all German cars do. Three factors evidently saved the group from becoming a fatal statistic, these were;-

i)   The speed of impact – 40mph
ii)   The Volkswagen re-inforced safety cage
iii)   There wasn't any oncoming traffic.

The latter would have significantly increased the chances of fatal consequences. The Fire Service were there. Three fire engines had arrived and they were meticulously and strategically working at the scene of operations, stabilising, managing the glass, operating the heavy cutting and spreading tools and casualty caring for Stacey and Fluffy.

'That driver almost killed us. I wanna hit the man. What the freakin' hell were you thinkin' of? You saw him didn't ya? On his mobile phone, without a care in the world.' Ash shouting out loudly in a furious state of mind, communicating with a gentleman who was acting as a witness.

'Yeah. Don't worry, I saw everything. That motherfocker almost killed ya. I'll testify for ya, no probs. Just give ya friends some moral support for the time being. I'll sit in mi car over there n speak to ya when ya ready. No rush!'

'Whats ya name mate?'

'It's Mushy. Mushy Pea.'

'Thanks. Mine's Ash.'

The firemen were taking the roof off, to Fluffy's disappointment, but ultimately, they had to cut him and Stacey out of the car. They'd removed the tailgate, so a fireman could climb through the back to lift up Stacey's head and stabilise her cervical spine. The Paramedics were working in tandem and being led by the Officer in Charge, the guy with a white helmet called Watch Commander Nodster. It was so strategic how they had two sections. An inner and outer cordon set up. The firemen in the inner cordon were working frantically around and inside the vehicle. They had to expose shut lines and peel and reveal the plastic fascia interior so that airbags and seat belt pre-tensioners wouldn't be activated, while they were spreading and cutting the doors. 'Are you gonna take the roof off?' asked Ash.

'Yeah. But just stand back please n stay wi the ambulance staff.' responded one of the firemen.

The paramedics had fitted an oxygen mask to Stacey's face and were giving her oxygen. There were a plethora of sounds from cracking, clonking and shattering, crushing, popping as the crew performed their duties. The scene was safe though, as they paid optimum attention to casualty care. Fluffy Donkey had also been given oxygen therapy, fitted a cervical spine collar to stabilise his neck also, and had covered him with a green protective sheet. One was also being placed over Stacey too. The reason for this, was solely to ensure that glass, dust, debris and other particles wouldn't cover the casualties and cause any uneccessary additional injury, panic or concern, as theese could be inhaled and ingested. Stacey was evidently in a great degree of pain, but it appeared to be the result of whiplash from side impact along with chest and side where the seatbelt had pulled tight, restricting central core movement. Ash was being comforted by one of the ambulance technicians, being asked to stay cool, however, understandably, he was absolutely incensed with the taxi driver for his atrocious wreckless act. The road had to be closed as the accident covered both sides and would have been too risky to leave open, plus it made it far easier for the Emergency Services to operate without any additional hazards.

'Cutting, cutting now.' Was a loud vocal command from one of the firemen cutting the front passenger side a post.

One of the guys was pouring water over the windscreen, while another had hit the middle of the screen to make a hole and then proceded to cut the bottom about two inches up with a glass saw. All the firemen who were around the car, had their helmet visors down to protect their eyes from debris. The incident appeared to run like clockwork.

'Aaaaaaaargh, aaaaaaaaargh. My knee. Are y-y-y-you OK Stace?' Fluffy Donkey was yelping out in pain and checking on Stacey's state of health.

'I'm, I'm, I'm, I'm doin' OK. Where, where, where am I?' she replied.

She was gradually drifting back into a state of consciousness, thankfully, but was obviously disorientated as a result of the accident.

'Everything's gonna be OK. So ya name's Stacey. How old are ya?' asked the fireman who was holding the back of her head to stabilise her neck.

'Twenty.'

'What d'ya do for a job?'

'I'm a sch, sch, school teacher.' she responded in a slurring voice.

'You've got a great pair of legs. You look very athletic,' said the fireman.

'Th-th-thanks I'm a part ti-ti-time athlete. What's your name?' she asked wincing in pain.

'I'm Stelios.'

'Are you Greek?'

'My mum's from Athens n dad's English. So yeah, half Greek.'

Stelios was flirting outrageously with Stacey, while casualty caring for her. She was an extremely attractive young lady, although, it was the usal sensitive mantra displayed by Emergency Service staff, used to re-assure, comfort and provide amount of hilarity which would certainly help to distract the injured and affected persons mind, hopefully alleviating an amount of pain.

'Where did you buy ya legs from then?' asked Stelios.

'I borrowed them for the day. I wanted to have some with roller blades on, but thought they'd be no use in a car. Normally they have spikes on the bottom.'

'That sounds quite kinky.'

'For ru, ru, ru, aaaargh, aaaaargh, my side! Sorry, I mean for runnin' n athletic events. I do athletics… heptathlon.'

'It's startin' to make sense now. When we've taken the roof off, we're gonna slide a board into the car, behind ya back and take you out. It's not quite a white knuckle ride, but it'll be an excitin' experience, edge of the seat stuff.'

This brought a chuckle from Stacey, which caused her to wince in pain. It created a slight twinge in her neck and aggravated her waist. Her back was a little sore, but thankfully it wasn't creating too much duress, thankfully. In the front, the paramedics had placed a cervical spine collar around Fluffy Donkey to also minimise head movement, as this could be detrimental to any potential injuries to that part of the anatomy. He was relieved to recieve oxygen, to enhance is breathing, although, extremely annoyed that due to a foolish moment of madness by the third party, he was saying farewell to his beloved Scirocco. Ultimately though, it was a massive relieve that the three of them, Ash, Joe and Stacey had managed to escape with their lives in tact. One of the Firemen was taking photographs with a camera.

'Are those photos he's takin' gonna be in some kinda Fire Service magazine?' asked Ash to the paramedic who was attending to him.

'They're been taken so that when you're all taken to the casualty department at Lillyford Park Hospital, it hugely assists the doctors with being aware of what potential injuries you may have,' answered the Ambulance Technician.

'Aaaah. That's a great idea isn't it?'

'It's fabulous. A massive help. They know what kind of impact the vehicles have had, so from that it tells them alot about the nature of the accident and the type of injuries that have been sustained. They'll have to have x-rays too.'

'Will I need an x-ray? I feel OK, but a l'il dizzy now and my neck's hurtin'.' said Ash.

'Just sit down in the ambulance please and I can check you over.'

'I just wanna get the phone number from the guy over there who witnessed the accident. Just give me a minute please.' Ash requested.

Ash walked over, slightly staggering towards Mushy Pea's white van. Mushy wound the window down,

'Ya lookin' a l'il heavy legged mate. Ya best stayin' wi the ambulance crew over there, because you don't wanna faint here.'

'I'll be OK I think. Just feelin' a l'il light headed. Can you give me ya number n then I can use ya as a witness.' replied Ash.

'Yeah, no probs.'

Ash took his phone out of his pocket and typed in his pin code lock number. So ya name's Mushy Pea. Ya not a batchelor are ya?' Joked Ash.

'The old ones are the best. No, I'm married with two kids and one goat.'

They both laughed in harmony.

'My numbers, o, seven, seven, three, four, one, five, six, three, two, four. Give me a call to let me know how ya doin' and I'll give ya my address details.'

'Many thanks Mushy. Take care n see ya later.'

'Yeah, you take good care too, and look after ya mates. Hope all go's well at the hospital.'

'Thanks.'

Ash staggered back to the ambulance and climbed in the back. The Ambulance Technician sat him down and used an instrument to check his blood pressure, measured his heart rate with a stethoscope. Ash was feeling a little faint and eventually slumped in the chair he was on. The technician gave him some oxygen therapy and checked his radial pulse by placing two fingers on his wrist. His pulse was good, averaging seventy beats per minute. He was very athletic, playing many sports from football to tennis, so it was normally alot lower, but obviously with the stress levels caused by the accident, it was higher. Meanwhile, the roof had been removed from Fluffy Donkey's Volkswagen.

In the back, they'd cut Stacey's seatbelt off and slid a board in behind her. The front passenger seat had been moved forward electronically, as the battery was still operating. Occasionally the Fire Service are reluctant to disconnect it, as it can assist them with their rescue operations. Five of them were working slowly and meticulously, ensuring Stacey was comfortable and carefully taken out of the vehicle. Stelios was at the head, supporting it, assisted by four others who were positioned at both sides, controlling her movement up towards the head of the board. Stacey, it appeared would be fine, apart from severe bruising and whiplash. She had trials in the next few months for the Indoor European Championships, so wanted to be in supreme physical condition for that. It's probable that she would have to take a few weeks off to recover from her injuries and to have some intensive massage on her neck, to ensure full mobility was restored. The paramedics had also inserted a saline drip into her arm, to boost her sodium levels, as she'd been knocked out by the impact of the accident, but thankfully she was still breathing.

'Ready, Steady, Slide,.' were the commands from Stelios at the head of the long board.

The person at the head had to communicate to fellow personnel to ensure they were all singing from the same hymn sheet. Not literally, but it was a good analogy emphasising the importance of the firemen working systematically, enabling a smooth renoval of the casualty out of the vehicle.

'Ooooow… My shin! Ouch. It's really sore.' she yelped out.

She'd banged her right leg on the rear of the front passenger seat on impact. It was causing her a great degree of pain, when they slid her up towards the top of the board.

'Sorry love. We have to make sure you're secure on the board, so we don't aggravate any possible injuries.' That was the voice of Percy Snapper, one of the more experienced members of the firefighting crew.

'It's OK, it's not your fault. You've all been fantastic. I don't even know what happened.'

'That black car over there, we believe he pulled out of that junction n banged straight into the side of ya. Someone saw him on his mobile. He's a taxi driver.' responded Percy Snapper.

'Ooooooh my God, thank the lord we're alive.' Stacey slurred, still in a state of disorientation.

She closed her eyes. A spirit must have been shining down on them offering protection. The firemen had lifted Stacey through the back of the car on the long board and in to the boot space with the tail on top of the rear seat. The fireman had re-organised themselves, and were able to lift Stacey through the boot and on to one of the stretchers placed at the side of the car, about five foot away inside the inner corden.

Fluffy Donkey was the next to be taken out. One of the firemen circled the car to ensure all the wedges and blocks were secure and another had secured a personal line to the accelerator pedal and the driver side door frame, therefore, when the door was opened, it created space, releasing his foot, allowing better movement of his legs, and enabling his seat to slide back automatically. When the pedal had been cut with the dedicated cutters, to prevent any problems. The steering cover was on, this was used to protect the casualty in case the steering wheel airbag was deployed accidentally. The driver's side front door had to be moved, meaning more space for the firemen to work in. The driver side door was cut, first of all, spreading the bottom hinges and then the top. *POP*, went the door as it had come away from hinges. The fireman holding the cutters, snipped the remaining wires, then the door was carried away to a wreckage dump created for debris, in the outer cordon. The firemen had made a cut at the bottom of the drivers side sill, along with squeezing the front side panel, following this one of them picked up a pair of spreaders and slid them into the gap that had been made.

'We're just going to perform a lift on the dashboard, to create some space enablin' you to move your feet and legs better. We're then going to slide in a board behind your back and then lift you out.' said the fireman who was about to lift the dashboard.

'Just get me out as soon as ya can. I'm startin' to feel a little claustrophobic. I don't care about my car now, I ju-ju-just... aaaaaaargh. I wanna get out.' Fluffy yelled out in pain, annoyance and frustration.

Compared to the sleek and sophisticated model before the accident, the Volkswagen had now been transformed into a convertible mangled wreck, , thanks to the mindless actions of the Lucky Star taxi driver. The dashboard was now being slowly lifted, as the fireman used the large imposing hydraulic powered spreading tool. It was placed into the small incision that had been made a few inches above the front of the A-post sill. The jaws of the spreaders were slowly opened, which opened the gap wider, forcing the dashboard up and forwards to ensure Fluffy Donkey's legs could be navigated safely out, under the steering column. Stelios asked Fluffy Donkey if he was ready for the seat to be slid backwards automatically.

'Yeah, go ahead. I'm burning up in here.'

It was highly likely that Joe had fractured his foot on one of the pedals on impact, as his body temperature was fluctuating between hot and cold. These were prominent fracture symptoms, besides pain, shallow breathing, pulse being rapid and weak, cold and clammy palms, nausea amongst others.

'I'm just going to recline the seat to make it easier for the boys to get a board in behind you,' said Stelios.

One of the guys had wrapped a previously cut seatbelt behind Joe's back, so he could pull him forward as the board was slid down his back towards his cocyx. Another fireman was going to place a tear drop shield in front of the long spinal board, this would make it a more fluent extrication. Joe was still inhaling a large quantity of oxygen, while being advised to relax and regulate his breathing, therefore, it would hopefully alleviate any unnecessary panic. In went the board, after the seat had been reclined. The fireman holding the seatbelt pulled Joe forwards gently to make the process easier. It must have taken no more than two minutes to ease him onto the board. The firemen were strategically placed around the board, acting with immense precision, all fully aware of their tasks. 'Ready, Steady, Slide,' was the command, from the guy at the head of the board, whose job it was to direct operations. It was a little easier than Stacey's removal, because they had the advantage of the internal electronics, where as the rear seat, didn't have that luxury, being a rigid structure. It could be folded downwards to create boot space, but in an extrication predicament, this would be fruitless. He was taken out and placed on a stretcher positioned at the side of the mangled wreckage. After removing his shoe and sock, the head paramedic took a look at Joe's foot quite extensively. He squeezed it, at which Joe let out a squeal reminiscent of a wounded pig. There was a large amount of swelling around the outside of the right ankle and the top of the same foot. He prodded it in various places, which was naturally highly sensitive and uncomfortable. The Ambulance Technician took out a crepe bandage from the trauma pack, split open the protective plastic bag and wrapped it around the lower part of Joe's legs, about three inches above the ankles. Two firemen raised Joe's legs slightly off the long board, to enable the bandage to be wrapped round more easily. After about three revolutions, the paramedic cut the bandage and secured it, tying it in a bow on the uninjured left side. The firemen attached the safety straps to the long board, clipping them on to the outer edges with the karibiner part and connecting them in the centre of the body. They had a seatbelt fastening mechanism. Joe was asked to place his hands together on his lower abdomen.

'I aint Wacko Jacko you know. I don't stroke mi crotch in public, especially in such an intimate settin'!'

'Ow.' said one of the firemen.

'Eeeee-hee.' replied Stelios.

This brought a ripple of laughter from the emergency service crews. The straps were placed over each shoulder diagonally, just under his hips and half way down his legs. They were then pulled taught, but not too tight to be restrictive. Throughout the process, a fireman had held the oxygen cylinder while it was attached to the air hose, which connected to the facemask. It was set to fifteen litres a minute. This was a setting to supplement natural atmospheric oxygen and to make the casualty as comfortble as possible, hoping to relax them, which would advantageously regulate and aid their breathing. The paramedic and ambulance technician took the brakes off the stretcher and started pushing it towards the ramp of the ambulance. They started to struggle as Joe was a sizeable specimen. Not implying he was overweight and carrying too many beef burgers in his stomach, but he was a powerful muscular gentleman, who was certainly tough to push uphill at six foot four inches tall. The right hand rear wheel suddenly buckled, fell off, a bolt popped out, with a washer falling to the floor and a spring catapulted off the tarmac into the side of Fluffy Donkey's car. It was a comical moment that wouldn't have looked out of place in a carry on film. As the firemen were making up all of their equipment, four of them quickly turned to assist the ambulance staff, lifting Joe up on the stretcher and into the back of the ambulance. Two of the drivers had filled out a patient survey form, to assist the paramedics, so they knew what state of health the casualties were in, also on arrival to hospital, this information was a huge help to doctors and nurses. It was also a legal document, which could be used in a court of law, if there were any complications and incorrect information written down, consequently potentially implicating personnel. The ambulance Stacey was in had now left the scene and was on route to Lillyford Park Hospital. The chocks, blocks, hydraulic cutting equipment, steering wheel cover, glass master saw, glass hammer, salvage sheets and other miscellaneous equipment was being removed from the scene and put back on the fire engines. Percy Snapper was brushing all the debris off the road and into the gutter, so it wouldn't be a hazard to other motorists, when the road was eventually re-opened. A police officer was still questioning the taxi driver. Joe's stretcher was now securely positioned in the back of the ambulance, brakes locked on, one wheel short, but thankfully it wasn't a necessity for a mechanic to replace the broken wheel in expresso style, reminiscent of a Formula One Grand Prix mechanic under pressure to perform instantaneously within ten seconds to ensure their car didn't lose too many places in the race. Ironically though, the next pit stop would be Lillyford Park Hospital. Ash sat down on a chair at the side of Fluffy Donkey and the paramedic, who was keeping an eye on the health state of the two wounded patients.

'Thanks for all your hard work guys, you've done a grand job! It's really appreciated.' said Watch Commander Nodster.

'I still can't believe what happened Fluffy. I could have dragged that driver outta his car n given him a ceremonious old fashioned one-two.' said Ash.

He was still furious, understandably, as it could have easily been a fatal accident. 'Don't worry Ash, you've escaped unscathed, apart from a l'il whiplash. I'm hurtin' from head to toe.' replied Fluffy Donkey.

'I keep encouraging you to come to the gym with me. If you weren't such a freak of nature, a super sized Goliath at a wapping seventeen stone n six foot four, you may have escaped without a scratch or a break.' Ash teased.

'If I could move, you'd be receivin' two hundred n five pounds of clenched hand to ya ribs, or maybe just a chin tickler.'

'Oooooooo. I didn't imply you were fat, just that you'd have escaped with less injuries. A wild bear in a telephone box would have more room?' said Ash.

The paramedic burst out with laughter along with Joe. It was the two of them engaging in their usual playful banter.

'You're OK Joe, possibly a fractured metatarsal, badly bruised ankle, knee, back, some whiplash and a sore head, where it's hit the side window,' re-assured the paramedic.

'You mean, his sheer physical cushionings acted as a buffer n minimised his injuries?'

'I'm gonna slap you when I can move,' growled Fluffy Donkey.

'I wouldn't quite put it like that. I'd just say, if he was a smaller build, his injuries may have been far worse.'

'Whats ya name mate?' asked Ash.

'It's Neil, Neil Single.'

'So ya like a super natural hero, or a special medical agent?' said Ash.

'You mean like Bond, James Bond.'

'Yes Neil,' replied Ash.

'Can't you knock him out with some anaesthetic Neil?' asked Fluffy Donkey.

'It'd be more than my job's worth. I could try and hypnotise him though?'

'Oooh please. That'd be a godsend. Just teasin' Ashilito.'

They were almost at the hospital, travelling on blue lights with sirens sounding, in hot pursuit of the ambulance that had left a couple of minutes earlier, that Stacey was being attended to in. They'd be fast tracked to the A & E doctor, who would give them all a full examination, before sending them down to the x-ray department, to check for any broken bones and head trauma. Both Ash and Fluffy Donkey enjoyed the experience of being driven at well above the speed limit, a given luxury of the Emergency Services when driving to an incident, or in the case of an ambulance, heading to a hospital, if circumstances dictated.

The taxi driver had been arrested, handcuffed and driven to the local Marlborough Police Station for questioning. He'd probably been over the limit after drinking excessively the night before.

The punishment if found guilty, the driver would face, would have severe implications, however, he was so fortunate with the outcome, of three wounded, but their injuries thankfully not life threatening and life time disabling. That was the hope anyway.

Chapter Nineteen

Hospital Night Fever, Night Fever

When they arrived at Lillyford Park Hospital, they were all escorted into A & E by ambulance technicians and paramedics, and greeted by nursing staff. The department was full, typical for a weekend. Drunks, punks, monks, people injured by masonry, objects inserted and stuck into skin from workmens' tools to stationery, men involved in fights, women wearing jeans to fishnet tights, sports persons, some injured while playing with racquets, others wrapped up warm with blankets to denim jackets, children screaming, a few grown up adults with eyes streaming, an old man sleeping, while his wife rested her head on his shoulder by leaning. All Fluffy Donkey, Stacey and Ash wanted was to be back home in bed, preparing for work on Monday morning.

They were all placed in cubicles next to each other, occassionally ooooo-ing and aaaarghing at the pain they were in. Thankfully Stacey's condition was improving and she was becoming more stable. She was the first of the three to be whisked down to the x-ray department. The boys sighed, as they couldn't understand why she was receiving female preferential treatment.

'Nurse, she was only knocked out for a few minutes.' said Fluffy Donkey.

'Fluffy, you were almost cryin' in pain. Try carryin' a baby for nine months n then delivering it.' responded Stacey.

She raised her voice to reply as she'd heard Joe complaining in the next cubicle. 'She isn't a young mother is she Ash?'

'Noooo. She's just bein' honest. You have been wingin' n yellin' out in pain. You've only broken a few hair strands n maybe ya metatarsal, R-three. Women have a stronger psyche and mental toughness compared to us so called macho men.' replied Ash.

'At least someone's sensitive and can relate to zee female gender. What's ya name?' asked the Nurse.

'I'm Ash, and you are?'

'I'm Genevieve, please to meet you.'

'Ya accent sounds very familiar. You must be from France.' Ash responded.

'Indeed, I'm from zee north of Fraaance. Bootiful, appy, exquisite gay Pa-ree. I love my ome, it's so special.'

She spoke with a sexy, sophisticated and cultured tone which Ash was instantly drawn to. It was a typical Parisian lilt, which was very endearing, but sounded a little harsh when the letter h was dropped. That was a common french speaking trait, as that letter is silent in their language.

'Have you been livin' here for long?' asked Ash.

'I've been ere for a good eight years. I did my nursing training back ome in France, then wanted to travel, see culture n zen apply for work. Zat is what brings me ere!'

'You're the hottest nurse I've ever seen! Are you from a volcanic island?'

'I wouldn't call Paris volcanique, but it possesses ot wezzer, especially in di summer time.'

'Just sit comfortably n relax Ash, ya like a proverbial dog on heat.'

'Relax Fluffy. Just play dead for a few minutes. I actually like you horizontal, at least ya under control. Ooooooo… What I could do to ya right now, God only knows. Ha Haaaaaaaaaaa.'

'I told you in the ambulance. Just wait till I'm mobile n on mi feet again, I'll…'

'You'll be an easier standin' target at six foot somethin' on crutches.' said Ash, chuckling.

'When I'm on two feet though, you'll be in trouble.'

'I think I'll be OK. You move like a blind slug, so won't have any trouble with droppin' ya with a sharp right hand!' teased Ash.

'Just you wait Ashilito. We'll see who's the real martial arts expert.'

'It ain't you. Did you manage to get that bronze medal at high school at papier mache makin'?'

'I'll papier mache ya head!'

'Don't be so aggressive, you need to rest n relax. I don't want you injurin' ya tongue while snarlin' n salivatin' like a rabid daaaaaawg.'

'I'll give ya one thing Ash, you've got a sense of humour. Problem being is, you dropped it outside! Ha Haaaaaaaaa.' replied Fluffy Donkey.

'You boys need to relax. It appears you were in a bad accident. I don't want any more of zee bloodshed, we ave enough to deal wiz on le weekend. Ya in zee best place and Genevieve will nurse you back to good ealth!'

'Yeah Genevieve, ya right. We're the best of friends, but he's just a l'il stressed, because his girlfriend was a l'il concussed in the accident n he's naturally concerned for her.'

'Is zat zee attractrive girl Stacey, oo's gone for er x-ray?'

'Yeah it is. But she defo aint my g-friend. I've only just met her in the last twenty four hours.'

'She's ot. If someting blossoms, it's meant to be. Be appy, you've all survived n ya in safe gentle ands.'

Stacey was back quite quickly from the x-ray department. The porter wheeled her back to join the two of them in casualty. She'd only been gone for about twenty minutes.

'Boys, I'm back, but have to stay in over night, because they wanna keep me under surveillance after me being knocked out. I should be allowed to leave in the mornin' though.'

'How's ya tibia, waist, chest n neck?' asked Fluffy Donkey.

'Leg's sore, just badly bruised though n not broken, so I'm delighted n relieved. At least I can get ready for the European Championships. Mi waist, chest n neck are sore n mi heads throbbin'. I just wanna close my eyes n sleep for twelve hours. I think I'm being moved to a young persons ward in thirty mins or so.'

'I think I'll be goin' home.' said Ash.

'If you can find ya way? I wouldn't want you injurin' yaself on route,' teased Fluffy Donkey.

The time was moving swiftly towards seven o'clock, outside it was warm and extremely beautiful. For once summer was the season it should be, not a fantasy destined, never to be realised. The sky was a stunning royal blue, accentuated by the cotton wool gracefully floating clouds, drifting slowly besides the potent rays of the tropically gleaming sun. It was if they were playing a game of peek-a-boo, as every now and then, the clouds would be disruptive and inconveniently cover the sun. Moments later, he would re-appear stronger than ever ready to embark on another phase of control. It was a warm twenty four degrees, which for this time of-mid evening in the United Kingdom, was a pleasurable joy. Just a shame this fine weather couldn't be more consistent, although, it was delightful to savour it while it lasted. After the torrential downpour that occurred a few days earlier, this was dancing sunbathing heaven. I've never seen anyone dance while sunbathing, however, but this could become a new concept of artistic movement. Definitions of this would be, when a person's body went into momentary muscle spasm, or when they were wafting away an irritating fly or other insect, or when they were listening to music, allowing their mind to melt away, while allowing any part of their anatomy to bop, twitch, jive or shimmy to the soothing sounds projecting from their state of the art modern phone gadget, i-pod, home stereo system, TV, passing car radio or the songs playing sweetly in their Red or Dead-head.

Back at Jammin' Boy's house Groundhog Day was coming to a conclusion. Jennifer and Annabelle were cosily slumped on the sofa, either side of the King of the house. Was that Felix or JB? It was JB of course, despite Felix thinking he ran the show. He actually did, as JB fussed over him daily and nightly. Jennifer and Annabelle were slurping their third glasses of red, quite staggering really, after the copious amounts they drank yesterday evening and in the early hours of this morning. Especially after the antics they'd engaged in with Ash and JB. More so Annabelle's naked bathroom appearance, which JB wouldn't be able to erase from his memory for many a year. Even worse for Annabelle, although it hopefully wouldn't go any further than the affected parties.

'Is it OK if me n Bella stay tonight? You may need a l'il company.' asked Jennifer.

'We've got school in di mornin'. It probably aint a good idea, because, I need mi beauty sleep n I don't wanna be kept awake all night.' replied JB.

'Bella n I can share ya bed.'

'Why would you wanna share mi bed, when you've got two other bedrooms to use. I make that one each. Menage a trois, n I don't mean three into one!'

'We may as well end the weekend in style. We could keep you hot in the middle of the sandwich. Un bocadillo con carne bueno!' responded Jennifer.

'Yeah Jen, ya right. I am good meat, but I don't feel like any bread tonight. I can leave dat till di mornin', wid a l'il helpin' o scrambled egg!' answered JB.

Jennifer was certainly very probing. Not to the satisfaction of JB. He wanted, quite simply, an evening of solitude, comfort and recuperation after a monster partying weekend extravaganza. Jennifer for some reason had this inclination that he was her territory, or at least, she wanted to make it that way.

He was defiant that it would not happen, even in her wildest dreams. What made it even worse was the fact that she and Annabelle had consumed over a bottle of red wine within the last two hours. They were probably still drunk from the binge fest and couldn't resist the temptation for more.

'Shall we go down to Lillyford Park n see how they're all doin'?' suggested Annabelle.

'I tink it's probably best if we let em phone us when dare ready. Plus it's gettin' late too. Fluffy said he'd be in touch.'

At the hospital, it was Fluffy Donkey's turn to head to the x-ray department to find out if he'd suffered any fractures or other internal complications. With the symptoms he was experiencing, it was highly likely that he'd broken a metartarsal, or maybe two. The hospital porter who had brought Stacey back, took Joe down there too, pushing his mobile bed, following the yellow line. He remained on the spine board, as they didn't want to move him, just in case he'd experienced any serious spinal trauma. Ash had moved into Stacey's cubicle to keep her company. The nurses had taken her off the spinal board and rested her gently back on the firm but comfortable bed. Genevieve had wandered away to attend to a few other patients and then returned to speak to Ash and Stacey.

'Are you OK Stacey?'

'Yeah thanks. Just badly bruised, but floatin' wounded. We're all so unbelievably lucky after the terrible crash, thank Jesus.'

'I am so appy n relieved for you all, you are very lucky. Ash, ow are you feeling?'

'I feel good, but just a l'il tired n dizzy. I think I'm just sufferin' from concussion.'

'You may all ave to stay in dis bootiful ospital tonight, because it won't be a good idea to be back ome. It's important zat you ave somebody to look after you. Dis is a perfect aven for now. Can I touch your air Ash?'

'Yeah ya right. Just in case any of us need assístance during the night, it's better stayin' here. Of course you can touch my air, as you say.'

'Merci beaucoup pour ca. Ooooooooooo la laaaaaaaaa, it feels so soft and so… so –oo smoove. It makes me very appy to touch it excited.'

'Ha Haaaaaaaaaa. I don't wanna make you that happy, as you're workin'. What'd make me a very happy chappy, would be, if… if… if you gave me your number.'

'I'm a professional woman. I can't grant you zat wish. But I can ask you to phone up casualty and ask for me. So in a few days, I expect you to do zat.'

'I'd love to. That's a deal.'

She licked her lips while washing her hands, winked and smiled very sexily at Ash. Stacey was astounded that Ash could attract a woman and work so quickly in a Casualty department. Totally amazing.

'Stacey, e's such an andsome young man. I look forward to see-ing im again very soon, I ope! I must go and do some more work. Take care both of you. Groses bise.'

Genevieve left their cubicle sporting a very sexy wiggle, as you could see her pert and petite bottom moving side to side as she walked. She was a very attractive woman, one mighty fine piece of ass. With short bobbed black hair, a few freckles on her face, hazel green eyes, a slender and shapely nose, kissable lips and a very curvaceous size eight body. She must have been about five foot four inches tall.

'You Romeo, Ash. It must have taken you a matter of fifteen minutes to produce chivalrous magic there. I'm flabbergasted. You rock,' Stacey said.

She smiled, laughed briefly, which was hard to do as her ribs were sore and her chest was tight. They knuckle touched each other, a cool symbol of appreciation. Fluffy Donkey was on the mobile bed, strapped to the spinal board in the x-ray department awaiting his turn. There were about ten people queueing up with a whole range of injuries from bloody noses, arms secured in slings, allergic reactions to bee stings, legs raised in wheelchairs, sprains, strains caused from playing sport to falling down stairs, heads swathed in bandages, cuts that could have been sustained by out of control canal boat anchorage, some with torn and blood stained shirts and others who looked unhurt. They were probably partners, family and friends who were there for moral support.

'Mr Sargent.'

Fluffy Donkey had momentarily drifted off while resting horizontally, as he could only twitch his legs and move his arms as he was securely fastened to the board. He was dreaming about the experience he'd had with Stacey, although it was rather more graphic than what had actually happened. He slid off her top while they kissed and caressed, rolling about on the four poster bed. He playfully smacked her bottom, which was as toned and as firm as a salted peanut. His hands moved around to the zip on her tiny skimpy shorts. He tugged gently sliding down to the zip end, popped open the button to reveal a wonderous mound of finely cultivated vaginal hair. She was commando. Instantaneously, his finely honed member was standing to attention with discipline and ready for action.

'Mr Sargent, Mr Sargent.'

'Ooooh... oooooh... uuuuum, yeah baby, yeah.'

'Mr Sargent, are you here?' asked the radiography.

'Oh my god. Let me peel off your...'

'Mr Sargent, what would you like to peel off?'

'Eeerrr... eeeerrr... hhhmmm... sooorry, sooorry! What would I like to peel off?'

'Yes Mr Sargent!'

'I'd like to peel off my clothes, get off this board and be able to lie more comfortably. Is it my turn now?' he asked.

Fluffy Donkey had been transfixed in a lucid dream about him and Stacey having sex for the first time. He was snoring softly, alerting everyone in the waiting area. People were laughing, even those with painful injuries managed to be energised for a few moments, as he seemed so content in his dreamworld experience. Especially when he was sleep talking and at that opportune moment the radiographer had walked out asking for her next patient, to be confronted with a summons to have potentially her clothes removed. It could have been a scene for a Carry On movie, hilarity personified.

'I thought for a moment you wanted to accost me and indulge in some inappropriate behaviour?' she replied.

She appeared to be serious, much to the embarassment of Joe.

'I was miles away then. It wasn't a proposition for you, I was dreaming. I'm really sorry if it came across wrong.'

'Apology accepted. You're a lucky man. I'm in a jovial mood today, so you get a Sabbath day reprieve. If it'd been a Monday, oh-oh!' she cajoled.

'Thank my lucky stars.'

'Let's get you in here then, for an examination. What shall I start peeling off first? Hhhhhmmmmm. I'll start with these straps.' said the radiographer.

She wheeled him in to the x-ray room. She stood behind the vertical screen and configured the machine. It was an impressive room. Virginal conventional white with state of the art innovative gadgets positioned around the room. It was very spacious, about eight by six metres in size. The x-ray machine could be moved backwards and forwards, also downwards and upwards on a telescopic extendable computerised rectangular pillar.

She took a few pictures at different angles, so they could get a peripheral angle It flashed several times. The room to fully kit out would have probably cost in the region of two hundred and fifty thousand pounds. Thankfully with spinal boards being translucent on an x-ray machine, it meant Fluffy Donkey could stay on it. They didn't want to move him, just in case he had suffered any potentially debilitating injuries to his spinal column.

'You can go now. Your x-rays will be given to you by the Doctor in the next thirty minutes. I'd love to penetrate your mind to see what enchanting dream you were having!' said the Radiographer.

'Many thanks for that. If you peel off ya uniform, of course in private, we could fantasise together?' he cheekily replied.

'I know it's almost the watershed, but I don't appreciate illicit smut in this department... Thank you!' she exclaimed.

A different hospital porter wheeled him back to casualty, to rejoin Stacey and Ash.

'Do you want to hop in this chair, so I can take you down for ya x-ray?' asked the porter.

'Yeah. Time to go peeps.'

Ash was the last one to be taken for his x-rays. Most probably he was just suffering from shock, whiplash and dizzyness. He'd managed to climb out of Joe's Volkswagen Scirocco, very luckily indeed. It was likely that he would also be staying in Lillyford Park Hospital over night as he wasn't really in a fit and healthy state to be returning home. Off Ash went, being pushed in a wheelchair.

'See you soon Ash.'

'Yeah, I shouldn't be too long Stace. See you n that reprobate shortly.'

'I'll give you sixteen plus of reprobate when I'm outta here,' responded Fluffy Donkey.

"How ya feelin' Stace?'

'OK Joe, just really tired. Mi body's achin' all over n mi head's still dizzy. I just wanna go to bed.'

'Snap. I could do with a hot cup of cocoa right now n then shut my eyes and not wake up till ten tomorrow morn.'

'That sounds like heaven. I could do with a neck massage Fluffy,' suggested Stacey.

'How the hell am I gonna give you a massage, when I'm strapped to this board, feeling like I'm gonna be catapulted skywards like a rocket launcher.'

'I didn't mean you, I meant a physio. You're an invalid at mo, so ya no use or ornament.'

'Don't make me laugh Stace. and please don't start giving me lip like that velcro sponge ball Ashilito.'

'Ha Haaaaaa. I won't. But I want ya to sort yaself out, because, I'm expectin' you to take me out on a date. We could go tobogganing?'

'Just because I can't move at the moment, doesn't mean I won't be fit, willing n able in a couple of weeks,' answered Fluffy Donkey.

As Ash was being pushed down the corridor to the x-ray department, they passed Genevieve. Was she stalking him? He certainly hoped so, as he was attracted to her radiant beauty. In fact, who wouldn't be? She was a sensational looking woman, who would be the perfect cure to anybody's worst day. Certainly asthetically anyway. She halted the porter and Ash in their tracks, while following the yellow line. It was as if they were off to see the wizard, the wonderful wizard of Oz.

'Allo mon amie. Are you now going for your x-a-ray?' said Genevieve.

'Hi Genevieve. Yeah, just to make sure mi head's still in tact and nothing's broken.'

'It looks to me zat everything is in tact. zose eyes are so bright, zat air is so soft n zat face is a bootiful shining light. Don't forget our pact Aaash!'

'Don't you worry. I promise. Scout's honour.' he replied.

'I look forward to it. Bye bye n take good care.'

'Bye Genevieve. See you later n take care too.'

'Not later tonight, but I ope, very soon.'

Ash did not have to wait too long either. Probably no longer than fifteen minutes, which was unusual, as waiting times in hospitals were normally approaching the four hour mark. That was from admission to treatment.

Stacey had been moved to ward forty which was in the Regal Wing of the hospital which was on the south side. It was on the third floor overlooking the city centre. There were three available beds in the ward, coincidentally in the same room, which was virtually unheard of. Usually hospitals were struggling to find additional beds, but not on this occasion. Thankfully as their injuries weren't deemed as being too serious, they weren't located in the Intensive Care Unit.

Joe had to be taken to the plaster department as the x-ray had shown that he'd fractured two metatarsals on his right foot, the fourth and fifth. They hadn't broken completely, which was a relief, as surgery would have been the favourable option. The cracks were in an identical position side by side and were about a centimetre in width. This had occured with the impact. Joe had unconventionally put his left foot on the foot brake consequently his right foot being dormant had lifted up at speed and crashed into the bottom of the accelerator pedal, this movement causing the fracture. If he'd used the appropriate right foot, it may not have happened. As his spinal column was in one piece, he could be removed from the long board. An Accident and Emergency nurse had come down to the plaster department to help take Fluffy Donkey off the board along with the plaster technician and orthapaedic Specialist.

Chapter Twenty

Boot-iful Banter

He was very sore, so it took him a few minutes before he could slowly move certain parts of his body, especially when he'd been on the board for a good two hours or more. They rolled him off the board and on to the mobile bed he'd been brought on by the hospital porter. After a few minutes of regaining his movement and re-generating blood flow with gentle exercises of flexing his arms, legs, fingers and toes, he managed to lift himself up with the help of the technician and the orthopaedic Specialist, swivel himself around so his legs were hanging off the side of the bed. He put his left foot down, while being held by the two guys, who helped him onto the bed in the plaster room. '
I see it's a quite-a badly swoll-en where you've given it a right-a good-a whack. These sto-ock car racers eh Jezza?' said the plaster specialist.

'Yeah, an expensive hobby I'd say Mikele. I wish I had that kinda money to go n mash cars up?' said the orthopaedic specialist.

'At least it keeps you boys… aaaaarrrgh. At least it keeps you guys in a job.' Yelled Fluffy Donkey.

'Soorree, I didn't meeean to cause soo muuch pain-a!' responded Mikele.

'Yeah, it hurts right there alright!'

'Whaat I'll do-a, is giiive you a boota, Italia-an style-a, whiich will elp you to walk-a muuch bet-ter,' confirmed Mikele.

'I don't mean to be rude Mikele, but why do you have a girls name?' asked Fluffy Donkey.

'What's your name?'

'Joe.'

'Oor. A bit-a like Josephine-a?' laughed Mikele.

'In Italy Josephine-a, the English name Michael is Mikele. I understand-a thaat the name-a Mikele in English, is Michaela. They do saay-a, that-a we all ave a little female inside us, Joe.'

'Aaaaargh. Aaaargh. Don't press it there again, it's agony.'

'Sorree Joe, but-a, are you a man-a or a mouse-a?' Apologised Mikele.

'Have you ever seen a six foot four inch mouse?'

'Only in-a fairy tales. But-a I've seen a four foot six one, right ere on the bed-a. You know what-a I mean-a Joe!'

'You've got quite a bit of humour Mikele. It's makin' me feel much better.'

'He does stand up comedy part time Joe and he uses my afro as the microphone. You know what I'm sayin'!' said Jerry.

Jerry was mixed race, light brown in complexion, six foot one inches tall, with a brown beauty spot on his left cheek and a neatly prepared baby afro, about four inches thick. Jerry and Mikele high fived and burst out into laughter following Jerry's comment.

'Are you sure you're not the comedian Jerry?' asked Joe.

'I don't have the same cultured, flowin' roman flair like Mikele. He's the archetypal Mambo Italiano. Hey, mambo, mambo italiano, hey mambo, mambo italiano.'

Jerry went into song and verse as if praising and bigging up his comrade. Initially Joe felt a little bit perturbed by the sarcastic comments flying from Mikele's mouth, but he soon realised it was solely playful banter and was a way of helping to alleviate the pain he was suffering.

'You walk-a like the guy from the wizard of Oz-a. What's iz name-a?' said Mikele.

'You mean the scarecrow Mikele?' suggested Jerry.

'No-a, but-a to be onest, every time I go near im, e looks-a frightened. Anybody would-a think-a I'm built like Rocky?!'

'Ha Haaaaaaaa.' chuckled Jerry.

'E's built like-a Ivan Drago, but e looks-a like-a big n gentle cuddly bear.'

'Are you tryin' to say I'm carryin' too many pounds?'

Jingle jangle, as if by magic a golden pound coin dropped to the floor and rolled underneath the bed.

'There's ya answer. You said it. Ya so flush-a with-a money, you drive-a stock cars n throw it away-a.'

Mikele picked up the coin and returned it to Joe who obligingly took it back.

'In fact boys, for the wonderful… aaaargh, work you do, could you donate it to one of ya hospital charities please. In fact, here's another two. It's not money for twenty minutes of stand up though.' Fluffy Donkey said smiling.

A lovely gesture by Joe, which was graciously accepted by Jerry and Mikele. Mikele measured Joe's foot and asked Jerry to take a size twelve out of one of the cupboards. Jerry unfastened it and Mikele used some antiseptic fragrance free wipes to clean some dried blood that had formed on his right foot. Both specialists wore personal protective latex gloves, as it was regulation that they had to have a barrier when being exposed to bodily fluids. He also used some cleansing wipes to give his foot a sweeter scent, as it smelt extremely sweaty.

KNOCK KNOCK.

'Come in.' answered Mikele.

A man dressed in green overalls opened the door and walked in.

'How ya doin' boys?' asked Neil Single.

'We're all good thanks, Neil, apart from this wounded one here. He'll be OK though. Just a couple of broken metasarsals to nurse back to good health,' replied Jerry.

'The coppers have arrested that taxi driver. Think he was over the limit, because they breathilised im. You're all lucky. Have your mates left you?'

'Yeah, they've deserted me n been given beds for the night. I'll hopefully be joinin' em shortly.'

'I'll take this board and be on my way. Send my regards to em. Must go, we're gettin another job. Take care. See ya.' said Neil the Paramedic.

'See ya. Many thanks for all ya help.' responded Joe.

'Take care Neil.'

124

'See you later Neil.' said Mikele.

'Sorry Mikele, what were you sayin' earlier on about that wizard of Oz character?' asked Joe.

'I was-a sayin', you're like-a the tin man-a. You're movin' like ya need-a some oil-a.'

'To be honest, I could do with a beautiful woman, smearin' massage oil me now and givin' me an hour of essential hands on.'

'I tink at di moment, all you need-a is love-a. Ha Haaaaaaaaa. Just like-a di Beatles. In fact-a, you could-a do with buyin'-a protective back protector, to look-a like-a di creature?'

'Ha Haaaaaaaaaa. Yeah man. It's all about creature comforts!' said Jerry.

Fluffy Donkey was thoroughly enjoying the humour and banter in the plaster room. It was certainly helping to alleviate some of the pain he was suffering. He felt like he was in a comedy club being entertained by fabulous stand ups. The charisma and rapport that Mikele and Jerry had was so infectious to others, so any patient passing through for treatment would always be energised and inspired by their warm and jovial nature. Mikele fitted the size twelve protective boot on to Joe's right foot. It was like a boot worn by Stormtroopers in the Star Wars movie. It was made of a hard plastic shell with an internal composition of foam and nylon for comfort. It had four air shells inside the boot which could be inflated using the side bulb that moulds to the foot. This provided compression, hence reducing swelling and accelerated rehabilitation. The advantages of this design as opposed to the traditional plaster of paris was that it could be removed, to allow the foot to be washed, helping to prevent ankle stiffness and muscle wastage. This promoted recovery far quicker than the older method. It also enabled patients to start applying an amount of pressure on the foot, as it gradually started to heal. This meant that crutches could be discarded far sooner.

'You're all ready now Joe. We'll get you a wheelchair and organise for a porter to take you to the ward. Mikele, could you find out where Joe needs to be taken please?' asked Jerry.

'Of course-a Fro Boy. No problem, right away boss,' responded Mikele.

'Fro Boy? Why d'ya call him that?' asked Fluffy Donkey rather puzzled.

'Eeeeerm, come on Joe, I'm not exactly bald am I and have a cool, chic and cultured baby afro. Some people just call me mic!'

'Eh! I don't understand.'

'Mic, short for microphone. Next time don't inhale too much of that laughing gas, it'll send you a little doolally.' Chuckled Jerry.

Mikele contacted the nurse station on the third floor of the Regal Wing to confirm that this was where Joe would be re-located. He eventually got through at the third time of asking and spoke to the Ward Sister, who confirmed that Joe would be staying there overnight. It was an observation ward that was for those who had experienced head trauma. It was a feeder ward to Neurology. After putting the phone down, Mikele told Joe he'd be re-uniting with Stacey and Ash at the other side of the hospital.

'The three amigos runnin' things-a.' said Mikele.

'That's how we roll Mikele. Just like those swashbucklin' swordsmen, the three musketeers.'

'I'm sure you wouldn't look outta place in Rome-a. You could light up the coloseum, what a spectacle!'

'At the moment, the only thing lightin' up is the whites of my eyes.'

'And the bones on your x-rays.' said Jerry.

They all burst out with laughter again in synchronised fashion.

KNOCK KNOCK…

'Come in-a,' said Mikele.

'Hi, I've just come to take a patient to the Regal Wing,.' said the porter.

'Thanks. That'll be me.'

'I didn't think it'd be anyone else. You're the only one here wearing a neck brace and a ski boot. Shall we hit the piste?' replied the porter.

'Have you ever seen a disabled one legged giant downhill skiing?' responded Joe.

'No, but I've seen one rolling down the mountains. Come on, let's be having you.'

Fluffy Donkey eased himself off the bed with the generous assistance from Mikele and Jerry, who gently and gracefully sat him down in the wheelchair.

'This is your imitation chairlift. Sorry it's not the real thing. Maybe your dreams'll take you there tonight eh?' said the porter.

'I hope so.'

'Take care Joe. Break a leg.' said Jerry.

'Look after yaself Joe. Buona notte. Don't-a get into any trouble. You can't run away-a, you can't skip-a and you can't hop-a, so the best-a recipe is-a, to relax-a and sleep-a. Get well soon-a and remember, knock yourself out-a! Ha Haaaaaaaa,' said Mikele.

He was a prize joker, always entertaining people with his addictive and soothing smooth mambo italiano charm. Mikele opened the door so the porter could wheel Joe through and into the corridor, en route to the modern, very stylish and attractive Regal Wing. It was seven floors high. It was a typical twenty first century breeze block construction covering a secure steel frame, giving it rigid integrity. It was a spectrum of colour externally, displaying art nouveaux pastel colours of lilac, turquoise and lemon in a large chequered pattern. It was extremely therapeutic and endearing for a hospital. Internally it was innovative and no expense had been spared to provide patients with the most pioneering treatment ranging from curing ingrowing toe nails to cancer. Thankfully it was a state funded facility and hadn't been kidnapped and sabotaged by the evil demons of privatisation. Besides being rigged with security keeping every inch apart from inside the toilets (a gross intrusion of privacy) under close surveillance, security guards patrolled every entrance. Respect to the Welfare State.

Ash had already been taken up to join Stacey, as his x-rays had shown little more than aligned bone with no displacement. He just suffered from mild concussion, aches, pains and light bruising. Stacey and Ash were awaiting Fluffy Donkey's imminent arrival. It would be no doubt welcomed with a light applause, but not too loud as it was approaching nine pm. The time had passed by briskly since their accident had occured at approximately five o'clock. They were all extremely tired after a hugely eventful last thirty hours. The delirious and euphoric highs suddenly descending and almost imploding with a near catastrophic low. Thankfully their health was still in tact, almost!

Fluffy Donkey was almost there, being escorted by the porter. He wasn't really in a talkative mood. He was exhausted and in need of precious rest after a terrifying ordeal. At least now he was nearly comfortable. The sooner he could relax and stretch out in bed, the better. The journey took about five minutes, as they had to travel from the north side in the opposite direction. He now had the opportunity to appreciate the beautiful aesthetics of the hospital. It had been revived over the last five years, as the government had plummeted millions into transforming it into a cosmetically enhanced facility. It was certainly held in high esteem throughout the country and was undoubtedly rated as the ultimate. Hospital. He was wheeled to the lifts and up to the third floor of the Regal Wing. They arrived at the entrance door of the observation ward and the porter pressed the intercom button to speak to one of the nursing staff.

Chapter 21

Staying Alive

'Hello, can I help you?' asked the nurse.

'Yeah, I've brought a gentleman up here in a wheelchair. What's your name mate?' asked the porter.

'What's my name? I'm the ward sister.'

'No, sorry, I'm speaking to the patient.' replied the porter.

'It's Joe. Joe Sargent, as in the copper.'

'Yeah, I heard that. Come in, you're under arrest.' said the ward sister.

The door clicked, so the porter wheeled through Joe. They travelled straight down the corridor to the nurses' station, which was a large desk on the ward. There were ten rooms on the ward, each having six beds and a few private rooms which were for patients with more severe head injuries, who were going through a transition, before being taken to Neurology.

'Hi Joe, I'm Sister Bliss, just call me Baby,' said the sister.

'Your name's Baby!' said Joe.

He looked at the porter, who in turn winked at him. They both magically started to bawl out like a new born baby.

'Haaaaa. That's funny, anyone would think you two were identical twins,. One slight problem, there's about ten inches between you,' laughed Sister Bliss.

'We're not that small,' answered the Porter.

'Speak for yaself, I've never had any complaints or problems, I've just been called Moby, Big, Monster and many more names,' said Joe.

'I'm talking about your height, not the nether regions of your anatomy. Why do you guys always seem to resort to smut talk?' said Sister Bliss.

They both looked quite sheepish and embarrassed.

'It's quite funny that ya named after hair care products Sister. Ya parents must av been psychic, when they ad ya.' said the Porter.

'I just think they thought I wouldn't be a flash in the pan, I'd be short and curly, no highlights, just the vogue and chic girl with colour, couture and full of volume!'

'Are you a walkin' hair care commercial?' asked the Porter.

'No, just one special Baby. Coocchie, coochie coooooo,' said the sister.

'Speaking of baby talk, I better get a move on, because my little ones are being babysat by mi Dad, so I need to get off. Where d'ya want him?' asked the porter.

'It's OK, don't worry, I'll sort him out. He looks like he needs mothering!' said the sister.

'Thanks, take care. See ya.'

'You too. Many thanks. Look after yaself.' said Joe.

The porter left with an empty wheelchair, ready to finish his shift and head home. It was quite a hybrid of activity on the ward, even at almost nine pm. Visiting hours were two till four in the afternoon and then for the second period of the day from six till eight thirty. As it was an observation ward, the nurses tended to be quite flexible, allowing visitors to stay a little later. It was reminiscent of a queue for public transport at peak period times, as there appeared to be a deluge at leaving time. Sister Bliss was just taking a few notes on Joe's medical card, before taking him to join Stacey and Ash in room seven. When she had finished, she wheeled him through to his bed, removed his cervical spine collar, as he no longer needed it, and pulled the cover back so he could be helped into bed. But firstly, he had to take his clothes off and put on a hospital gown. He needed a hand, as his range of movement was limited due to muscle and bone soreness. Sister Bliss had to take the protective boot off his right foot, so his trousers could be taken off. She slipped his boxer shorts off and looked the other way, also giving him a hand with his shirt. She put his arms through the front of the backless gown and herded him into bed.

'Ha Ha, Ha, Ha, Stayin' Alive, Stayin' Alive, Ha, Ha, Ha, Ha, Stayin' Alive, Stayin' Alive.' sang Fluffy Donkey.

He was now in more jovial spirits at being re-united with Ash and Stacey. The pair of them joined in with the encore of the Bee Gees seventies classic. Despite them all being exhausted, weak and injured, they managed a momentary injection of zest. It didn't last too long though, as Sister Bliss asked them to lower the tones, with other people resting and others sleeping. Fluffy Donkey's phone started to ring out loudly.

'Damn, I better put it on silent. It's JB.'

Sister Bliss walked over to the room as she'd heard the phone ringing from the corridor, as she was walking round checking on other patients.

'Can you make sure that all phones are on silent please? Respect those that are sleeping. Thanks.'

'That's tellin' you Fluffy.' said Stacey.

'Being put in check once again Fluffy.'

'Don't you start Ashinaldo. You've already got a huge right hook on order.'

'I didn't know I was gonna be impersonatin' Long John Silver in pantomime,' replied Ash.

'Just you wait. It'll be droppin' you to ya knees.'

'Ha Haaaaaaaa. Learn to walk first you invalid,' chuckled Ash.

'Boys, relax n stop gettin' so argumentative. I'll start parading as a round card girl if ya not careful.' said Stacey.

'Uuuuuum uuuuuuum. What a lovely prospect and proposition. I can't wait to see that, It'll certainly cheer me up n be a sight for sore eyes,' answered Fluffy Donkey.

'You never know, one day could be your lucky one!' said Stacey..

Eventually as the phone had rang off when JB had called, he phoned back a minute later, as he wanted to know how the crew were.

'Yes JB, how ya doin'?' asked Fluffy Donkey.

'Are you been serious man, don't ya mean, ow you doin' n di rest o di crew?'

'We're all good thanks. Nothin' too serious in terms of injuries, apart from I've broken two metatarsals on mi right foot. The two outside ones. They've given me a kinda ski boot, which is so comfy.'

'Ows ya ed n ting?'

'Mi head's quite sore along with mi neck, back, right knee and chest where the seatbelt pulled tight,' replied Fluffy Donkey.

'Most importantly, you've all escaped virtually unscathed. I'm so relieved, well, I mean, we're all relieved.'

'Love you all!' said Jennifer.

'Look after yourselves. Glad and really happy y'all safe n walkin' wounded,' said Annabelle.

They both shouted out from JB's living room, which Fluffy Donkey could hear. It brought a smile to his lips. After the experiences they'd had, it was the least he could do.

'We're virtually walkin' wounded, apart from my back's as stiff as a piece of concrete,' Fluffy said, disgruntled.

'They should tro ya back in di cement mixer den,' laughed JB.

'I can't wait till I'm fit n healthy again, because Achinaldo's gonna receive some donkey tail swishin' damage.'

'Are you two fallin' out man?'

'No, but he just keeps teasin' me, because I'm like the tin man from the wizard of Oz. In fact, when I saw the orthopaedic and plaster specialists, they said the same thing. Hopefully though, Stacey can provide me with some good oils,' responded Fluffy Donkey.

'Excuse me Fluffy. We haven't even been out for a date yet, so a massage is way down the line.'

'I'll get over you, I know I will, because I'm the King of wishful thinking,' Fluffy Donkey sang.

'You'll get over me? You have to get with me first. Talk about a prelude to disaster! You're history tin man,' laughed Stacey.

'Geeeeez, is there a magnet drawing arguments in here tonight, or are we just all restless?' asked Ash.

'Don't you get involved again.' said Fluffy Donkey.

'Come on, let's have a three way?' suggested Ash.

'Eeeeerm. A three way? This girl aint easy n certainly no broke ass slapper! Refined as a finely chiseled diamond, I'll let you know.'

'Noooooo. Not a *ménage a trois*, I mean a three way argument.'

'I say, let's just get some sleep.' suggested Fluffy Donkey.

'Are you fa real man? I've been on di phone wid you for di las five minutes, n ya squabblin' like fishermens wives man. Ave a l'il decency n talk to mi, when I'm on di other end o di line! Raaaaarse claaaaaart!' JB said rather bemused.

'Sorry man. It's just, mi head's a l'il dizzy, I'm tired, frustrated, in pain n I've got these two comedians distractin' me.'

'I'll give you comedian. When I comedy roundhouse ya ed!' said JB.

'Can you all please settle down and keep the noise to a minimum? It isn't a party ward, it's Sunday, just have a bit of respect for the other patients,' said Sister Bliss.

They all apologised profusely. 'Yeah, let's get some shut eye. I think we all need it,' said Fluffy Donkey.

'That's the best thing you've said all day Joe,' said Ash.

'Pphhhhhhhhh,' replied Fluffy Donkey.

He puffed his cheeks out and appeared that he was very quickly coming to the end of his tether. He decided the best form of defence was silent treatment, not wanting to provoke a response from Ash.

'I must go JB. The Ward Sister's wantin' us to relax n recuperate.'

'It makes sense. Just take tings easy n take di weight off ya left foot n back. After di eve you've all ad, it's important to wind down man.'

'Ya right. Take care n don't abuse Jen and Bella.'

'Ooooooo... I so easily could, but it's not very professional.'

'If you were a true playboy, you'd relish the fruitful delights,' responded Fluffy Donkey.

'It's so temptin', but you ave to realise, we all work together n it could be fraught wid problems.'

'It didn't stop you this morn with Jen,' said Fluffy Donkey.

'I tried mi ardest to resist, but Jen was di epitome of a wild tigress, unrelentin', stalkin' er prey, pouncin' n diggin' er claws into succulent human flesh.'

'Speak for yaself. I wouldn't really call you succulent. Ha Haaaaaaa. Right, I must go Brother. See you really soon Jammin'!'

'Don't get trapped in dere. Make sure dere's a way out.'

'Yeaaaah JB, I'll be out sooner than you think. I hope in a few days! See ya,' said Fluffy Donkey.

'Big PHAT love to y'all. Take great care n enjoy a liquidised diet. Ha haaaaaaaa,' laughed JB.

Peace was restored as Fluffy Donkey ended the call. He was finding it extremely uncomfortable as he couldn't roll over on to his side or front, which was his normal sleeping position. They all said goodnight to one another. A nurse had brought their medication, ranging from mild ibuprofen to Fluffy Donkey's stronger co-codamol. The nurse had also closed the blinds and turned the lights out. It was time for them all to embark on a dreamworld adventure, the perfect cure after a highly turbulent day. Monday morning was approaching on the horizon, and Stacey certainly wouldn't be gracing Oatmill High with her presence in the morning. Sister Bliss would phone in sick for her.

Chapter 22

Tough Nut to Crack

Back at JB's house in Honeyville, JB, Jennifer and Annabelle were discussing the Groundhog Day film experience. They all agreed that it would be a horrible experience with every day being like any other and it would demotivate, induce stress, frustration, stagnation and for some with fragile characters, potentially suicidal tendencies.

'I'm so relieved Fluffy, Ash and Stacey have managed to escape virtually unscathed, apart from a l'il whiplash, broken metatarsals and severe bruisin'!' said Jennifer.

'Yeah man, it could o been so much worse, ya know,' responded JB.

'I think, as a celebration, we should all get naked n enjoy some good lovin'?' suggested Jennifer.

'Don't ya think enough naked bodies have been seen this weekend Jen?'

'Come on, Bella. It's only a bit of fun!' replied Jennifer.

'If you n JB wanna savour some sensuous sexploration, good luck. Go ahead.'

'No Bella. We've ad our fun, it's now time fa you two beautiful ladies to ed off ome. Dis afro boy needs precious R n R fa di mornin'. It's almost di summer olidays, but I ave to maintain mi professionalism. Opefully, mi traits can rub off on you,' said JB.

'We could stay over night, have some real fun n then head off home before school, in the mornin'?' suggested Jennifer.

'What l'il bit of NO and SLEEP, don't you understand Jen?'

'I know, but I just don't understand after such a special partyin' weekend, why we just can't have some more fun.'

'You two can go out n party n ave some more fun, but fa me, it's bed solo. No more proposals of an indecent nature, tank you!' replied JB.

'I'm hearin' you JB. We all need to recuperate after a monster marathon shindig. It's almost summer holidays, so I'm sure we can organise another spectacular. Jen, let's get off n give JB a l'il single man's pleasure!' said Annabelle.

'Ooooo, I know, but just wanna stroke mi hands all over his sculptured, athletic body. It's lush.'

'Jen, all dis flattery won't get you any further. I'm grateful for di compliments, but NO literally means NO.'

Jennifer ran her fingers through JB's silky soft afro while kissing and licking his right ear. It sent shivers down his spine and goose bumps started to rapidly appear all over his body, just like hundreds of rabbits popping their heads out of their burrows at hearing the pitter patter light vibrations of many lizards above.

'Jeeeeeeeen. It aint gonna work lady. I need to be in bed by ten. You girls can order a taxi. Let's just ope it's a more enjoyable journey dan di other crew's,' said JB.

Annabelle had made her way to the toilet. She phoned a cab while she was up there.

'How long Bella?' asked Jennifer.

'Should be here in fifteen mins.'

'Sorry to be a pain in the booty Jammin', but you know I fancy the pants off ya.'

'I'm so grateful ya know. I find you really attractive, but it ain't healthy, because, people 'will start to talk at work. I don't wanna make our lives uncomfortable. Dis mornin' was a one off. I eventually broke mi resistance because of ya persistence n infinite beauty. You're a hot gal, but tings can't possibly run. If one of us leaves Oatmill, it could be a different story,' said JB.

'I'm sure we could keep it low profile. Why would anyone need to find out?' asked Jennifer.

'Tink about it Jen. Realistically, ow are we gonna manage to keep tings under wraps, apart from beneath di bedsheets?'

'We'd make a great couple.'

'It's all fantasy dough. If anyting appens in di future, good, if not so be it!' answered JB.

A car sounded its horn outside. It was probably the taxi for Jennifer and Annabelle. JB peered through the curtains to see. Indeed it was a Lucky Star taxi.

'Ladies, ya taxi's ere already. Dat was quick, widin ten minutes.'

'Comin',' shouted down Annabelle.

Jennifer put her shoes on, gave JB a gigantic long hug, also managing to press her lips against his, engaging in a short sensuous kiss.

'Geez, get a room you too.'

'We're being kicked out Bella, so there's no chance of that tonight.'

'Ladies, we all need our beauty sleep fa work tomorrow mornin'.'

'Speak for yourself JB. I feel n look at least a seven outta ten, don't ya think Bella?'

'I'd give you one,' said Bella.

'I'm not gonna come outta the closet n tip the velvet, maybe next week though.' responded Jennifer.

'Come on ladies, get gone. Give me a call please when you get ome. We don't want any more patients in casualty. Ave a good night sleep n I'll see you both in di mornin'.'

'Thanks for everything JB. You've been a sensational host. Sorry about the mornin' bathroom streak.'

'Don't apologise Bella. It was a sight for sore eyes. I'm gettin' goose bumps as we speak,' he said chuckling.

'I know, but I feel embarassed.'

'Bella, embarrassed? You n that word don't go together,' responded Jennifer.

'It was the effects of alcohol. I don't normally display public nudity, apart from bathin' topless on holiday.'

'Bella, who you kiddin'? Ya only shy when you first meet someone. After that, anything goes.' laughed Jennifer.

'What a total misconception. You know that ain't true Jen. That was a one off n unintentional. I didn't expect anyone to be up.'

'JB was certainly up, at the sight of you in the bathroom. Uuuuuum uuuuuum.'

Jennifer at the precise moment, put her hands on Annabelle firm buttocks, squeezing her cheeks through the yellow floral dress.

'Jen, we agreed to those shenanigans next week, not now,' said Annabelle.

'Ladies, time to go. The taxi's pippin'.'

'OK. We know when we're not wanted. Take care Jammin', see you tomorrow. Thanks for everythin' n more.'

'No worries Jen. Feeling's mutual. See ya tomorrow, take care lady.'

'Bye JB. Till tomorrow. Thanks again,' said Annabelle.

'Ya welcome Bella. Laters.'

The girls trotted along the driveway towards the cab, shoes clinking and clonking on the paving stones. Giggles and laughs rang out from the girls. They opened the gate, then closed it firmly.

PING!

The sound reverberated, enough to make Felix's ears suddenly stand on end. He'd been hiding upstairs, catching up on some precious sleep, after a restless night with the commotion occuring both up and downstairs. Outside, the taxi door slammed and the driver pulled away. The girls didn't live too far away. They both shared a plush apartment on the edge of Marlborough. JB was so relieved. He could now relax after the crazy and hectic exploits of the past thirty or so hours. He locked the door and made sure every window downstairs was secure, before setting the burglar alarm, turning all the lights and appliances off downstairs and making his way to the bathroom. Felix had followed him upstairs and was fussing around him, swishing his tail gently against JB's bare legs. He could quite easily have been a catwalk model, Felix. JB gazed at himself in the mirror, running his fingers through his fro and said assertively,

'I'm lookin' mighty fine, sharp n slick, Jennifer was so damn lucky to savour the length of my candle stick.'

Rather pleased with himself, however, still concerned by the effect it would have on Jennifer, as earlier throughout the evening, she was constantly hinting at more sexual shenanigans. Many a man would have succumbed to her astounding attractiveness, but JB was a man of devout principle and had resisted temptation. He brushed his teeth, the vibrating head of the toothbrush rotating frantically as it cleaned his pristine gleaming enamel. Felix began to purr very loudly, as every time he heard the sound of the toothbrush, his ears pricked up, his heart began to slow down, he walked backwards and forwards in strategic fashion, as if stalking his prey.

They had a special and precious friendship, better than any human being, because JB could trust Felix implicitly. After teeth brushing, JB rinsed his face several times with cold water, dried it, turned the light off, walked to the bedroom, closed the blue velvet curtains, took his clothes off and jumped into his cosy double bed, alone. *What a relief*, he thought, being able to sleep dreamily without any distractions. It was a very humid evening, so JB left the window partly open and settled down to sleep, pulling the quilt off the bed, laying in the crucifix position on his back. Felix jumped on to the bed and slept on the silk navy blue quilt which was hanging on the left bottom corner. Felix loved the cool sensation the quilt gave.

Chapter 23

Monday Morning Blues

Bbrrrrr… Bbrrrrrrrrr. JB's alarm clocked sounded. Felix's ears pricked up, but he was virtually unmoved, still in deep sleep mode. JB rolled over and snoozed it. He sighed deeply, knowing it was almost time to get up and get ready for work on Monday morning. He was still exhausted after the weekend exploits and would relish yet another long sleep tonight. Monday was almost as good as Fridays, as he had only one lesson more, including a quadruple first thing. It was seven am, so he normally snoozed his alarm twice, with it sounding at ten minute intervals. The only time he got up at seven am prompt, was when he had to wash his afro. Thankfully this morning wasn't one of those days, as he'd washed it towards the end of last week. He tossed and turned, wanting to delay the inevitable waking up. He loved his job at Oatmill High School, but just couldn't be bothered or motivated today.

Eventually, after snoozing the alarm twice, he woke up at the third time of asking, seven twenty precisely. He stretched his arms out above his horizontally lying body, clicked his fingers, kicked his legs to promote some blood circulation and energise himself and then let out a huge roar, lion style, which made Felix jump off the bed in fright.

'Sorry Felix, dat wasn't intentional, but mi eds tired, mi body's limp n I don't wanna be walkin' all gangsta today, draggin' mi foot seal stylie, or walkin' like a chimp.'

Miaaoooooow. A loud good morning from Felix, followed by a long Olympic Sprinter style, pre race stretch. Two legs out in front and two to the back, Felix was also ready for the day ahead, ready to torment and aggravate Petra the pedigree pussy cat.. JB rolled out of bed like an SAS soldier performing a controlled, graceful and rapid combat manoevre on a tour of duty behind enemy lines, before opening fire on an unsuspecting victim.

BANG!

He crashed to the floor. All that serenity and artistic prowess stood for nothing, as the landing was rather embarrassing. Thankfully, apart from Felix, there was no-one else there to witness the disaster. He opened up the curtains and pushed the fire escape window open after unlocking the safety catch, by pressing it down and twisting the handle. The weather was glorious once more. Sun beaming down, sky = a magnificent blue with a few white cotton wool clouds slowly drifting to the east. The breeze was so refreshing as it passed into the bedroom. JB went to the bathroom to check himself out, relieve his bladder and wash his face. Following bathroom duties, he skipped his way downstairs, opening the the blinds in the living room and the ones in the kitchen, then de-activated the burglar alarm. He just had time to have a quick breakfast. What should he devour? Marvellous nutritious muesli, traditional toast with margarine and apricot jam or a beautiful succulent bacon buttie? After a brief discussion in his mind, he opted for the muesli with a creamy and scrumptious low fat yoghurt decorated with fresh blueberries and honey on top. He pulled the muesli out of the cupboard, yoghurt and blueberries from the fridge and prepared a delectable meal. He was conscious of the time, as he was normally living life on the proverbial edge, rarely on time, apart from for work, although, in the last few weeks he'd been spoken to by John the head of year for a few late arrivals.

He sat down at the oval shaped pine wood kitchen table to eat his breakfast. Felix jumped on the table, only to be pushed off by JB's flailing hand. He placed the navy cereal bowl that was overflowing with creamy luscious yogurt with a few streams of honey running down the side of it, on the table. Felix was miaowing frantically, as he could smell the yoghurt. As it was irritable to cats' stomachs in large quantities, JB got up and put a small amount in his bowl. There was a seperate bowl of cat biscuits that were chicken and lamb flavour. They were Felix's daytime nibbles which contained calcium, helping to strengthen his teeth. JB was savouring his mouthwatering breakfast, absolutely delicious. He preferred to have that compared to any other morning kickstarting delight. Felix was lapping up the creamy goodness of his yoghurt treat. JB wasn't messing around with his cereal this morning, it was shovelled down his throat at a frantic place, which would no doubt induce indegestion. He normally took his time with his food, enjoying the array of flavours. He didn't want to be reprimanded by the head of year. His reputation was certainly highly revered, but he was by no stretch of the imagination untouchable. Muesli down the hatch, he stood up and took his bowl over to the sink, ran the cold tap and poured himself a large glass of water. He drank that in a virtual flash, following that moment of rehydration, he ran the hot water, squirted some washing up liquid into the bowl and washed up the pots.

He ran upstairs with Felix in his wake, wanting to play with him as usual. He was still naked, so went to his bedroom wardrobe, opened the door and chose his clothes. Today he decided to opt for a shocking pink shirt, black Zara trousers with a pinstripe down the sides reminiscent of a snooker players. It was finished off with white gold heart cuff links, a white tie fastened Windsor style, a pair of black cotton socks with silver lips on the outside and under the trousers a confortable pair of white Calvin Klein boxers.

He normally smeared on some coco butter, a daily ritual, but because he had snoozed the alarm twice, meant time had been lost usually used for his morning shower. He hadn't forgotten, it's just that time was of the essence. He closed the bedroom window and then went to the bathroom to brush his teeth. His electric toothbrush as always made Felix purr when it sounded, like a woman's treasured sex toy. Quite apt in the sense of a pleasured pussy. After brushing his teeth, he stroked Felix momentarily with his foot and checked his iPhone. It was seven forty five. He had to hurry, as the bus ride was normally at least thirty five minutes, pending traffic. He rinsed his face, squirted on his favourite Issey Miyake cologne, , looked glancing in the mirror, dried his face, re-fastened his fro into a pony tail and put on his stocking cap, He jogged back to the bedroom and pulled out a pair of Louis Vuitton sleek black lace up shoes and made his way downstairs. He slipped his shoes on, tied the laces, put some more water in

Felix's bowl and set the burglar alarm. He picked up his man sack and door keys, opened the door, locked it, jogged to the gate and as he was closing it, the number seven bus was just approaching the stop. Not a great start to the morning, maximising the chances of pulling a muscle, hamstring or thigh, but he had to catch the bus. He shot off like a greyhound out of the traps, absolutely flying to the stop which was about eighty metres away. Thankfully the queue was quite long, probably about ten people, which halted the bus in its tracks, just enough time enabling JB to slow down, wipe his brow, jump on and show his bus pass.

'Wow man, dat was a scramble. Just made it.' he said.

'That sprint would have given me a heart attack.' replied the driver.

As he lifted his head up, he saw his friend C-Man sitting at the back of the bus in the right hand corner. There were quite a few spaces, so JB made his way to sit by his side.

'C-Man, what appenin' bredder? Ya late dis morn, you sleep in?'

'Mean. I thought I deserved a lie in, after a hectic weekend. Where d'ya get to?' asked C-Man.

'Boy, what a weekend. We partied to di max. Ad a BBQ at my yard wid a few friends n den went to a friend's birthday from work. Eaded to Starstruck in Marlborough, lived it up, got our grooves on n ad a few liquors boy. Di whole crew enjoyed it. What did you do?'

'I went to the gym, hung with my parents, watched a few movies n played five-a-side football.'

'Any decent movies?'

'Yeah, Mr and Mrs Smith with Brad Pitt n Angelina Jolie. A good watch, I'd recommend it Jammin'.'

'I've eard about it, but never seen it man, gi me a low down.'

'It's meeeeeeaaaan! It's about a married couple who work as assassins. One big problem though. Their relationship becomes booooring and they're both hired for competing Agencies who are required to kill each other. It's well worth a watch Jammin'. I'll lend it to ya.'

'Respect. It sounds like a really edgy, excitin' n grippin' plot. I ad a licence to thrill dis weekend, not quite di same as Brangelina wid one to kill. Some o di crew came back to mine after Starstruck n we ad a mini after party.'

'Where was my invite?'

'Sorry man. I couldn't because Tom, one o di school teachers, said we could only bring two friends. Was gonna bell ya, but promised to go out wid Ash n Joe a couple of weeks ago. Don't worry, you weren't bein' neglected man.'

'It's alright, I'm tryin' to save money anyway, because I wanna go to America in July. Don't have too much disposable cash at mo.'

'Yeah man. We all ave priorities, n mine was to blank you dis weekend,' teased JB.

'Joker. You know that DVD I just told you about, you can buy it online. Ha Haaaaaaa,' responded C-Man.

'You just said I could borrow it?'

'I did, but I've changed mi mind. Ransom money.'

'Lord, you aven't been gettin' tips off dem two assassins av ya? Ya deadly man.'

'I might change mi mind again. Must be all that Bucks Fizz.' said C-Man.

'Don't let your indecision, take you from behind, trust your inner vision, don't let others change your mind,' sang JB.

'Meeeeeeaaaaaan. For that eighties classic, I'm gonna give you the benefit of the doubt. I'll lend you that DVD. You've just been released. Ha Haaaaaaaaa.'

'Lord, it's just like playin' monopoly n bein' released from prison! Pheeeeeeeew, I'm di lucky one.'

'Today you've been extremely lucky, tomorrow, I wouldn't be so sure!' C-Man said, chuckling.

The journey appeared a lot quicker today, which was bizarre as it wasn't the summer holidays for another three weeks. Maybe because JB and C-Man were entertaining and amusing themselves as per usual, so the time passed by quickly. As the saying goes, 'Time flies when you're having fun.' JB certainly did at the weekend. He was having flashbacks about his dalliance with Jennifer and thinking she was one phenomenally hot woman.

'You OK Jammin'? You look deep in thought.'

'Yeah man, sorry, jus tinkin' about weekend exploits.'

'You mean, sexploits, don't ya?' replied C-Man.

'Excuse me!' said a voice in front.

'Did you ear dat C-Man?'

'Yeah, I don't know who it was!'

'Can ya keep ya dirty talk to the bedroom or behind closed doors please? You boys don't change, do ya!'

'You swine. Rocca, what's appenin'?'

'Things are sweet n all the better for seein' you Jammin',' responded Rocca.

It was Rocca Fello, a very good friend of JB's. They hadn't seen each other for a while because Rocca had been travelling for three months around Latin America.

'Ow was ya trip to Latin America den?' asked JB.

'You'll never believe! Ooooooooow.'

'I don't wanna know now, because you just said, keep ya dirty talk to di bedroom or behind closed doors.'

'Meeeeeeeeaaaaaaan. This sounds juicy. We're behind closed doors on the bus, so surely you can reveal all, until someone else hops on?' suggested C-Man.

'Mikey, I will, but later. I suppose I can tell you about the weather, the cultures and the people.'

'Come on den Rocca, spill di proverbial beans.' said JB.

'The weather's beautiful man, the culture, yeah. They're all so passionate and loyal, being Catholics. People can't do enough for ya, but you have to be careful, because there's a lot of poverty and with that comes crime unfortunately. I felt genuine love out there though, especially in places like Mexico, Colombia, Peru etc. If you make an effort to speak Spanish, they adore you. I wanna go back.'

'It sounds incredible man. Why dint you take me?' asked JB.

'You know why! You couldn't get time off in school term time n I couldn't get enough holiday in the summer hols. Next time I go, I'll make sure ya on board.'

'Meeeeeeaaaaaan, I think I'll come along too.' said C-Man.

'For sure Spunky Monkey.' replied Rocca.

Spunky Monkey was a nickname given to C-Man. He was a very good goalkeeper, so his friends associated him with the legendary English goalkeeper, David Seaman. Initially when that name arose, from the depths of the testicles, he said, 'Balls!' Quite apt, being a goalkeeper and having to match, punch and save the ball, the name, just like semen, stuck! He actually grew to like it, always bringing a smile to his face.

'We'll have to look at goin' next year then.'

'Ow about dis summer ols?' replied JB.

'I don't know whether I could get any more time off though. I've just taken a three month sabbatical.'

'Surely ya bosses 'l be flexible n understand ya gonna rock it wid Jammin', Spunky Monkey n crew!'

'We'll have to wait n see. Let me get back into the swing of things for a month, n then I'll ask. Need to get settled n keep mi boss sweet n hopefully, things 'l be alright!' said Rocca.

Rocca worked as a Graphic Designer. You could tell he loved art as he had a sleeve of decorative tattoos on his right arm and body. He was olive skinnedthanks to his Italian heritage. He was very slick, smooth and refined, typical traits associated with the country shaped like an old boot. 'Ow does it feel to be back to work dis mornin' Rocca?' asked JB.

'Boy, it's tough after three months livin' it up. This mornin', I didn't wanna get up. If ya can imagine, every mornin' scorchin' sunshine, bright blue sky, beaches full of some of the most adorable sights, purely scintillatin'. Now n again, I'd wake up n slurp a tequila sunrise or mojito. Luscious to the max.'

'It sounds unbelievably meeeean! Mojitos and minxes, a latin banquet.' said C-Man.

'OMG! I'm just imaginin' seein' undreds n thousands of Jennifers.'

'Who's she?' asked Rocca.

'She's one o di teachers at our school dat came out Sat night. She's ot property boy, but persistent to di max.'

'If she's hot, what's the problem?' asked C-Man.

'Di problem is, we're both at di same school n it ain't ideal. She's a good girl too, but mi ead don't need any complications.'

'Ya too moral n respectful Jammin'. Just have some fun n enjoy the delights.' said C-Man.

'I did on Sunday mornin'. We get along well, but I don't want a relationship n especially not wid a gal at our school. It spells to me… Danger Danger, high voltage.'

'If you came to Latin America with ya bro Rocca n crew, we'd have the time of our lives. It's like an adventure playground. Too many rides n some are white knuckle! Ha Haaaa Haaaaaaa.'

'Rocca, I'd be livin' like a monk over dere. Mi chastity belt would be in mi case n I'd be on lock down. I can't stop tinkin' about dis Latvian godess dat came to our school a couple o weeks ago! She's di bomb boy. Never seen anyting so ooot. Need to hunt er down like a bounty killer,' replied JB.

The journey went by quickly as the boys were in full voice and vibrant to say it was early on Monday morning. Rocca was travelling a little further than C-Man and JB. He worked on the edge of Oatmill in the next town called Mangoville. It was a fruity place, which is apparently why the name was given hundreds of years ago. There were many boulevards decorated with apple and pear trees. It was very popular for visitors as it was a surburban orchard. It was like a national treasure attracting people from all over the country. A museum was built and opened about thirty years ago, that was all about the history of the village. An exceedingly delicious apple and pear cake made in Mangoville was exported all over the world. It was rather bizarre the name, especially when it wasn't famous for the exotic fruit, but juicy apples and pears.

It was eight fifteen, so it had taken less than thirty five minutes. JB and C-Man got off the bus near Oatmill and said goodbye to Rocca. 'See you soon. Enjoy ya first day back n don't work too hard,' said JB.

'I won't. I'll do the bare minimum today, n get back into the swing of things.' responded Rocca.

'Take care mate,' said C-Man.

'You too. Get ready for our hispanic holiday.'

'Don't worry, I will Rocca.'

They hopped off the bus and walked the short journey to Oatmill ready to embark on another eventful day. C-Man was grateful for his short six month contract that had inspired him and instilled confidence, especially when work opportunities weren't plentiful at the height of the recession. C-Man had been in and out of work for a couple of years following his return from a year travelling around Australia. He was a highly skilled joiner, but because he'd changed careers five years earlier, it was always tough to acquire work as he hadn't been established for a long period of time. Most of his work was through Employment Agencies or through the local Lillyford City Council. He was developing a successful reputation for himself though, this would hopefully enhance the prospects of obtaining longer term and eventually more permanent employment. When they reached the school entrance they separated, JB heading to the staff room and C-Man to his location, which was an empty classroom used by contractors. A lot of the skirting boards, some of the doors, lockers and cupboards needed maintaining and repairing. The school had only been open two years, but unfortunately was showing signs of wear and tear. A combination of this and neglect had contributed to the deteoration. C-Man and his fellow joiners were working hard to repair the damage. It was a gigantic school, so that's why the contract was for six months. Also to save money, the school had opted to use the Council as opposed to a private contractor.

JB got to the staff room for about eight twenty am, which gave him time to have a cup of herbal tea before the working week started. He only had five lessons today, a quadruple and a single after lunch.

'Mornin' all, how ya doin'?' said JB.

'I'm great thanks. What a party. Starstruck was absolutely rocking and you were busting some good moves, JB along with Jen.' said Bethany.

'You know I like to be di king o di dancefloor n I gave Jen di privilege o bein' mi queen!'

'I was certainly the queen of your castle at the weekend Jammin'!' replied Jennifer.

'Indeed you were. Mi dancefloor queen.'

Jennifer beamed a huge smile at JB and winked at him. He returned the compliment and stuck his thumb up at her. She was looking stunning, wearing a black pencil skirt to just above her knees, two inch black heels and a white frilly blouse. He was taken a back by the incredible sight. Her hair was tied up in a beehive which certainly exposed her chiseled facial features. JB was in dreamworld, still mesmerised and bamboozled by their sexually erotic shenanigans that occured yesterday morning.

'The kettle's boiled and your ginger and camomile with spiced apple are in your favourite Cool Man rasta cup.' said Bethany.

'Many tanks Beth. Could you give me a massage too Beth, I'm achin' so much since di weekend.'

'I'll give you a quick shoulder massage now if you want?' suggested Bethany.

'Oh yeah, please Beth. I need it desperately.'

He was evidently teasing Jennifer as he knew she'd be increasingly jealous of his antics. Bethany was quite ordinary looking, a Plain Jane. She had shoulder length light brown hair, dark brown eyes, c-cup bust and a petite but shapely figure. JB put his man sack down and sat on the chair, taking a few slurps of his herbal tea. Bethany firmly pressed her fingers into his muscular shoulders, massaging the sizable knots, spreading them outwards, trying to reduce them. Jennifer pretended she hadn't seen this, said bye and headed to her class. Bethany's breasts were pushing into his back, which was arousing him and putting a gigantic smile on his face as he closed his eyes. Ding-a-ling-aling, ding-a-ling-aling, the piercing shrill of the morning school bell sounded.

'Oh, what a shame. Dat was divine Beth. Same again at lunchtime eh?' proposed JB.

'If you're lucky, I may be inclined to give you some extra? Better dash to class,' answered Bethany.

'Many tanx Beth. I look forward to deja-vu lady. See ya later.'

'Yeah, will do Jammin'. Enjoy your morning session.'

'Don't worry, I intend to,' replied JB.

They both left for their respective classrooms. JB to his customary form classroom six. He picked up his rasta man cup, three quarters full of camomile with spiced apple and ginger, as he walked hurriedly along the corridor.

Chapter 24

Learn a Lesson the Hard Way

He reached the classroom and opened the door.

'Mornin' all, I ope we're all ready after weekend wonders.'

It was received with a chorus of groans.

'It can't be dat bad, you've ad two days to recover from las week n it's almost di summer hols!' he responded.

He placed his cup on his front desk, put his man sack down at the side and looked in his drawers for the appropriate register. Today's quadruple lesson was with year eleven pupils who were the fifteen and sixteen year olds. It was Monday 20th June and their English exam was all continuous coursework, so many were quite relieved that they didn't have to revise for it.

'Dis is ya last lesson o di term, so from next week it's ya two weeks study leave. All ya course work's done fa di year, so today, use di time wisely n revise fa dem exams.'

They were all suddenly rather boisterous, within the space of moments, after being subdued and lacking in vitality at the start of the week. Probably, most of it was down to the fact that their GCSE exams were about to start, so a combination of anxiety and esteem issues had led to de-motivation.

'What I would say to ya peeps is, ya can only do ya best, so don't worry about failure. Dat ain't in di script. It's all about success n strivin' fa greatness. Opefully dat'll elp ya relax n prepare yaselves. If ya don't pass any, you can re-take em, but just to warn ya, negativity breeds misfortune.'

'I like those words sir. Talk about inspiration. I'm gonna right that down n memorise it. Can you put it on the smart board please?' said Errol Jackson.

'Yeah, no probs Errol.'

'Sir, were you out partyin' Saturday night at Starstruck?' asked Jimmy Jones.

'I ad a most fabulous weekend Jimmy, but I'm not gonna discuss my partyin' adventures wid you.'

'Why not Sir?'

'Because it's none of ya business. What I decide to do in mi spare time, is my prerogative.'

'I heard you were lipsin' up Miss Luis Cortada.'

'Jimmy, as I explained to ya, whatever I do in mi own time concerns me n no-one else.' replied JB.

'Apparently you were dancin' rather sensually, suggestively n raunchily wi Miss Luis Cortada.'

'Jimmy, can ya jus settle down, relax n quieten ya mout please.'

'Yeah, sorry Sir.'

'Right den peeps, di register. Are we all ready, sittin' comfortably and concentratin'?' asked JB.

'Jessica Bradley.'

'Sir.'

'Jeremiah Stirling.'

'Here Sir.'

'Rudi Rampling.'

'Yes Sir.'

'Lucy Rawlinson.'

'Yes Sir.'

'Dickie Long.'

'Here Sir.'

'HAAAAAAA, HAAAAAAA, HAAAAAAAAA, HAAAAAAAAA.' Shrieks of laughter from the class.

'Settle down please peeps,' said JB.

'Dickie, are you long or short today? Hopefully not too hard n standing to attention at the thought of Miss Luis Cortada sensuously movin' n groovin' with Sir,' shouted Jimmy Jones.

'Shut up Jimmy. Have a l'il bit o respect,' responded Dickie.

'Jimmy, dats di last warnin' for ya. I don't expect you to disrespect a fellow pupil n certainly not in my lessons. I know ya di class joker n like to improve spirits, but those kinda comments won't be tolerated. Understood.'

'Yes Sir. Sorry about dat. I din't mean to disrespect di boy,' said Jimmy.

'Jimmy, can you go to see Mr Robertson please. I've given you a few chances dis mornin' n you've taken advantage of every one. To make tings even worse, you start mimickin' me!' Ordered JB.

'Sir, I'm really genuinely sorry, I didn't mean to offend.' Pleaded Jimmy.

A few tears started to roll down his cheeks, as the prospect of having a meeting with Mr Robertson beckoned. Mr Robertson was an ex Scottish International Rugby Union player. He was six foot five inches tall, of a muscular build, weighing in at seventeen stone and a few pounds. He could certainly be imposing vocally, never mind physically. He was a very receptive person, but wouldn't stand for any immoral and disrespectful behaviour to a fellow pupil, let alone a teacher. His morals were very strong and he was known as 'The Cruncher', because in his rugby playing days, he loved a tackle. Many an opponent had been carried off the field of play as a result of a debilitating tackle. He was a tough specimen and held in high esteem by ex players, officials and supporters.

'Jimmy, you apologised di first time n den you decided to rub mi face in it. You not only insulted Dickie, you den proceeded to offend me. You ave to learn di ard way. Away you go to see Mr Robertson.' answered JB.

'Ooooooooooooooooooooooooooooo.' A sudden hum sounded in the classroom.

'Where was I? Errol Jackson.'

'Here sir.'

'Jimmy Jones. Off to see The Cruncher,' JB muttered.

'BOOOOOOOOOOOOOOOOOOOM,' said Errol Jackson.

'Relax please Errol.'

'My apologies Sir. I'm just not envying Jimmy, havin' to visit Mr Robertson.'

'Me neither Errol. Let it be a good lesson to im!' replied JB.

'The thing is Sir. Ya the fairest teacher I've ever had the pleasure of being taught by. Ya always understandin', sensitive, sincere, helpful n as flexible as a ruler Sir,' said Errol.

'Like a ruler Errol?' questioned JB.

'Yes Sir.'

'I wouldn't compare myself to Joseph Stalin, Idi Amin, Saddam Hussain etc. More of a Kofi Annan.. I like to be a pacifist, endeavourin' to restore peace and unity in di face of conflict n adversity.'

'Yeah man. I'd say ya defo a Tsar of that true description Sir. I didn't mean that kinda ruler tho, I meant like a helix one. Those that you draw straight lines with.' replied Errol.

'Ha Haaaaaaaaa. Sorry Errol, a slight misunderstandin' dere. Many tanx for dat different analogy. Ya not gonna start callin' me 'Shatterproof' are ya?' joked JB.

'No Sir. Bomb proof,' responded Errol.

'BAAAAANG... BAAAANG.' Jeremiah Stirling and Rudi Rampling simultaneously crashed their hands down on their desks, to imitate the sound of an explosion.

'Aaaaaaaaaaaaaaargh. My hand's in agony,' said Rudi Rampling.

'Dat'l teach ya. Go to di toilet n run it under di cold tap,' Advised JB.

'Lord, your hands are soft. Why don't you go n join Jimmy Jones in Mr Robertson's office. That'l be a rather icy reception.' said Jeremiah Stirling.

HAAAAA... HAAAAAAAAA... HAAAAAAAAAA. Cries of laughter from the class.

'Order, order, can we please refrain from silly and rather daft antics please, while I'm taking the register. It is most shameful behaviour. One should not have to re-iterate this after the misdemeanours of one of your faithful companions lead to unfortunate punishment after a moment of skulduggery.' said JB..

After the commotion that had occured, JB had finished reading out the register, peace had been restored and the class took out their books for various subjects and started to revise.

'Sir, you promised to write that inspirational phrase on the board.' said Errol Jackson.

'Yees Errol, I did, I'll do dat now fa y'all.'

JB wrote the phrase down on the smart board.

'NEGATIVITY BREEDS MISFORTUNE.'

'Dis should make y'all realise ow positive minded you ave to be, despite sometimes feelin' disillusioned, demoralised n apprehensive. Ultimately, believe in yaself n it'l encourage you to succeed in life. When you ave optimistic thoughts, it elps to drive you on in ya quest fa greatness! Ere's a l'il song I wrote, gotta sing it, note for note, Don't woooorry, be happy, ooooooo-

ooooooohooo, oooooohoooo hoooo...' JB ended his words of wisdom with singing Bobby McFerrin's huge global track from the late eighties.

Some of the class started to join in, which became a joyous and beautiful soulful melody. After most of them feeling rather subdued with it being exam season, also the first day back after the weekend. It was a sudden transformation, the calm after the Jimmy Jones storm, suddenly ascending into a most attractive rainbow of vocal pleasure.

A minute walk away around a few corners and down a long corridor, sat Jimmy (on his proverbial Jack) Jones. He had knocked on Mr Robertson's door, in response had been told to wait outside until it was time to be welcomed in. Probably not the operative word though, as when Jimmy told Mr Robertson what had happened, inevitable he would be deeply offended and undoubtedly livid. Jimmy was a trembling nervous wreck, sweating noticeably, shaking and twitching. Mr Robertson would probably be incensed initially, imposing himself to instill fear into Jimmy, then he would conversely start to relax and psycho analyse his behaviour. Mr Robertson had a Masters Degree in Human Psychology, so his position as Head of Year was advantageous, as he was a placid man and never abused his authority. He had superb social skills, a warming demeanour, until somebody crossed him.

Back in the classroom the pupils had eventually settled down after the register and had started to work on revision for their impending exams. Schools always had two weeks study leave prior to their final GCSE exams, but for some reason, today was the final day of a full curriculum before this period. This would be the last time Jammin' Boy would teach Year Eleven pupils as alot of them would be heading off to college and employment, although a handful would probably go into the sixth Form. He was hugely disappointed as a good rapport had been developed over the last few years. It was always emotional for the kids at school as most were uncertain of their futures and upset to be leaving behind their school experiences, teachers, lifestyle and the precious secondary school legacy. JB gazed out of the window, transfixed on a seagull that kept hovering, swooping down and then gliding. It had probably seen a creature down below and was preparing to clasp its claws on a rodent, oblivious to the danger above. Eventually, it swooped down, lifted up a piece of tasty morsel and flew away at a rapid speed. For some reason, watching wildlife outside reminded him that he had to phone Fluffy Donkey to find out how he was. He would have to wait another hour though, until morning break. He pulled his phone out of his pocket, unlocked it by typing in the security pin code, pressed the phone symbol and scrolled down his contact to Fluffy. He chose the message option and started to type.

'Yes Fluffy, what appenin' bredder? Is di foot feelin' a l'il sore? What's di quality o di nurses like, any tasty flavour?! (Followed by a smiley symbol with its tongue out). Ows Ash n Stacey doin'? Enjoy di orrible ospital food n break a leg (which he thought was quite comical, as Fluffy had already fractured a couple of metartarsals). Peace, Health, Harmony n PHAT Love.'

He sent the message, awaiting hopefully, a reasonably prompt response. He then surfed his phone, looked at photos he'd taken on Saturday night at Starstruck and browsed at the BBC News articles.

Meanwhile, Jimmy Jones was still sitting outside Mr Robertson's office, sweating and extremely nervous, awaiting the wrath from the Head of Year.

'Come in. Take a seat son. What can I do for you?' asked Mr Robertson.

'I've been sent here by Mr Herbert.' replied Jimmy.

'What have you done? Is it for hard work and excellent results, or for bad behaviour? Your eyes look a little red, so I'm assuming it's for the latter!'

'Yeah sir, ya right. Mr Herbert was takin' the register n I made a few silly comments.'

'Comments like what, Jimmy?'

'Weeell… weeell… weeeell,' stuttered Jimmy.

'Well what? Tell me, son!'

'Silly comments about Dickie Long sir!'

'Dickie Long, now that's a name for you! So I guess you've been shafted for it!'

'Ha Haaaaaaa. You could say that sir.'

'I don't find it very funny, Jimmy son. In fact, I'm very annoyed about this. It's not the first time you've been in trouble for those kind of jibes. It's almost the end of term and you've let not only yourself down, but your class and Mr Herbert too.' responded Mr Robertson.

'I'm really sorry sir.'

'If you're that sorry, I expect a bit more conviction in your voice and a sincere apology. Alright son. You're lucky you've caught me on a good day. I suggest you return to your class and apologise sincerely to Mr Herbert and wipe your eyes, son. Here! Take one of these with you.'

It was quite funny, as Mr Robertson used the word 'son' a lot. Anyone would think he was their father. He actually had two children himself, but they were both girls. Jimmy was extremely fortunate that he hadn't been given a ceremonious telling off by the Head.

'I'm genuinely really sorry sir. I didn't mean to offend Mr Herbert and you. Sometimes I need to be a little more tactful,' said Jimmy.

He took the tissue from Mr Robertson, wiped his eyes with it, stood up, walked towards the door, opened it and walked out, allowing it to close, as it was a self closing fire safety door.. Jimmy Jones made his way back from Mr Robertson's office, walking with a spring in his step, his head held higher than twenty minutes ago, as he was relieved at the reprieve. Detention was usually a given reprimand for insolence and disrespect. He could now return to classroom number six and concentrate on his essential revision with the rest of the class. He decided to pass by the toilet first, as the anxiety had induced his bladder. He was now walking with confidence and aplomb, transformed by Mr Robertson's lenient treatment.

Back in the class, JB's iPhone vibrated. It was a responding message from Fluffy Donkey. He read it, head bowed and intrigued by the reply, hoping that everything was OK at Lillyford Park Hospital.

'Yes Jammin', everything's good here, apart from my foot's really painful, even tho I'm using cocodemol. Me, Stacey and Ash are being discharged this morn. Should be out in an hour or 2. I'll call ya later n we could maybe hook up 2nite? Peace n PHAT Love-Fluffers.'

The morning was passing by very quickly, or so it seemed. JB was thinking about that potential adventure to Latin America with Rocca Fello, C-Man and crew. Besides that, he closed his eyes momentarily and started having flashbacks to the Latvian woman who had visited the school last week. He had to do a little bit of research to find out exactly where she worked in Latvia and also if she was due to visit Oatmill High in the future. What a challenge this would be. He was fascinated by her culture, consumed by her infinite beauty and was desperate, well, maybe a slight exaggeration, but he wanted to see her again. They hadn't spoken, just quite simply had eye contact in the corridor. This blew his mind, as she was the hottest woman he'd seen in a long time. Jennifer was hot, but the Latvian woman was off the scale for him. A sudden vibration occurred on his desk. He opened his eyes and realised it was his mum ringing. It was on silent. He would have to phone her back later in the day, as now would be rather inappropriate. At the same moment, the classroom door opened and in walked Jimmy.

'Welcome back Jimmy.'

'Hi sir!'

'What action has Mr Robertson taken den?' asked JB.

'He jus said I had to apologise to you for disrespectin' you. He said he was in a good mood and wouldn't give me any more punishment n I was a lucky boy. I'm really sorry sir.'

'Damn right. On another day it could ave been a different outcome boy. Ya one lucky fella. Go n take a seat.' responded JB.

As Jimmy started walking towards his desk,

Ding-a-ling-a-ling, ding-a-ling-a-ling, the school bell sounded and it was the end of the morning session. His mum's watch or clock must have been a little ahead of schedule, that's why she had phoned him before class finished. She was very meticulous with everything she did and had his class timetable blue tacked to the inside of one of her cupboards, so she knew when was the best time to phone him throughout the course of the week. He decided that he'd call her back either at dinner time or later this evening.

'Close your books n go n enjoy ya break, I'll see you in thirty minutes.' said JB.

Everyone closed their books and made their way out to the playground or the record club.

Chapter 25

Hands on Approach

JB picked up his man sack and made his way to the staff room. He was looking forward to resuming his antics with Bethany, her breasts pushed into his back while she soothingly massaged his shoulders. He reached the staff room in a couple of minutes, slowed down by having to evade the stampede of all the children making their way outside for break time. He was zig zagging and side stepping reminiscent of a fleet footed Rugby League stand off, not like Mr Robertson who was pure power, driving with robust, devastating and brutal force. If you asked Mr Robertson about his Rugby Union playing repetoire, he would just say, he was known as The Cruncher. Whenever he coached the Rugby Team at Oatmill, he would always instill within the players to take no prisoners.

'Are you having your favourite herbal tea Jammin'?' asked Bethany.

'Please Beth. Can ya tro some ginger in dere too n den work on mi shoulders n neck again.'

'OMG, how many more demands are you going to make?' asked Bethany.

'What else are you prepared to do?' teased JB.

'Be careful Beth, don't let him try n seduce ya!' warned Jennifer.

'Oooooo Jen, the art of seduction on a Monday. Might be a sensuous and fabulous end to a manic Monday,.' said Bethany.

Jennifer was so unbelievably jealous of Bethany, especially when she was fussing over JB, then again who wouldn't be? He was a single, confident, intelligent, charismatic and handsome young man with everything going for him.

'Jasmine, what appened on Sunday mornin' wid Tom's bro?' asked JB.

'He took me home n we had an entertaining morning. Ya brother's well hot Tom. He made my nipples stand on end n sent shivers down my spine.'

'I don't need to know about all the particulars Jaz.' replied Tom.

'I know, but he has the x-factor. We're going out for a meal Friday night, I'm well excited.'

'Don't you abuse him n spit him out Jaz. He's freshly out of a relationship n just wants to have fun.'

'I know Tom. Don't you worry. He's a tasty piece of fresh meat n will be relished, nourished n devoured! Ha Haaaaaaaa,' said Jasmine.

'Tom, if I was you, I'd make sure dat Ethan wears a chastity belt, because Jaz 'll corrupt im to di max. Dat girl's highly dangerous, she'll give im an eart attack,' said JB.

'Joker. You think ya funny? I do quite like ya wit though. You need a good slappin' sometimes Jammin!' responded Jasmine.

'Uuuuuuuum… I see ya gettin' kinky again. Just wait till after di watershed, we don't want any disasters n public displays of sauciness!'

'You know me Jammin', a clean cut girl next door.'

'Who you kiddin'?'

'True. You can't kid a kidder can ya.'

'Especially not di king of female behaviour. I knew I should o been a social psychologist. Just call me Hitch!' replied JB.

'Ha haaaaaa. More like a bad boy biatch!' laughed Jasmine.

'Anyway Beth, can I ave my massage please?'

'I was wondering when you were going to ask again!'

'I did mention it when I first came in n you asked me what erbal tea I wanted, remember?'

'Yeah, I do. Just kiddin'.'

'Dat makes tree kidders ere den!' said JB.

'I wouldn't quite call myself a kid, Jammin', more like a Nanny Goat, motherin' you boys!' responded Jasmine.

'I must admit Jaz, you are quite the Agony Aunt,' said Bethany.

'Anyway Beth, come on, we've only got another twenty five mins, lady,' said JB.

'Relax man, keep your fro in tact. Can someone close that window please, we don't want his hair blowing off.'

'Are you tryin' to say I've gotta toupé Beth?'

'Noooo. I just don't want you gettin' frustrated n losin' it outta the window.'

'Haaaaaaa. Funny lady. Let's do dis den. Mi shoulders n back are still tight.'

Jennifer was sitting quietly in the corner engrossed in her book. You could tell she was incredibly jealous, although endeavouring to pretend she hadn't heard any of JB and Beth's flirtatious conversation. She raised her eyebrows and peered over the top of her book as soon as JB mentioned massage. In her mind she was fantasising about their breathtaking encounter that started on the toilet and then progressed to the bathroom sink. Pure unadulterated sexual pleasure. At least she'd had the luxury of an intimate experience with JB, whereas with Bethany it was exclusively a hands on act without frivolity, although when her breasts pushed against his back, JB had visions of a different kind. Bethany carried her cup of traditional English PG Tips tea over to the chair JB was relaxing in. She took a slurp from the cup, almost sounding like a scary horror movie creature of alien proportions, not very classy. She thought the temperature had lowered, hence taking too large an amount and then having to spit it out, because it was so hot.

'Aaaaaaaaaaargh,' she yelled.

She had burnt the roof of her mouth and tongue with the tea. She briskly walked over to the sink to pour herself a glass of corporation cold pop to cool down her smouldering palate.

'Effin' hell! That was absolutely scorching.'

'Are you OK Beth?' asked Jennifer.

She chuckled to herself, as she thought it was a little bit of subconscious karma, jealous that she was entertaining JB.

'Yeeeeaaah, I'll be fine thanks Jen. Just a stupid thing to do really. When handlin' somethin' hot, it's always wise to cool it down first,' she responded.

'I know the feeling,' said Jennifer, referring to her shenanigans with JB, unbeknown to Bethany.

'Where were we? Right Jammin', you ready?'

'I've been waitin' fa di las five minutes. When ya ready, ya can put ya ealin' ands on di nape o mi achin' neck?' said JB.

'Alright, I'm comin'!'

'OMG Beth! I think it's the wrong time n place to be producin' some furry cup magic. Leave it till after school n when ya behind closed doors. We don't want ya havin' a screamin' orgasm here in the staff room. Leave that till the weekend. Oooooooooo, I enjoyed one of those after ya birthday bash Tom! Ya brother's hot!' said Jasmine.

'Jaz, they don't call me you. I'm more of a subtle and discreet saucy devil. I keep mi thoughts in mi mind, you know me.'

'I bet you're a real minx in the bedroom.'

'Probably only after a few drinks.' said Bethany.

Bethany enjoyed a little staff room friendly banter with Jasmine, but she was by no stretch of the imagination in the same vein as her. That girl was too hot to handle and too cold to hold. A rebel without a cause, a female predator! Always on the rampage in search of fresh tasty male meat, not a cannibal, just a female animal. At last, JB managed to be on the receiving end of his massage after the breaktime staff room drama of jealous Jennifer, burning Bethany and jovial Jasmine. Bethany's soft hands gently kneaded the powerful muscles in JB's neck and shoulders. He closed his eyes as the sensations sent shivers down his spine and made goose bumps start to rapidly bubble all over his skin. Her fingers and hands moved in circular motions, breaking down the lumps and bumps.It was so soothing, making him smile and his heart beat slightly faster than the average eighty to a hundred beats a minute. He was so relaxed that a mini stream of saliva started to dribble from the edge of his lips. He suddenly shuddered and woke himself up.

'What time is it?'

'It's almost time to return to class. Twenty five past ten.' answered Bethany.

'Geez, already. Where di time go man?'

'Do I look like a man Jammin'?' asked Bethany.

'It's just a figure of speech Beth.'

'Is that a sliver of a silver stream down the side of ya mouth Jammin?' asked Jasmine.

'Yeah, can't a man ave a dribble in peace sometimes, widowt bein' disturbed or reminded of iz subconscious abits. I bet you experienced a bit more dan a dribble on Sunday mornin'. Someting like a volcanic eruption from a dark wet crevice! Ha haaaaaa.' .

'I'm not gonna share my sordid secrets with you, I'll leave that to Jen.' said Jasmine.

'Why ya bringin' me into this personal equation? What gives you the impression we share our secrets? We're good friends that's all, n occassionally indulge in a sensuous dance, like on Saturday night. Anyway, stop deflectin' the topic of convo, what did actually happen with Ethan?' responded Jennifer.

Tom was slightly taken a back, looking rather embarassed at the prospect of potentially hearing how his brother had fraternised with Jasmine. Saved by the bell! Ding-a-ling, ding-a-ling, sounded the bell, indicating it was time to return to class, after a quick fire thirty minutes.

'Oh no, I can't believe it's dat time already, I was lovin' dat. Ya hands are so soothin' Beth, I tink we may need a part trois? suggested JB.

'JB, I can't believe ya tryin' to pull ya Hitch manoevres on Beth.' said Jasmine.

'No chance woman. Dey don't call me di predator. You're dat creature in di movie. Always huntin' fa snacks. I get mine between meals, not human consumption.' replied JB.

All the teachers finished what they were doing and headed back to their classrooms. JB moved quite lethargically, as the massage had lured him into a semi deep trance. He shook his head profusely, slapped his cheeks with his hands, rubbed his thighs, jumped up five times, reminiscent of a hopping frog, trying to energise himself before walking out of the staff room.

Chapter 26

Swan Song

Back to classroom number six to resume his English lesson. You couldn't really call it a lesson, as it was just pre-study leave revision. Hopefully there wouldn't be any misdemeanours in the final hour and a half before lunchtime. Jimmy Jones was back with a vengeance, hopefully rejuvenated and relaxed after being disciplined by Mr Robertson during the early morning session. He was the class joker, but sometimes took his humour to the next level and could be rather irritating and antagonising. As they had finished their break, the class seemed more relaxed, or maybe it was the apprehension and nervous tension of exam fever. Some of the subjects didn't involve exams, just continuous coursework, core subjects like Modular Science, English Language and Literature.

JB's phoned vibrated. It was Fluffy Donkey saying they'd all been discharged from Hospital. They were catching a cab back home. They all lived quite close to JB, so would be home in ten to fifteen minutes. They were all planning on heading to Fluffy Donkey's appartment, where Ash was going to cook up an African culinary storm. They all needed a huge pick me up after their near death experience.

Back in the class, all the kids had their heads down, engrossed in their text books, revising intensely, or so it seemed. JB was going to respond to Fluffy's text and then take a wander around the class to make sure they were all investing their time wisely and not doodling and time wasting.

'Yes Flufster, pleased to ear dat y'all bn kicked out o di ospital n once again u land on ya big feet. So ya gonna try n serenade Stacey? Dat'll b n interestin' sight when ya both crocked. She aint dat badly urt, so surely she'l literally wet nurse ya dis avo n make ya fur stand on end. Don't try n take advantage of er, bkoz, she's a respectable gal. Treat er like di lady she is, bkoz, we're not all crazy animals like u! Ha Ha Haaaaaaaaa. Bigup di walkin' wounded fa me. May c ya 2nite? Peace, Health n PHAT Love-JB ;-))!'

It was inevitable JB would receive a prompt response, especially when he had tormented Fluffy Donkey, which was a prevalent factor of their friendship. Forever taunting, antagonising and teasing. It was all good natured though and brought them really close together. They had been close friends since Primary School. JB stood up from his seat, pondered momentarily and then after scratching his fro through his tightly fitted stocking cap, started to walk very gracefully around the class, twisting and turning between the double desks which were strategically positioned in a near perfect formation. It was reminiscent of German conditioning, efficient and immaculately presented. He was intrigued at the different revision techniques the class were using, some using bullet points, others using pneumonics and lists, where as the more intelligent ones just read and had the ability to retain the information with Einsteinesque intelligence quotion.

'Errol, what ya doin' boy?'

'Just drawing characters sir. I need to make sure I'm ready for me art exam. We get one and a half hours to draw our foreground view,.' replied Errol Brown.

'Ahaaa. I'll let you off den. I tought you were doodlin' n wastin' precious time,' replied JB.

'I need a little time, to think it over, I need a little space, just on my own, I need a little time, to find my freedom, I need a little time…' sang Errol Brown.

'Funny how quick the milk turns sour, isn't it, isn't it? Your face has been lookin' like that for hours, hasn't it, hasn't it?' responded JB.

'Promises, promises turn to dust, wedding bells just turn to rust, trust into mis-truuuuust,' JB and Errol Brown harmonised.

'WOOOOOO-WOOOOOO-OOOOOOOOOO.' Rapturous applause from the class.

'Sir, you should be a music teacher too. That voice is PHAT. YUUUUUUUUU-HUUUUUUUUUUUU,' shouted Jimmy Jones.

'That's the bomb sir. You certainly don't have a face for radio,' said Jessica Bradley.

'Excuse me Jessie, what does dat mean?' asked JB.

'It means sir, that ya beauty would be wasted on the radio, because you wouldn't see ya face. Hence, a face for TV.'

'What a beautiful comment Jessie. I guess ya wantin' brownie points for ya English coursework. Are ya tryin' to flatter me?' asked JB.

'No sir, just being honest,' responded Jessie Bradley.

Wolf whistles and howls entwined with foot stamping and table bashing started to shake the windows and move the door.

'Order, order, quiet please.' Bellowed JB.

He crashed his hand down on Errol Brown's desk with a bone jangling thud that restored silence virtually immediately. Jessica Bradley's cheeks had gone a startling and striking bright red following the class cheers and whistles.

'You look like a beetroot Jessie.' said Rudi Rampling.

'Are you tryin' to say, my face looks like a big bruise? Well, thankyou very much Rudi, at least I don't look like a pizza. Mister Al Fungí.' replied Jessica Bradley.

Rudi was absolutely furious, his face bulging, cheeks bright red, body tense and tight and yellow heads looking like they were going to explode.

'Why ya being so cynical Jessie? We can't all have perfect faces. Just a shame yours isn't as hot as ya ass! OW-OOOOOOOOOOOO. At least I can get rid of my spots with chemicals, what would you do?! A face transplant!' responded Rudi Rampling.

Jessica suddenly became very upset, lips blubbering, tears beginning to roll down her cheeks. 'Where did all dis suddenly come from. We've been avin' a good mornin' wid only one mishap. Why d'ya ave to spoil yaselves?' asked JB.

'Sir, I was only sayin' she looked like a beetroot, because her cheeks had gone bright red. I wasn't being callous about her appearance. She's a pretty girl, but just sometimes has to watch her mouth.' answered Rudi Rampling.

Lucy Rawlinson stood up and went over to Jessica to console and comfort her. 'I didn't mean it Rudi, I'm really sorry,' replied Jessica Bradley.

'Apology accepted. Just think with ya brain before you speak sometimes.'

Rudi really fancied Jessica and the feeling was definitely mutual, although they pissed each other off quite frequently. It was like a love hate relationship.

'I thought you too fancied each other?' teased Errol Brown.

HAAAA HAAAAAA HAAAAAAAA. Came cries of laughter from the class.

They both started to blush a little. Jessica's tears had began to dry up, with the help of her cardigan arm sleeve. She stuck her tongue out at Rudi in a playful manner. In return he rolled his tongue around his lips and flirted outrageously with her.

'Can we please get back to revision n refrain from dis childish stupidness? Dere's no need for it. I wanna see tears of joy n celebrations in di next few weeks, embracin' di end of ya exams, preparin' fa ya summer olidays peeps.' said JB.

'Damn right sir, we need a l'il more togetherness after the mornin's shenanigans!' said Errol Brown.

'Dat's di spirit young man. Ooooo, how I do love a sensible and most prudent approach to life. Philosophical potent prowess young chap!' said JB with English eloquence.

JB quite nonchantly with a skip in his step, walked back to his desk and sat down. He pressed his iPhone home button to check the time. It was almost half past eleven, just thirty and a few minutes before dinner time, when he would possibly phone his Mum for a catch up. With all the antics that had occured, sing songs, doodling art, tears of sadness, sledging, comforting and re-assurance, the time had once again virtually flown by. During JB's lessons, there was always some drama or excitement occurring. He had this evident aura that appeared to always magnetise his captive audience..

Fluffy Donkey had inevitably responded to the earlier text of torment and impudence. JB unlocked his phone and browsed through the text. It read,

'JB, you joker n afro haired doughnut, we may be walkin' wounded now, but when I've got my hands on ya, you'll be joinin' the invalid society. Would've been nice for you to pick us up from hospital n not left us to get a cab? Re: Stacey, I could do with some good lovin' off her! ;-) Before, I see ya, I just may have savoured a volcanic eruption, all over her toned n pert breasts! Ha Haaaaaaaa. I need somethin' to cheer me up, especially when we almost went to heaven n back...Speakin' of heaven, what a sight, Me n Stacey rockin', rollin' n ridin'! ;-) Speak later face ache. Fluffy.'

JB chuckled to himself and couldn't believe the filthy mind Fluffy had, feeling so wanton with Stacey. He obviously felt neglected after JB and Ash had savoured their frivolous indulgence on Saturday night/Sunday morning, thanks to Jennifer and Annabelle. JB was plotting his response. He thought about holding Fluffy Donkey to ransom and threatening to tell Stacey what he'd texted! Oooooo, that would be so cruel, but would certainly have Fluffy eating out of the palm of his hand, just like a sixteenth century peasant with a princess. Good idea! Or to deter him from Stacey, call his bluff and say he'd already savoured the fruits of her athletic allure. Both scenarios would antagonise and frustrate Mr Sargent. He decided he was gonna hold him to ransom as this would irritate and worry him more, especially as the prospect of Stacey finding out what had been typed in a text would leave her aghast at Joe's thoughts, albeit, it could even arouse her as she probably would want to climb on top of him, when that eventual moment arose. Currently that was not the case though, as she wasn't a typical floozy, she possessed decorum, refinement, elegance and sophistication, or at least, so she portrayed in a professional capacity.

'Dat's it, dat's it, I'm gonna make im squirm wi dat tret, n den e aint gonna treat me wi makin' me buckle wid a big bone crunchin' body shot.' JB thought.

His iPhone screen flashed again. This time it was a message from Ash. JB unlocked his phone and read,

'How ya doin' JB, hope ya good brother. Just leavin' Lillyford Park now n catchin' a cab to Fluffy's. Stacey promised to cook up a storm in the kitchen n I think Joe's hopin' for some therapeutic dessert. He said he wants to volcanically erupt over her assets! Ha Haaaa. He's lost his mojo, it must be approachin' half a year since his last conquest. Knowin' his luck, he'll probably cream his panties first? Right, Stacey's back with us after a loo stop, we're dashin'. Say hi to Bella for me! ;-)) Speak later, Peace-Ashilito.'

'Hhhhmmmmmm... Interestin'?! I've got some dirt to dish on Fluffy now, I think those ransom demands are provin' to be rather prudent,' he thought.

It was staggering that Fluffy Donkey could be so blasé, but then again, himself, JB and Ash were close, so any illicit thoughts wouldn't be aired in public like dirty linen. JB had other ideas, but wouldn't be prepared to jeopardise their special friendship for flippant and disregarding comments about a fellow teacher, let alone embarassing her. He didn't know Stacey well enough to share innermost thoughts, despite her working at the school. She was a friend, but closer to Annabelle, Jasmine and Jennifer. JB still thought it would be a good trick to play on Joe after all the jibes he'd been giving him recently. His response read,

'Yes Flufster, Enjoy ya avo wid Ash n Stace, but b careful, I don't want ya embarassin' yaself. About Stace, is it defo Game On, d'ya think? I just tink u'v bn a bit disrespectful wi ya comments earlier! I don't wanna scupper ya chances, but I feel I ave a duty to protect er, especially when she's a fellow teacher n good friend! I don't tink she'd take it too kindly, findin' out u wanna volcanically erupt all over her pert breasts?! ;-O Den again, if u play dem cards right, I'll big u up to di max! ;-) What d'ya tink 1 legged Donkey Balls?? Peace n PHAT Love-JB.'

He sent it, awaiting another audacious and cynical response. JB checked his e-mails on his phone and browsed through the BBC News articles, wanting to find out what had been happening in the world within the last twenty four hours. His phone vibrated again and lit up. Guess who?! It was of course no other than... Bethany.

'Do you want to experience another warm, sensuous and soothing massage at lunchtime? X B. ;-)'

JB almost fell off his chair. He expected it to be Fluffy's sarcastic reply, but never in his wildest dreams, did he expect Bethany to be texting him. He smiled, extremely content and simply responded,

'Deal. X ;-P'

He was a little bored now, as there was no teaching to do, just keeping the kids under supervision. At least it was a privileged treat, as normally he would be educating them with some riveting English literature or watching a film about one of their assignments like Animal Farm, Buddy or Macbeth.

Eventually Joe did respond to JB's blackmail threats.

'FUCK OFF!'

JB was slightly taken a back, as he definitely had the upper hand in this power struggle:-

'Choose ya words carefully hop-a-long Fluffy. I could make or break ya wishes! ;-)'

He sent a subtle and advisory reply to Joe, who would hopefully heed the words of wisdom. Ding-a-ling-a-ling-ding-a-ling-a-ling, the lunchtime bell sounded and it was massage time for JB as a lunch dessert and for the kids, playtime.

'Pick up all ya text books, belongin's, keep revisin' ard, enjoy ya study leave, be safe n take tings easy. Tanks for a fantastic few years, good luck wi ya exams n see y'all around school,' said JB.

As the Year Eleven pupils picked up their bags, jackets and books, stood up off their chairs, pushed them under their respective tables and walked towards the classroom six door. Every one of them thanked Mr Herbert (JB), either giving him a high five or a knuckle touch as they left. JB was happy to see them all growing up into more responsible adolescents, even Jimmy Jones, Jessica Bradley and Rudi Rampling had their moments. The transition of puberty was certainly having an impact, with hormones flipping, testosterone gripping, attitude tipping, but all in all, they were a good bunch of kids and Mr Herbert was sad to say farewell. As soon as everyone had said their goodbyes, he skipped to his desk to pick up his phone, placing it in his trouser pocket, and checked for his jacket, but he hadn't brought one today with it being a warm twenty four degrees. He pushed his chair under the desk, headed to the door, pulled it open and walked down the corridor towards the staff room, where he would eventually relish the healing hands of Bethany. He felt his phone vibrate in his pocket, which had to be Fluffy Donkey's text response. He pulled out his phone, reminiscent of a wild wild West cowboy in Quick Draw McGraw style, gun released, cocked and bang! He unlocked the phone and pressed the message,

'RUDE BOY CABBAGE JB, Can't believe ya holding me to ransom?? I owe you for this match up, but don't worry, I'm still gonna clock you to the jaw with a humdinging right hook! ;-)) Just reached home, sitting on the sofa with Ash and Stacey's floating around like an angel fussing over us both. Her ass is as tight as a coconut, so ripe n ready to be stroked, groped n Oooooo la laaaaaaaaa! She oozes so much sex appeal, my sacks about to explode!! ;-O Anyway, apologies for the expletives, but don't think you can hold me hostage for too long, because the sooner I'm mobile n two footed again, Troubles gonna come knocking on ya door! Be warned! Have a great day n see ya 2nite maybe?'

JB chuckled to himself with a large beaming smile upon his face. He responded to Fluffy,

'Bring it on, I'll be waitin' for ya! ;-)))'

'Oh, I'm so sorry.' he said as he bumped into a group of kids heading swiftly for the canteen.

One of them smiled, hunched his shoulders n gave Mr Herbert the peace sign gesture with two fingers nearest the thumb held apart and raised, palm facing. If it would have been the other way, fireworks would certainly have exploded. Mr Herbert was a very tolerant young man, but resented insolence, rudeness and ill manners. He made his way to the staff room, opened the door,

'Yes yes peeps, whats happenin'?'

'All good Jammin'. Especially now you're here,' said Jennifer.

'Here comes the booooy, yeeeeeaaaa-haaaay,' replied Bethany.

'Yes JB, Good afternoon sir,' responded Tom.

'Here comes trouble,' answered Jasmine.

'Dat troubles just back flipped, somersaulted and spiralled right back at ya in a tuck to ya chest… BOOOOOOOOM!' replied JB.

It was five past noon and the staff room was as atmospheric as per usual. A real hybrid of activity, kettle boiling, magazines and books being read, Teachers munching on their lunch, happy and jovial banter amongst the troupe, cupboard doors being opened and closed, the dripping of the sink tap, which still hadn't been repaired.

'I'm gonna get on the phone n get a plumber out, because that tap's been leakin' for well over a week. Pain in the damn booty!' said Jasmine.

'That's not the only pain in the booty Jaz!' teased Annabelle.

'OUCH,' said Tom.

'Are you OK Tom?' asked Bethany.

'Yep, it's just mi haemmorhoid pokin' through.'

'Ooooo, you're disgusting Tom.'

'Ha Haaaaaa…Just like mi bro Ethan last Saturday night, cavortin', kissin' n caressin' in Starstruck like a sex hungry teenager with a lady we all know! I use lady in the loosest sense o the word!' responded Tom.

He looked at Bethany and glanced over at Jasmine as she was nibbling away at her sweet and juicy looking corn on the cob.

'Why ya lookin' at me n winkin' Tom?' asked Jasmine.

'I'd rather you finished what you were eatin' first before speakin'. I don't wanna see a phallic re-run of the kinda tricks you got up to with our kid Jaz.' teased Tom.

'And what exactly would you know? OMG, it's the etiquette police over there.'

'Our kid's already told me about some of ya saucy shenanigans, apparently hotter than Dijon mustard?'

'I wouldn't compare miself to a French mustard, but I would say I'm quite spicy like a chorizo sausage.'

'You like sausage alright. Especially the larger size,' laughed Tom.

'Can we have a little bit of calm in here pleaso, I don't think we need to be recitin' the kama-sutra at lunch time. I know it's quite hot outside, but let's try n keep it cool inside,' said Bethany.

'Yeah, ya right Beth. I could do wi ya healin' ands on mi neck n shoulders again dough.'

'Let me finish my dinner first n then if ya lucky, I may soothe those aches n pains again. As I just said though, I don't want temperatures bubbling too high after Jaz n Tom's sex talk.'

'I only want an innocent massage Beth. Don't worry, I won't be askin' fa any extras, dat's unless, you were offerin'?' said JB, hoping to provoke a reaction from Jennifer.

'Hhhmmmmm… Interestin' proposition. I wouldn't wanna step on Jen's toes though.'

'It's OK Beth, Jammin's already nibbled some o them off, a few more injured ones won't make any difference.' responded Jennifer.

She'd evidently been offended and hurt by some of Bethany's comments. She was only joking though and didn't have any intention of squeezing in between Jennifer and JB, but then again, a threesome. The proverbial *ménage a trois*? Jammin' Boy certainly wouldn't mind, Beth probably wouldn't either as she quite fancied him, unbeknown to Jennifer. Undoubtedly though, Jennifer would have something to say about that, but then again, so would Mr Herbert. He didn't want any more extra curricular liaisons with Ms Luis-Cortada, so that prospect would most probably be a non starter, just like a pedigree Grand National horse pulling up lame in the warm up. The chemistry was visible between JB and Bethany, although both played it down.

'Don't worry Jen, I'm only jokin' about extras with JB, he isn't my territory,' she emphasised.

'I know you're only joking Beth. I'm not worried about that.'

Jennifer stood up from her comfy swivel leather chair, walked towards Bethany, held her arms out in front of her, both embracing in a warm, re-assuring friendly hug. JB was thinking how he would love to be the piece of meat in that tasty sandwich.

'Ladies, I don't want ya to fight over mi, I'm not dat special. Just an average six outta ten Joe,' said JB.

'I'd give you one.' said Jennifer, laughing out loudly.

'I think I'd probably give you at least a seven,' replied Bethany.

'I'd give you a clip round the ear Jammin', for ya mischievousness,' said Jasmine.

'Ladies, please stop ya flattery, ya makin' a black man blush. Mi ears are turnin' pink.'

'Do ya ears really go pink when you blush Jammin'?' asked Jasmine.

'Come ere n ave a look.'

Jasmine got up off the cosy three seater couch and walked over to JB, standing behind him. She was scrutinising his ear lobes looking for signs of pinky redness. In the meantime, Tom had taken a pink balloon out of one of the cupboards, blown it up and quietly tip toed his way behind Jasmine. 'I still can't see any pinkness on ya ear Jammin'?' she said puzzled.

'It's just dere.'

'Maybe it's a little hard wi the sun shinin' through the window, or maybe mi eye sight's deteoratin'?' said Jasmine.

'Put ya eyes a l'il closer n den you'll see.'

'Oh yeah, I can see it now. How bizarre! Is that just with brown people?'

'I tink so.'

'How about black people?'

'I tink dere tongue goes pinker?'

'Seriously! How weird.'

'BANG!'

Tom pricked the balloon, which made Jasmine jump about an inch off the floor. She also took a step backwards and almost fell over, banging into the cupboards behind her. All the Teachers in the staff room were in fits of laughter, high fiving each other and loving the fact that Jasmine was now hysterical.

'Ya all evil. Yeeeeaaah. Resident Evil!' said JB.

He picked up the burst pink balloon and placed it on his tongue. 'Look ere Jaz.'

'Oh, go away you.'

'Dere ya go.'

'Why've you got a balloon on ya tongue?' asked Jasmine.

'Because I'm black n not brown. When I fill in a questionnaire n it asks you fa di ethnic origin, dere's no box fa brown Caribbean, so I state black. I'm also showin' ya dat when black people blush, dere tongue goes pinker!'

'You joker Jammin',' Said Jasmine.

'Dats why I'm a prankster. Anyway, dat was ya lover's bro Tom n not my fault!'

'He ain't my lover, we only met Sat night n had a l'il fun, don't dramatise Jammin'!'

'I aren't, but to be onest, you were like newly weds. Ya couldn't keep ya ands off each other.'

'He's a hot chap, what d'ya expect.'

Everybody was enjoying their lunch while being entertained by someone. Considering it was a Monday, the staff room was full of vigour and abundant energy. JB decided to text his mum to ask if she wanted to come around to his in the week for a catch up.

'Ow ya doin' Momma? If ya free this week, d'ya wanna come round for dinner? Just savourin' lunch at mo, back in class at two for one lesson of English. Can't wait, the summer hols are on the horizon. Speak soon, Lots of love JB XX.'

'Come on Beth, lunchtime'll soon be over. Come n put ya ealin' ands on mi neck please.'

'Relax JB. You're so demandin' today! What's happened to you? You're normally so composed, cool and easy going, has someone excited ya?'

'Noooo. I'm just desperate fa ya soothin' ands Beth.'

He was such a smooth Romeo, some would label him a lothario of love with a sleek, glowing and twinkling silver tongue. He certainly possessed the *je ne sais quoi* chivalry and charisma with the ladies. Beth walked over to JB's chair, slapped him gently and playfully on the side of the face, asked him to unbutton his pink shirt and loosen his tie.

'Ooooo, dat feels just right. If I fall asleep, please wake me up.'

'Don't worry Jammin', I will.' replied Beth.

He was so excited by her touch, that his middle man started to make a few twitches in the depths of his pants. He was visualising how pleasurable it would be to undress Beth seductively to unveil her statuesque body. She was of a similar stature to Jennifer, but considerably shorter. Her breasts were perfectly formed, or so it appeared through her yellow blouse. It was slightly translucent, so you could just about see her bright yellow bra underneath. Again like this morning, her breasts pushed against JB's back, which made him extremely happy indeed. Within a few minutes he was once again drifting off to sleep, as her therapeutic hands were so soft and smooth, similar to JB's skin. Like a baby's bottom.

Chapter 27

Chill with the Still

Several hours later, after a relatively short day for JB, with five lessons of English, he was back home relaxing and planning what to do this evening. He felt quite rejuvenated after his weekend exploits, today's massage sessions with Bethany. He momentarily reminisced about her soft and therapeutic hands. He was starting to feel a slight tremor in his boxer shorts at the sensation of Bethany's firm, curvacious and beautiful breasts pressing themselves against the top of his back.

'I feeeeel good, da-na-na-na-na-na-na, I feeeeel good, da-na-na-na-na-na-na, so good, hurgh, hurgh, so fine, hurgh, hurgh n so reet petite.' he sang, collaborating James Brown with Jackie Wilson.

Felix's ears twitched and he raised his head, as JB started shaking on the sofa. He was lying on the three piece sofa watching something he had taped earlier on Sky plus. It was a documentary about Muhammed Ali, a biography highlighting his glittering illustrious career in the world of boxing. JB was a huge boxing fan. He enjoyed the training for fitness, but wasn't too keen on sparring, as he prided himself on his appearance and was adverse to being subjected to pain and facial disfigurement. His role as a teacher wouldn't really be partial to bruises when it was a profession requiring child contact. JB was a bit of a sissy really, priding himself on his appearance and would be quite squeamish at the sight of his own blood, let alone anyone elses.

Felix was sitting cosily again after being disturbed by his singing a few minutes ago, perched between his legs near his bottom, as JB was on his front resting his head, right cheek against the cushion gazing at the TV. He paused the documentary as he wanted to phone his mum. He tapped the home button, typed in the pin code and selected contacts. He selected the missed call option, scrolled down to Mum, pressed call and opted for the loud speaker feature. It rang a few times and then his mum picked the phone up.

'Hello.' she said.

'Mammita, it's me, ow ya doin'?'

'I'm great thanks, I've just been doing a spot of gardening!'

'Orticultural armony eh. You can come round n do mine if ya like?'

'What did your last servant die of?'

'Ard work, it was Wednesday's child...'

'Ha Haaaa. You think you're funny?'

'Yeah Momma, absolutely hilarious! What are you doin' dis week?'

'I'll be keeping fit at the gym, some more gardening and a little shopping.'

'Good. I just wondered if ya wanted to come to mine fa dinner on Wednesday or Thursday?'

'Yeah, that'd be great thanks! What are you doing now?'

'Ius chillin' on di sofa watchin' a Muhammed Ali documentary n keepin' Felix occupied.'

'Is he behaving himself?'

'Yeah, if e doesn't, I give im some water squirtin' treatment, fireman stylie.'

'Ha Haaa. I'll come round Thursday evening if that's OK with you.'

'I'll consult Felix, but I don't envisage any problems. E just miaowed n said as long e can rest in is usual place, ya welcome.'

'OK, it's a deal. I'll see you Thursday evening then. Is six alright?'

'Yeah, dat's fine Momma, no probs. Ave a relaxin' night n I'll see ya then. Bye.'

'Yeah, take care. Bye son. Love you.'

'Love you too Momma.'

He ended the call and then decided to text Fluffy Donkey to find out what the plan for tonight was. It was approaching five pm and he was feeling quite peckish. He was hoping he could have a nibble of some of the food that Stacey would have cooked for Fluffy and Ash, that was, if there was any left. Fluffy knew JB was probably going to go round later on, so being the selfless person he was, inevitable he would have some spare in the oven. JB's text read,

'Yes Fluffster, what appenin'? I ope ya chillin' on di sofa wid Ash n Stacey restin' ya poorly foot. I'm relaxin' watchin' a doccy about the legendary Ali at mo. Shall I come round to your's fa 7ish n also, will dere be some food fa me brother?'

He pressed the send button and waited for a reply, which from Joe was usually virtually immediately. JB was feeling revitalised but tired after his first day back at Oatmill High.. It was only a month away from the Summer holidays now, so most of the teachers were starting to struggle physically and mentally. People think it's so easy, being a teacher, but unless you've worked in that domain, you can't empathise. It was extremely rewarding, but also at times very demanding with alot of time devoted to lesson planning and preparation. It got easier with time, like any vocation, because people began to grow into their roles, but at the beginning it was a culture shock having to concentrate for long periods of time, adhering to the curriculum, stimulating the minds of the children and acting as a coach, mentor, confidante andfriend.

JB had been a teacher at Oatmill for a good seven years. He'd completed a teaching degree and then progressed to a years PGCE (Post Graduate Certificate of Education), which enabled him to be fully qualified. Throughout his PGCE, he did a placement at Oatmill High School and received rave reviews from the then Head Teacher Mr Coronation. His nickname was chicken. He didn't have features resembling poultry, but the name was given to a type of seasoned West Indian chicken, so the name stuck. He retired three years ago in 2007, which was a huge loss to the school, as he had been there for twenty years at the old school. He often came in to the school though, to act as an Agony Uncle, as he had a very cool, relaxed and endearing demeanour. He would work with children that were remedial, disadvantaged or had behavioural problems. His conversion rate was about ninety percent. He was held in such high esteem by his fellow teachers, hence the reason why he was re-employed. He had received an OBE for his commitment and dedication to inspiring and providing better provision for disenchanted kids. He patented a charity called Children's Chance which had become instrumental throughout the educational system of the United Kingdom. He was voted in as the Ambassador by the Charity's committee. He only worked a couple of days a week, because he enjoyed his regular round of golf, giving him a perfect business/pleasure lifestyle. Unfortunately he hadn't had the opportunity to be the head teacher at the new modern state of the art school, because it wasn't complete while he was in charge, however, he was made an honourary member and had the privilege of opening Oatmill High alongside the Mayor of Lillyford. He had acquired all his glittering accolades in the twilight of his career, pre-retirement. This demonstrated that with extremely hard work, enterprise and innovation, success could be achieved at a later stage of life, when the majority of people settle for comfort and don't challenge themselves in order to reach their lifetime aspirations. Mr Coronation was a walking inspiration, a silver fox, an educational icon, a knight in shining armour, a living legend.

JB's phone lit up and vibrated. It was Fluffy's response, 'Get your ass over here and come n look after ya brothers. We need some light entertainment. Come for 7 and Stacey'll heat you up a treat. Peace!'

His belly started to rumble. Felix's ears twitched and pricked up. He let out a mini squeal and yawned, before digging his claws into JB's butt cheeks.

'OOOOW! Ya damn fool, get off mi ass. OOOUCH! I ain't Petra ya know. Get in di kitchen n I'll sort ya food out soon.'

Felix miaowed, swished his tail and puffed it up. He wasn't too happy about JB shouting at him, especially when he didn't mean to dig his sharp claws into his sensitive flesh. 'I'm gonna give you a manicure tomorrow. Dem claws are like spears n not Britney… Bethany, hit me baby one more time!' he sang.

He definitely wanted to have some fun with Bethany, but the same problems could occur as they may with Jennifer. JB didn't want to be pursued by too many more female Teachers at Oatmill High, even though he had only slept with Jennifer, it could become a contagious mouthwatering challenge. Call it a sex educational conquest! He was finding it very tough to get Bethany out of his mind. She'd made a monumental impact after alleviating the soreness in his neck and shoulders with a few splendid massages. He was fantasising about her fabulous breasts pushing themselves gently into his back again, as he was dozing on the sofa. He unbuttoned her tightly fitting yellow blouse, button by button while sensuously kissing her lips and running his fingers through her light brown shoulder length hair. He gently slid off the blouse, exposing her tanned light brown complexion revealing a lacy yellow underwired bra that showed off the wonderful contours of her sizeable breasts. While still kissing her soft and smooth lips passionately, his left hand moved around to her back, gently brushing against her right shoulder. His right hand stroked her right torso just above the top of the bra, occassionally sliding its way down towards her breast and nipple. His touch was sending waves of shivers all the way down her spine, forcing her buttocks to intermittently spasm as if she was experiencing an earth shattering orgasm. Her tight hipster skinny jeans looked as if they had been paint sprayed on, as they were so figure hugging. His large member was pushing its way forcefully against her crotch, as they started to dry hump each other.

Bethany's eyes momentarily opened, glistening under the bedroom spotlights, resembling a reddish brown Charneleon gemstone. His right hand then slipped its way into the depths of her left bra cup, fondling her areola and protruding firm nipple. He pulled his hand out, inserted his fingers into her mouth. She sucked, licked and nibbled them, before he once again inserted them into the bra cup. They were now writhing around on the bed, the temperature soaring, intensity increased in highly erotic interlude.

'Miiiaaaaaaow.'

JB's body shuddered, his eyes opening, his nose twitching.

'Geeeez, sorry Felix, I was fast away in dreamworld. What time is it?' he asked the vacant space in the living room.

His heart racing at a frantic pace as he seriously thought he was about to have passionate intercourse with Bethany. He shook his head, gave out a massive sigh, checked his iPhone for the time. He must have slept for a good forty minutes as the time was now five fifty six. The Muhammed Ali documentary had now finished, so JB managed to lift himself off the sofa and head to the kitchen to feed Felix, who wasn't very happy about being squirted with water, so looked rather folorn. JB took out some beef and liver Whiskas from the cupboard, opened the lid and spooned a small portion out with the designated cat food fork. He then banged the clumps that were congealed in between the prongs, back into the tin and then put a plastic tin cover on top. He threw some Iams cat biscuits down into the cat bowl too, to give Felix some good nutritious sustenance. He poured some fresh cold water into his bowl and then went upstairs to get ready. He was distracted by the appealing double bed, so decided to dive on it for fifteen minutes more rest. He was finding it really hard to motivate himself after a shortish first day back at school. He set his alarm for six fifteen pm.

He sprawled out on top of the quilt on his back in the crucifix position and closed his eyes. No sooner had he fallen asleep, he was woken suddenly by his alarm. He turned it off straight away, rolled over to the side of the bed, sat up on the edge of it, stretched his arms out above his head simultaneously lifting his legs in harmony to ninety degrees. After his wake up stretch, he stood up, removed all of his clothes and jogged to the bathroom. He opened the top window to minimise the steam effect, placed his swimming cap on, stepped into the shower basin, rotated the knob and turned the water on.

He rotated the shower head to jet spray, as he wanted it to hit all the aching muscles that Bethany had massaged earlier. It was at just the right temperature, warm and soothing. He was loving the sensation as the water propelled itself on to his toned skin. He re-positioned the jet for a few moments while he squirted his favourite mango foamburst onto his body. He spread it all over his body with firm circular motions, making sure he cleaned his bottom, the top of his back and in between his toes. When he'd lathered his body and face, he moved back under the powerful jet spray. Within ten minutes he was finished, out he hopped on to the virginal white slate tiled floor, pulling the navy blue towel off the silver heated rail, proceeding to dry his skin. He whipped off his swimming cap and hung it to dry just over the knob that changes the water temperature. He was really looking forward to hooking up with Joe, Ash and Stacey, especially warming to the idea of tasting Stacey's culinary delights. He was hoping with her Family's ethnic origin from the Caribbean it would be a mouthwatering meal of spicy proportions. After drying his skin fully, taking care to do in between his toes, he opened the bathroom cabinet and took out his favourite replenishing sweet fragranced cream of Palmer's cocoa butter, pressed the top open, and started to squirt and massage it into his skin. When he had finished creaming his body, he swilled and gargled some Listerine mouthwash in his mouth for about thirty seconds, before spitting it out. He made his way back to the bedroom to get dresssed for his evening rendezvous with Joe, Ash and Stacey. He slid open the left hand side of his wardrobe to peruse the many clothes he had to wear.

'Boy, what should I trow on man? So many choices, anybody would tink I was a woman!' he chuckled.

He pulled out a pair of comfortable light blue Levis 501 jeans, a plain light lemon t-shirt, a light blue cardigan with a puffy collar fastened with silver duffel coat style buttons, a pair of white Calvin Klein boxer shorts and some plain black cotton socks. The time was fastly approaching seven, so he quickly got himself ready. He took out a pair of white Converse Allstar lace up pumps from the bottom of the wardrobe and slid the door closed. He decided to spray on some of his favourite Issey Miyake eau de toilette, made sure the upstairs windows and doors were all closed, before jogging downstairs. He went into the room and turned off the television and Sky box, tidied the sofa cushions up, pulled the horizontal blinds closed and walked out of the lounge, closing the door behind him. Felix appeared to have forgiven him for the water squirting experience earlier and started to walk around him, brushing his fur against JB's legs and swishing his tail from side to side. JB slipped on his Converse pumps and then picked Felix up, giving him a big kiss on the top of his head. He then placed him on the floor, before setting the burglar alarm. BEEP BEEP BEEP. He dashed to the door, unlocked it, opened it and closed it behind him, saying bye to Felix. He locked the door and waited for the acknowledgement of the double beep to confirm the alarm had set.

Chapter 28

Fluffy Love

He walked to the gates at the end of the driveway, opened them and then climbed into his sleek and elegant Audi 1.8L A3 black sports coupé. He never used materialism to attract the ladies anyway, just his jovial, infectious and addictive charisma which invariable seemed to work. He never chased girls. The magnetism always appeared to lure them in. He started the engine, revved it a little, turned on the stereo system and pumped out some old school garage music before driving onto the main road. The traffic was sparse as rush hour had ended a while ago. JB was tapping his steering wheel and moving his body from side to side as he drove to Fluffy Donkey's, who lived ten minutes away just on the edge of Fruitville.

'Wid a little bit o luck, we can make it tru di nite, wid a little bit o luck I can make you feel alright.' he sang.

He pulled up outside Fluffy Donkey's at bang on seven pm. Joe would be impressed. JB had a habit of being fashionably late, so this was a huge surprise. He parked the car in a spare space outside the modern four storey apartments, climbed out, shut the door and locked it with the key sensor. He walked to the entrance door and pressed number thirty four which was on the top floor. It buzzed.

'Hello, who is it?' asked Ash.

'Who d'ya tink it is hermano?'

'Wayhay, up ya come brother.'

'Tanks Ashilito!'

JB opened the entrance door and walked up the four flights of stairs. It smelt of lavender. The cleaners had obviously been today to spruce up the communal areas. JB knocked on the door, it opened.

'Yes brother, what's happenin'?'

'I'm all good Ash, just tired after di ectic weekend. It's OK for some. You tree playin' truant ay. Easy life.'

'Thankfully I'm self employed as you know, so I'll just take a few days off to clear this whiplash.'

'How dare you Jammin'? I haven't had a day off sick since I started my placement at Oatmill. You bad boy, that's slanderous,' shouted Stacey from the living room.

Ash and JB hugged in the hallway, before JB took off his trainers and put them in the store cupboard.

'You big afro haired specimen of love, come in here n give Fluffy a squeeze.' shouted Joe.

'Yes Flufster, ow ya feelin', you too Stace?'

'I'm doing well Jammin' thanks, mi back's a l'il sore and mi neck's tender, but apart from that, I should be able to start training in seven to ten days,' replied Stacey.

'Ow about school?'

'I should be back next week. We've only got a month left then, before the summer holidays n the end of mi PGCE.'

'You'll be OK Stace. I just ope dey give you a permanent contract at Oatmill.'

'Yeah, so do I.'

Stacey stood up from the sofa, JB walked over and gave her a gentle hug. Ash sat himself down in the cosy black leather chair.

'Are you goin' skiing, Fluffy, wi dat boot on?'

'I'll whack a ski around ya legs Jammin'!'

'Break a leg. Oooops…Ha Ha Haaaaaa. You already ave, let's ope you don't damage di udder one.' chuckled JB.

JB shook Joe's hand, gave him a knuckle touch and leaned onto the three seater sofa and gave him a gentle hug.

'Pooooh, what's dat smell?'

'That's the delicious dinner Stacey's kindly made!' responded Joe.

'It ain't dat I can smell, its sometin' else. It ain't ya arm pits is it Fluffy?'

'Ya gonna get it Jammin', when I'm back, fit, willin' n able.'

'Just jokin' Fluffy. It must be ya cologne, dat eau de toilette, or in English, toilet water! Ha Haaaaaaaa.'

'This is too expensive for you. Ash got it for me from duty free last time he travelled.'

'Is it dat Hermes, hermano?'

'Yeah Jammin'. The finest refinest fragrance. It costs about a hundred pounds a bottle.'

'Did Fluffy raid a bank to pay ya back?'

'Correct Jammin.' I raided my piggy bank. Just sit ya ass down there at the table and feed ya face n shut ya mouth!'

'I'll feed ya face wid a left hook Fluffy.'

'When ya ready JB, when ya ready!'

Stacey went into the kitchen to dish up a delight for JB. It smelt absolutely stunningly spectacular.

'I've got a selection of movies for us to watch Jammin'. The Untouchables, Pulp Fiction, Gangs of New York, I Love You, Man, Avatar or He's Just Not That Into You! Take ya pick after you've eaten dinner.'

'I tink I'll go for Avatar or She's Just Not That Into You!'

'It's He's Just Not That Into You.'

'I know, but I'm just sayin', she's just not that into you Fluffy. If you catch my drift?'

'Watch ya mouth man. Ya only jealous Jammin'!'

'Jealous, be serious man. You've gone almost five months widowt sex. Ya a virtual monk.'

'Sometimes you'll realise, it's quite healthy to cleanse ya sexual soul n revert to the Monastery.'

'I'm cleansed Fluffy, I've just ad a shower!'

'Ha Ha Ha Haaaaaaaaaaaa,' laughed Ash.

'Sssshhhhhhhh, I think Stacey's coming in.' said Joe.

'Yeah, that's OK, and you're comin' out!'

The atmosphere was really jovial and had been lifted to another dimension since JB's arrival. The three of them were very tight, just like waist and limb squeezing skinny jeans. Not in the sky rocket (pocket), but a very close special friendship. They regularly teased each other. To outsiders, it would possibly appear that there was friction, but it was just the way they were. Tormenting, teasing and playing pranks. Sometimes they acted like mischievious teenagers, always trying to get one over on the other. Certain outsiders might also be curious about their sexual orientation, as they all sporadically exhibited camp tendencies.

'Stacey, dis smells absolutely delicious. Can't wait to stick mi teet into it like a dog on a bone. What is it?'

'It's a wonderful spicy Mexican dish. Burritos.'

'Doesn't dat mean donkey in spanish?'

'Yes JB, very funny and very clever. Now shut ya mouth n enjoy the mouthwatering flavours.'

'Fluffy, why d'ya take tings to eart at times? I only said it's donkey in Spanish! Eeeeeeeee-aaaaaaaaaaw.'

'Don't worry Joe, I'll cheer ya spirits up later.'

'Hhhhhmmm, that sounds interesting! What's ya plan?'

'You'll just have to wait n see.' replied Stacey.

'That treat surely can't be as spicy as the burritos you've made?' Questioned Joe.

'You'll just have to wait n see.'

'We're all being treated today with special surprises. The perfect tonic after a turbulent last twenty four hours.'

'Yeah, ya right Ash. I got di shock of mi life earlier today, when Beth decided to give me a shoulder massage. Dat g as soothin' n ealin' ands, believe me, extra special. I felt a goose bump or two on di back o mi neck, besides mi fro almost jumpin' on to di ceilin'!'

'Who's one lucky man?'

'I'd call miself blessed Joe, just like you peeps today bein' entertained n mothered by Stace.'

'Guaranteed JB. I think we should propose a toast peeps.'

'I tell you what Joe, why don't we crack open a bottle of wine n celebrate all being here to tell the tale, after a fortunate escape yesterday?'

'Ash, that's a perfect idea. Stacey, would you kindly mind doing the honours? Just take any bottle of plonk from the kitchen wine rack.'

'Gents, don't ya think I've done enough for ya today already?'

'Weeeeell, almost, but we're thirsty n some of us are a little light headed still.'

'I was also in the accident ya know!'

'I know, but you don't mind d'ya?'

'Peeps, don't worry, I'll do it, seein' as I'm di most mobile one o di crew.'

169

'Ya dinner's gonna go cold though.'

'It's OK Stace, it's scorchin' ot, so I'll let it cool a l'il n pour y'all a glass,' JB answered.

JB went into the kitchen, while Stacey set the table for him. She placed a knife and fork on the wooden table either side of the light beige cork placemat. She went into the kitchen to get a few condiments for JB, like guacamole, hot and spicy salsa dip, sour cream and some black pepper. JB was pulling out a vintage deep Chilean red from the wine rack, which was built into the cupboards, holding twelve bottles. He opened the kitchen drawer and took out a bottle opener.

'Don't take too long JB, you need to eat ya food before it gets cold.'

'I will. I'll be two minutes. Where are di wine glasses?'

'Just above ya head in that cupboard. Move ya head to the side n I'll get them for ya.'

Stacey took four bulbed glasses out of the cupboard that had slender long six inch stems.

'Tanks Stace.'

'It's alright.'

'When you gonna be back at work?'

'Prob next Monday. I wanna take a week off to make sure I'm right. I've also got trials for the Indoor European Athletics Championships in August, so I wanna qualify for those.'

'You'll be alright wi plenty o essential rest n recuperation.'

JB had uncorked the wine bottle and carried it through to the living room, while Stacey carried the glasses through and placed them on the glass coffee table.

'Let's open the wine and celebrate life.'

JB poured the sumptuous Chilean red vintage wine into each of the four glasses.

'Yeah, damn right Stace. I wanna propose a toast to say tanks to di Lord or whoever exists up dere in di sky. Tanks fa protectin' mi special friends, tanks for enablin' dem to go on survivin' n strivin' fa greatness in di face of adversity. Bigin' y'all up n wishin' success, ealth, appiness, protection n PHAT love always. Peace n armony.'

They all clinked and clonked glasses, smiled and took a sip of the wine.

'CHEEEEEERS, SALUD, NA ZDORÓVYE!' JB pulled out his chair, sat down at the table and pulled himself into it, for dining comfort. He picked up his cutlery and began to cut into the burritos. Stacey had used fresh chicken breasts, peppers, mushrooms, fresh chillies, onions, courgette, mexican beans, hot pepper sauce, fresh yogurt, lemon, lime and a secret sauce ingredient. His mouth was watering as the taste was divinely scrumptious. He had a dish of rice and red kidney beans too, which he poured to the side of the burritos, along with a glass bowl of succulent leafy salad garnished with balsamic vinegar.

'Stace, dis is sensational, almost as ot as Jen's booty. WOUCH! I can't believe it, tasty, ot n spicy. A perfect exotic dish at di end of a long day, n to spend it wid mi friends. Ultra special!'

'It's OK Jammin' I thought after the last twenty four hours of emotional heartache, it was the least I could do for y'all.'

'That's the least you could've done? Ya damn right Stace, I could've had a head to toe massage!'

'Listen Fluffy. You were so lucky to move n groove the night before last with me n then, let alone, share a living room with me and for a triple whammy, I've come to ya appartment n cooked for the boys!'

'Ya right Stace, maybe I'm expecting a l'il too much!'

'No ya not Joe, she just said it was the least she could do for us!' laughed Ash.

JB was relishing the beautiful cuisine that Stacey had kindly prepared. It had definitely livened up their spirits after the crash and hospital overnight stay. He was licking his lips and savouring every piece of flavour on his palate. Just looking at his facial expression gave a stark reminder to a woman titillated by a pair of strategically placed love eggs, vibrating frantically on the inside front wall of the knickers, rubbing sensuously against a dripping wet wanton vagina. He was such an animated individual who relished virtually every aspect of life.

'What are we gonna watch then?' asked Ash.

'It must be I Love You Man or He's Just Not That Into You!'

'I love you too man!' said JB.

'I thought you loved us both?' answered Joe.

'OK, I was a l'il economical wi da truth. I do, but I ain't gonna marry any of ya.'

'Not even if I pull out a packet of Haribos?'

'Fluffy, dat's a totally different proposition. I might jus be tempted... Eeeeeee-Aaaaaaaaw.'

JB was in his element, still enjoying the burritos with rice, beans and salad.

'Stace, I knew you'd make sure di rice was made wid peas.'

'Peas?'

'Yes Fluffy. Dat's what I said. Peas.'

'Stace used red kidney beans. A typical West Indian delicacy.'

'Yeah man, I know dat. In di Caribbean dere called peas dough.'

'Right, that's why they say rice n peas.'

'That was the name of that witness I took details from yesterday Joe. He was called Mushy Peas. I've got his details in my phone, so I'll write them down so you can give him a call and use details when you eventually fill in ya car insurance details.'

'Many thanks Ashilito. I'll just do that. By the way, how many details did you get? I've never known anyone be so addictive to the word details? Ha Haaaaaaa!'

'OMG. Just because I pay so much attention to details, does that concern you? Silence. Hmmmm. Still nothing? I take that as a no then!'

'Chill out now man. I'm not JB. Unless you wanna start a three way war?' said Ash.

'Right gents. I'm gonna make a decision for the movie. You peeps just can't make ya minds up!' said Stacey.

'Hang on Stace, whose house is it? You've done enough for us. Women's Lib's now over.'

'Don't be so chauvinistic Joe.'

'Nooooo. I don't mean it like that. I just think you need to sit down, relax and enjoy the evening.'

Stacey agreed, slightly bemused, sat down next to Joe and slapped his right thigh.

'OUCH! Why ya being so abusive?'

'You haven't seen nothin' yet. The best is yet to come!'

'Oooooo. Is that a promise or just an idle threat?'

'You'll have to wait till later.'

'Hhhhmmmmm. Interesting!' replied Joe.

'If you play ya cards right, it could be your lucky night.'

'Shall we get the movie on then?' asked Ash.

'Good idea man.'

JB had just finished his dinner and not left a drop. He hadn't licked the plate, but it looked like it had been cleaned by a cat, as it was quite clean, apart from a few remnants of food. He took a sip of his wine.

'Are we all ready den?'

'Yeah, now you've finished.'

'Stace, dat was absolutely sensational, I feel like I'm in dreamland. I've never tasted burritos of dat igh quality. All di ingredients used to perfection. OMG.'

'Many thanks Jammin'. Mi Mum taught me all I know. When you have parents from the Caribbean like you JB, it's a privileged culinary genetic trait.'

JB stood up and took his crockery and cutlery into the kitchen.

'Just leave em on the side Jammin,' shouted Stacey.

'It's OK, I'll wash em.'

'Just leave em in there.'

'No probs Stace,' responded JB.

JB decided to run some hot water into the washing up bowl, squirt some Fairy Liquid in and proceded to wash the pots.

'Come on JB, ya not washin' ya fro in there are ya?' asked Ash.

'Noooo. Just da pots.'

'The movies goin' on,' shouted Stacey.

JB started to hurry up with the washing up and placed his pots in the drainer. He tipped the soapy water down the sink, sprayed some Dettol that was on the side, onto the neighbouring work surface and then cleaned it with a cloth. When he had finished, he made his way into the living room. He sat down in the black leather comfortable chair, after picking up his half full glass of Chilean Rioja from the living room table.

'What DVD ave ya chosen?'

'Wait n see Jammin'. You'll love it man.'

'Oh, that one.'

'Be patient, just like we were for about sixteen or so hours last night n this morn in the hospital.'

The trailers were playing first, so JB's suspense was prolonged.

'Geez man, I can't wait any longer, di suspense is killin' me.'

'It'll be worth the wait JB, I promise,' said Stacey.

Fluffy Donkey and Stacey were sat cosily on the black three seater leather sofa, while Ash and JB had their own single ones. There were four trailers before the movie started on the DVD that Stacey had chosen. Apart from Stacey, none of the guys knew which movie she had opted for.

'Why don't we have a l'il bet on which movie we're gonna be watchin'?' said Joe.

'Sounds like a good idea Fluffy.'

'Yeah man, I'm down wi dat too. Shall we say two pounds each?'

'Let's make it a bit more exciting n go for a big beehiver fiver.' suggested Ash.

'Lord, you boys ave dollars to burn. OK den, you've twisted mi arm Ash, a fiver it is.'

They all shook hands to confirm they were all in on the betting pact.

'I'm gonna say, She's Just Not That into You.'

'It's He's Just Not That into You JB. How many times do I need to remind you?'

'I'm just teasin' Fluffy.'

'I'm gonna take a pop at Avatar.' said Ash.

'I reckon, I Love You, Man,' said Joe.

'Aaaaw, tank you. I never expected you to confess ya love fa me in dis intimate environment. It must be di result after ya near death experience yesterday. I jus wanna say also Fluffy, I love you man.' answered JB.

'Many thanks brother. Let's hug it out bitch!'

JB and Fluffy Donkey hugged. JB stood up from his cosy armchair and walked over and put his arms around Joe, which was quite tough to do, as he was a huge strapping six foot something

'Yeah Man, bring ya money to me. I knew it all along.'

'Ha haaaaaaa. That's the trailer for He's Just Not That into You JB.'

'Damn. Alright, I'll settle down. I'm gettin' too excited wid all dis suspense. I better and over mi dollars right now den.'

'They're coming to me JB. It's all about the Sci Fi fabulous blockbuster Avatar.'

'I think y'all barkin' up the wrong tree. My bets certainly a strong outsider. Come oooooon!'

The trailers appeared to be going on for ever. They were becoming a little restless now and wanting to get their hands on an extra ten pounds. Who would be the lucky one?

'Shall we start a drum roll man, dis suspense is beginnin' to irritate me now. Stace, can you jus forward wind it gal?'

'Fluffy, would you like me to wind it?'

Joe was slightly taken a back, although his green eyes lit up at the prospect of Stacey winding her body around his midriff and crotch region. He was wearing a pair of loosely fitting grey jogging bottoms that he had changed into when they returned from hospital earlier today. Thankfully he also had a pair of boxer shorts, because his erect middle man was becoming visible through the material of his bottoms. Not literally poking through, but slightly upraised, displaying the shape of the happy chappy.

'Eeeerm, yeeeeaaah, yeeeeaah, but not now! I'm looking forward to winning this money from these two reprobates,' replied Joe, slightly stuttering.

He lifted up a yellow cushion and placed it strategically on his lap to hide the bulge endeavouring to catapult itself out into the open.

'I can't believe you'd rather choose a DVD over me windin' n grindin' upon ya.' said Stacey.

'Noooo, noooooo! I don't mean it like that, I just think we're all settled, comfortable n ready to watch this hugely anticipated movie.'

'Excuses, excuses, but good answer. I'll give you the benefit of the doubt on this occasion!'

'Don't you worry Stace, I'll make it up to ya.'

'You've nothin' to make up for, apart from returnin' the compliment n winin' n dinin' me at my place!'

'When mi back isn't so sore, I'll obligingly cater for your every need!'

'Promises, promises,' said Stacey smiling.

'Aaargh! I better take two of those cocodamols to relieve the pain in mi foot. It's a l'il sore and its four hours since I took the last two.'

'You shouldn't be drinkin', Fluffy, if ya on medication!'

'Jammin', I deserve a glass of wine after the heartache of the last twenty four hours. I need one to relax me too, otherwise I'll be giving you a body crunchin' right. A l'il rib tickler.'

'Blah, blah, blah. Don't promise what ya can't deliver. Ain't dat right Stace?'

'Damn right JB. Let's see if he can entertain me with his refined culinary prowess? Maybe he'll just conjure up a basic poached egg on toast a la carte with a dash of cress and some herbs sprinkled on top?'

'Don't you worry Stace. You'll be begging for more!'

'Ooooooo, sounds enticin'!' laughed Stacey.

'Can you two leave ya sensuous behaviour to di bedroom, ya sendin' a shiver down mi spine n Fluffy appy to see ya! Ha Haaaaaaaaaa.'

'Hold it down cowboy. Is that why you've put the cushion on ya crotch Joe, to hide ya excitement?' asked Ash.

'Stop it! I just feel comfortable with it placed there, just in case one of you boys throws something at me.'

'What... Like a dirty rotten torn dish cloth?'

'I'll trow more dan dat at im Ash. It'd be a custard pie wid cream!'

'You boys are hilarious. The entertainment's free too. How lucky am I. Sit Down comedy in the comfort of Fluffy's home.'

'Ere we go. Whose scooped di dirty cash?'

Dreamworks Pictures. It was I Love You, Man. '

You hooooooo. Show me the colour of ya money you two. I knew it.'

'You deserve it Joe. To be honest, I was gonna donate five pounds for ya club foot fund anyway,' said Ash.

'Yeah, n I was gonna give ya a fiver for the glass back foundation. Ha haaaaaaaa!'

'Stop all the birds eye potato waffle n hand it over to the Daddy!' said Joe.

'It seems a bit ironic though. Are ya sure you weren't in on dis Stace? It jus seems too good to be true... He can't take iz eyes off a you, you feel like heaven to touch, e wants to old you so much...'

'I need you baby, if it's quite alright, I need you baby to walk those lonely nights, I love you baby, trustin' me when I say it's OK...' sang Ash and JB in harmony.

They were lyrics from Lauryn Hill's huge selling track, *You're Just Too Good To Be True*. Quite an impressive rendition too. Stacey was tapping her foot and Joe was slapping his thigh gently, while closing his eyes.

'Wouch! Is that a subliminal message?'

'Surely it can't be Ash. It's jus too good to be true!'

'Haaaaaa haaaaaaaaa.' laughed Ash.

JB and Ash were mocking Fluffy Donkey again, as he appeared to be quite smitten with Stacey. She was only a baby at twenty one years of age, seven years his junior. He hadn't had sex for approximately five months, but besides wanting to be a visitor in her knickers, he did, so it would seem, have a soft spot for her. Considering he had only first met her on Saturday at JB's BBQ, there was an attraction there and the feeling was certainly very mutual. The movie was displaying the opening credits as Stacey slowly started to slide her body closer towards Joe's on the three seater sofa. Joe's left hand started to meander towards the naked flesh of her athletically toned and honed right thigh. It began to run itself along the outer bottom edge of her hot pants, brushing gently with her skin. Her thighs began displaying goose bumps, reminiscent of a Braille written placard. She leant her head on to his masterful left shoulder and stretched her neck to kiss him on the left cheek.

'I didn't know Lou Ferrigno was in this?' said Ash.

'Whos' e?' asked JB.

'It's the Incredible Hulk.'

'Yeah man, I know who dat is!'

'Are you two quite comfortable over there?'

'Yeah, we're just fine Ash, thanks.'

'If you wanted to get a l'il cosier, I could fetch ya quilt in from the bedroom?' suggested Ash.

'It's quite warm here Ash. I'll just use Fluffy's body heat. Sssssssssssss... schmooooooookin' hot. He's like a furnace.' said Stacey.

'Lord! Get a room you two.'

'We've got a large living room here.'

'Sure have Joe,' replied Stacey.

'What kinda room were you talking about JB?'

'I tought more of an intimate location, like a boudoir bredder!'

'I have two bedrooms, but no boudoir. I suppose I could turn it into one though? What d'ya think Stace?'

'Yeah, why not! We could make that happen if you were forthcoming?'

'Ha Haaaaaaaaa. Dat's so funny.'

'What is?' asked Stacey.

'Fluffy bein' forth cummin' Oooops, I mean comin'!

'I don't understand? Where's the punchline?'

'Di punchlines in di word Stace. I don't tink ya dat naive? Den again, I keep forgettin' ya only a baby at twenty!'

'Baaby?'

'Yeah gal. Ya in ya infancy in di workin' world after finishin' uni.'

'I'm twenty two next month.'.

'Ya certainly all woman, but ya still young. Ya barely outta nappies!' chuckled JB.

'Hmmmmmm. I think you can safely say I grew outta nappies nearly two decades ago!'

'If dat's di case, why's ya skin still like a baby's bum?' asked JB.

'Probably because as a lady should, or young girl... I nourish, nurture n exfoliate my skin n treat it with respect. My mum always told me, to treat it like a precious treasured rare flower. Cherish it n don't chastise n abuse it!'

'Oooooooh. What an interestin' philosophy. I've never seen mi skin as a precious treasured flower, jus a priceless exclusive gem, di kind dat only a few select women can afford!'

'I see we've got some interesting objects in here then. Let's just call you both floral stones!'

'I'd say more like stoned flowers. Only a few select women can afford? You mean those in the gutter that are desperate for a helping hand out,' said Joe.

'Are you tryin' to say I'm high on drugs?'

'Noooooo Stace! You're the sunshine flower n JB's stoned!'

'Ooooooo... I'll let you off. Don't forget, I promised to wind n grind upon you later, so you better tread with extreme caution Fluffy.'

'Charmin' Fluffy! Ya sayin' I'm stoned? Jus because I'm black n from di Caribbean, ya implyin' dat I smoke di ganja, man! When ya better, I'll give you a stoned right cross to di jaw, n den we'll see who's floatin'! Also, it's you dats been celibate for di las so many years! Ooops, sorry, I mean months!'

'Are we supposed to be watchin' a movie, or are you gonna continue to talk n sledge each other all the way through?' said Ash.

'I aint desperate, Jammin' n don't dispose myself easily to the ladies.'

'Ya intimidated o women dats why, bumper claart! Anyway Ash, ya right man. Hush up ya mout Fluffy, we've got a movie to watch!'

Joe was almost spitting feathers at the insults flying across from JB once again. Thankfully though, Stacey had used her soothing feminine allure to seduce the boys into becoming engrossed in the DVD she had chosen.

JB hurried into the kitchen to pour himself a glass of water, as he was driving and didn't want to be over the limit when he made his way back home.

'Would anyone else like any warter?' he asked in his native Kittician patois.

'I'm OK thanks Jammin'!'

'No thank you JB,' said Stacey.

'Get me a bucket and then I can throw it over ya head!'

'No worries. One bucket of warter comin' right up. D'ya want dirty warter or clean, cold and fresh from di kitchen?'

'Just a glass will do thanks!'

'Yeah man!'

JB pulled two glasses out from a cupboard above the kitchen sink, turned the handle to the right for cold as it was mixer tap, meaning it ran hot and cold by sliding the chrome handle to the appropriate side. He filled up both glasses when the water was cold enough, turned the tap off and took the ice tray out of the freezer compartment. He pushed a handful of them from below, forcing them out of the tray and then plopped them into each glass, before putting the tray back in the freezer and closed the door and returning to the living room.

'Dere ya go Fluffy. I Love You, Man.'

'At the moment I wanna give you a fist of fives, but am too stiff to move!'

'Boooy, is dat why you've got di yellow cushion positioned over ya crotch? Stacey's Midas touch is certainly workin' wonders! Ha Haaaaaaaa.'

'Ha haaaaaaa. Nice one Jammin'!' responded Ash.

'Booooys. Quiet please. If you haven't already noticed, there's a movie playing!' said Stacey.

Joe had a real look of disdain and was engrossed in a transfixed glare at JB, obviously incensed by a comment he had made. JB was enjoying the start of the movie with eyes on the large fifty inch wide screen black LCD TV set in the corner of the room. He momentarily turned his head towards Joe, expecting him to be relishing the movie also, however, Joe was still eyeballing JB, mouth swirling, right index finger twirling, cheeks contorted and looking as if he wanted to rip his head off. JB winked, nodded and stuck his thumb up at Joe, expecting him to acknowledge him, but no, the raging bull was the look on Fluffy Burrito's face. In JB's mind, he started to sing the song Elton John released in 1983, *I Guess That's Why They Call It The Blues*. It reached number four in the UK music charts.

'And I Guess That's Why They Call It The Blues, laughing like children, living like lovers, rolling like thunder under the covers…!'

JB was rather happy with himself, but couldn't understand why Joe was so antagonised? Talk about oblivion. Most probably it was the insinuation that Fluffy was stiff under the yellow cushion he was holding on his crotch. Joe hadn't taken to the comment too kindly! About an hour into the movie, a strange noise was sounding at a slightly lower tone than the TV volume. Everyone was totally engrossed in the movie, apart from JB, who was irritated by the unusual sound. He looked around the living room, trying to identify the perculiar noise. He glanced at Ash. He was smiling, displaying his gleaming ivory enamel. He looked over at Stacey and Joe. It was Fluffy Donkey. He was resting his weary head on Stacey's shoulder with his eyes closed and mouth wide open. That was the answer, Fluffy Donkey making a strange gargling sound, as if he was cleaning his palate with mouthwash.

'Fluffy, are ya watchin' dis man, or jus garglin' weird songs?' asked JB.

He leant over the arm of the black leather chair he was sitting in and made a kind of high pitched mouse like squeal. Joe shuddered, moved his head to his right and mumbled something.

'Uuuurgh.'

He then continued to gargle. 'Fluffy! Shush now man. We're tryin' to watch di movie if you aven't already noticed.'

'Whaaaat?'

'I said, we're tryin' to watch dis movie man, hush up ya mout now n keep ya eyes open.'

'Shut it man.'

'You shut it and watch. It was your choice o movie n snoozin'. If you wanna snooze, go to ya bedroom!'

'I must have just drifted off. Sorry peeps.'

'Stace, ya must o put sometin' strong in dem burritos, you've knocked im out.'

'I'll knock you out man,' said Joe.

'Sssshhhhh Fluffy. Just relax n rest. You're tired after the chaotic last twenty four hours or so,' responded Stacey.

A few moments silence followed.

'What was dat special ingredient den Stace?'

'Just some of my extra special hot n spicy sentiments. Maybe the pepper I used was sleepin' powder, not ground corns?'

'It certainly worked n shut im up for a while. You go girl.'

'I hope he aint gonna be sleeping too long, because I promised him that lap dance,' said Stacey.

'Don't worry, I'm wide awake now. It must have been my body subconciously giving me an evening siesta.'

'How long's di movie on fa?'

'Is it about two hours?' asked Ash.

'Just a little shorter than that. It's been on for an hour already. I think it's an hour n forty five mins, give or take five.'

'Thanks Stace,' replied Ash.

'Oooooooh, I tought you were sleepin' too?'

'No man. Just totally engrossed in fab comedy.'

'Damn right Ashilito, dis is a classic. I tought Fluffy was rehearsin' for a part in di sequel wi dem crazy assed garglin' noises?'

'Yeah, so did I.'

'Funny one boys,' responded Joe.

'Oh, ya actually awake now?'

'Yeah, keepin' my eyes on you Jammin'.'

'Keep dem on di screen, I'm not on di box tonight.'

'Maybe not, but I'll box you when I'm better.'

'Tell me sometin' new. All dese idle treats man.'

'Come on boys, relax again n watch,' said Stacey.

She paused the movie and rewound it back, as they had missed the last five minutes due to all the chatter. JB had seen the movie before, so he decided to fly a text to Beth. He was having yet even more fantasies about becoming embroiled in a passionate interlude with her. They had never had any dalliance, apart from her massaging his neck and shoulders earlier today. He was so reluctant to become involved with any fellow teachers at Oatmill High, but after his erotic encounter with Jennifer he was obsessed with working his way through the staff. A slight exaggeration, as he wasn't attracted to all employees at the school. He would have to be extremely careful though, as he didn't want to develop a reputation as being a lothario, as potentially it could have a detrimental effect on him attaining a higher profile position at Oatmill. He had aspirations to be a Head of Year and eventually a Head Teacher. He thoroughly enjoyed his work at the school and was a huge success with his passion, application and charisma, besides several other traits that endeared him to his fellow teachers and pupils past and present.

He began to type his text to Beth. Nothing too complicated, just a tantalising one suggesting another sensuous experience tomorrow during breaktime.

'Beth, ow ya doin' lady? Jus chillin' at mi mates wid Stacey n Ash. I've got a big smile on mi face after enjoyin' ya massages earlier today. Fancy a repeat performance tomorrow?'

He hoped she would respond in a positive manner, but obviously didn't want to indicate he fancied her, or just plain and simply wanted to be a presence inside her knickers. In his mind he possessed some incredibly dirty sexual thoughts. Saying that, who didn't? The Pope, The Queen Lizzie Windsor, the President of the United States of America would all experience those thoughts at some stage of their working days. They were human, after all. Time passed by and it was fast approaching ten o'clock. The movie after all the rewinding, pausing, communicative, sledging and gurgling distractions, had just finished.

'What happens now then Fluffy?' asked Ash.

'I'd say it's about time you all French Connection UK'd off..'

'Dere's no need to be so abrupt n rude now man!' JB replied sucking his teeth in typical West Indian style.

'After all the slavver you've given me in the last two days, that's how I feel right now. I make you dinner, provide you with wine, buy you BBQ Essentials and that's the thanks I get?'

'Relax now man. Is dat ya rant over wid now? Don't be so sensitive, even dough you got a glass back n dodgy foot. Oh yeah, n ya neck's like Robocop. Sorry Stacey, but Fluffy's mi bitch, e jus as deze moods every now n den!'

'That's alright Jammin', you could say tonight, I'll take ya place n be his Queen Bitch!'

She prodded Joe's left thigh and tickled his left armpit. 'Ouch! No, no, noooooo. Don't make me wriggle, because mi back's still sore and I don't wanna aggravate my neck. Maybe my Queen Bitch will have to sleep in the spare room or on the sofa tonight?' chuckled Joe, slightly straining.

'Where did you expect me to sleep?'

'On the floor in a sleeping bag.'

'Ooooooh…Charmin'! You mean, I don't even deserve the luxury n supreme comfort of ya spare double bed?'

'Of course you do, I'm only teasing!'

'Exactly what I'll be doin' when you receive your lap dance, that is, if I think you deserve it? Hhhhmmmmm.'

'I've been ever so good to you, surely it's a yes!'

'Maaaaan… Look at ya! Pinin' already. It's only been two days. Get yaselves to Gretna or Las Vegas. To me, it sounds like an act o desperation! Ha Haaaaaaaaa.'

'Hhhmmmmm… Yeah, I must agree JB, he is a l'il hungry!'

'Nooo! I'd say, more like, STARVIN', hyena stylie!'

'He's like the proverbial huntsman.'

'You mean, like one o dem dangerous Australian spiders Ash?'

'You got it. Exactly like that. The man smells danger, or should I say…'

'He is danger!'

JB and Ash ironically said the same thing at the same time. The dynamic duo, reminiscent of Batman and Robin, Starsky and Hutch, Superman and Superwoman, Jekyll and Hyde and Jam and Bread.

'I'm gonna go n let you two tuck each other in. Don't wanna be gettin' in da way of any tin man clinches.'

'I think there's more chance of the two of them winning the lottery. It feels quite cold in here, I don't sense any passion? Come here JB, give me a hug.' said Ash teasingly.

'Isn't it about time you two did one?'

'Alright, we get di hint Fluffy. Many tanx for a most wonderous mexicano speciality Stace n tanks for arf decent ospitality Joe. Next time, make sure I ave a tree course meal, wid a knuckle sandwich fa starters.'

'I can organise that. No probs. Come here n give ya close friend a hug. No tongues though.'

JB stood up from the armchair, walked over to Joe and gave him a sincere hug, without squeezing too tightly as he was still feeling sore from the accident. JB stood on his tip toes and licked Joe's ear.

'Uuuuuuurgh! Do ya mind. That's not what I bargained for. A kiss would've been sufficient.'

'Bend down den.'

'Lord, how flexible d'ya think I am. When I start yoga I'll be able to reach four foot. Ha haaaa.'

'What ya sayin'?'

'I'm saying that you're a short ass!'

'You're di donkey. Eeeeeeee-aaaaaaaaaw. El burrito sensacional. Plus I'm almost six foot.'

'You'll be six foot under when I'm fit and healthy again, dropping ya with a big haymaker.'

'Promises, promises.'

'Just you wait midget.'

'Anyway, it's time to go. Jus make sure ya friend's workin' tonight. I don't want im lettin' ya down.'

'Which friend's that?'

'Dat one dats been neglected recently. E's in quarantine. E ain't rabid is e?'

'Ooooh, that friend. Don't worry, he's been well looked after. Fed and watered on a regular basis.'

'Ha haaaaaaaa. Dats quite hilarious fa you. E's been watered alright, but me don't know about fed. E mus o lost weight wid all dis dietin'!' said JB smugly.

'Come on, let's be having you.'

'Many thanks Fluffy and Stace for fabulous hospitality. Next time though, can you put a muzzle on the gargling animal please.'

'Ha haaaaa. I'll send him to captivity next time.'

Ash and JB walked to the hallway, after both hugging Joe and saying their goodbyes. Stacey escorted them, as Joe was feeling a little sore.

'Where are ya shoes boys?'

'In di store cupboard.'

Stacey opened the door and took them out..They put their shoes on and both gave Stacey a hug and a kiss on both cheeks.. Stacey unlocked the door and saw them both out.

'Take care Stace. Opefully see ya next Monday. Don't let im violate you in dere. Slap im into shape.' laughed JB.

'Don't you worry, he's in safe hands n can't move very far.'

'Take advantage of him,' whispered Ash.

'Ooooooooo, you're so cruel. I'll see what I can do though.' replied Stacey.

Stacey closed and then locked the door behind Ash and JB and went back into the living room for a virtual eleventh hour of pure possibly, unadulterated pleasure. Considering Joe's state of health and fatigue, shenanigans of a sexual and sensuous nature were probably off limits.

JB and Ash walked down the four flights of stairs to the front entrance appartment complex door, to the car park. They hugged each other, knuckle touched and said their goodbyes until the next time, which would be within the week, most probably.

Ash walked towards his car, JB to his, climbing in almost simultaneously as they were parked close by. JB turned on his ignition and turned the heater on full to the hot side, as it was quite a cool night. Before driving away, he pulled his phone out of his pocket to see if Beth had responded. His phone had been on silent throughout the movie I Love You, Man as a mark of respect, so as not to disturb anyone. Although, there were many distractions with Joe's dream state gurgling and sledging between him and JB. He typed in the pin code to unlock his phone and not surprisingly, Beth had responded. He read,

'I'm great thx Jammin', was also thinkin' how enjoyable it would be for you to return the compliment! ;-)) Name a time and a place, n not in school time. Call it extra curricular, if you like! ;-P Xx'

He puffed his cheeks out and let out a big sigh.

'Geez man, she means business. Wow, excitin' stuff eh. Lord, mi ed's feelin' all dizzy.'

He took the handbreak off and drove back to his place in Honeyville.

Chapter 29

Mamma Mia

It was Thursday evening already. The last three days had flown by, since JB had been wined and dined by Stacey at Joe's flat. He was on the bus heading back home, deciding what to prepare for tea. His mum was coming round at seven pm. He had to go to the supermarket to buy the essential ingredients. JB had two brothers called Delroy and Douvelle and a sister called Tyresia-Marianna. Delroy was a thirty three year old plumber, Douvelle was a thirty four year old property developer and his sister Tyresia-Marianna was a thirty two year old doctor of medicine. Their mum was a very young fifty two year old called Cheribelle. She married her late husband Sugar when they were eighteen, thirty six years ago. Sugar had tragically passed away seven years ago, due to a brain tumour. It was diagnosed eventually, after dismissive doctors had attributed his persistent headaches, loss of appetite and fatigue to stress, as opposed to referring him to a neuro consultant immediately as a precautionary measure. Consequently and tragically, when he was eventually referred, a brain tumour was diagnosed, this being the most aggressive, graded four. It was because he had collapsed a couple of times at home within a few days, which seriously concerned and upset Cheribelle. She decided to use intuition and took him down to the local casualty department at Lillyford Park Hospital. After having various tests and x-rays within a few hours, the news was delivered to Sugar and Cheribelle, which was devastating. After having neurosurgery and radiotherapy within the space of four months, he had a relapse. The family had been forever optimistic and believed that Sugar would manage to perform a mini miracle and overcome adversity, surviving this trauma. But fate prevailed and he tragically passed a month later in February 2003.

JB was almost at his destination, Tesco's supermarket. He had to get off the number seven bus half a mile from where he lived, in order to buy food shopping for tonight's meal he was going to prepare for his mum. The supermarket was new, having only being opened a few months ago. Compared to most of the other supermarket chains, Tesco was considerably cheaper, so was extremely popular. Being the height of the recession, people had to economise wherever they could, avoiding a carbon footprint and being eco-friendly by using push bikes, car sharing, catching the bus, walking or running. The bus was packed as it was rush hour and the heavy downpour half an hour earlier had meant most people travelling on the number seven had been caught in the midst of it. Jackets were silky looking with streams of water droplets, trousers and skirts sodden uncomfortable, shoes squelching and squeaking, hair dishevelled, the stale odour of cigarette smoke from sodden clothing, sweet scented perfume and unpleasant breath meandering into the atmosphere. JB had left school at four thirty pm, as he had worked a little later, besides he'd enjoyed an after school herbal tea with Bethany in the staff room. That was the real reason he was later heading home. Bethany gave him the pleasure of yet another neck and shoulder massage, but this time, he returned the compliment and did the same for her, apart from one extra special extra curricular treat, a head massage. Some of his very own reiki. They were getting a long very well, although JB knew that if anything happened between them, in terms of sexual behaviour, it would only be fleeting. After his shenanigans with Jennifer at the weekend, he was feeling incredibly horny and intent on relishing some fun with his fellow female teachers. He knew it was unethical, but he found the challenge so incredibly exciting. Bethany also knew that any fornication between the two of them would only be brief. She was quite willing for a no strings attached dalliance with Oatmill's King Romeo. They still hadn't finalised their eagerly waited rendezvous away from Oatmill High School, but no doubt, it was in the pipeline.

He had to get his mind on food shopping, as his stop was next. The bell rang and the bus stopping sign appeared on the LCD parallel to the middle doors on the bottom deck. JB had managed to find a seat at the back of the bus in the corner, the warmer area, as the engine was located at the rear. Thankfully he was dry, as he had decided to take an umbrella to school with him today, plus he had also managed to get to the bus shelter before the heavens opened fully. He was a stickler for checking the weather forecast on a day to day basis. He stood up and the plumpish gentleman to his left hand side moved his knees to the left to enable JB to squeeze past. He made his way to the middle doors, as the bus was pulling in to the stop layby. The doors opened and about ten people got off. JB being his usual courteous self, allowed three or four people coming down from the top deck to get off before him. Eventually, he hopped off.

It was a warmish June evening, with a cloudy covered sky with a few outbreaks of blue and the sunshine endeavouring to force its way through. JB loosened his tie, took off his dark green bomber jacket, folded it up and placed it in his man sack. He was looking distinguished, wearing a white cotton short sleeved shirt, black tailored trousers with a dark grey pin stripe down each side, a thin black belt with a large stainless steel buckle at the front, a v-necked black woollen tank top and a dark green silk tie. His look was finished off with a pair of white Converse Allstars, the ones he wore on Monday evening when he went for dinner at Joe's. His hair was slicked back and tied in a pony tail, emitting a sweet scent of hair mayonnaise.

He crossed the road in between slow moving early evening traffic and made his way to the entrance of Tesco. It was approaching five pm, he had to get a jiggle on, as his Mum would be coming round in two hours. He walked briskly through the car park towards the front entrance automatic doors. He delved into his trouser pocket, pulling out his wallet. He opened it and took a pound coin out. He walked over to the trolley hangar, inserted the coin into the slot, which unlocked the safety chain, enabling him to reverse it out, spin it around and push it towards the store entrance doors.

'Phew, tank god dese wheels are workin' properly n not buckled. Dat's one o di first times in ages I've ad a decent trolley!'

'Yeah, it always seems to happen to me too. Let's high fiiive to thaaat!' said an elderly northern Irish gentleman.

JB gave the guy a high five.

'Yeah man. Dis could be a good shoppin' spree!'

'I sincerely hoope so.' replied the Irish gentleman.

JB waved goodbye to the Irish gentleman and walked into the store, pushing his trustworthy trolley through the automatic sliding doors. He was pondering what to make, so many decisions. A warm evening meal? Fish, meat, tofu (even though his mum wasn't a vegetarian)? A cold summer salad with a starter of soup and croutons or warm crusty baguette with balsamic vinegar and olive oil dip? Maybe a dessert too?

'Hhhhmmmm,' he said quietly to himself.

He pushed the trolley along the fresh fruit and vegetable aisles and picked up a mix of four lemons and limes, ginger, juicy blackberries, courgette, a clump of lemongrass, a bunch of ripe vine tomatoes, mange tout and baby corns, garlic and herb croutons and a punnet of sweet strawberries. His palate was starting to produce a petri dish amount of saliva, as he was being seduced by the glorious attractive mosaic colours of sumptuous fresh and flavoursome nutritious delights. He was in a really buoyant mood, as he was hosting his mum for dinner, the weekend was once again on the horizon, the short term weather forecast was a scorcher and he was intrigued and excited at a potential rendezvous with Beth.

He picked up two packets of mozzarella, a punnet of mediterranean olives with anti pasti comprising of black and green olives and,sundried tomatoes. He was about to prepare a real culinary storm, a proverbial cyclone in the kitchen his mum would relish and cherish. It would have a similar devastating impact as a Category four storm with Cheribelle's gullet trembling, saliva flooding the mouth, culminating in being blown away. He was spinning his trolley one eighty degrees, sliding it to the left, gliding it to the right with such nonchalance, as if he was performing a powerful and purposeful pasa doble! He was hoping his rapid progress wasn't going to be interrupted by someone he knew. Tonight of all nights, he wanted to be literally, in and out. A wham bam thankyou mam! He made his way briskly to the bread section and swiftly picked up a crispy fresh baguette.

'Wooow. Dat's amazin' man. I love di smell o fresh bread.'

'I agree. It takes me baack to those days in Belfaast when I was a wee nippeer. Fresh sweet scented breead, Danish pastries... Totally spellbinding!' said a voice over JB's shoulder.

It made JB jump. It was the same Irish guy he had chatted briefly to outside the store.

'It was di same fa me back in di Caribbean as a young bwoy. Enjoy ya night, take care.'

He now put his foot down as if he was driving a Formula One Grand Prix car around a track trying to record a fastest lap time. He picked up two sirloin steaks, a handful of Ainsley Harriot's cous cous that were on offer at two for a pound. He thought he would buy a cheesecake treat, turning it into a three course special. He spun the trolley round, just thankfully missing an elderly lady with his trolley. She didn't see him, so no need for an apology, maybe because she had just turned into another aisle which saved her from being involved in a trolley carnage, hit and run. Of course though, worst case scenario, JD would have administered first aid.

'Phew, dat was a close shave!' he mumbled.

He picked up the old school traditional lemon cheesecake, making his way towards the checkout.

'Before I check dese tings out, I better get some ice cream too.'

He had to turn right and head back towards the dessert aisle. He stopped at the ice cream fridge freezers. So many different kinds to choose from. Should he buy Haagen Dazs, Ben and Jerry's, Walls? Which flavour should he opt for? Too many choices! In the end, he opted for a generic vanilla, Tesco's own. He was now satisfied, he'd bought all the essentials. It was quite busy, with it being the rush hour run for white, blue collar workers et al finishing their working day. A till just became available as a lady had finished paying and wheeled her trolley away. It was the only checkout of twenty, so it was his lucky day with God, Allah, Buddha or whoever else was on his side. Probably his late father Sugar, floating above providing him with lifetime spiritual protection and inspiration.

'Hi, how ya doin'?' said the guy at the checkout.

'I'm great tanks n you?'

'I'm good thanks. I can't wait till home time though. Would you like a hand with your packing?'

'No, I'll be OK tanks.'

'I'll wait til you've loaded the conveyor belt.'

'Well tanks a lot. Ya very kind. Some o di assistants don't wait fa ya, dey jus start, don't ask ya fa elp n slide tings tru to di end! Dat really frustrates mi. Manners n respect cost a noting.' responded JB.

'It's so easy, just a little customer care.'

The checkout assistant was called Bolly. He was an Asian man, probably in his late twenties to early thirites. He was wearing a white turban of cotton silk which was wound neatly and perfectly around his head. His facial hair was expertly shaped with sideburns pointing southward and a well manicured moustache and goatee. You could tell he took pride in his appearance. He wore a white long sleeved shirt with dark blue pinstripes, a navy blue cravat and plain nylon jacket with dark blue trousers. JB had placed his trolley at the end of the conveyor belt slide, tucked into the side so he could bag up his items and place them straight in.

BEEP... BEEP... BEEP, sounded the scanner as Bolly put items through, one by one.

'Is dat ya real name?' asked JB.

'No man. It's my nick-name. When I was young, my mother n father had dreams of me becoming a Bollywood superstar, so they nick-named me Bolly. My real name's Baljit.'

'Pleased to meet ya Baljit,' said JB winking at him.

'What's your name?'

'Dey call me Jammin' Boy, but mi real name's Duane.'

'Jammin' Boy! I like that name. Are you a musician?'

'No man. I'm a school teacher at Oatmill High.'

'Is that the one near Fruitville?'

'Yeah man, it's just next door to dere.'

'I hear it's a very good school with rave OFSTED reviews.'

'Yeah, it's rated very highly,' responded JB.

'That's twenty four pounds and seven pence please.'

JB took his wallet out of his pocket, opened it and slid his visa debit card out. He then inserted it into the chip and pin machine and keyed in his pin number, placing his right hand round the machine, so no-one could see it.

'Tanks.'

'Would you like cash back?'

'No tanks, jus mi card.'

'Haaaaaa haaaaaa,' laughed Baljit.

JB took his card out of the machine took his receipt from Baljit.

'Many tanks, take care n ave a good night.'

'Many thanks. You too. Bye.'

JB walked to his trolley putting his visa debit card back in his wallet, placing it back in his pocket, nodded to Baljit.

'Bye.'

He pushed his trolley towards the entrance, thankfully he only had three bags that weren't that heavy, so he could manage to walk the short half mile distance home. It was almost five thirty pm, where had the time disappeared to. He had to hurry, as he wanted to prepare dinner and relax. It wouldn't take long to make though, thirty minutes at most.

For the starter he was going to prepare the olives with anti pasti and fresh sliced baguette to dip into balsamic vinegar and olive oil. The main course would comprise of two delicious and incredibly juicy sirloin steaks with a side garnishing of mange tout, baby corns, courgette, chopped lemongrass, peppers, ginger finely skinned and sliced, the citrus juices of lemon and lime, mixed tinned beans, garlic and onion, finished off with a splodging of hot pepper sauce. Dessert would be traditional lemon cheesecake. After putting his trolley back amongst its relatives under the sheltered stand, he walked briskly towards his cosy abode. He managed to make it home before five forty five pm, quick timing. He didn't want to mess around, as his Mum was always punctual, unlike him. When he returned home, after unlocking the back door, opening it, de-activating the burglar alarm, he let Felix out for an early evening run, closed the door, placed the shopping bags full of food next to the cooker hobs and dashed upstairs to get changed.

He undressed and threw his clothes onto the bed quilt and slid his legs into a pair of dark blue Nike jogging bottoms. He put on a plain dark green t-shirt that was from H and M. He was at ease and so comfortable in loose fitting sportswear. At least the house appeared lived in now, with him leaving the landing and downstairs hallway lights on, clothes on the bed and food bags on the side. Because he was very tidy, before he returned from work, anyone could have easily mistaken it for a showhome. He was really happy that his mum was coming round for dinner as it had been a few weeks since he last saw her. He made his way to the kitchen, poured some water into the kettle and pressed the button to boil it. He unpacked the food essentials from the bags, put the two steaks, strawberries, blackberries, mozzarella cheese, anti pasta and cheesecake into the fridge to keep cool and placed the ice cream in the freezer. He closed the light brown horizontal wooden blinds and turned on the hob light. He started to chop the vegetables, starting with a large onion he took out of a kitchen cupboard. He used a medium sized knife from the block at the side of the hob, where his knives were kept. He chopped away, singing to himself in his mind, wiggling his bottom from side to side. After the onion had been finely chopped into tiny squares, he poured some olive oil into the wok resting on the right hand side front hob and turned on the heat to mark three, throwing the onions in. He turned on the hot water tap, squirted in some lemon zested Persil washing up liquid and filled up the bowl in the sink, therefore, he could quite simply dip his hands in to wash them when they were covered in uncooked food particles. It was predominantly for when he had pawed and scored the steak sirloins. He also ran a little bit of cold water into the bowl, so he didn't scald his hands.

The clock was ticking and Cheribelle would be arriving in about an hour. The onions were starting to brown nicely, so JB began to chop the multi-coloured peppers into squares, he placed three cloves of garlic into the crusher without stripping them naked. After seeing this technique on a cookery programme months ago, he was so pleased with himself, as the garlic crusher forced the cold combating vegetable out of their clothes, a kitchen display of indecency. He threw the garlic, sliced peppers, mixed beans and courgette into the wok as he was going to shallow fry the steaks when his Mum arrived, otherwise they'd be ready way too early and wouldn't taste as scrumptiously delicious. He would lace them with pepper, fresh lime and lemon juice with a dribbling of hot pepper sauce to give them more of an explosive kick. The texture would be a finger licking, mouth tingling medium rare, brown on the outside and a healthy beautiful pink in the middle. He turned on the heat extractor, to take away the steam ascending from the wok. It looked like part of a spaceship about to take off to another galaxy, although it had been securely fixed to the wall, above the hob, so there wouldn't be a chance of it going anywhere. He walked over to the fridge, opened it and took out the juicy succulent looking sirloin steaks, closed the fridge and then peeled off the cellophane from the polystyrene tray. He scored them with a sharp knife, dipped his right hand into the hot water in the sink, took it out, shaking off the soap suds, before drying it. He went back to the fridge and took out a lemon and a lime, took a sharp serated edged knife from the rack, dug the grooves into each piece of fruit simultaneously using forward and backward motions. The zesty scent rose into the air, momentarily hypnotising his nasal cavity. One by one he squeezed the juices of the citrus goodness over the steaks, allowing it to permeate deep within the scored grooves of the meat. He sprinkled some black peppercorns over too, then opened one of the top cupboards and took out a bottle of hot pepper sauce. He unscrewed the lid, ooooooooooh, what a super spicy aroma. He drizzled some pepper sauce over both steaks, spinning them over to ensure most parts received some of the flavour enhancing sauce. Time was ticking and Cheribelle would soon be here. Felix started to jump up and scratch the outside of the kitchen front door, besides howling outside. He'd been attracted to the meat feast to be devoured by JB and Mother.

'OK cat... Jus chill out. Come tru di catflap and I'll be wid you in a tickety boo.'

Felix was now starting to scratch frantically at the door, desperate to gnaw away at a juicy piece of rump. Unfortunately that luxury was for the Herbert clan. Felix was part of that, but would have to be content with a whole tin of tuna fish. JB fully immersed his hands in the still hot soap sudded water and washed his hands thoroughly. He took them out, dried them and placed a pan lid from the drainer over the marinating meaty goodness. 'Why don't ya use di flap, ya dumb cat? In ya come den ya docile ting.' JB said, unlocking and opening the door.

Felix came bounding in, dashing backwards and forwards like a vociferous carnivore sniffing the scent of blood with no visible prey in sight. For some unknown reason, he wouldn't always use the cat flap, a most peculiar trait. He was now howling so loudly, desperate for his dinner. Fingers and everything else crossed, he would be satisfied with a full tin of tuna, or maybe not. He was now crouching on his hind legs, preparing to jump up on to the work surface at the side of the hob. JB again opened the cupboard to the left of the hob, above at head height and took out a tin of Prince's tuna. He pulled out the tin opener from the drawer below that cupboard and wound away, turning the handle after securely fitting it to the tin. Hey presto, it was now open and Felix's evening dining session was about to begin. It would be washed down with some ice cold water. JB knelt down and picked up Felix's food dish and placed it on the work surface next to the sink and forked out the tuna flakes into it. He scraped virtually every piece of the flavoursome fish into the bowl. He picked the bowl up and placed it down on the floor to the left of the internal kitchen door. One more ear piercing miaow, as he briskly trotted towards his bowl, rubbing against JB's leg and swishing his tail. He was now in his element, wolfing down the tuna flakes as if there was no tomorrow.

'Relax now cat, you'll give yaself indegestion eatin' like dat. I know ya enjoyin' it, but ave some dinin' etiquette ya wild creature.'

Felix couldn't care less, as long as he had some refined cuisine in his dish, that's all that mattered. JB had an assortment of wines situated in the stainless steel wine racks that were above the top cupboards. He stood on his tip toes and pulled a bottle of rich ruby cabernet sauvignon red down. It was a screw top, so he didn't need to take out the curly wurly bottle opener and force the cork out. The name Cabernet Sauvignon derives from seventeenth century France. A chance meeting, reminiscent of the movie Sliding Doors, where two grapes were acquainted, Cabernet Franc and Sauvignon Blanc. They eloped on a vine and consummated their affection, therefore, the rest is history. This wine is now undoubtedly one of the most popular types in the world. JB adored a sumptuous glass of wine and it was the perfect opportunity with his mother's rendez-vous. He was feeling a little tired after another busy working week, although with it being GCSE revision time for year eleven pupils it was a less hectic time, as his role became more supervisory and advisory, although he still taught English to younger age groups. The summer holidays were on the horizon with only a few weeks left after this one.

SWISH... SWISH...

His mobile phone sounded. It was the wind text alert that he had on his iPhone. He glanced across at it. Another message from Bethany. His face lit up, made even brighter by the kitchen lights. He was extremely happy and really wanton, anticipating a secret date with her. He turned the heat for the onions down low, as there was no rush. His mum would be arriving in just short of three quarters of an hour. He sat down at the table and unlocked his phone and selected his messages. He opened the most recent one from Beth. He read intently, scrolling down with his eyes, which were becoming startled at how suggestive she was being. She was undressing ready for a hot bath and stating how she was stepping into it cautiously and wanting JB to massage the soapy bubbly water into her back and the nape of her neck. She suggested they meet up on Saturday afternoon for a game of pool, ten pin bowling, retail therapy or a few alcoholic beverages, maybe all four? JB was astounded as they had never been intimate, apart from a few relaxing shoulder and neck massages in the staff room at break times. She appeared to have such a firm, toned and curvaceous petite body, so seeing her naked… OMG, in the bath! JB could only fantasise at the moment, but hoped that would become a distinct reality. He was plotting his response.

MIAOW, MIAOW, came the loud and piercing noise from Felix.

'Damn cat, just go n lie down n take di weight off dem paws. You've just ad a full tin o tuna, so ya not gettin' any more jus yet n you can leave dem steaks alone too.'

He would have to put Felix in the living room or outside again, otherwise he was going to be a domestic cat nuisance, or more like the feral kind. Should he be coy, should he be flirtatious, should he be sensuous or should he be intimately sexual with his text reply to Beth? He thought, probably tactful, witty, flirtatious and decorous, as he didn't want to appear too keen and smutty, even though his thoughts were that.

'Beth, I'm so jealous of you bein' in the bath all by yaself. Di water mus be appy at sharin' di bath wid you. Of all di tings in di bathroom, I'd love to be ya sponge, so I could soak up all di water. I reckon we should do a l'il shoppin' n den ave a few drinks Sat avo/eve. Mi mums comin' over in forty mins, so jus conjurin' up a tree course meal. Maybe you could do di same fa me? A massage fa dessert too. I'm fully clothed, as bein' di naked chef aint really appropriate fa dinin' wid Mum. Njoy rest of ya eve, c u 2mro. X ;-))'

He slid his chair backwards and climbed up off it. He walked towards the hobs.

'Don't you dere boy. In fact, you've ad ya dinner, so I'm gonna lock you in di livin' room outta di way, so you can't create any mischief.'

He picked Felix up, pushed the kitchen door open, walked into the hallway, opened the living room door, walked in and dropped him from about three foot. Felix immediately turned round and tried to squeeze through the door and back into the kitchen, but JB was far too quick for him. He opened the door just wide enough to squeeze through, not allowing Felix to follow. He then pulled the door closed behind him. Almost straight away, Felix was scratching away and howling, wanting to follow JB into the kitchen, as he was desperate for a piece of juicy and succulent steak. JB's phone sounded again… SWISH… SWISH!

Unsurprisingly it was a response from Beth. A little shiver flashed down his spine at break neck speed. Telephone text tennis was definitely hotting up. She said how she was dribbling soapy water over her body while being sat up in the bath. How hot she was, but in the presence of JB would be reaching boiling point.

'Wish you were here now. You could pour me a glass of wine, offer me a chocolate and be my tall, dark and handsome stranger.'

Was she hinting at role playing, was she wanting him to seduce her sensuously or just indulge in unadulterated hardcore explicit fornication? His mind was racing twenty to the dozen. Whatever the outcome, he was looking forward to shopping with her this Saturday afternoon along with any additional potential extras. It would be entertaining to say the least. To relieve his mind from the impending frivolity, he decided to pour himself a glass of Casillero Del Diablo which was a Chilean Cabernet Sauvignon, deep, rich and immensely fruity. He unscrewed the top, opened the cupboard full of different types of glasses and took two out and placed them on the work surface. He poured himself a glass and filled it just over half full. The glass was a statuesque design and if it were a model, it would be a super one at the very least. Seven o'clock would soon be here, so he took out a griddle pan for the sumptuous sirloin steaks and then slid the long sizeable baguette from its protective sheath and placed it on the bread board. He took out the bread knife from the block and walked over to the fridge, opened it, crouched down and took out some butter. Creamy and delicious Lurpak. Uuuum uuuuum! He began to cut the baguette into small slices and then placed them in a round blue and dark grey ceramic dish he had taken out earlier. In between slicing the bread and placing it in the bowl, he gave the onions, peppers, courgette, mixed beans and garlic a stir. They were done, but he wanted to keep them warm, that's why he left the hob on, but turned down low. He took a few sips of his wine.

'Dat's di bomb man. I love dat wine, it's so juicy n sweet, prob just like Beth's breasts n body. Oooooo-haaaaaaaa. Felix, ya missin' out cat, not on di wine, but di sirloins. Ha haaaaaaa.'

That was a little bit cruel to Felix, but he couldn't hear him through both closed doors. Speaking of loins, the prospect of being amongst Beth's was mouthwatering to say the very least. Possibly very juicy like the fresh cut of beef. His mind had to return to his three course dinner as Mum would be here in ten minutes or so. He picked up the bottle of Balsamic vinegar that was to the left of the hob along with the olive oil. He took out two small rectangular shallow white ceramic bowls to pour the concoction of oil and vinegar in for the sliced baguette to dip in. He was now bursting for the toilet, so left everything in situ, picked up his phone, opened the kitchen door and dashed upstairs. As he passed the living room door, he noticed Felix was thankfully distracted rolling around on the floor with his favourite toy, or so it seemed. He just made it to the toilet, switching the light on outside the door, lifting the lid up, pulling his jogging pants down, sitting down and squirting faster than the speed of light. It's probably a good job he sat down lady like, otherwise there could have been a toxic flood all over the bathroom floor. Imagine the stench and then having to clean it all up. Uuuuuuuurgh. He wiped himself with a few sheets of toilet roll, shook his manhood a few times, stood up, pulled his pants up, placed the lid down and flushed the toilet. He washed his hands with some creamed soap and warm water and then made his way downstairs after turning the tap off. He was so unbelievably hungry, licking his lips like a hungry hippo. As he passed the living room door which was glass partitioned, he glanced in to see Felix still rolling around with what he first thought was a toy. He opened the door.

'Feliiiiiiix! What d'ya tink ya playin' at cat!'

He picked up the water spray that was on the marble fire place hearth, and squirted him with it. Felix had only bitten off part of a Yukka plant leaf and was chewing it profusely and spitting out the remnants on the floor boards. JB wasn't a happy man. He almost drenched Felix with the water, which resulted in him being bemused. Hopefully it would teach him a powerful lesson and he wouldn't make the same mistake twice. Felix took the treatment really offensively and resigned to cowering away in the corner of the room, shaking his fur profusely to dry himself out. He cut a folorn feline figure, licking his fur and miaowing loudly. JB jogged upstairs to the airing cupboard to get him a towel to dry his fur, obviously he wasn't capable of drying himself apart from air dry. He took out a thick fluffy dark grey towel, threw it over his shoulder and trotted back downstairs to Felix's rescue. He was rolling around on the wooden floor trying to self dry. JB opened up the towel and smothered Felix in it. Eventually he started to return to his normal self and began to purr.

'Dat's better boy. Dere's no need to go on di rampage because you can't ave any steak. It's damn expensive, but den again, you wouldn't know wid me payin' all di bills. I don't expect you to understand when ya a kept catty watty!'

JB crouched down and gave him a kiss on his virtually dried belly, rubbed it, picked him up and nuzzled him. He then put him down, allowing Felix to go for a crazy mad frantic run. He dashed backwards, forwards, sideways like a possessed creature. JB forgot where he was and what he was doing before having to intervene an animal plant attack.

'Dat's right, I better put some olives n anti n uncle pasti in a bowl as an hors d'oeuvres. Momma'll love dat.'

He moved back into the kitchen, washed his hands after touching Felix, dried them and took out the olives and antipasta from the fridge and put the whole portion into a small rounded blue and grey bowl. He still hadn't set the table yet, so before placing the bowls containing anti pasta, array of oils and sliced baguette on the oval sculptured masterpiece, he took cork place mats and cutlery out of the respective drawers and placed them down. Now he could decorate the table with a beautiful assortment of colours. He was looking forward to seeing his mum as it had been a few weeks.

Chapter 30

Dinner Date

He heard the front gates being opened and shortly after the soft revving of an engine, an indication that she was here. The engine was turned off, door opening and then slamming shut, followed by a double beep of his mum locking the doors and activating the immobiliser.

He couldn't hear any footsteps, but the gentle knock of the door.

'Who is it?'

'What d'ya mean, who is it?' asked Cheribelle.

'Oooh, is it you Momma?'

'Of course it's me. Couldn't you tell by the sound of the car engine and immobiliser?' she asked.

'Mum, am I supposed to be able to identify every car engine n immobiliser? I'm not a car engine spottin' anorak!'

'You wouldn't look out of place though wearing an orange anorak and a thick rimmed pair of Scooby Doo Velma sized glasses. Ha Haaaaaaaaaa.'

'Ha Haaaaaa Mum. Very funny!' responded JB.

'So what's cooking son?'

'Take ya shoes off, don ya slippers, off wi di jacket n savour a glass o di finest refinest Casillero Del Diablo, it tastes divine.'

JB took his mum's jacket and hung it up in the hallway on the coat racks.

'It's warm in here, can't you open a window to cool it down?'

'Probably because you've ad ya jacket on, dat's why ya feelin' like toast.'

'I think it's the heat from the hob and my hot blooded son.'

'Ha Haaaaa. Stop it Mum, don't embarass me!'

'Weeell son, I never know where you are with the ladies. You change as often as I change my knickers, so that's often. Ha haaaaaaaa.'

'I don't need to know how often, but I hope it's daily!'

'Get me that drink you promised anyway.'

'Comin' right up.'

JB put the griddle pan on the hob and turned the heat on full, so he could sizzle the sirloin in a few minutes. He poured a small amount of olive oil into the pan and then poured a glass of red for Cheribelle.

'What d'ya tink?'

'Uuuuum. It's sensational. Ya Dad would love this.'

'E can ave a drink up above wid us. To di Erbert crew, ealth, appiness and PHAT love to y'all! Cheers Momma!'

'Cheers to you too Duane.'

'It sounds so funny Mum, when ya call me Duane. I'm jus so used to Jammin' or JB.'

'You were christened Duane, so you should be proud of that name.'

'I am, but jus prefer mi nicknames.'

'The youth of today, eh.'

'Aaaaw… tanks Mum, dat's a real compliment bein' referred to as a yout at my age, just touchin' di tip of tirty!'

The griddle pan was starting to smoke now as the heat was scorching. He flipped both steaks in, dinner was almost ready. Cheribelle sat down at the table and made herself comfortable. JB opened the top cuboard, took a box of matches out, closed it and walked over to the table to light the vanilla and chocolate candle, struck the match, the flame glowed, so he lit it and then wafted it out. He wet the match in the bowl of soapy water in the sink and then threw it in the bin.

'Would you like ya starter now?'

'Ooo… yes please.'

'Comin' right up.'

He took a large plate out of the drainer and put the sliced baguette on and carried it over to the table. He then went back to the work surface and took the grey and blue bowl with olives and anti pasti over to the table, so his Mum could tuck into the starter.

'Uuuuum, this looks absolutely delicious, crikey. I love anti-pasti.'

'I sometimes wonder why dey don't call it uncle pasti? Really baffles me.'

'Why would they call it uncle pasti when it's anti?'

'Well fa me Momma, it's sexist ya kno. It ain't right dat since women got di vote tirty or forty odd years ago, you get everyting ya own way dese days. I mean look at child custody, abortion rights etc. I tought we were livin' in times of equality?'

'Duuuaaaane, me n your Dad brought you up with respect, high morals, dignity and integrity, so I don't expect you becoming a sexist pig… OINK… OINK. Ha haaaaaa.'

'Ya so funny. Whenever ya click ya fingers you expect men to jump, n not just off a chair or di sofa, but over di ighest of urdles,' he said sucking his teeth.

'Wine please.'

JB clicked his fingers, 'Yes Momma, ere it comes at last. Talk about exclusive V.I.P. luxury treatment by And-Air.'

He poured the Cabernet Sauvignon into the bulbous glass, pulled a piece of kitchen roll off the reel near the cooker, wiped the rim and then took the three quarter full glass to his mum. He dashed back to the hob, flicked the steaks over as they were sizzling away in the griddle pan. They looked to be cooked almost perfectly on the under side and a rich rosy pink in the middle. He re-checked the mix of beans, onions, peppers and courgette in the wok, took off the lid and gave them another stir. They had been simmering for a good twenty minutes and were ready to be served. He turned the heat off, replaced the lid and moved the wok to an empty hob.

'These nibbles are delicious Duane.'

'Dere called hors d'oeuvres Mum,' he said in a French accent.

'OK son. I know my cuisine, but just for you…These hors d'oeuvres are sensational. Uuuuuum. The drizzling of balsamic and olive oil gives them a more flavoursome taste, mixed in with the uncle pasti.'

'Now we're talkin'. Ya startin' to make perfect sense!'

JB took some kitchen foil out one of the kitchen drawers, pulled it out and then ripped a one foot piece on the serated edge of the box. He took the scrumptious sirloin steaks out of the griddle pan and placed them on the foil and wrapped them up to keep them warm. He joined his Mum at the table and tucked into the tasty french baguette slices with dip and anti pasti.

'Wow, dese are so damn tasty. Ya know what we cud ave done wid.'

'Tell me Duane.'

'Some anchovy's trown into di mix. A more salty n stingin' taste to it.'

'You're right, it would have given more of a sharpness, but still, they're scrumptious.'

JB and Cheribelle were relishing their starter and savouring the rich essences of the red wine. They chatted about family and reminisced about when Dad was alive. Laughing and joking, thoroughly enjoying their quality time together. The steaks were cooked absolutely perfectly, dark brown on the outside and a juicy, succulent and mouthwatering bright pink in the middle. A divine médium rare.

'Oooooh, this is out of this world Duane. Thankfully some of the traits your Dad and I taught you have worked wonders. The pepper on the steak gives it a spicier taste along with the drizzling of hot pepper sauce.' Cheribelle said licking her lips.

'Dat's ow I work wonders on mi girls Momma, dine n lime em.'

'Liming' was a West Indian term for dancing. In the West Indies there are many spoken dialects, all a form of the English language. Another word for dialect in the West Indies is Creole. The language is English with an African influence as West Indians migrated from there in the seventeenth century. West African migration led to West Indian islands developing their own languages due to the 'slave trade', where new inhabitants began working on sugar plantations! Saint Kitts is a tiny island in the heart of the Caribbean with forty thousand residents. It's located in amongst the Leeward Islands, the other group of Islands are called Winward Isles. Saint Kitts otherwise known as St. Christopher also has a sibling, similar to JB, although he had three. Nevis is the sister island situated over the Caribbean Sea water two miles away across a shallow channel called 'The Narrows.'

JB had added some cous cous too. He had boiled it in hot water on the hob, when it was ready he mixed the courgette, onions, mixed beans and peppers in the same pan. It looked an attractive spectrum of colour. The steak was easy to cut because of the perfect texture, not quite like a knife through Lurpak butter, just slightly tougher. JB's phone sounded again with its normal customised text SWISH.

'Duane, can't you put your phone on silent while you're at the dinner table?'

'Mum, I'm not dinin' at a restaurant wi di most decorous, select n refined o company, I'm in mi own ouse, drinkin' mi own wine, munchin' mi own food n angin' wid mi Momma. Dere's no reason fa mi to be discrete.'

'Good point well made son. Still, I want to savour Mother and Son time tonight without any distractions.'

'Ows dat gonna appen wen Felix is next door?'

'I forgot to ask, where he is. Are you going to let him in?'

'I've saved im a l'il piece of rump, so yeah, e can come in n eat dat.'

JB slid his chair backwards, stood up and walked towards the internal kitchen door, opened it, moved into the hallway and opened the living room door.

'MIAOW... MIAOW!

'Hello beautiful, how you doing?' asked Cheribelle.

Felix scampered over to her, starting to purr loudly, swishing his tail side to side and rubbing his chin against her open hand.

'Come ere now boy, enjoy dis delicious piece o meat.'

JB quickly cut up a chunk of steak into small pieces and put it in Felix's dish. No messing around now, he bounded over to the delicacy and started chewing away like there was no tomorrow.

'He's enjoying that.'

'You kno what e's like Mum, e enjoys everyting. Can you believe it, before you came, e was munchin' on dat yukka plant. I ad to spray im wi di water.'

'Was that while you were preparing dinner?'

'Yeah man.'

'How many times do I need to tell you, I'm not a man. Maybe I'm becoming hormonally challenged in my older years, but I'm still very feminine.'

'You know it's just a figure of speech.'

'Yeah woman.' Cheribelle mimicked him.

'Ha haaaaa. I see you aven't lost ya humour.'

The food smelt absolutely ravishingly divine. The scent was drifting effortlessly through the airwaves, it was so hypnotising, if it was a drug it would have been hallucinogenic and worth millions to underground international cartels. The Cabernet Sauvignon was flowing, the fur on Felix's body appeared to be growing while the eyes of JB and Cheribelle were brightly glowing. The food was being consumed with elegant etiquette, although they were wolfing it down like a teenager desperate to get out and play with his friends, it would not have mattered. They weren't exactly dining at a blue michelin five star restaurant. So who cared, however, eating with refinement was always the preferred style, especially when Cheribelle and the late Sugar had taught their four children that trait.

'Uuuuuuum. This is finger licking, lip smackingly delicious. You'd make some lucky lady a fabulous husband. When are you gonna find someone?'

'Mum, I'm jus enjoyin' miself at di moment, it's di least o mi worries. When di right woman ascends from di emergin' distance, possessin' di right traits, I'll know she's di one.' said JB with aplomb.

'You're approaching thirty, so I thought you'd be wanting a woman on your arm?'

'Mum, it ain't important. You n Dad were married young, but times ave now changed, it's a new generation ya know.'

'I know that, but still, you don't wanna be a bachelor into your forties do ya?'

'Dere's no pressure. If I am, den so be it. I will say dough, I saw dis stunnin' n sensational woman at Oatmill di udder week. Boy, she di ottest ting I seen fa years. Our eyes met along di corridor, but I didn't stop to get er name. Apparently she was visitin' from Latvia fa dis cultural week we ad. I need to track er down someow, like a clinical assassin. Jus call me Bridget Fonda. Ha haaaaaa.'

'Well son, if she's in Latvia, that won't work will it?' said Cheribelle.

'Ya never know, she may be plannin' on emigratin' ere. Dere part o di European Union too, so she don't need a visa.'

'Can't you be sensible and think about someone closer to home? There are lots of beautiful women in Lillyford, Marlborough and other suburbs close by. You've also got Mangoville and Fruitville if you prefer more exotic and cultural ladies.'

'Que sera, sera, whatever will be, will be, the future's not ours to see, que sera, sera!' JB sang.

'If I had mystical powers, Duane, you'd be married with children already.'

'Thankfully ya don't. Pheeeew, what a relief,' sighed JB.

'Ooooo, the baguette tastes out of this world when you mix it with the cous cous sauce from the beans and steak.' said Cheribelle dreamily.

'Yeah, di juices all work together in dere own exquisite way.'

The second and main course was almost finished, so the traditional lemon cheesecake was next on the edible hitlist, while Felix had his mind on some more steak, but that was finished.

MIAOW... MIAOW.

'Ya can jus relax in di room n let ya belly settle now. You've ad today's taste tinglin' treat.'

'What delight do we have for dessert?'

'One of ya favourites. Traditional lemon cheesecake wid fresh cream or ice, take ya pick.'

'That sounds awfully yummy,' Cheribelle replied in a posh accent.

'Oooh, Mother, it will be incredibly divinely, delectably delicious, I say,' responded JB.

'Just out of curiosity though, didn't you say with fresh cream or ice?' Cheribelle replied, rather puzzled.

'I did Mum. Ice cream, not ice. Dat'd be a weird blend fa dessert.'

Cheribelle's plate was now like a ghost town, while JB was finishing the last remnants of his main course, his plate looking more like a crowded village with hundreds of pieces of cous cous mixed in with beans, vegetables and a half eaten slice of discoloured baguette, looken rather sodden, covered in balsamic, olive oil and hot pepper sauce from the steak.

'I'm ready for my dessert, with ice please. Oops, I mean ice with a little splashing of cream, but not the fresh kind.'

'Funny woman.'

'One loves to engage in a l'il humour from time to time.'

'You've missed ya vacation.'

'Vacation? I'm going with the girls this summer.'

'OK, I meant vocation.'

'What are you doing this year, besides hunting down that Latvian lady?'

'I'm possibly gonna ead to Europe or Latin America wid Rocca, Ash, Fluffy Donkey and C-Man n anyone else dat wants to travel wid us.'

'Any ideas?'

'I'd love to go to Mexico, Brazil, Argentina n a few other Latin countries, or maybe jus chillout in Californ-IA on Venice Beach n den maybe pass tru Las Vegas. Dat'd be amazin', dem golden beaches, bronzed honeys, crystal clear waters, blue skies n unbroken sunshine. Wouch, I'm dreamin' already,' said JB smiling like a Cheshire cat.

'That sounds fab. Have you asked Delroy and Douvelle if they want to join ya?'

'No, not yet. I tink Delroy would wanna come, but probably not Douvelle. Plus I don't tink is girlfriend'd be too keen on di idea.'

'You may be surprised, because he tells me she's going away with her girlfriends this year.'

'Seriously!' JB responded in a state of shock.

'I know! I was dumbfounded when he told me. She isn't the right girl for him, she's far too possessive.'

'I've always tought di same ting. I'd be delighted if e came. We'd ave a real blast.'

'Apparently she's going away to celebrate one of her friends thirtieth birthdays.'

'Dat seems a l'il weird when she's always been reluctant to let im jet off wid is friends. I don't trust er. She's too much of a diva fa me Momma.'

'Yeah, I totally agree with you. I'm so pleased he never got a house with her, she's trouble.'

'It was di best ting e did, buyin' n renovatin' ouses to earn some good money for investments.'

'I'm so relieved too. She was always so insistant for them to buy a place together, but thankfully he's so switched on, he never succumbed.'

'Damn right!'

'Jenna's now hinting that she wants to start a family.'

'No man.'

'There you go again.'

'Oooops... Sorry, I mean woman... Mum... I ope e's sensible, because she's di kinda girl dat could dupe im.'

'My thoughts entirely.'

'At least fa once, we're on di same ymn sheet! Ha haaaaaa.'

'Are you going to finish your dinner? It's going to be cold otherwise.'

'OK Mum. I know ya intin' ya want ya cheesecake. I'll urry up n finish.'

'Don't rush, enjoy it. I wouldn't want to start without you anyway.'

JB resumed with the remainder of his dinner. Cheribelle was so looking forward to the lemon cheesecake, her favourite dessert. JB had three reasons to be happy. He was delighted to host his Mum for dinner. He was excited at the prospect of a rendezvous with Beth at the weekend. The summer holidays were rapidly approaching on the horizon. He was even more delirious that his two brothers Delroy and Douvelle might be joining him and his friends too, for an international boys' adventure. If his two brothers joined the holidaying entourage, they'd have an absolute scream. JB, Delroy and Douvelle were all so lively, they made a sparking plug appear lifeless.

'I better phone di bros dem, to discuss possible oliday aunts. We'll probably get a las minute cancellation, because it'll be far cheaper.'

'You can surf the Internet or check deals on teletext, they have some fantastic offers.'

'Good idea, it could save us a fortune.'

'If you don't hurry up with that dinner, I'm going to attack it myself.'

'Sorry Mum, I know ya droolin' over dat cheesecake.'

JB continued devouring his cous cous, last piece of rump steak and vegetables. Cheribelle was beginning to feel restless, as he was taking an eternity to finish. In his defence, his Mum did tend to eat at a ridiculously unhealthy sprinting pace. That's why she always struggled with indigestion. How could she actually enjoy food when it was shovelled down the throat at record breaking tempo? The taste buds would surely barely get the opportunity to savour and experience the tantalising array of flavours most people who ate at a sensible speed would enjoy.

'My Lord, you've eventually finished. You took your time,' Cheribelle commented.

'Mum, di difference is, I take mi time so I can savour every l'il juicy drop, where as you attack n devour like a rampant carnivore who asn't eaten fa weeks.'

'Less of your cheek, Duane.'

'It's true. Food's dere to be enjoyed n relished, not to be abused.'

'Speaking of which, cut the cheesecake so I can abuse that,' said Cheribelle, laughing.

'Momma, ya gonna adore dis. It's Tesco's own. I bought it from di one in Unnyville.'

'How many times have I encouraged you to use your h's. I thought after all these years, you may have started to pick them up off the floor. You've dropped so many over the years.'

'They've probably been rescued by the ambulance staff n taken to di ospital fa life savin' treatment. I keep tryin' to pick em up, but dey're jus too evvy fa me.'

'When you teach do you use them?'

'It's di only time I do, some o di time anyway, as I need to encourage to kids to speak properly n express demselves wid proper articulate English language.'

'I'd love to be a fly on the wall in the classroom, I'm sure it'd be like watching a sitcom, with entertainment by the minute.'

'You'd be in ya element at di back o di class. I wouldn't charge you fa di performance either. Free comedy at Oatmill High. Ha haaaaaaaa.'

What a huge relief, it was now dessert time and Cheribelle had the mouthwatering prospect of enjoying the delicious lemon cheesecake that JB was raving about.

'I can't believe you didn't make your own, you've got the ability son.'

'Many tanks. I know, it's jus dat, after di busy weekend wid partyin' for Tom's thirtieth birthday n den di accident involvin' Fluffy Donkey, Ashilito n

Stacey, den bein' back at work, I aven't ad di chance. Next time dough Mum, I promise I'll make it all from scratch.'

'I look forward to that experience.'

JB pushed his chair backwards, stood up and took the plates to the sink, ready for washing. He had a dishwasher, but preferred the traditional method of washing by hand and occasionally donned a pair of marigolds. He opened the fridge, taking out the beautiful smelling cheesecake. It looked yummy. He placed it down on the work surface next to the cooker and then took a knife out of the knife block. He removed all the packaging and the sweet scent started to ascend towards his nasal cavity.

'Wouch, dat's di proverbial bomb. If it was a drug I'd be igher dan di ighest Stateside skyscraper. As some people say, dat's di dog's balearics.'

'Duaaaaaane! Watch your tongue now. In fact I've got a good mind to throw your head into that bowl of soapy water! It's disgusting language.'

'Dog's balearics! Ow is dat disgustin' behaviour. It ain't an expletive.'

'Duaaaaane! Please, refrain from that talk.'

'Ooooo-K Mum. Dog's bollocks!'

'That's a lot better. Just call them what they are. Don't use all these modern associations, when you can use the right words.'

'So ya gonna encourage me to use the word bollocks as opposed to balearics, which is a more respectable analogy. You know I don't like swearin' n use di decorum dat you n Dad taught me.'

'You're right son. I was only joking. Come on then, sort the cheesecake out!' laughed Cheribelle.

'Yeah, I'm right on it. A big lion size piece comin' right up.'

JB threw the packaging in the bin, apart from the tray it was placed in. He cut the cake into quarters, the knife working that bit harder to work its way through the hardened biscuit base crumbs. He opened the cutlery drawer and took out the triangular shaped stainless steel spatula to scoop up a piece for him and his mum and then shut it. He turned around and took two small plates from the dish drainer and put them next to the hob alongside the cheesecake. He lifted one piece out at a time and placed them on each plate. He took them over to the table and put them down.

Meanwhile in the living room, Felix was snuggled up on the couch, resting on a light brown cotton cushion, probably dreaming about his antics with his girlfriend Petra.

'Would ya like another glass o wine?'

'I can't because I'm driving.'

'You can stay in di spare room if ya like.'

'In fact I think I will and then I can relax, without having to drive home.'

'Good. I'll give ya dat second glass o wine den.'

'Please. Also, haven't you forgotten something?'

'Apart from mi mind, I don't tink so!' JB said rather puzzled.

'Think again. Come on, you even mentioned to me about half an hour ago.'

'Eeeeerrrrm. I can't tink, remind me!'

'You doughnut.'

'You tryin' to say I'm full o sugar wid a tasty jammy centre?'

'Nooo. You've got a short term memory. You asked me if I wanted fresh cream or ice cream with the cheesecake. Dooooh!'

'Ooooops. Must be di effects o dat first glass o wine. It's quite strong at tirteen point five percent. Sorry! What would ya like den?'

'I'll go for ice cream please.'

'Dat makes two of us. Is standard vanilla alright fa ya?'

'That'll be perfect thank you.'

JB bent down, opened the freezer and took out the vanilla ice cream. He closed the door and then opened the cutlery drawer once more to take out the ice cream scoop. He picked up the bottle of Cabernet Sauvignon, ice cream and scoop taking them to the kitchen table. 'Dere ya go Momma, cheesecake a la Tesco, Cabernet Sauvignon and the cream of the crop.'

'At last Duane, I never thought this moment was going to arrive.' Cheribelle said sarcastically.

JB placed a plate of cheesecake on both cork mats for him and his mum. He poured another glass of wine for his mum and one for himself as they had both finished theirs. He took the lid off the ice cream, picked up the stainless steel scoop and dug it into the ice cream.

'It's too ard at di moment, I'm gonna ave to leave it a few mins mum.'

'I thought you might have taken it out of the freezer twenty minutes or so ago?'

'I was so engrossed in convo wid you n mi scrumptious rump n vegetable erbs wid cous cous.'

'Because you were eating at snail pace. I did keep hinting, but you dismissed me.'

'Because I don't wolf it down like a hyena, I take mi time n enjoy di delights of all dem flavours!'

'Have a little more respect for your precious mother. Don't be so rude!' Cheribelle remarked disaprovingly.

'If ya gonna imply dat I eat like a snail, what's wrong wi me sayin' you munch like a wild dog? It's jus di same. Only because ya older dan me you infer it's disrespectful. We're both grown adults, so respect should be reciprocated.'

'I do respect you son, but accusing a woman of eating like a wild dog isn't exactly respectful is it?'

'Yeah Mum, ya right. Sorry bout dat, but you do eat damn quick! Dat's why you get indigestion so often.'

'Let us digress please and stop making analogies to wild creatures great and small.'

'Ow's di cheesecake?'

'It tastes really nice, but I'm not going to eat any more until the ice cream's softer.'

'Let me try it again wi da scoop.'

'Aaaaaah, Result. That looks a lot softer now.'

'It's just about prrrrrrfect. Felix would love dis!'

As if by magic, the strong predator senses of the domesticated pedigree cat had drawn him into the kitchen.

MIAOW... MIAOW!

'OK Flixy, I'll put you some in ya bowl.'

'You treat him like a king. You better be careful though, otherwise he'll be getting fat.'

'E gets plenty of exercise, so e'll be mighty fine.'

JB put two scoops on his mum's plate and two scoops on his own. It looked a delicious delight next to the pastel shaded lemon cheesecake. They both dug their spoons into the soft and creamy cheesecake.

'This is delicious Duane, but I know you can do just as good a job yourself.'

'Many tanks Mum. I probably could, but dint ave di time tonight, as I ad to go to di supermarket straight from school. I'm definitely gonna make one though, next time.'

'You've acquired your culinary skills from your beloved mother.'

'True, but I also got some from mi dad too.'

'Let's propose a toast to your dad.'

'Dat's a good idea. Dad, we love you incredibly, wish you cud be ere to enjoy dis, tanks fa all di qualities you've provided n all di humorous experiences our lives ave been littered wid. One love always, rest in peace.'

They clinked their wine glasses together, said,

'Cheers, to Dad,' and had a big sip of the wine. The cheesecake was being enjoyed by both and was rapidly being eaten by Cheribelle, while JB was slowly cutting away and eating the tasty dessert. They were both feeling quite tired after a long day. JB had been up since about seven thirty-ish while Cheribelle had worked a full day at the small charity shop situated in Lillyford city centre. She worked nine till five on Wednesday and Thursday. This gave her alot of freedom, which she enjoyed, keeping her busy along with regular visits to the gym and attending various courses ranging from knitting to sewing to cooking to D.I.Y. His mum had always been active, regularly working out at the local Virgin Active gym, attending various fitness classes from body pump to spin to pilates, and spending down time in the spa area, an ideal therapeutic forum for chilling. Since her husband Sugar had passed away, over seven years ago, she had immersed herself in various arts and crafts, which gave her the perfect opportunity to divert her attentions into positive elements. Sugar and Cheribelle had been inseparable for about thirty five years, meeting in the Caribbean in 1968 when Cheribelle and Sugar were both in their late teens. Cheribelle had travelled over there on a family holiday, they met and had a romance, which fortunately blossomed. They went virtually everywhere together, enjoying a successful and pleasurable life until tragedy struck in 2002. They had brought up their four children with good moral values, ethics that were important to enable them to be responsible, respectful, honest, sensitive and obedient people. These traits had been instrumental in giving Douvelle, Delroy, Tyresia-Marianna and Duane a good grounding in life, thus enhancing their lives in both a social and professional capacity.

JB was starting to drift off momentarily.

'Duaaaane, you're falling asleep. Do you want to wake up with a face full of cream?'

'Eeerm. So… so… so… sorry Mum. I tink I was jus dosin' a l'il. Mus be di effects of all di kids, wearin' mi out.'

'I'd probably attribute it to the girls in your life tiring you out. The strong flavoursome red wine along with another long day at work,' said Cheribelle, laughing.

'I don't ave any girls in mi life, apart from you n Tyresia! Di wine's defo avin' an effect dough.'

'Hmmmm... So who have you been frantically texting tonight then?'

'Oh... Dat's just a friend from school.'

'What's her name?'

'She's called Bethany, Beth fa short.'

'I can see she's more than a friend with that smirk on your face,' said Cheribelle.

'No Mum, we're jus friends, but she's a good girl.'

'That's what you need in your life, some stability, love... Someone to look after you.'

'Dat's why I've got you.'

'Duane, you're not a Mummy's boy, you're a responsible and successful young man, but you can't go out and party for ever.'

'Dere's no rush ya know. When it appens, it appens. Dem quality ladies are ard to find dese days, I probably need a faith ealer. Ha haaaaaaa.'

'You need a heel alright. One kicking up your backside,' said Cheribelle.

'Mum, dat cud be construed as child abuse. I don't tink I need to be subjected to dat behaviour. Eels are OK in di outside world n di bedroom, n maybe di kitchen, but not in di room or bathroom. Haaaaaaa haaaaaaa.'

'I think I'd be slightly concerned if I saw eels in the house. I know cockneys love the jellied kind, but certainly not for me. They're disgusting slippery creatures.'

'Muuuuum! What ya talkin' about?'

'You mentioned about eels being worn in the most obscure places?'

'Muuuum! You said I needed an eel up di backside! Dat's perverse too. I ope ya not advocatin' incestuous means?? Mi exit ole's solely fa defacatin' n breakin' wind, but not fa any crazy bestiality insertions of a foreign kind.'

'Duaaaaaane! I'm talking about footwear, not slippery creatures that live in waterways.'

'Geeeeeeez! Now ya tell me!'

'I think your mind's working overtime. Too many creative and enterprising assignments for your students.'

'No Mum, I jus miseard what you said.'

'Probably because your head's St. Elsewhere. You're too engrossed in texting your lady friend.'

'I've only sent a few texts tonight. I'm jus tired after another long week at work n dis wine's goin' straight to mi ead.'

They continued to enjoy the scrumptious flavours of the cheesecake with vanilla ice cream. The ice cream gave the dessert a more soothing touch. They were almost finished, JB struggling to keep his eyes open, Cheribelle still alert and wanting to watch some late night TV. After their three course meal, it was time to wash the dishes, sit down and relax. Upstairs to the supreme comfort of bed was the ideal recipe for JB. Cheribelle placed her stainless steel dessert spoon on to the empty plate that had a slithery light dressing of ice cream remnants left, entwined with cheesecake crumb base bits. The spoon handle clanged against the edge of the plate, soon followed by JB's, which was rather astounding, as he normally ate slowly.

'That was absolutely sensational. Next time, I look forward to experiencing the divine, distinguished and delectable delight of my son's very own homemade cheesecake, as opposed to the packaged supermarket version.'

'Yeah Mum. I promise you I will. It's just a l'il difficult when I'm slavin' all day n den ave to ead to Tesco's to buy las minute provisions.'

'Still Duane, you excelled as usual. The main course was of a very high standard and the starter was a lovely tasty number.'

'Many tanks Mum. I enjoyed it too.'

They both pulled their chairs out from under the table, picked their plates up and carried them to the sink.

'I'll wash, Mum n you can dry.'

'Deal.'

JB emptied the cold foamy water into the sink, turned on the hot water tap, picked up the Persil lemon washing up liquid and squirted some into the bowl. He turned on the cold tap slowly too, to make sure he had the perfect mix, not scorching hot, but warm enough to kill bacteria and clean the utensils. When the bowl was three quarters full, he turned both taps off, and swirled his hands around to agitate the washing up liquid until he was happy with the consistency. He possessed some obscure traits when it came to various tasks. It was a mild form of obsessive compulsive disorder. Cheribelle picked up the tea towel and waited for him to place items in the drainer. One by one he thoroughly cleaned, making sure that all particles of food had disappeared from the crockery and cutlery.

'You're taking your time Duane, can you get a move on? At this rate we'll still be here at pumpkin time.'

'Dere's no rush, it ain't a race to finish Mum!'

'I know, but I'd like to sit down, relax and watch some late night tele.'

'I feel like goin' straight to bed. Mi eyes are strugglin' to stay open n mi legs feel ready to collapse.'

'You can collapse on the sofa while we watch something.'

'Muuuum, I don't wanna be stayin' up too late, it's a school night n I need mi beauty zzzzz's. It's almost nine o'clock.'

'Surely you can manage at least another half an hour?' said Cheribelle.

'Dat's probably di maximum n den I'm in dreamworld.'

'I know where your mind will be.'

'Where's dat den?'

'Immersed in seductive shenanigans with one of your ladies.'

'I don't ave any ladies at di mo.'

'Swear!'

'Mum, you brought me up wid respect, moral decency n integrity. Why di ell am I gonna swear in front of di most precious woman in mi life!'

'You just did!'

'Rubbish. I'd never do dat.'

'You just said the word rhyming with swell.'

'Oooops… Soooooorry, it jus slipped out.'

'I bet it isn't the only thing that slipped out recently is it?'

'I'm not gonna engage in dat kinda conversation wid you. It's a l'il personal!'

'Oooooo-k… But I'm right aren't I?'

JB started to blush, Cheribelle could tell because his eyeballs started to roll and he momentarily looked away, as he couldn't give her eye contact. She slapped the tea towel against his legs with a thwacking sound. She was an expert at that. Twisting the tea towel tightly and then striking an object, usually the victim's legs with a quick cresciendo of noise.

'OOOOOUUUUCH! What was dat fa?'

'Evading the question.'

'Mum, jus dry dem pots up please, I'm sleepy.'

'Yeeeees your honour and Royal Highness!'

They continued washing and drying up as the perfect dynamic duo while engrossed in family banter. Clink, clonk, clank, as JB nonchantly placed the pots into the draining bank.

'D'ya want another glass o wine Mum?'

'Oooooo… I think that would be too good to resist. TGIF tomorrow and I'm not working, so yeeeees please.'

'Put dese pots away den.'

'Less of the cheek you. I'm not open to bribes, apart from paying you to stay up and keep your eyes open?'

'Mmmmm… I'm open to offers, but mi ead's sayin' sleep n mi eyes are cravin' dreamworld.'

'I know you've got another half an hour in you.'

'I tink ya arf an our's in di next time zone, because mi ead n body are ahead o schedule. Why don't we hit di sack, as fa me it's an early rise again n den di weekend off.'

'Pour us a glass each, we can relax in the living room and see how it goes. No TV, just music and quality Mother and Son chat.'

Eventually all the crockery and cutlery had been washed, dried and put away in the cupboard, JB had wiped down the work surfaces with a cloth sprayed with Dettol, gave the cork place mats to Cheribelle, who returned them to the appropriate kitchen drawer. JB poured the remaining contents of the wine bottle into both glasses, giving them each almost a full glass. As JB was always immensely optimistic, the proverb the glass is always half full was rather prudent. JB blew the candle out, turned the kitchen lights off and double checked to ensure all the appropriate switches were turned off, apart from those designed to be left on. He followed his mum into the living room. She carried the two glasses of wine through, pushing open the kitchen door and turning right, pushing the living room door open too. She sat on the three piece sofa facing the forty two inch wide screen TV, crouched down and put her glass of wine down, along with JB's. She literally jumped back into the sumptuously comfortable chocolate brown sofa, lifting her legs up in the air as if she was being thrown off a bucking bronco at a fairground. JB picked up both glasses, passing one to his Mum and placing him down to the right of where he was going to sit.

'Would ya like to watch a l'il tele?'

'I don't mind son, I thought we agreed not to? We can do that or chill out here and listen to some music.'

'I'll put some music on di TV. Ow about Radio Five live, dey always ave interestin' late night topical debates.'

Felix jumped up on to Cheribelle's lap after he'd been having a rest in front of the wood burner. It wasn't on, but his house always retained a lot of natural heat. JB turned on the TV and scrolled through the channel options and selected Radio Five.

'Dis is interestin'. A debate about what sleepin' in socks says about ya.'

'You don't sleep in them do you Duane?'

'Noooo Momma, only if mi feet are cold n I'm savin' money on eatin' central.'

'You're eating central, please explain?' asked Cheribelle.

'OK Mum, central heating,' he said.

'That's better. I can understand you now.'

JB was born in St. Kitts after his Mum decided to emigrate there about forty one years ago, after having a holiday romance with Sugar. Cheribelle met Sugar there after a family holiday and after struggling to maintain a long distance relationship on returning to the UK, she decided to take a risk and the plunge to make it work in 1969, a year later. She was only eighteen, but felt she had nothing to loose and was desperate to be with Sugar who had stolen her heart. They raised all four of their children in St. Kitts. Douvelle, the eldest, had been born in 1976. They moved back to England as a family in 1984 when JB was almost four, to enable the children to have a better education and more fruitful job prospects. They experienced a difficult first few years together, as back in the 60s and 70s, mixed race relationships were taboo. A proportion of people frowned upon them being together and subjected Cheribelle to unpleasant bigoted comments such as White Trash and Onky. Sugar would always confront the perpetrators who normally quickly retracted and apologised for their obscenities. Occasionally Sugar would resort to a more hands on approach, often resulting in the offender being on the receiving end of a flurry of left and rights. Sugar could handle himself alright, although he was more of a pacifist and would only indulge in violent behaviour if he felt there was no alternative. He was from a large family and being one of half a dozen brothers, had to regularly protect and defend himself as sibling fights were common.

His brothers acted like local vigilantes and were respected and revered by the local community. If any misdemeanours occurred and people were violated, they would investigate, endeavouring to ensure the perpetrators would be punished. Sugar was an aspiring design electonical engineer with a high intellect, a trait inherent in his family. They were all academically sound, several emigrating to the United States to pursue scholarships and a more modernised standard of living. The continent of North America was thriving, ethnically diverse, technologically innovative and a pioneer of scientific research and development. 'Duaaaane, Duaaaaane, wake up or go to bed!'

'Wha, wha, what?'

'Either open your eyes or go upstairs to bed. You're roaring like a wild beast.'

'It's probably Felix. E's a noisy cat at times.'

'I can safely say, Felix is purring on my knee and was getting restless at the deafening noises you were making.'

'Sorry Mum. It mus be di wine makin' me troat groan.'

'You don't need to apologise, it's normal, especially amongst you men.'

'I've eard you snore in di past. One time I tought dere was a tractor in di ouse.'

'Have a little respect for your elders.'

'I do Mum, but you look younger dan me, so I don't need to.'

'Watch your mouth, but thanks for the flattery!'

JB rubbed his eyes, let out a gigantic yawn, stretched his arms above his head, stood up gingerly off the sofa, bent down, picked up his glass and slid the Cabernet Sauvignon down his throat.

'Duaaaaaane! Why you treatin' dat wine like a shot?' she said in a Kittician accent, mimicking JB.

'Ha Haaaaaaa. Dat sounded so funny, you speakin' patois! I drink it like a shot, because I wanna hit dreamworld n knock miself out n not wake up till sevenish.'

'That's a good point.'

'He walked over to Cheribelle, leaned over her and gave her a smacking kiss on the right cheek, stroked Felix's head and kissed him on the top of the nose. He twitched his ears, shook his head and miaowed as if to say,

'Don't disturb me.'

'Night Mum. Dere's some fresh linen on di bed, jus turn off di tele please before you come up, n close di kitchen n room doors.'

'Don't worry, I will. Night son.'

'You ave ya spare keys fa di ouse, so let yaself out when you want tomorrow. I'll be leavin' at about seven thirtyish, so won't disturb ya.'

'OK.'

'Sleep well Mum.'

'You too. Thanks for a beautiful night. Take care and I'll see you very soon.'

'Yeah Mum, look forward to it. Can you set di burglar alarm again too, please.'

'Don't worry, I'll do it. What's the code again?'

'It's Douvelle's birth date n year.'

'That's it. Thanks. Night night.'

'Night again.'

Felix had re-adjusted himself on Cheribelle's lap and was purring away loudly, obviously extremely content. JB made his way upstairs to the bathroom. He turned the light on, picked up his electric toothbrush, unscrewed the cap off the toothpaste tube and slowly and meticulously squirted a pea sized amount onto his Oral B brush. He put the cap back on, turned the cold water tap on, held his brush under briefly and pressed the button to turn it on. Away it buzzed, lifting it up to begin brushing his pearly whites. Downstairs, his mum was engrossed in the crazy radio debate about why people wore socks in bed and what it said about their personality. Whether or not you agreed with the thoughts of the public, presenter and studio guests, it was enlightening to say the least. The time was fast approaching ten fifteen pm. JB finished brushing his teeth, and removed his clothing, placing them neatly on the floor and climbed into bed. It was unusual for him to be in bed earlier than eleven o'clock, but a long week, following a hectic birthday weekend with Tom and crew, along with a few glasses of strong rich ruby red Sauvignon had worn him out. Thank God It's Friday… Almost. Within no time he was out for the count.

Chapter 31

Thank God It's Friday

Bbbbbrrrrrrrrr… bbbbrrrrrrrrr…

JB's iPhone alarm clock sounded dead on seven am. He rolled over. 'Damn man, I can't believe it, time to pick up mi ead n body already.'

Felix was lying comfortably on top of the quilt sleeping, until JB disturbed him. JB snoozed his alarm for the conventional ten minutes and decided to have an extra five minutes in bed, as he couldn't motivate himself to get up just yet.

'Tank God it's Friday,' he mumbled.

He wiped the right hand side of his mouth and cheek on the cotton bed sheet, as he could feel a slither of saliva running down towards his neck. Today was a relaxing one, as he only had four lessons of English followed by a free afternoon. To finish off the day, he was going to go to his ritual yoga class in the early evening. That was as long as he could manage to keep his eyes open after a tiring week. Tomorrow was his heavily anticipated rendezvous with Bethany, an exciting proposition. Surprisingly he managed to get out of bed before the ten minute snooze alarm sounded again. This was unusual as he only did this normally if he was going to have a morning shower, or shampoo and condition his afro, but not this morning. He would do it tomorrow in preparation for his date with Bethany. JB pulled himself up into a seated position, stroked Felix on the head, stretched his arms above his head, pulled the quilt back and slowly eased his way out of bed. He walked around the bed to the curtains and opened them. The sun was shining powerfully through the window, what a glorious start to the final day of the working week.

'I feel good, na na na na na na na, I feel good, you know dat I would… so good, uh uh, so fine, uh uh, I've got you, na na na na!' sang JB croakily.

He did a little dancing jig near the window, smiled widely, excited about the weekend's prospects. It was Friday the twenty forth of June and approaching seven ten am. The day had started off majestically, with a clear blue sky, sun a powerful beaming yellow. JB was feeling on fire, in the sense where he was on top of the world, radiating intense energy and ready to possibly seduce and serenade Bethany tomorrow afternoon. His alarm sounded again, so he swiped his phone to cancel it. It was Yoga Friday, so that would help to soothe and relax his zen mind state, enabling him to be revitalised and recuperated ready for tomorrow. Zen derives from the Japanese word Dzyen which is modern mandarin, meaning meditative state of absorption. Yoga was a fabulous recreation to help any person alleviate mental stress and muscular tension. JB had been going to classes regularly for several years now. It was an ideal end to the week after dealing with the mental demands of teaching full time. The classes were held at his local gym, Virgin Active, where his mum went too.

Normally he would go downstairs without a stitch of clothing on apart from his cotton stocking cap which he wore normally for bed to keep his afro tidy. He only had to afro comb his hair if he'd shampooed and conditioned it, done while blowdrying or if he wanted to let the proverbial jungle beast out of captivity. He usually washed it every one to two weeks. He opened the double wardrobe by sliding the door open and pulling out his dark grey fluffy warm and cosy dressing gown. He put it on, remembering to fasten the waist belt, as he didn't want to give his Mum an almighty fright. I don't think she would have been too happy to have seen his middle member swinging around loosely between his legs.

'Mum, are you awake?'

There was no response, so he assumed she was still sleeping soundly. He didn't want to wake her when it was so early in the morning. He went to the bathroom to wash his face and wake himself up properly. He pushed the door open, moved to the sink, turned the cold water tap, bent over and cupped his hands allowing a mini pool of water to collect so he could throw it over his face. He had a ritual, usually repeating this act three times. He turned the tap off and turned to the heated aluminium radiador/towel rail to wipe his dripping face dry on a charcoal grey towel. He then jogged downstairs, making his way to the kitchen, opening the kitchen door. He opened the blinds to let some sunlight in and then took a tin of Felix's chicken and liver Whiskas out of the cupboard. It had a peel off tin, which made it easier and less time consuming. He took it off and threw it in the bin in the corner, just under the burglar alarm panel. It was one of those expensive aluminium Brabantias with a press top flip lid. JB liked his cool, hip and modern gadgets. He picked up the stainless steel cat fork, carried the tin of cat food and fork to Felix's bowl and gouged out about a human adult handful of food. He banged the remnants of food from the fork and back into the tin. Felix came bounding downstairs as he could smell the scent of his morning delight from the first floor. Not an appetising odour for humans, just for the animal fraternity. JB took the two thirds full tin and fork to the sink, he put the fork in the sink at the side of the washing up bowl, picked up the hygienic tin plastic cover and placed it over the tin, before putting it back in the fridge. At the same time he took out a fresh pot of natural yoghurt and carton of fresh blueberries.

'Dese are luscious man. A l'il bit o fresh slippery unny n away we go. Dat's strange! Di burglar alarm asn't started beepin'. Hmmmm....I bet Mum forgot to set it.'

Break ins weren't that common in Honeyville, although last Sunday morning someone had broken into a car close by. It was a relatively safe neighbourhood and the main perpetrator of crime was the notorious cat burglar. Working their strategic covert espionage magic, penetrating cat flaps and stealing enemies' food. Hopefully Felix had more decorum than that, but realistically, the chances were remote as he loved to scale curtains as a kitten and was still to this date, occasionally mischievous. JB was picking at the juicy blueberries that were just in date, relishing the delicious flavour.

'I better stop dis, pull out di muesli n get dis cereal well n truly whacked up.'

He opened the cupboard door above his main work surface at head height and took out the bag of natural unsweetened muesli. He kept it securely shut with a bag fastening clip, allowing it to remain air tight. He removed the clip holding the corner of the bag, placed it on the work surface, bent down to open another cupboard door, as he needed a bowl to mix his nutritious concoction of morning goodness. He took a navy blue and grey bowl, placed it on the work surface and closed the cupboard door with his foot. He poured a healthy portion into the bowl, flipped off the yoghurt pot plastic cover, spooned several dollops of creamy goodness over his cereal.

'Raaas claaaart! Damn man, I've lost mi bananas. What di ell am I playin' at? Better slice a banana n trow it on top n mix it right in dere.'

He skipped to the fruit basket and broke a ripened large seven inch banana off a bunch of five.

'Yeah man, Beth's gonna savour some goodness of a similar size tomorrow. Booyaka sha, people di dance n some dem romance.'

He was rather optimistic, expecting to slip in between Bethany's body and her knickers, if she was wearing any. For all JB knew, she might go commando, expecting the sexually gratifying inevitable, or perhaps, maybe not. She was a respectable girl, but JB had this magnetic attribute of being able to seduce and corrupt the most respectable girls. He peeled the banana, threw the skin in the Brabantia bin, pressing the lid to flip it open, then closing it. He pulled the cutlery drawer open, took out a dining knife, shoved it shut with his thigh in a rapid martial art manoevres, as if he was dropping an opponent to his knees. Buckling with a deadly bone jangling debilitating shot. He quickly sliced the banana dropping it in with effortless grace, picking up the spoon to mix the ingredients, before scattering a blueberry bomb on to the appetising dish. To finish it off, he unscrewed the lid off the honey pot, tilted it over the bowl and watched it smoothly start to flow. He had to swirl it around making decorative artistic patterns as if he was designing a Gaudi masterpiece. When he'd poured enough, he tilted the jar more upright until the honey eventually came to a stop. He moved his finger around the top of the jar to ensure no residue would drip down the side, making a small sticky pool on the work surface.

At least he could now savour the wondrous brekkie. Felix was slip slopping away, enjoying his chicken and liver morning starter. JB knew he was missing something.

'O.M.G. mi eads so scatty dis mornin', it mus be di effects o dat Cabernet Sauvignon las night. Dat's why I don't like to drink on a school night. Mudder corruptin' me. At least it's Friday n I only ave to survive four lessons n den di weekend. Yeah man. I need some o dat sparkling water Flix, to cure mi fuzzy ead n dat aint jus mi fro!'

He opened the fridge door, took a two litre bottle of sparkling water out, opened the glass cupboard and pulled out a large pint sized one, closing both with slick style. He poured the water into the glass, virtually to the brim and carried the bowl of cereal goodness and water to the table. He was on schedule to catch the bus shortly after seven thirty am. He pulled the chair out, his usual one, put his breakfast down, sat down, jumped the chair in and started to eat.

'Dis is di dream brekkie as well as dat one di Latvian girl left di recipe fa. Ow I'd love to share dat palatable pleasure, along wi di food.'

It was seven twenty am, so he still had enough time to finish his cereal, drink his water, brush his teeth and get himself dressed after smearing sweet scented cocoa butter all over his body. The muesli was going down very quickly, at a similar speed to the way Cheribelle ate, so he was slightly rude and hypocritical last night after insinuating she ate like a wild creature. In no time the bowl was empty, apart from a few remnants of moist yoghurt soiled wheat, entwined with sticky honey. He scraped it clean, slid his chair back out from the oval table, stood up, kneed it back in with his right, picked up his crockery and took it to the sink. He placed them both in the bowl, turned on the hot water tap and ran it to soak the cereal bowl and glass. He flipped the lid of the washing up liquid and squirted a small amount in to help agitate the grease until his mum came downstairs and cleaned up after him. In his defence, he normally washed up straight away, however, he knew that his mum had a relaxing day today so would possibly do a little summer cleaning for him. The cheek of him, exploiting his mother's graciousness. He dashed upstairs to the bathroom to brush his pearly whites. He put a slurry of paste on his electric brush, turned on the cold water tap to moisten the texture, turned on the brush and away he buzzed. His brush had a timer on it, so when the mandatory two minutes was up, the red light on it flashed. How technology had evolved, compared to even five years ago when a conventional hand held brush was all there was. The only excitement was choosing the colour, brand and texture of head, whether it being soft, medium or hard bristled.

'Duuaaaane, are you gonna turn off the tap, because you're wasting a lot of water?'

'Me can no ere ya.'

The second spare bedroom door opened, JB could hear the noise as the bottom of it brushed lightly against the carpet.

'I said, why don't you turn off the water tap? You waste so much by leaving it running, it's expensive!'

'JB turned off his brush, dried it on the charcoal dark grey towel and put it back on the charging unit which wasn't plugged in.

'Muuum, relax woman, I can't speak wid a mout full o foam.' he blurted and gargled.

He spat out the mixture of toothpaste and cold water, crouched down so his head was just above sink height, drooped it under the tap allowing cold water to run into his mouth, before swirling it around and then spitting it out.

'Did you hear what I said?'

'A good mornin' would be more appreciated. Ow ya feelin'? Ope ya gonna ave a beautiful TGIF.'

'What's TGIF?' asked Cheribelle.

'Use ya imagination. It's quite self explanatory Mudder. Thank God it's Friday!'

'One, watch your tongue, two, speak more clearly, three, stop speaking in street jibe and four...' she retorted.

THWACK...

She lifted up his dressing gown and smacked him powerfully on the back of his right leg.

'Ouch! What was dat fooor?' he responded angrily.

'Sometimes you need to have far much more respect for your Mother!'

'Ow can I ere ya, when I'm brushin' mi teeth n also, it's early in di mornin' n ya know it takes me twenty minutes or so to come round n get mi ead right!'

'OK. You're forgiven this time.' Cheribelle said smirking.

'I need to get a move on, because mi bus is due at seven tirty five-ish.'

'Hurry up then.'

She threw her arms around his back, giving him a gigantic tight hug. JB returned the compliment.

'Right, let me go, time's o di essence.'

His Mum turned the cold water tap off as JB had accidentally left it running.

'What did I say to you about the water? You don't listen do you? I should leave you to learn the hard way, because I know your Dad would have done exactly that.'

JB grunted under his breath, released his hands and arms from his mum's body, walked passed her, turned round and smacked her on the bottom. She was wearing a pair of light cotton pyjamas, but couldn't really feel his playful smack.

'Oooooo, are you being kinky?'

'Don't be so disgustin'! Ya mi Mudder, not mi gal.'

'Haaa Haaaaaa.' laughed Cheribelle.

JB walked to his bedroom, took off his dressing gown, slid open the wardrobe door and placed it back on the hanger.

'What shall I wear today?'

He picked up the container of cocoa butter, flicked open the lid and squirted a large amount into his left hand. He rubbed his hands together, spreading the load and started smearing it all over his body, arms, stomach, chest, legs and feet. He squirted some more onto his hand and finished off covering the bits he'd missed, apart from the middle of his back.

'I need to invent some kinda device dat let's ya put cream into dis part. Backside man. It's so irritatin' when you can't reach dat.'

'Duaaane, Are you talking to yourself?'

'No Mum, you mus be earin' tings!' he said chuckling.

'You mean, you're going senile.'

He put the lid back on the container, placed it on the bedside table and walked back to the wardrobe. He took out a pristine white cotton short sleeved shirt, a purple silk tie and a pair of black trousers with a purple pin stripe down each side. They were a very elegant pair and would certainly receive comments at school today. He pulled out an attractive lilac front buttoned cardigan from his jumper shelf,. He was looking jazzy, smooth and sharp to say the least. He was looking forward to arousing an interest from Bethany before their date tomorrow that none of the other teachers were aware of. They were going to keep it hush hush, because they didn't want to attract attention to themselves. It was probably the perfect scenario, quite covert and under cover, espionage style, as everyone knew a dalliance had occurred with JB and Jennifer, the two Js. He crouched down and took out a pair of dull black mole skin rounded toe lace up shoes, stood up, took out a slender cylindrical bottle of Giorgio Armani and squirted it on either side of his neck, his arms and wrists, before rubbing them together. He placed the bottle back, slid shut the door and made his way downstairs.

'Take care Mum. See ya soon. Can you remember to put on di burglar alarm before ya go, because you forgot las night?'

'Did I?'

'Yeah man.'

'You mean, yeah woman. Oooops, sorry Duane. I promise I'll remember before I leave.'

'Tank you Mum. I'll come round to yours next week fa dinner, if dat's OK?'

'Of course you can son. As long as you show Mum some respect and bring her a bouquet of flowers.'

'You'll be granted wid respect, but flowers, it depends on which way di winds blowin'!'

'Get gone you. Take care and see you very soon. Come here a moment please.'

'I'm rushing Mum.'

'One second.'

He turned round almost at the bottom of the stairs and jogged back up to the landing with moleskin shoes in hand. He pushed open the second spare bedroom door,

'What is it Mum?'

'What d'ya mean, what is it?' she questioned his words.

'Weeell, I'm in a mad rush n it's seven thirty one, mi bus is due in four minutes.'

'Hush ya mouth n give ya Mum a massive squeeze, please.'

'Now ya makin' sense.'

'Right, I'm dashin' Momma. Love ya. See ya next week.'

'Take care son. Be good, be safe and enjoy yourself!'

He, jogged to the bedroom door, opened it and hurried down the stairs for at least the third time this morning.

MIAOW... MIAOW.

'Felix, go n see ya Mum, I ave to get gone to work now.'

He bent down and put his shoes on, tying them securely. He picked up his man sack that was hanging over one of the kitchen chairs, threw it over his shoulder, opened the cutlery drawer and took the house keys out, closed it, opened the door, turned the kitchen light off and walked out. He slammed it shut, locked it and ran to the garden gate. He opened the garden gate frantically, like a man possessed, as he was a little behind schedule. He skipped through, closed it behind him and sprinted to the bus stop. Thankfully the queue was long, the bus was just indicating as it pulled into the stop. It was only a seventy five metre dash, so not too far. He didn't want to pull a muscle. It was early morning and his muscles were cold. The weather was beautiful, sun shining powerfully down on to the gradually busy developing streets, rebounding off the surface and appearing to radiate energy and vibrance to most of those below. Vehicles were passing by, driven by delivery drivers taking their first consignment to its rightful destination, to leather clad persons with helmets on motorbikes and car drivers heading to and from work on the final day of the week. There were others that cared about the carbon foot print and decided to travel by bus, others by foot and others by bicycle. Millions around the world were embracing the greenhouse effect with open arms, reminiscent of the United Nations original 'Peacemaker', Kofi Anan, contributing towards a better planet, recycling cartons, bottles and paper, whereas other neglecting inconsiderate global 'Jack Asses', disrespecting, abusing and helping to corrode the wondrous Planet Earth.

JB made it to the bus stop with consummate ease, slowing down to a leisurely trot after sprinting at an early morning break neck pace. He wiped a glimmering bead of sweat from his forehead with his hand, clipped open his man sack, pulling out his metro card. The queue was down to JB and an elederly woman, probably in her eighties.

'Could ya give me ya hand young man and help me onto bus?' she spoke in a strange broken accent.

'Yeah, it's alright, course I will.' replied JB.

She had a brown walking stick in one hand, her navy blue hand bag strapped over the opposite shoulder.

'Be gentle will ya, I'm not a strong young bird ya know.'

'Ya not too much older dough. I'm sure you turn n ead or two!'

'What is it wit youth o today? You can't pronounce words proply, slack use o English language. The words head, not ead and dough's what you bake to make bread. Thanks fa lovely compliment tho, ow sweet o ya, you Romeo. I bet you have those ladies eatin' outta palm o ya hand.'

'God, I'm ere givin' you an and, n you criticize mi English. Dat's what I teach. You don't exactly speak di Queens's English do ya.'

She sighed heavily,

'Can you not use Lord's name in vain please. He's given us these pleasures in life, so don't disrespect im.'

'Ya right. Sorry bout dat. What's ya name darlin'?'

'Mi name's Ethel, but ya can call me Ethsy. That's mi nickname. Did ya say ya were an English teacher?'

'Yeah Ethsy, dat's right.'

'I think ya might need some more lessons yaself young man.'

JB laughed, because her English was certainly far from perfect, but she was old and regimented and typically probably thought she was never wrong.

'Come ooooon. We're not chillin' on a Sunday mornin', I'll be behind schedule if you don't get a move on!' said the bus driver.

'Can't ya see, I'm a little old lady? Have a bit o respect. Don't anger an older lady with a cane in er hand. Otherwise I'll have to bend you over mi knee!'

'Sorry love, it's just you're both too busy birds eye potato wafflin'. Get on the bus n then continue to chatter.'

'Maaaan, di lady's older, ya can see dat. It'll take as long as it takes man, so don't try n rush er. Patience is a virtue n if ya behind time, ya can still make it up. Chill man.'

'You heard im, cool down mister bus driver.'

'OK you two. Get a move on then.' said the driver.

'Wait a minute.' A yelp came from the street.

The driver closed his doors and was about to set off, but not until JB had escorted Ethel to her seat. She had just taken her free bus pass out of her handbag and shown it to the driver.

BANG, BANG, the door shook as a late passenger had just sprinted to the bus. JB turned round to look along with other passengers. It was C Man.

'Driver, dat's mi friend, can you let im on please?' shouted JB.

'He should have got here on time. As I just told you, I don't wanna be behind schedule.'

'We both heard that. Open those doors before I hit ya wi this stick,' shouted Ethel in an angry voice.

JB had just sat her down next to the middle doors, seats designated for elderly, disabled and mothers with prams or pushchairs. The driver was just about to pull off, but had second thoughts after Ethel's high octane threat. The driver didn't even respond to Ethels demand verbally, he just instaneously opened the door.

'Thanks driver. I almost thought I was gonna miss it.'

'It's your lucky day.'

C Man took his metro card out of his pocket and showed it to the driver, who nodded, looked in his near side mirror, glanced into his off side one, indicated and slowly pulled out.

'Yeah man, what's appenin' C Man?'

'I'm all good Jammin'. Phew, thought I'd only just gone n missed it.'

'Ya a lucky man, it's only because I threatened that driver wi mi stick.'

'Meeeeeeaaaaan. Some of those drivers don't have any respect do they.'

'C Man, dis is Ethel.'

'What did I tell ya. It's Ethsy,' she jumped in, giving JB a stern stare.

'Hi Ethsy, I'm C Man.'

They shook hands.

'Are you a sailor then?'

'No love, I'm a joiner.'

'Good fa you. It's not easy at the mo wi the blasted Government n a lack of jobs.'

'I know. I'm lucky, I've got a six month contract at the school where JB works.'

'Jammin', JB, which is ya real name?' asked Ethel.

'Mi real name's Duane, but I was nicknamed Jammin' or JB many years ago.'

'What a strange concoction o names. We've got a guy that's like a doughnut, wi jam in n another one who's Captain Pugwash. I bet you two have got some magic wi those young ladies out there, if you know what I mean.'

'D'ya fancy comin' to yoga tonight at Virgin?'

'Yoooga?? Are you for real. That's for sissy's n camp men!'

'Watch ya mouth C Man. I used to do a lot o yoga when I was younger, it's great fa ya suppleness n helps ya relax. It's so de-stressing. You look as if ya need some. Ya too stiff when ya walk, I almost thought ya were that robot. What d'ya call him?'

'Which one?'

'That one from Star Wars!'

'R2D2?' Guessed JB.

'No, the other one.'

'Storm Trooper?' said C Man.

'Nooooo. R2D2's friend.'

'Ooooh, im. E's called C3PO.'

'That's the one. Thanks Jammin', Yeeeah, you walk like him C Man.'

'Thanks! Charmin'!'

'I'm only tryin' to help ya. I'm just sayin', you need to loosen up a bit.'

'Footloose, footloose, kick off ya Sunday shoes, please, Louiiise, pull me offa my knees,' sang JB.

'Jaaaack, get baaack, c'mon before we crack,' sang C Man.

'Lose your blues, everybody cut footloose,' Ethel joined in.

'Footloose, kick off ya Sunday shoes,' came a crescendo of vocals from other passengers.

Some were humming, some singing in tune with others way out, but what a way to start Friday morning. All appeared to be in fabulous jovial spirits. When the singing accompaniment eventually faded out like a CD album between songs, a rapturous applause reverberated around the bus downstairs.

'Woo-huuuuuu,' came cries from upstairs.

'Yeeeeeaaaaah… Yeeeeee-haaaaaa.'

'Thaaat hits the spoooooot.'

What an impulsive minute or two of harmony, which seldom occurs, especially in a public environment.

'Absolutely bloody marvellous,' yelled the driver.

Whistles came from a few passengers on the bus. The driver wasn't complimenting the passengers, however, because in the road about a hundred metres ahead there appeared to be orange and white traffic cones put strategically across the road. It didn't look like the work of construction workers though, as there was no initial road sign warning, which systematically occurred.

'I can't believe it, that driver's happy fa once.' Mumbled Ethel.

'I'm totally shocked. What appened dere I wonder?'

'He must have been impressed wi the singing.' replied C Man.

'Is everyting OK driver?' asked JB.

A big huff and puff came from the driver's booth. He slowed down, putting his hazard warning lights on, bringing the bus to a gradual stop. His safety protective booth door was slung open, him jumping off his seat and almost being hit by the door as it rebounded off the side internal wall. He just managed to stop it by holding his hands out in front of his face. He had to return to his dashboard to open the front doors. He trotted off for about thirty seconds or so and then returned. Passengers who couldn't see clearly were baffled and bamboozled by the escapade. Other's were chatting amongst themselves, others listening to the radio or music on their modern gadgets, some reading from their kindles while others flicked through a conventional paper book or glossy magazine.

'Sorry about that. Some blinkin' fool had decided to put traffic cones in the middle of the road for a laugh. I moved them, so it's all sorted now,' he said to the passengers downstairs.

He opened his booth door, which was slightly ajar, climbed back into his seat, switched off the hazard lights, started the engine and pulled away.

'He's a grumpy fellow is that one. Anyone would think he had the world on his shoulders.'

'E's got several passengers above im, upstairs, so you could say e ad part o di world on dem!' chuckled JB.

'Ya quite a sharp boy Jammin' one. I bet the kids at school love ya.'

'Maybe some o dem like me n a few o dem love me.'

'Oooooooo... If only I was fifty odd years younger. I'd have to teach you to speak better though.'

'Ow d'ya know I don't like a more mature woman?'

'I think I'm just a l'il bit older than mature. I'm pushing a hundred n no good to anybody. If I worked at a zoo, they'd throw me out to the lions.'

'I bet you'd taste good though, after all dem years o curin'. Meat fa di king o di jungle.'

JB then put his hand to his mouth and emulated Tarzan,

'AAAAAARGH... AAAAAAAAARGH... AAAARGH... AAARGH... AARGH.'

'Hey mate, you should audition for a role in the circus!' said the man sitting behind.

'Meeeeeeaaaaan! I've always said that. A circus, yeah, that's where the clown belongs! Haaaa Haaaaa. I'll shake ya hand to that mate, I've been saying that for years!'

'Oooooo, that Circus Master could tame this pussy cat any day,' responded Ethel.

It was an entertaining and jovial morning bus adventure to Oatmill for JB and C Man. Shenanigans with the bus driver, conversations with Ethel and song singing on the number seven bus.

This early part of the Friday journey was now over. JB leaned forward and pressed the red bell which was mounted on the pole that ran from the lower deck floor to the ceiling.

'Are ya leavin' me now?'

'Sorry Ethsy, me gotta run now n teach bad English to dem kids.' he joked.

'Charmin' young man. You help me on board, use all that chivalry, tease me n then spit me out. I was hopin' ya were gonna take me round market n entertain me, as well as being a baggage handler!'

'If I could, I would, but a man as good educatin' work to do!'

'How about you then sailor boy?' asked Ethel.

'I've got to go n play with me wood. I'm working at the same school.'

'I'm sure they won't miss ya today. Give me ya piece of wood to play with.'

As she smiled open mouthed at C Man, her top set of false teeth fell about an inch down from the top of her mouth, before she wrestled them back with her jaw.

'If it'd been a Saturday, I would love, but we've got a lot of work on, so I can't,' he said aghast at the sight of her dentures.

'I suppose I'd better find another toyboy in Lillyford market. Oooooo, I can get me hands on someones cucumber.'

'Ya might have problems biting n chewing it love,' said C Man cheekily.

'Don't you worry bout me, I'll suck it like a lollipop.'

The bus slowed down and stopped. JB and C Man along with some of the pupils at Oatmill High got off the bus as the doors opened.

'Take care Ethsy, see ya next time,' said JB.

'Take care love n enjoy ya fruit n veg picking!'

'I will C Man and I'd love to taste some o yours.'

As the middle doors on the bus opened, JB and C Man looked at each other in pure amazement.

'Dat woman's weird wid all dat crazy assed sexual behaviour.'

'She's just old n wants to enjoy bit of good company. I bet she's lonely n is holding on to her small portion of virtually deceased libido.'

'Yeah man, but dat was undecorous, smutty n beyond di realms of repulsion man!'

They both turned round to wave goodbye to Ethel. As they did, she responded, waved, put her left index finger in her mouth sucking it as if it was a phallic symbol. Her top dentures once again momentarily dropped downwards from her mouth. Not the most attractive sight by any stretch of the imagination.

'Anyone would think you were a saint Jammin' n never indulged in erotic, titillating and suggestive gestures?'

'I'm not denyin' dat man, but dere are time n places. On di bus early on a mornin', n by an agein' granny. Come on man, you ave to accept dat it's inappropriate n crude!'

'JB, just relax man. Anyone would think you were a monk n were the most righteous man in the whole world?'

'Weeell… I'm di second most behind you sir!' laughed JB.

'Good point well made.'

'Anyway, let's skip di crazy conversations about toothless, perversed, desperate and sex starved n frustrated O.A.P.s. I don't wanna ave nightmares tonight about Ethsy goin' down on me! It's enough to give a young ealthy man an eart attack.'

'I just wanna emphasise though, you're a damn rascal sinner who portrays to be the male epitome of Mother Theresa!'

'Ya only jealous because ya know mi fro makes di ladies go crazy. Don't feel left out, ya can ave a stroke if ya like? Just like Ethsy runnin' er ands all over di dirty fruit n veg in Lillyford market. I can't believe you even turned down di opportunity of escourtin' er round. Gigolo star! Ha Haaaaaaa,' teased JB.

JB playfully punched C Man to his side, provoking him to respond by pulling JB's black stocking cap off.

'I said you were jealous o mi fro. Go on den, ave a touch.'

JB picked it up off the floor, dusted it down with his left hand and placed it neatly back over his funky neatly presented afro. He pulled it down tightly over the clumped pony tail just below the top of his head

'Why would I wanna touch that? One, I don't know where it's been n two, it's probably a perfect breeding ground for a whole host of creatures great n small!'

They briskly walked the short journey from the bus stop to the school. JB told C Man about his impending date with Bethany tomorrow afternoon, while C Man was trying to tempt JB to hang out with him and other friends. People like Barnestormer Darude, Biddy Biddy Bad Boy, Eugene, Dezmundo, Dee Dee, Slinky, McDoughnut Ball Ead, Paddy, Bollywood Superstar, Reggie the Dentist, L'il Donkey, Lion, Ish Bish Bash Bosh, El Beattle, L'il Onion, Mister Primitive, Adidas Alluring Awesome Avenger, The Cat, Wondrous Woolly, Chucky the Castaway Kid, The Cobra, Tony Muai Thai, Seffi the Egyptian Warrior, Savaaarge, Casino Royale, Sebba the Mauritian Model, Cross Fit Collossus M.R. The Wolfpack-G-Man and Dré Dog, Janis the Super Model, Mister McGuire the tennis Titan, The Clinical Potent Marksman, Yamster Hamster, Sugar Ray Jay, The Sean Penn lookalike surfing Stalwart to name many more than a few! He knew the best offer was entertaining the alluring, attractive and foxy Bethany. He savoured a raucous time last weekend for Tom's thirtieth, so was looking forward to a quieter one. However, he was still hoping for another sexual encounter with yet another teacher from Oatmill High. They reached the school entrance, hugged it out tightly, high fived and knuckle touched before going their seperate ways. Despite all the teasing, tormenting and harassing, they were very close. To outsiders it probably looked on the contrary, as the jibes appeared to be relentless. Only they knew differently.

Chapter 32

Staff Room Banter

JB made his way to the staff room as the time approached quarter past eight. He was a little ahead of schedule, so had time to have a quick herbal tea before the start of Friday morning lessons with Year Ten pupils. He reached the staff room and was about to push the door open, when it opened inwards. He fell forwards, almost knocking Bethany over. He fell into her outstretched arms as she managed to save him from embarassment.

'Geeeeez, who'd have believed it! You couldn't have scripted that better.'

'Boy, dat could ave been far worse wid me fallin' flat on mi face on di floor!'

'Thankfully for your sake an angel rescued you from disaster,' she said, winking.

'Good mornin' Beth n good mornin' everybody.'

What a dramatic start to the day. Her neck emitted a beautiful sensuous odour that hypnotised JB.

'Good morning to you Jammin'.' replied Bethany.

'What perfume are ya wearin'? It smells.....incredible!' said JB, puffing out his cheeks in startlement.

'It's Guilty by Gucci.'

'Woucha! It smells of a bloomin' summer orchard. Let me ave another sniff.'

'Sure.'

After withdrawing from the unexpected staff room clinch, JB tilted his head forward again into Bethany's neck to inhale the adorable scent of her perfume. He held his nose there for a few seconds, pulled away, shook his head and said,

'I'm glad to be alive! Woo-hooooooo.'

Bethany walked out of the room and Jennifer gave him a cold chilling transfixed stare that cut straight through human flesh.

'What's wrong Jen?'

'*Nada. No problemo su puto. Increíble totale,*' she said.

This meant, 'nothing, no problem you whore. Totally incredible.' She saw Bethany as a threat to her gladiator and was becoming very territorial, even though JB didn't belong to anyone. He was one of Oatmill's most eligible bachelors who was relishing his freedom.

'Jen, dere's no need fa dat kinda talk. I've only smelt a woman's perfume, its ardly commitin' a criminal offence!'

'I can see the deviousness in ya eyes. Why are you tryin' to make me so jealous?' said Jennifer.

'I'm not woman. Relax now. We're all friends, so dere's no need fa any jealousy n animosity is dere!'

'True. Sorry Jammin', I'm just feelin' a little under the weather.'

'If ya not feelin' too good, go ome. It's no use bein' ere if ya weak ya know.'

'I'll be OK. It's just that time, you know… Women's issues.'

'Boy, talk about explosions in di nether region. Sounds like Mary.'

'Yeah. It's defo a bloody one!'

'Too much info, thanks Jen,' said Jasmine.

What a relief Jennifer was unaware of JB's rendezvous with Bethany tomorrow. They would have to keep a relatively low profile, just in case their paths crossed. JB didn't want to create any conflict and jeopardise the friendships he had with Jennifer and Bethany, however, if news got out about their covert undercover espionage type secret tryst, World War Three could be predicted.

'Is dat fa me Bella?'

'Yeah. Enjoy it, I promise it's not been spiked with any laxatives. Right Jen?' Annabelle answered nodding and smirking at Jennifer.

'So what ya sayin' is, drink at ya own risk?'

'Honestly, it's safe to drink.'

'If you're a fish,' said Tom.

JB picked up his rasta man mug, smelt it to see if he could detect any foreign bodies in there. Not like a dead blue bottle or wasp, just something that could give him an upset stomach. He decided to risk it. It hadn't been tampered with, the ladies were just teasing him, although I think Jennifer wished she had duped him. In her mind, he deserved it, for playing her off against Bethany. He still had fifteen minutes to spare, as he had arrived five minutes earlier than his usual time of eight twenty am. His mug of herbal tea was piping hot, so he held it with both hands, lifting it to his mouth, blowing it and taking tiny sips, so not to scauld his lips and palet. It tasted good.

'Dis special secret ingredients delicious Jen, or should I say Bella. Is it a joint recipe?'

'If ya not careful, it could be a recipe for disaster Jammin'!'

'Why y'all gangin' up on mi dis mornin'? All I've done is fallen into di arms of a woman n sniffed er perfume, it's ardly a public order offence.'

'Jammin', just have a l'il more tact, love.' said Jasmine.

'You know JB, the hallmarks of a diplomat!' responded Annabelle.

'Yeah alright. You girls are on di warpath, so I guess I'm gonna ave an amnesty. Which weapon d'ya want first?'

'Ooooo, I'd love to get mi hands on ya rifle! Is it still fully loaded n ready for action?' said Jen.

'It's locked away in its holster at mo. I don't wanna fire any bullets round ere, it could be deadly.'

'Maybe that's why bloody Mary's happened with Jennifer?' sid Jasmine.

'Eeeerm… Didn't you say too much info earlier Jas? Talk about hypocritical.'

'Jeeeen, ya not the only woman that has a menstrual cycle.'

'That's quite apt Jas. Men-strual cycle. It's a woman's subliminal way of saying… Right, I'm gonna ride away from this male testosterone zone. Give me four or five days of exile,' said Tom, laughing.

'I like that Tom. Super analogy!' said Jennifer.

'You know me, always thinking outside the box, so to speak.'

'You never fail to amaze me Tom. That's why I'm attracted to ya brother Ethan. He's got similar traits to you.'

'I'd like to think though, I'm the brains of the family n he's the beauty.'

'Are ya jokin'? You exuuuude beauty also. I mean… look at ya. Ya drop dead!' said Jasmine.

'Oooooooof! I think I need to go for a cold shower or can someone please bring me a fan.'

'You'll be OK Tom. I'm one of ya biggest fans. Don't you worry,' said Jennifer.

JB chuckled discreetly under his breath. Jennifer looked over towards JB, smiled, trotted over to Tom and gave him a big hug and a kiss on the cheek for good measure.

'Stop it Jen! You'll give yaself a bad name. Don't ruin ya teachin' reputation, they've sacked people for less.' said Jasmine smirking.

Tom responded and also threw his arms around Jennifer, engaging in a moment of attentiveness and affection. The staff room door opened, in walked Bethany.

'You look sharp and chic this morning. I love the deep purple tie, accentuated with the lilac cardigan,' said Bethany.

'I didn't see the lilac pin stripe down the side of ya trousers. Yeah, I agree, lookin' gooood,' said Annabelle.

'Well, thank you ladies. I try n make n effort every now n den.'

Ding-a-ling-a-ling, Ding-a-ling-a-ling. The school bell sounded with its customary piercing shrill.

'Let's get to work fellow educating egotists,' said Jasper.

'Speak for yaself Jasper. I'm far from an egotist. Confident n always aimin' to get what I want, but I'd say, more of a confident Charlie's Angel… Question, tell me what you think about me, I buy my own car n I buy my own ring…' said Jasmine, going into singing mode.

'The shoes I'm wearin', I've got it, the car I'm drivin', I got it,' sang Annabelle.

'All the women who independent, throw your hands up at me!' sang Jennifer.

'All the ladies, truly faithful, throw your hands up at me!' sang Bethany.

'Good work ladies of true independence during (Period-ic Menstrual Times). Ha Haaaaa,' hollered Jasper.

'Let's go Charlie's Angels n T-Birds, its showtime!' said JB.

All the remaning teachers in the staff room started to head towards their respective class rooms. JB picked up his man sack, threw it over his right shoulder, rasta man mug in hand and followed the educational cavalry, walking to his form class room six. The corridors were virtually empty, just a handful of pupils walking, others dashing with bags, satchels in hand, in different directions to ensure they would arrive just in time for the start of the register. JB moved briskly, even though his class room wasn't too far away. He pulled down the handle and pushed open the door, which creaked as usual. He greeted his pupils.

'Mornin' all, ow we doin'?'

'Good morning Mr Herbert.'

'Shall we try again, as dat was a l'il hollow. Take two. Good mornin' all.'

'Good mornin' Mr Herbert.' A more forceful and lively response.

'Are you all ready fa di weekend?'

'Yes sir,' sounded the chorus.

'Dat's a more vibrant n pleasant response! Let mi take di register den.'

He took his mansack off his shoulder and placed it down at the side of his front desk. He pulled his chair out and sat down, before shuffling in under the desk. He took the key out of his man sack, leaned to the side, unlocked the the drawer with the register in, took it out, before closing it and then put it on the desk. He opened the Year Ten register and began.

'Jonny Basnett.'

'Here.'

'Rebecca Button.'

'Here.'

'Jessica Stropsville.'

'Here.'

'Alessandro Romeo.'

'Here.'

'Aspen Colarado.'

'Here.'

'Sally Worsnop.'

'Here.'

'Jameel Taylor.'

'Sir.'

'Frankie Arpegio.'

'Sir.'

'Peaches Longley.'

'Here.'

'Leonardo Caprio.'

'Here.'

'Jemima Saltfish.'

'Sir.'

'Jack Fulton. Are you open or closed today?'

'Here sir. I'm open all hours, unless I'm sleeping.'

A crescendo of laughter reverberated around the room.

'OK peeps, let's jus settle down please.'

'I'm loving the dress code today Mr Herbert. You're looking sharper than an alligator's teeth.'

'Well, tank you Jack. Dat's a glowin' compliment. Ya lookin' slick too.'

'Thank you sir.'

JB continued with the register, until all thirty names had been called out.

'Today, di plan is to go into creative cultured Calypso mode. I'd like y'all to write a story about what Calypso means to you. Make it flamboyant, make it unique n make it hot wid a l'il dancin' diva-ness.'

'Calypso, isn't that one of those juicy lollipops?'

'Jemima it ain't just any old Tom, Diick and Arry lollipop. Its di ones daat ave-a coloured paper tube wrapper! You know-a, you ave-a to squeeze at di bottom and push it up-a!' said Alessandro.

'I tink ya both barkin' up di wrong tree, because you wouldn't find it any wood or forest. It ain't frozen, it's spicy n so damn hot. It's a dance genre, not a frozen lollipop,' replied JB.

'Ha Ha Ha-Ha Ha! You two don't know what Calypso is?' asked Sally.

'I wasn't too sure to be onest wid you, but I didn't thiiink it was an ice pop.'

'You thought it was exactly the thing I said,' responded Jemma unconvincingly.

'Nooooo… I never! A Calippo is a frozen ice pop, not a Calypso!' laughed Alessandro.

'OK peeps, can we just now settle down please, cool off, but don't freeze n den turn up di eat wid some calypso free flowin' writin' style, refinement n flair! Me soul on fire, party people feelin' HOT HOT HOT. What to dooooo on a night like dis, music sweeeeet, I can't resist, we neeeeeed a party song, a fundamental jam, so we go rum bum bum bum.'

JB was in such a buoyant mood because it was Friday, he was going to yoga class and ultimately because he was spending time with Bethany tomorrow afternoon. He got up off his chair and started dancing around the classroom, shuffling his feet forwards and shaking his bottom from side to side. This was a typical West Indian Calypso dance. He was electric, ready to ignite the flammability of Bethany. Could it be the ideal explosive mixture?

'Sir, why are you shakin' ya bottom so quickly as if you ave ants-a in ya pants-a?' asked Alessandro.

'Dis is di way we dance in di Caribbean to Calypso. You ave to wiggle ya body n shuffle forwards or sideways. You can mention dese kinda traits in ya stories.'

'That's so sexy sir!'

'Jessica, I wouldn't n don't need to know if di way I dance is sexy, n ope not to you! I'm ya teacher, not ya boyfriend!'

'That's Alessandro sir!' shouted Frankie.

'Dat ain't my business Frankie. I'm ere to educate you, instill confidence, inspire, discipline, motivate and elp sculpture y'all into respectful, decent n moral human beings. You could call it a partnership wid ya parents n guardians!'

'What d'ya mean sir?'

'Well Frankie, you ave opefully a special relationship wid ya parents, so I'm a substitute parent, guardian, friend, mentor, coach n confidante ere at di school. You should feel free to speak to me about anyting. Of course I would never force ya, but I'm ere to make ya journey tru school easier.'

'I understand sir. I always feel comfortable talking to you, because you're so helpful, honest, kind and understanding. Some of the teachers here at Oatmill are so inconsiderate and don't treat you proper.'

'You mean properly Frankie,' said JB in his posh accent.

'Exactly sir.'

'Jessica, is there someting you wanna share wi di class?'

'No sir!'

Jessica was extremely embarrassed and her cheeks had rapidly become a bright scarlet red. It was the announcement by Frankie that Alessandro and her were officially an item.

'There is sir.' shouted Frankie.

'I don't tink it concerns you. Alessandro, d'ya know anyting about dis circumstance?'

'It's true sir.'

'Frankie, keep-a ya nose out man-a,' said Alessandro sternly.

'Why are you trying to hide the truth though, Alessandro? It's nothing to be a shamed of!'

'Why should I be ashamed-a?'

'Jessica's a beautiful girl, very attractive and cool. If you're not going out with her, I wouldn't mind!' he smiled and giggled.

'Sir it's not true. I kissed him at a party that's all.'

'Ooooh, please tell us more!' enticed JB.

'That was all sir. Just an innocent kiss.'

'I bet.'

'Frankie. I'm not the kinda girl you think I am. I don't do those kinda things. I'm an innocent fifteen year old who has no intention in doin' that until I'm at least sixteen n with the right person.'

'Respect Jessica. You're a very responsible n respectful girl. In today's society, people don't seem to understand n realise dat sex under di age of sixteen is wrong. Di legal limit's dere for a purpose, because it's tought dat people can't make sensible informed choices and aren't emotionally ready for intercourse. Anyway peeps, I don't want any of you girls avin' babies at dis age. Ya far too young n also you'd be gettin' yaself n di boy in question into trouble! I don't wanna be a godfather either!'

'I totally agree sir. I don't intend on losing my virginity till I'm married.'

'Frankie, if you choose to wait till ya forty, it's a long time! No one's implyin' dat you ave to wait dat long. Just sixteen or over n when ya ready fa dat experience! Anyway, we're bein' distracted by shenanigans between Jessica n Alessandro, so let's get back to creative writin' about Calypso dancin' culture!' said JB.

The morning was passing by quite quickly. At breaktime, JB decided to stay in the classroom as he wanted to keep a low profile and not give Jennifer any ammunition for firing bullets, as she already had a hunch that he had a passing interest in Bethany. In covert undercover espionage style, he decided to get himself a refill of herbal tea before the first morning bell had sounded, therefore, it meant he didn't have to engage in any uncomfortable circumstances with Jennifer, although he would have to face the music and dance at some stage, unless he was going to hibernate. It had only become awkward as for some inexplicable reason, Jennifer had been jealous at JB falling through the staff room door into Bethany's arms this morning before register. It was ironic, however, as any of the teachers could have opened the door at that opportune moment. Jennifer felt jilted after last week's shenanigans during Tom's birthday bash, when she had stalked her prey like a lioness in the jungle, attacking with predatory prowess. After having mind blowing intercourse back at JB's following a smouldering day and evening in which they intimately savoured without any frivolity, just flirtation until they shared JB's sacred sleeping sanctuary.

As JB was now on the rampage with Bethany, so he hoped when Saturday eventually came in more ways than one. A highly charged explosive, explicit and erotic interlude was at the top of his agenda, the feeling not guaranteed to be mutual. He had made his way for that herbal refill quite briskly, as he had realised just in the nick of time, the bell would imminently sound. Thankfully the walk was only down the corridor from classroom six, so he didn't have far to travel. It was simple, in and out with a pull of the water boiler leaver for good measure, a dip into the honey jar, followed by a quick drop, plop and stir. As soon as he had returned to the classroom the bell had sounded. Talk about perfect timing. As it was a double bubble bumper English lesson for Year Ten pupils on a Friday morning, in other words, two double lessons totalling three hours, taking them to lunch and JB to his ritual afternoon off.

After school today, he would come home and relax for a few hours, before driving to Virgin Active for his evening yoga class which was for an hour, starting at six pm. During the second double lesson of English, he decided to drop Bethany a text to find out how her morning was going.

'Yes Beth, ow ya doin'? R u njoyin' di mornin' so far? I've decided for us to go n shoot some pool 2mro avo, if dats OK wid u. Ya probably a hustler, ready, willin' n able to crucify me! JESUS. Ooops, dat's a l'il naughty of me, apologies fa blasphemin' di Lord's prodigal son! Dress code-Sophisticated, sartorially elegant n sexy chic. Peace-Jammin' X.'

He was thinking about what garments of pure panache he should wear. He had a wardrobe stacked with clothes, so had a very diverse choice.

'Opefully di weather'll be warm, so I can dress down a l'il but still exude class and decorum!' he mumbled under his breath.

'Are you OK sir?'

'Yeah Frankie, why d'ya ask dat?'

'Because you were muttering to yourself.'

'Was I?'

'You defo were. My Dad once told me that anybody that talks to themselves are on the first step to the delusional asylum!' Frankie laughed.

'I can safely say, I'm far from delusional, jus illuminal.'

'Ya always lightin' up our lives sir.' said Peaches.

'Dat's such a glowin' compliment. If ya not careful, ya gonna make me blush.'

'How d'ya know if a person with dark skin's blushing?'

'I don't know Peaches, ow d'ya know if a person wi dark skin's blushin'?'

'Shine a torch on their skin.'

'Is that supposed to be a joke Peaches?' asked Leonardo.

'Yes Leo.'

'Well it's absolute trash. Did ya pull it outta one of last year's Christmas crackers n save it for a special day?'

'No Leo, it's instilled in my brain.' answered Peaches abruptly.

'Ya probably better off openin' ya head up, puttin' a mini JCD inside n draggin' out the junk n then replacin' it with some better quality jokes!'

'Who d'ya think you are? The only joke here is you. Why would you be named after a famous actor? You've nothing in common with Leonardo Di Caprio, apart from your names are similar n you're a mucky blonde!' said Peaches scathingly.

A ripple of laughter reverberated around the classroom.

'Oooops Leo, you're taking a titanic fall. If I were you, I'd quit while ya sinking. Someone'll throw-a you a life raft. Ha haaaaa,' said Alessandro.

'Dat's enough now boys n girls. If you put as much energy into ya work, you'd all be flyin' high wid A stars. Can't we go tru a lesson widowt barrackin', teasin' n humiliatin'?'

'Exactly sir. Some of them are sooooo childish. They need to grow up!'

'Dat's very true, well said Jessica.'

The class heeded the advice from Jessica and once again became immersed in their assignment about the flamboyance and energy of Calypso music and not the mouthwatering juicy fruits of Calippo lollipops. JB started to flick through the BBC News pages on his iPhone, curious as to what was going on around the world. As usual, it was the proverbial doom and gloom with very few articles being of a positive and pleasant nature. Until he saw a headline, '999 Pussy Rescue.' He pressed down on the article headline with his left index finger to open the page, he then started to read. It was all about a heroic dog that had seen a baby kitten drowning in a river. While camping in Minnesota, the dog had been taken out for a walk by his owner, who had let him off the lead for some good exercise. Almost fatefully as the stretch of river became very fast flowing shortly before it hit a waterfall that lead into Lake Superior. The dog had wanted to cool off on a very hot day, so went in for a swim. He had seen something floating down stream, so paddled out to investigate. In a moment of sheer panick, the owner had shouted for help after seeing his dog in a precarious position. The dog appropriately named Hero, had managed to grab hold of the object in the water, before being dragged across to the near side banking of the river. Miraculously after looking rather ominous, the dog and object became caught in an eddy.

They were so fortunate as this was their only saviour unless they against all odds would have survived a sixty foot waterfall drop? Several fellow campers were dashing backwards and forwards in a state of panick, deciphering what action to take. One guy had managed to get his hands on a long telescopic rescue pole with a rubber noose on the end. It was just long enough to reach the stranded dog and kitten. The noble man had guided the pole into the river and managed to attach the noose around the dog's neck, dragging both animals to safety. The man, Gee Loupey, was being held by other campers in a tug of war stance to ensure he wasn't dragged into the water. Gee Loupey said, 'I don't know what happened, I just heard all these shouts and cries for help, so ran along to find out what was going on. I picked up this yellow rescue pole I stumbled over and just did what I had to do. Before I knew it, a dog and kitten were safely at the river side. It's just lovely.'

JB was smiling from cheek to cheek at the gallant, bold and heroic efforts of Gee Loupey. A modern day Tarzan. Gee Loupey decided to keep the kitten and named it Lucky. What an inspirationally beautiful story for once, thought JB. His phone vibrated as it was on silent, a text response from Bethany.

'Yes Jammin', do you want to jammin' with me? ;-)) The mornings bn good thx. U'll have ya work cut out 2mro, bkoz, just like u said, I am a pool playing hustler. It'l be a reall ball. Lol. Possibly a l'il food n drink after, if u behave yaself? ;-P What u doin' for lunch? Xx

It was ten minutes to midday, so he had to think about lunch. He hadn't brought any food today, but there was plenty in the staff room cupboards. He responded,

'Yes Beth, I'm in fa di game of mi life, if ya dat good. I may ave to overload ya drinks wid more liquor to affect ya performance?? Otherwise jus put u off? Lol. Jus gonna ave some pasta, pesto n tuna wid some olives fa lunch. C u in 10. High 5. X'

JB stood up and walked around the classroom checking on the work they'd done so far. He was impressed by the imagination, creativity and inventiveness of their stories about the Calypso culture.

'Dere are some really interestin' stories about di Calypsonian culture. I'm gonna relish readin' dem. Put ya pens down, give ya wrists a rest, kick ya feet off n let dat stiffness disappear, shake ya eads, pull ya chairs back, stand up n jog on di spot.'

'We're all gonna be runnin' for our lunch-a sir.'

'Well, I ope not runnin', but maybe a l'il spring in ya step, in prep for a nutritious dinner Alessandro!'

JB winked at Alessandro, who in return, winked back.

'Take care all, ave a fabulous weekend n I'll see y'all nex Friday mornin'!'

'Take care sir.'

'Have a great weekend Mr Herbert.'

'Live it up sir.'

'Make di most of it.'

'Savour it Mr Herbert.'

'Happy weekenders sir!'

Ding-a-ling-aling-Ding-a-ling-a-ling sounded the school dinner time bell.

'Off you go peeps. Enjoy ya lunch n ave a sensational weekender n make sure you behave yaselves.'

The class made their way to the corridor outside, heading in different directions to fulfil lunch arrangements, whether that being a potted meat or chicken salad sandwich, a bag of smokey bacon crisps, a healthy and nutritious dinner in the canteen, a piece of fruit or a sneaky cigarette for the more rebellious ones. Hopefully most of them would be more inclined to have a tasty fulfilling meal that would keep them satiated till tea time. JB knew which of his pupils were headstrong, disciplined and single minded and which just followed the crowd due to impressionable weak willed traits. In time, as maturity manifested itself, most would be more inclined to make informed, sensible, strategic and productive choices, although some might be on the downward spiral to crime and destruction. JB had fortunately had the love, compassion, wisdom and secure guidance of his parents Cheribelle and Sugar, these enabling him to blossom into a model human being, although like everyone, he had traits that were irritating to some and antagonising to others. No matter who you are in life, you can't be liked and loved by the entire world. Some people will be able to identify with you and others won't. A philosophy JB's parents told him was, 'Treat people how you expect to be treated, otherwise, treat people as they treat you!'

JB closed the register, opened the designated desk drawer and placed it in there, closed it and locked it, placing the bunch of keys in his man sack. He pulled his chair out, stood up and made his way to the staff room, not forgetting to take his rasta man mug with him.

Chapter 33

LUNCH MUNCH

He was wondering what fireworks he may be likely to encounter, even though Jennifer had apologised for her earlier temperamental behaviour before morning class. He waded through the busy corridors, weaving in and out like a high flying fleet footed rugby playing winger, until he reached the staff room door. This time though, quite fortunately, there would be no deja-vu, falling into Bethany. sizeable c-cup mound. He pushed the door open, to be welcomed by pleasantries. There were about ten teachers in there, preparing their dinners and drinks, some already sat down watching the news on TV or engrossed in magazine articles from Marie Claire to Men's Health.

'What's happenin' Jammin'?'

'I'm all good tanx Jaz. Just ad a productive mornin' wi di year ten kids. I gave em a project to work on.'

'Ooooo, sounds interestin', tell us more!'

'I asked em to write a story about di Calypso culture.'

'Uuuuuum… Oo la laaa! Is that what you n Jen were dancin' to n Saturday night? Hot n so so spicy!' responded Jasmine with a massive grin on her face.

'Dat was just a l'il pasa doble n cha cha cha!'

'It certainly was cha cha cha JB,' answered Jennifer.

Bethany glanced across, turning and lifting her head up momentarily from her magazine, catching JB's gaze, winking, smirking and continuing to read her article. JB smiled back.

'Why d'you seem so happy with yaself? That's such a suspicious grin, don't cha think Jen?'

'Can't a man be so appy wid life, does e need a suspicious ulterior motive Jaz?' answered JB sternly.

'No, I agree with ya, but ya just look like the cat that got the cream!'

Tom started coughing vigorously, almost choking.

'Speaking about cats getting the cream, how about pussy go lightly over there? Talk about hypocrisy! Have you spoken to Ethan this week?'

'Who? JB or me?' replied Jasmine.

'Think logically Jaz. Who had the car parked in their garage last weekend?'

'Don't be so disgustin' Tom. As a matter of fact, we're hookin' up tomorrow day.'

'Oooooo, tell me more!'

'It doesn't concern you Mr Chrysler. We're probs gonna go for a bite to eat somewhere outta town.'

JB had poured some penne pasta into a saucepan and started to boil it with hot water.

'Phew!' he muttered under his breath.

He was so relieved that he and Bethany wouldn't bump into Ethan and Jasmine. He was also hopeful that out of anyone, they wouldn't see Jennifer, as that would really set the cat amongst the pigeons. We all know what impact a cat would have on most types of small to medium sized birds. To put it mildly, spitting feathers just for starters.

'Does anyone want a drink?'

'I'll have one please JB.' answered Tom.

'Can I have a strong black coffee please, Jammin',' asked Bethany.

'I'm OK thanks Jammin'! Don't they normally say, the drink you prefer resembles the kinda man or woman ya like?'

'I've never eard dat Jaz.'

'I was readin' about it last week Jammin'. They call it a subconscious attraction!'

'Isn't dat so generic Jaz?'

'Nooo, how is it? If ya think most of us have a preference. Some like a weak drink, some love a strong one, some prefer it with a few sugars, others with honey n me, I love a Screamin' Orgasm or a Long Deep Screw!' laughed Jasmine.

'I thought you were talkin' about drinks Jaz n not ya preferred sexual antics?'

'I was Jammin'. A Long Deep Screw's a juicy cocktail.'

'We all know you ad one o dem at di weekend don't we!' Highlighted JB.

'That's a cocktail that I drank yeah.'

'Can we change the subject please n talk about something else, like conservation of global wildlife or the recycling process? I don't wanna hear about Kama Sutra positions involving my brother, thanks,' said Tom.

'Ooooh, relax Tom. Don't be such a prude!'

'Let's be frank though Jaz, it's now lunchtime, so I don't need to hear about fresh meat while I'm digging my teeth into this wholesome, tasty n nutritious tuna salad sandwich.'

'I was only talkin' about drinks n sayin' how they subconsciously symbolised the kinda person you like. It was Jammin' who mentioned about fraternisin' n frolickin' with ya brother, not me! Mi mind's not always thinkin' about sex.'

'Maybe not, but most of the time it is!' said Tom assertively.

JB gave his pasta a stir as the water was bubbling, almost ready to drain down the sink. He opened the cupboard and took out a jar of hot pepper sauce, salt and black pepper. He opened the fridge door and took a jar of green pesto, a jar of pitted green olives, half a fresh lemon and lime that had been wrapped in clingfilm. He nudged the door shut with his right knee.

'Did anyone read dat story about di dog dat saved di baby kitten n ad to be pulled ashore in Minnesota dis week?'

'Yeah, I read about it Jammin'. A remarkable story and thankfully that tiny whirlpool intervened and prevented them from dropping down the waterfall to near certain death. So funny too, the dog being called Hero. You couldn't have scripted it,' replied Bethany.

'It was such a lovely success story fa once n great to get eadline news as opposed to di customary doom n gloom.'

'Totally!'

Bethany lowered her head once again, to browse through the glossy pages of her Marie Claire magazine. His pasta was now ready, so he turned the heat off and drained the hot water down the sink, being careful not to allow any penne convicts to plot an escape route to safer ground, before facing the death penalty in JB's hungry mouth. He used the saucepan lid to ensure no escapees could flee. He placed the pan back on the hob on a different ring, flipped the top off the pesto jar, picked up a tea spoon from the dish drainer and gouged out a few portions. He then unscrewed the top off the hot pepper sauce jar and drizzled a small amount into the bowl of yellow pasta, ensuring he didn't overload it with palate burning spice. He put the tops back on the respective jars, picked up a more serrated knife from the drainer, unravelled the citrus fruits from their protective clingfilm and sliced them, before cutting them in half and squeezing their juices all over the bowl contents. He managed to prevent any pips from the lemon sabotaging the delights. He flicked the cold water tap and ran the fruits underneath to wash away any bacterial pesticides, as he was going to flavour his herbal tea with them. Off with the olive jar and using the same knife after scooping out a dozen or so green balls, he meticulously sliced them all a few times onto a plate. He then threw them into the gradually growing tasty concoction. He sprinkled on some salt and black pepper and then stirred all the ingredients thoroughly around.

'Uuuuuuuum, dis looks delicious. Can't wait to devour dis delicacy.'

'Are you goin' senile Jammin'?'

'No, why Jaz?' he asked curiously.

'Because it appears that ya talkin' under ya breath n that's the first sign of madness!'

'I tink I'm already slightly mad Jaz, so dere's no surprise dere is dere!'

'Ya can say that again!'

'I tink I'm already slightly mad Jaz, so dere's no surprise dere is dere!' said JB.

'You didn't have to repeat it, it's just a figure of speech, you joker!'

'JB, are you gonna make the drinks then?'

'Relax now man. Gi me a bit more time, because I need to re-fill di kettle n sort dis pasta out. Comin' right up in two minutes.'

'It might be quicker if we make it ourselves.' suggested Tom.

'No Tom, it's nice to be looked after. Let JB be the butler.'

'You're right Beth, just get a move on please though Jammin', our mouths are almost dry.'

'It'll be ready when it's ready.'

JB refilled the kettle, flicked the leaver and turned it on to boil. He opened the crockery cupboard, took a bowl out, closed the door and rinsed it under the cold water tap. He took two cups out of the drainer for Tom and Bethany.

'Can I have decaff coffee please JB?' asked Bethany.

'Of course ya can.'

He unscrewed the top off the decaffeinated coffee jar, picked up the tea spoon and scooped it into the granules taking out a heaped spoon.

'I'll have one of those two please JB.'

'Comin' right up Tom.'

He repeated the process for Tom and took out another heaped tea spoon of decaffeinated granuled coffee.

'Don't forget the sugar with mine.'

'Ow many?'

'Just one please.'

The kettle had boiled, the switch clicked off automatically. JB lifted a flat spoon of brown sugar out of the pot and dropped it into Tom's cup. He had chosen two floral ones for Bethany and Tom. Pansies for Tom and sunflowers for Bethany. He poured the hot water into the cups, stirred the ingredients and then took them over to Tom and Bethany who were sitting on the couches near the TV.

'Dere ya both go.'

'Thanks Jammin'!'

'No probs Beth. Dis'll opefully perk you up fa di rest o di afternoon.'

'I hope so!'

'Why have you given me the cup with pansies on it?'

'I jus tought di flowers would lift up di rest o ya Friday.'

'Are you sure your not implying I'm gay?'

'Sometimes you ave very camp traits, but don't be offended. Ya probably a backstreet boy n don't know it? Ha haaaaaaa.'

'You've got room to talk with the way you occassionally walk n talk. You wiggle your ass sometimes like ya craving a bit of booty love!' laughed Tom.

'Di only bit o booty love I'm gonna receive is a sensuous slap n smack to mi cheeks. Booty love ain't di way I roll. Den again, if she's interested in some rear canal lovin', it could be on di agenda?'

'Whooooo?' asked Tom.

'Jennifer, so tell us more about ya weekend sexploits then?' said Jasmine.

'I'd rather leave that for behind closed doors Jaz. I don't really think it's appropriate to care n share wi the whole staff room do you?' responded Jennifer.

'Nooo, but you can tell me later though!'

'Maybe yes, maybe no!'

'Don't be a spoil sport Jen.'

'Shhhhhhh… Jaz. So what happened with Ethan then?' she turned the conversation on its head.

'I'm not gonna tell you here!'

'Snap. So you totally understand then, don't cha?'

'Yeah, ya right Jen.'

'No-one Tom!'

'Come on Jammin', there must be some lucky lady of late!'

'I leave dat fa special occasions Tom.'

'You mean like birthdays n Christmas?'

'You'll never know! Anyway, ow are di drinks?'

'Mine's delicious thanks!' Bethany said winking suggestively at JB.

'I'd prefer a bit more sugar in mine Jammin', but it'll do thanks.'

'Next time, make ya own Tom n don't treat me as ya slave,' said JB.

'You should be so lucky,' said Tom with a wink.

JB mixed his pasta ingredients with a fork vigorously in the bowl, to make sure all the flavours were fused and enhanced in the pan. He took the pan off the hob and started to shovel all the contents into the large white bowl. It looked absolutely scrumptious. He licked his lips with excitement. He scraped virtually every last piece of pasta and remnants into the bowl and then flicked the cold water tap and ran the bowl under there, removing most of the remaining residue and then filled it up with water to soak. He once again opened the crockery cupboard and took out a large mug with Mr Lazy on the side, from the Mister Men cartoons. That was a perfect explanation for how he felt. It was gonna be one hell of a lazy free lesson period afternoon. He put the mug down, opened the box of camomile and spiced apple teas, pulled out a bag and dunked it in the mug. He poured in the hot water from the kettle that was now a little cooler, albeit still hot, unscrewed the honey jar top, inserted the same tea spoon he'd used for the coffee and lifted out the contents, before swirling it around the spoon to ensure there was no dribble factor down the side of the jar or on the work surface. He plunked it into the the mug of herbal tea and gave it a good stir. He took the spoon out and dropped it in the saucepan in the sink. He tucked the fork he had used earlier well and truly into the pasta, to make sure it didn't fall out, carrying the bowl and mug of tea to the four foot high round table, before putting them down and then sat down. All of the other teachers were either sat on one of the sofas or chairs, reading or watching the news on TV.

'Beth looks ravishing,' he thought.

She was wearing a tight black pencil skirt, side zip up two inch heel ankle boots with a fold over flap and designer silver button, a lemon blouse and black buttoned up cardigan. You could see the shape of her c-cup breasts, which JB hoped to possibly be rather intimate with tomorrow. Her look was very refined and svelte. He pulled his iPhone out of his trouser pocket, pressed the home button which then displayed the pin lock, so he typed in the code to open the phone, as he wanted to browse the Internet. He wanted to find other activities to do besides possibly shopping and food. He thought Ten Pin Bowling would be a great way to have some fun, or of course shooting some pool. Bethany did imply she was a bit of a pool hustler, so that was the obvious choice, also retail therapy maybe wasn't a great idea, as there was far more chance of them being seen out together and rumours inevitably being spread by pupils or teachers. He ran a Google search on Pool Halls in Marlborough. Two came up, Elbow Rooms and Eight Ball. JB thought the better one of the two would be Eight Ball, as it wasn't as popular as the chain Elbow Rooms, so there was less chance of them being seen. He had been to Eight Ball before and really enjoyed it, although it ended embarassingly badly when C-Man had been ejected for being sick all over the lilac pool table cloth. To make matters worse, a few of the pockets had been covered with a river mix of pepperoni pizza and jaeger bombs, so they had decided to charge him fifty pounds for the damage. The Deputy Manager at the time had been quite young, so JB and friends had managed to sweet talk her and promise C-Man would return with the remainder of the bill. He had paid a tenner there and then, as that was the only change he had. This happened several years ago, so hopefully now, the Management had changed. It was a hilarious night from what JB remembered, that had started out with a few social daytime drinks, progressing into some pool playing forfeits. As C-Man was rather worse for wear quite early on, he was the proverbial pool playing bait. Every shot you missed or every time you fouled, you had to down a jaeger bomb in one. It was a special promotional offer, so they were priced at two pounds fifty each. You could arguably accuse the venue of being partly accountable, as they were supplying cheaper drinks, successfully acquiring more custom, but consequently being left with sick on their hands, or in this instance, slurried all over one of their tables.

The decision had been made, so he texted Bethany to confirm.

'Yes Beth, ow ya doin'? Ya lookin' hot 2day, n I especially like ya lemon blouse n pencil skirt. W-oucha! ;-)) Don't turn round as it may make it a l'il obvious. Jus bn lookin' at activities fa 2mro n decided we're gonna go to Eight Ball in Marlborough. Good pool tables, music n tasty tucker. Njoy di rest of ya TGIF. Jammin' Hot. X ;-))'

He sent it. Within moments Bethany was opening her handbag as she'd felt a vibration coming from between her legs. The bag was placed between her chic shoes and sent a mini tremor from her feet to the inside of her thighs. JB saw her shudder momentarily, turn her head to her right and then left, just to see what everyone else was doing. She had an intuition it may be JB, so wanted to make sure the coast was clear. Annabelle was to her right, totally engrossed in her book and Tom was sitting on her left, reading an edition of Men's Fitness. She lifted her bag up on to her lap, unzipped it, pulling out her phone to check to see if it was indeed her phone that had vibrated. The screen was lit up, so she knew it was. She unlocked it and read the message. Smiling broadly.

'You seem really pleased with yaself Beth, what's happened?' asked Annabelle.

'I'm just reading a joke a friend sent me earlier.'

'Tell us then!'

'OK, are y'all ready?'

'READY.' A chorus response from the teaching entourage.

'Here goes… Dustman calls to collect Dustbin. He knocks on the door and a Chinese man comes out. Where's ya bin? Chinese man says, I bin in di bedroom. Dustman says, No where is your dust bin? Chinese man says, I jus told you, I Dust Bin in di bedroom, Dustman says, NO, where is your wheelie bin? Chinese man says, OK, I Wheelie bin havin' a wank!'

'Ha haaaaaaaaa. Dat's absolutely ilarious.' JB laughed hysterically, almost choking on his pasta.

'Ha haaaaaaa. That's brill Beth.' Says Jasmine.

'Talk about wheelie wheelie funny Beth,' said Tom.

'I like that Beth. It aint just a has bin,.' said Annabelle.

'Eeeeerm, what d'ya mean Bella?'

'You know when you say something's a has been, it means they're now past it. So, I mean it's a dust bin n not a has bin. It's all about the here n now.'

'I get ya Bella, ya starting to make sense now. Ya took your time, or you could say, you've bin a while!' replied Bethany.

Tom had stood up and given JB a few slaps on the back as he was struggling to regain his breath after almost choking on his pasta after Bethany's hilariously funny joke.

'Many tanks Tom, dat's a lot better. I'll ave another slurp o mi tea.'

'No probs JB. Virtually anything for you. Especially when you made such an enjoyable coffee.'

'Tanks. I tought ya were dissatisfied it took so long?'

'I was only joking with ya.'

'You are di king o humour.'

'I think Beth must be the queen then?' said Tom.

'I'd say, probably just the princess, or maybe lady in waiting?' chuckled Beth.

'How's the pasta goin' down, apart from the wrong hole?'

'It's delicious, when I can actually taste it n not spit it out. It's really spicy, do you want to try some?'

'Yeah, why not. I'll just get a fork from the drainer.'

Tom walked over to the sink and picked up a clean fork from the drainer, bringing it back to the table so he could taste JB's spicy pasta mix.

'Delve ya fork in dere n taste a piece o dis.'

Tom plunged his fork into the bowl mix.

'OMG, dat is what I call HOOOOOOT! Oooooooo la laaaaaaaaaaaa. Why didn't you make me some of that?'

'One you dint ask n two, am I ya slave? Nex time I might treat ya!' said JB.

'Oh thank you kind sir! If you were a butler, I'd definitely hire you.'

'Ya so gracious Tom. If I needed a cleaner, I'd defo hire you!'

'What makes you say that?'

'Because if I dint stop ya, you'd ave cleaned up mi bowl o pasta!'

'You rascal you!'

'I ain't no rascal, jus speakin' di truth n sometimes it urts! Ooooooow.'

'What are you doing this weekend?'

'Probably gonna hang wid Fluffy Donkey n Ash Tray, maybe grab some food or just ave a quiet night in at one of our places. I could host a poker night? If I do, would ya be intrested?'

'Yeah, defo. I don't know how to play, so you'd have to show me.'

'I'm sure one of di sharks could give you a stronger bite n make you a more formidable player!'

'Are y'all quite good then?'

'I'd say miself, Ash and Fluffy ave all been rather successful down di local casino and also overseas, if you know what I mean good sir!'

'What d'ya mean by overseas?'

'Weeeell Tomothy… You know, after hours with a good old fashioned Royal Flush and a good run of bevy of beauties. I'd call that a pocket full of aces sir,' said JB in his most refined voice.

'I'm sure you could all teach me the basics, hone my skills and enable me to be a successful poker prince.'

'I'm sure we could try.'

'Yeah, please give me a holler if it's game on like donkey kong.'

'When as donkey kong rhymed wid on Tom? Ya mean all on like a Romeo don?'

'Something like that!'

'What's everyone else doin' dis weekend?' asked JB.

'I'm probably gonna go for a spa beauty treatment experience with my Mum n Bella. Does anyone else wanna come?' responded Jennifer.

JB smiled and was so excited inside, because that meant that one part of the CCTV wouldn't be functioning locally this weekend.

'Dat's an away win.' he thought.

'I'd love to Jen, but Ethan's gonna take me away for the weekend.'

'Ooooo-ooooo! Sounds like a dirty weekend to me Jaz!' said Beth.

'It'll just be a clean one, bedsheet n all.'

'Hhhhmmmm! In whose eyes? They'll only be clean when you first arrive and after you've left!'

'You know I'm a good girl Beth.'

'In your mind,' answered Bethany.

'Anyway, what are you doin' Beth?'

'Probably going to have a quiet one with family and catching up on some marking. I might get to throw a few rich glasses of wine in there too, if I'm lucky.'

'I've got a trip away wi the boys. We're gonna go to my favourite bonnie Scotland n spend a wee time in Edinburgh. I can't wait, but it's gonna be a wee bit messy wi di rugby laads,' said John.

'I suppose dere'l be a lot of scrummin' down den wid a few rucks trown in.'

'Weell, ya know JB. Lads on di laaash wi some lady action too, is a distinct possibility!'

'You'll ave an amazin' time livin' it up in di naughty north.'

JB continued forking into his delicious dinner, relishing every mouthful, until the bowl was virtually empty. JB's phone vibrated on the table. He hoped Bethany hadn't replied to the recent text he'd sent her, as Jennifer had decided to sit down next to him at the table.

'Senorita Luis-Cortada, ow can I be of assistance to ya?'

'You could kindly massage my shoulders, they're feelin' tired after the long workin' week.'

'Ya drive a hard bargain girl! If I decline, what will ya do?' he asked.

'Ya life ain't worth it Mister Herbert. I'd advise you to comply, otherwise oh my, oh my!'

'Meanin'?'

'Just get on with it please!' she demanded.

She turned her chair round to face the TV, so he could nestle in behind her to give a soothing, therapeutic and pleasurable massage. He turned his chair around too, so it was identical to hers, shovelling in the last heaped forkful of pasta, clinking the bowl as the fork dropped in, swirling the arm around the edge until it came to a sudden stop. He licked a couple of fingers on his left hand, as they were sprinkled with a small amount of his lunch residue.

'Dat hit di spot perfectly!'

'Ya hands are gonna do exactly the same to my neck n shoulders!' she purred, almost cat like.

Jennifer thought her behaviour would make Bethany jealous, especially after her receiving massages from JB throughout the course of the week. Bethany knew all about Jennifer's desires to insert her talons into JB, but hoped he'd be reluctant to succumb to her evident charm. She was phenomenally attractive, but too desperate to succeed with her quest for his heart. Bethany was very subtle, reserved and pensive and would never blatantly pursue a love interest. She was very much the old fashioned girl, who would allow things to develop naturally. Jennifer was incomparable to Jasmine, as she was explicitly man hungry, although she had been hunting for his ass for god knows how long! Bethany was wise enough to know that if any relationship manifested itself with JB and Jennifer, it wouldn't last, as she'd probably be too manipulative and suffocating. JB would inevitably be discouraged and driven away by this.

After licking his fingers clean, he pressed them into the top of her shoulders, kneading away at the tenderness, knotted areas, breaking down the tension and making her feel a whole lot better.

'Ow's dis fa ya?'

'Ooooooh, its pure heaven! Oooooo baby d'ya know what it's worth, oooo heaven is a place on earth...' sang Jennifer.

'Who sang dat song now, me can't remember?'

'Belinda Carlisle!' shouted Jasmine.

'Nooooo, it was Brenda.' said Tom.

'That might be her sister, but it certainly isn't her!'

'Right Jaz, I'm gonna Google it. Shall we put a wager on it?'

'Yeah, an Ayrton Senna.'

'I'd prefer a Lady Godiva! Speaking of which...'

'And ya point is Tom?' said Jasmine.

'Nothing. Yeah, oops, I mean, make it an Ayrton Senna then. The winner takes it all.'

'In my sky rocket. Yippeeeeeeee.'

'Wait a minute you two. I'll check it on my phone!'

John started to search on the Internet on his phone.

'Heaven on Earth was sang by... Wait for it. That wee lassy from the State of Californ I Ayy. Hollywood, Los Angeles to be precise! Birth name... get ready for the drum roll.....bam bam bam bam bam... Born Belinda Jo Carlisle on seventeeth of August 1958!'

'Yeeee-haaaaaaaa. Just give the Ayrton Senna to ya brother for some drinks over the weekend! In fact, No, I'll take it thanks. Ya win some, ya lose some! Happy Friday Tomothy!' chuckled Jasmine.

'That was just a pure fluke Jaz! D'ya fancy a double or quits wager?'

'That's the problem when people gamble. They lose n then they jus wanna keep spendin' money to get back in the black. Just stay in the red Tom, it's only an Ayrton Senna. We can have another bet next week, but I'm retirin' a tenner up!' she said smiling like a Cheshire cat.

'Oooo, that's so good Jammin'. Ya makin' the hairs on my neck stand on end.'

'I didn't realise dey were so big. Dere like mini tarantulas, it must be ya olive skin accentuatin' di look!'

'Watch ya mouth! *Callate, callate!*' barked Jennifer.

This meant 'shut up' in Spanish.

'I was only bein' truthful, sometimes it urts!' laughed JB.

'Whenever have I been so cynical to you? I'm always pleasant, respectful n complimentary!'

'I know, I was jus jokin' though! Don't take everytin' so seriously.'

'You better take it back then n make amends, because I was feelin' on cloud nine n suddenly I'm fallin' outta the sky!'

'I'm takin' it right back as we speak. PUUTT.'

'What are ya doin'?'

'I've just spat out di words, sucked dem back in again, flown beneath di clouds n caught ya before you it di ground. Jus call me Superman!'

'Oooooo, oooooh, ooooooo, that's so tender n masterful!' said Jennifer.

Bethany raised her head, turned round and said,

'Why don't you two just get a room?'

'We've got one here Beth. We get quite excited with public displays of affection. You can watch if ya like?'

'Nooo thank you. I think I'll give that one a miss. Are you two officially an item now?'

'I'd say, I'm an item n she's one too. I'm on di top shelf n she can't quite reach me!' said JB laughing wildly.

Jennifer turned round suddenly, as she'd been offended by JB's arrogant nonchalance.

'Ya too good for me are you? You weren't sayin' that on Sunday mornin' were you! *Estas muy arrogante, basta!*'

This meant, 'You're very arrogant, enough!'

'What are ya talkin' about Jen? Sunday mornin' I was di epitome of Lionel Richie.'

'That's why Iiii'm eeeeeaaaasaaaay, easy like a Sunday mooorniii-iin',' sang Jasmine.

'If I were you Jaz, I'd give yourself a bit more credibility, because Ethan doesn't like easy riders....Ooooops, Freudian slip, I mean easy ladies!'

'Tooom! D'ya want a sharp tongue slashin' across ya face too?'

'I didn't see Jen do that did you?'

'OUCH! Watch it Jen, dat tongue's as sharp as a brand new razor,' said JB.

'Ya lucky I'm not shavin' ya throat! I mean your neck, because I'd probably cut straight through ya carotid artery.'

'Tank di Lord n is Prodigal Son I'm behind ya den. What a relief!'

'I was only teasing you Jaz. Have ya not heard the sayin', never a true word said in jest?'

'That's a point Jaz.'

'What d'ya mean, that's a point?'

'I mean, I didn't mean to say that! I don't really mean you're easy!'

Tom glanced at JB and grinned as he walked over to the sink taking his cup to be washed. JB knew exactly what Tom meant, and he surely wasn't being economical with the truth, as Jasmine was definitely easy! Jennifer had started to relax now as there was no response. It appeared she had drifted off into an unconscious state, the effect of JB's soft, warm and strong hands.

'Jen, are you still wid us?'

'Uuuurgh!' she muttered.

'I said, are you still wid us?'

'Yeeeaaaah,' came a faint response.

JB continued the massage from the nape of her neck to beyond her hair line. Everyone else apart from Tom was lounging on the sofas or in the armchairs watching TV still or reading.

'D'ya want ya rasta man mug washing JB?'

'Yeah, please Tom. Opefully dat may bring ya some luck fa di weekend.'

'I need some, especially after losing that tenner to Jaz.'

'If dat poker night appens, I'll defo be in touch!'

'I hope it does, because I'd like to learn how to play properly!'

'Fa di time bein' as part o ya prep, do some research on di net!'

'Good idea! I'll do just that.'

'Your hands are so soothing Jammin'. I could do with hirin' them out most days of the week, n absolute godsend.'

'Oh, you've woken up now! I tought it seemed so peaceful!'

'As I said to you earlier, watch ya tongue.'

'I don't recall you sayin' dat, jus dis comment about basta, whoever e is!' said JB with a snigger.

'Yeeees, you've remembered! I said enough n shut up, which appeared to have worked for ten minutes or so.'

'Considerin' you've been sleepin' fa di las twenty five, I tink ya timin's slightly out, don't you?'

'All I can say is, ya hands could heal broken skin. That was so dreamy Jammin',' said Jennifer, attempting to lure a response out of Bethany.

Bethany knew she'd have JB all to herself tomorrow, so found no reason to respond to Jennifer's antics of antagonising behaviour.

'When's Stace back?' asked Annabelle.

'Supposed to be Monday Bella.'

'How's she doing?'

'Fluffy said she's real good. By all acounts, virtually back to normal n excited about returnin' to school.'

'Did Fluffy manage to experience the Stace factor then?'

'I don't know, e jus said dey ad a fabulous eve.'

'Rubbish, as if he wouldn't have told you about their shenanigans. You're tight!' said Annabelle.

'Dat's jus di way mi trousers ang!'

'No, you joker. I mean you're tight like family, so he must have told you more!'

'Dat's all e said! I'm jus teasin' ya Bella.'

'I'll have to ask Stace myself then!' said Annabelle, frustrated.

'It'l all come out in di wash!'

'Hmmmmm, let's see.'

JB knew everything that had occurred, as they disclosed all their intimate personal details. The truth of the matter is, as Stacey was a refined and respectable young lady, they'd indulged in frivolity but stopped short of full sex. In other words, Fluffy Donkey had savoured the full English breakfast without the grilled sausage. He said Stacey had wanted to have a few more dates and not have sex until she was ready,.on the contrary with a proportion of girls these days. Their knickers are on for no longer than two minutes, what happened to the old Christian beliefs? Not all girls were like this, but it seemed common place for one night stands to occur.

It was almost time for the afternoon classes, so the teachers were starting to organise themselves, closing books, magazines, washing and drying pots, zipping or fastening their bags up ready for the Friday finale. JB was going to have a siesta and sprawl himself over one of the three seater sofas, as he was feeling exhausted and wanted to be ready for yoga later tonight. Ding-a-ling-ling, Ding-a-ling-a-ling shrilled the school bell. It was one o'clock already. Chaos corridor time once again.

'Take care all. Enjoy ya avo classes n savour di weekend.' shouted JB.

Faint replies of bye and take care too, came from the departing entourage. Bethany waved goodbye, smiled sexily and winked at him, knowing they were going to be re-acquainted the following day. He winked back. Jennifer stood up wearily off her chair, pushed it in, turned round to face JB and threw her arms out enticing him to give her a loving embrace. He shuffled his chair out from under the table, stood up, pushed it in, nodded, walked towards her and hugged it out.

'I'm sorry JB, I've been a little moody today, it's just that time! Do you forgive me?'

'Maybe? Just as long as it doesn't continue,' he threatened.

'I promise! Give me a kiss!'

She leant forward towards his face, closed her eyes and placed her moist lips on his. She could taste the strawberry Lipsyl and the spicy taste of pasta on his tongue as they suddenly began to kiss passionately. He was totally taken aback and after a few moments had to withdraw, as this was wholly inappropriate and totally unexpected. Fortunately as he took a couple of steps backwards, the staff room door opened and in walked Mr Robertson.

'What are you two still doin' here?'

'I've got di afternoon off. It's my Friday ritual, John.'

'I was just packin' away my things n headin' to class!' replied Jennifer blushing.

'Miss Luis-Cortada, scurry away then. You don't want thoose kids waiting for ya!'

'I'm on my way!'

'Come on then, get a moooove on!' smiled John.

What a lucky escape. JB was incredibly relieved.

'Ave you forgotten sometin' John?'

'Besides my sanity, my favourite mug. If I wasn't so knowledgable, I'd have thought the two of youuu were indulgin' in some skulduggery! Ha haaaaaa. Thankfully, I know you better Mr Herbert.'

'Why the formal names John?'

'Because it's class tiime, so I can't be calling my teachers by their first names!'

'Forever di professional Mister Robertson.'

'You know me Mister Herbert!' said John.

He walked over to the crockery cupboard, opened it and took out his favourite mug, closed the door, walked towards the staff room door,

'Take care Mister Herbert and have a fantaaastic weekend!'

'Di same to you!'

JB was so ultra relieved that that scene hadn't happened ten seconds earlier.

'PHEEEEW MAN, what a lucky escape! Dat girl's danger! Ow relieved am I!'

He trotted over to the three seater sofa and army style rolled over the top sighing loudly, thanking his lucky stars.. He was still in a state of absolute shock and couldn't believe how wreckless, and foolish Jennifer's antics had been. JB was held in high esteem at the school, he certainly didn't want his reputation being tarnished, being disciplined and worst case scenario, being sent down the road with his tail trapped between his legs, begging for a reprieve. In other words, being sacked. This would be heartbreaking for him. In reality, they would have both been reprimanded, possibly suspended for a few weeks, pending an investigation, but best case scenario, Mr Robertson would have given them both a ticking off and advised them to cavort in a non educational environment. Thankfully, no punishment would be given, as Mr Robertson was totally oblivious and only saw them two foot or so apart, so had no evidence anyway. JB and Jennifer would have contested any allegations if they had been witnessed in an intimate clinch during school hours. It was also risky, as one of the children could have potentially seen the kiss from across the corridor, as the bottom of the windows in the staff room were four foot from the floor. It would have been desperately unlucky for that scenario to have occrured, because most of the children were in their respective classrooms ready for the afternoon lessons to begin. It still wasn't beyond the realms of possibility, so JB and Jennifer had the rest of the school day, the weekend and the early part of next week, to stew on it. JB wasn't unduly worried, as he knew Jennifer had forced herself on him and would refute any allegations vociferously.

Now it was time for him to chill and enjoy the luxury of his customary free lesson afternoon. He sat up and unlaced his mole skin moccasins and slipped them off, allowing his feet to breathe. The TV was still on, so he turned the volume down, straddled his legs over the sofa arm, spreading himself out along the length. He was so supremely comfortable. He smiled, rolled over on to his side, with his back against the sofa. He took his phone out of his pocket, pressed the home button, typed in the security pin code lock number, selected the clock icon and then set his alarm for two thirty pm. He was going to enjoy a soothing siesta for an hour and a half. Within five minutes he had drifted away into a beautiful relaxing sleep.

Chapter 34

Pre Yoga Siesta

It was time for JB to relax. He had returned home for three thirty pm, after enjoying his afternoon siesta in the comfort of the Oatmigh High School staff room on a supremely comfortable leather sofa. He felt more rejuvenated, especially with his ritual Friday afternoon off and down time. He stroked Felix, who was nestled happily on his lap on the sofa in the living room. JB had inserted his phone into the docking port and selected a soothing therapeutic album from his iTunes selection. It was a medley of mind floating animal sound instrumentals, heaven on earth. It was four thirty pm, so he had to soon get ready for yoga, which he was looking forward to. This would be the perfect tonic end to a hectic week. For him, it was a light muscle stretching hors d'oeuvre before the hearty and sumptuous weekend banquet with Bethany. Felix was purring loudly, content with his king being home administering some preciously deserved loving time. Throughout the course of the day, Felix would spend most of his time entertaining himself by either hanging outside with Petra, his Persian Godess, or chasing shadows, his tail or sleeping for hours on end. He was very easily pleased, normally by JB or Petra, although they had a rather tempestuous relationship, reminiscent of childhood sweethearts, fighting incessantly or loving immensely. Teenagers probably didn't really understand the true meaning of love, as usually lust was a replacement for this emotion, although in their eyes, they were hopelessly devoted in an unequivocal sense. JB knew about lust, as he fancied the pants off Jennifer and indeed had managed to remove them from her statuesque body last weekend. This weekend, it was Bethany's turn. The difference is, he found her more attractive inside and out, because she hadn't made a concerted effort to woo him, whereas conversely, Jennifer had, which made her less attractive to him.

He was drifting smoothly on the sofa, when his phone swished, momentarily muting the music volume, before returning to normal. He heard it subconsciously, his head twitching along with Felix's ears. His alarm had been set for five pm, so he still had another half an hour of relaxation, until his preparation for a relaxing hour of stretching, flexing, controlled deep breathing, which would alleviate any potential vexation.

Chapter] 35

Yoga Time

Bbbbrrrrrrrrr, bbbbrrrrrrrrrr, the alarm on JB's iPhone sounded, it was five o'clock, which meant he had to start getting ready. The music melodies had been halted by the sound of the glockenspiel alarm. It sounded like JB and Felix were in a percussioned orchestra. He gently eased Felix off his knee. He reluctantly stood up and slowly climbed off JB's lap and onto the oak wooden floor, turned back and looked at his owner, miaowing loudly with discontent. How dare JB disturb him, when he was in a deep relaxed and pleasurable sleep? He was extemely unhappy. JB stretched his arms above his head, shook his head to wake himself up, straightened and raised his legs, so they were sofa high, kicked his feet briskly, re-bent his knees and then stood up using his leg strength without holding on. He walked over to the docking port, picked up his phone, swiped it to turn the alarm off, inserted the lock pin code and turned the music off. He noticed Rocca had texted him, so he read it. Rocca wanted to know what he was doing this evening.

'Yes JB, what's happenin' brother? R ya free 2nite or u got plans? Could do with a night out or gym. Let me know. Peace! ;-)) x'

He closed the text app, pressed the phone icon, selected Rocca and called him. The phone rang a few times until Rocca answered.

'Yes Rocca, what appenin' bred? I'm goin' to yoga in tirty minutes, what ya sayin'? I can pick you up if ya intrested.'

Rocca agreed.

'Make sure ya ready n bring a pair o swimmin' shorts or speedos n ya towel. Don't forget ya flop flips too, because dem athletes foot n veruca germs'll be dancin' around reeady fa some victims to pry on. Peace, see you in tirty.'

JB ended the call, put the phone in his trouser pocket and went into the kitchen. Felix was swishing his tail and rubbing up against his legs, circling him as if he was a shark homing in on its prey. JB bent down and took the lid off the large tub of chicken and lamb cat biscuits, dug the scoop part of the way into the depths and took out half a bowl size full. He spun around while still crouching low and poured them into Felix's bowl. He turned round and placed the scoop back amongst the mix, then replaced the lid. He walked over to the sink, turned on the hot water tap touching it with the hand that hadn't been in contact with the cat biscuits, squirted some washing up liquid on to his right hand, rubbed them together and rinsed both hands under the tap before it became too hot. He massaged the Fairy liquid bottle with both hands, smearing some of the lather onto it and then rinsing it under the water. He placed the bottle at the side of the sink and turned off the tap. Felix was munching away at the biscuits, enjoying the flavoursome taste. JB took a glass out of the drainer, turned on the cold water tap, running for a few seconds till it was ice cold, before filling the glass up He turned off the tap and then drank it rapidly, placed it down on the side and then jogged upstairs. He went into his bedroom, opened the sliding wardrobe doors and started to remove his clothes. He put the lilac cardigan back on a coathanger, his trousers on another. He pulled out a pair of reasonably tight light blue Nike shorts that hung just above the knee, a pair of baggy navy blue jogging bottoms, white t-shirt and light grey hoodie. He would be dressed in Nike sportwear apart from the white vest and plain t-shirt. He took out a tight white Umbro sports vest off one of the shelves and put it on, before throwing on the t-shirt and hoodie. He was now dressed to impress with his figure hugging yoga wear. It was approaching quarter past five, so he would leave the house in about fifteen minutes. He sprayed some of his Giorgio Armani eau de toilette on to his neck and his left wrist before rubbing them together like an ant cleaning its legs. He wanted to smell good, hoping to maybe lure another lady into his personal space, but not to have the same effect as it had with Jennifer earlier in the day, with the dangerous staff room liaison. He slid closed the wardrobe door, left the bedroom before closing the door fully, making his way to the bathroom for a last minute toilet stop. Felix had bounded upstairs after munching most of his evening biscuit meal and started fussing around JB. After being disconsolate and irritated by JB when he disturbed his sleep several minutes earlier, he'd now come to his senses, displaying affection. JB jumped up off the toilet, momentarily shocking Felix, whose tail puffed up and swished against his legs. He pulled his underpants, shorts and jogging bottoms up, turned round, closed the toilet lid and flushed the toilet. He turned the sink tap on and washed his hands, squirting some soap into his palms in the process.

'Yippeeeeeeeeeeee! A bit o yoga wid Rocca, back home, chillin' den party time tomorrow wid Beth. Dats what I call a weekend of trills to di max. Yeah man.'

He turned the tap off and dried his hands, left the bathroom, pulled the door to.

'MIAOOOOOOOOOW! MIAOOOOOOOOOOW!'

'What's wrong na Felix?'

He'd only gone and almost trapped Felix's head between the door and the bathroom wall. He turned round, gently pushed the bathroom door back open. Felix was staring back at him with terrified eyes, fur all puffed up like a porcupines needles.

'MIAOOOOOOOW!'

'I'm so sorry Flix, I tought you'd dashed downstairs.'

JB picked him up and cradled him in his arms like a baby, rocking him gently from side to side, stroking his fur, trying to relax and ease his nerves. A second later, or with the door being pulled harder, it could have quite easily broken Felix's neck or caused him concussion. Thankfully, it was a near miss and all was well, apart from Felix's bowel contents loosened a little. JB could smell the unpleasant odour as Felix had dropped a bomb.

'Pooooooo, dat stinks man! I tink ya need to go to di toilet. I don't want business on mi ands.'

Felix was purring quite loudly, as he felt secure in JB's arms and relieved that he wasn't unconsious. JB placed him down, as he had to pick up his towel and swimming shorts for the pool and jacuzzi afterwards. He went into the airing cupboard bedroom where Ash and Annabelle had slept last weekend, opened the door and took out a warm fluffy dark blue long beach towel and a pair of medium length black Nike swimming shorts that were hanging over the hot water pipe. He closed the door, left the bedroom and closed that door to, making sure Felix wasn't in a precarious position. He eventually made his way downstairs, towel and shorts in hand, Felix in hot pursuit. As it was a few days after the summer solstice, he didn't need to bother with putting his lights on a timer, as it wouldn't be dark until ten thirty pm ish. His head was in a tiz was, as he'd forgotten his sports bag. He ran upstairs to his bedroom, opened the door, slid the wardrobe door across and pulled out his Virgin Active complimentary bag that was equipped with a spare swimming cap, Lynx deodorant, Palmer's cocoa butter body cream, security padlock, entrance ID card, black jelly shoes, a spare afro comb and special formula African shampoo and conditioner for his funky afro. He placed his dark blue fluffy towel and swimming shorts into the bag. He closed the wardrobe and bedroom door and jogged downstairs once more, opening the kitchen door. Felix was alongside him, not wanting to leave him alone.

'I'll let you out, so ya can go n play wid Petra for a couple o hours.'

'Miaaaoooow.'

Felix had a happy look on his face which was a huge relief as a few minutes earlier, his fur was puffed and he was in a state of shock. JB slipped on his Nike Air waffle trainers. He was now ready for yoga time with his good friend Rocca. He picked up his iPhone and car keys that were on the work top in the kitchen and his rucksack, pressed the button to disarm the alarm and immobilizer. It squeaked like a child's air filled toy. The alarm had to be set to ensure the house had a source of deterrent. He walked to the panel, keyed in the code, the alarm started to beep quickly, JB and Felix dashing to the door. He unlocked it, avoiding Felix's head this time as he pulled the handle down and opened the door. Felix scurried out, squeezing himself between JB and the washing machine. He closed the door and locked it before the alarm was activated, stood with his ear to the door, just to make sure it had set.

He walked to the front gates, opened them, jogged to his Audi and opened the driver's side door. He climbed in, threw his bag on the rear seat, closed the door, put his keys in the ignition, gave it a little gas and away he drove out through the gates. Not literally, but through the gap they'd left. He pulled over just outside the house, opened the door, jumped out, dashing to the gates to close them and foolishly leaving the engine running. He returned to the car that was growling to itself, as if it was frustrated at being left alone by its owner. Re-united, JB was behind the wheel and away he drove, heading to Rocca's place. It was five thirty pm, thirty minutes before the start of the yoga class. JB's car stereo was playing a medley of house anthems on Dream FM, a pirate station. He was bouncing slightly side to side, relishing the music that was pumping out, enhanced by the heavy bass sound. He had his driver side window wound down a couple of inches so pedestrians could hear the tunes and probably felt the vibrations through their body. Heads looked up, alerted by the music, intrigued or irritated by the boom boom boom! The journey to Rocca's was five minutes to the suburb of Fruitville. The sights were a delight as JB cruised through Friday early evening traffic. Men dressed in suits, women in tight dresses, some with blouse and skirt finished off with elegant shoes or ankle boots. The weather was a warm twenty degrees, about seventy Fahrenheit. As a lot of people had finished work at four, the norm for a Friday with certain organisations and companies, rush hour was almost ending.

JB pulled into the front of the apartment complex outside Rocca's. JB took his phone out of his pocket, unlocked it, selected the phone icon, choosing the call register and pressed Rocca's details. It began to ring.

'Yeah man, you ready? I'm outside waitin' for ya. Come on, let's ave some bro-mance n savour some supple specialness.'

'On mi way.'

JB was stationary, or should I say, his Audi was, however, mini jumping due to the sound of the heavy bass sound reverberating through the vehicle and aggravating neighbours. He had his eyes closed, arms and hands being thrown to the left, to the right, elbows bent and then straightened as his finger tips hit the ceiling. Occassionally clenching his fists and shaking his head from side to side, engrossed and enjoying the music. TAP… TAP… TAP… JB thought it was part of the musical track. TAP… TAP… TAP, once more. This time JB opened his eyes and turned to his right.

'Ow ya doin' love?'

'Turn that riff raff down. I've got a baby granddaughter in there who I'm looking after and I don't want her to be disturbed by that boom boom boom.'

An old lady who must have been at least three score and ten, but looked considerably older with a heavily wrinkled face that made a crinkle cut crisp look as if it had had a facelift and botox. She had a cigarette in hand and was puffing like an old steam train.

'Oooooh, I'm so sorry, I din't realise it was so loud. Can I apologise profusely fa dat,' JB answered, turning the stereo volume down.

'You're all the same you lot!'

'EXCUSE ME, WHAT D'YA MEAN BY DAT?'

JB was incensed, he rarely lost his cool, but interpreted that comment as a racial jibe from the elderly lady.

'I mean, you guys with these expensive racing cars are always playing ya music loud. If I was twenty years younger, I'd have jumped in the car and joined you. But not at my old age, not on ya Nelly.'

'I'm not di stereotypical boy racer, I ave a secure stable n respectable job. I tought ya were bein' racist fa a moment?'

'Me! Racist! My granddaughter's mixed race, because my daughter's married to a black man. I'm the least racist person there is.'

'Oooops… I'm so sorry fa dat. It jus seemed like a derisive comment initially. I don't mean to cause any offence.'

'It's OK, don't worry about that. What d'ya do for a living?' she asked.

'I'm a teacher at di local high school.'

'Which one?'

'Oatmill High.'

'I'll be phoning up to speak to the headteacher on Monday morning.'

'What fa?' JB replied concerned and puzzled.

'To tell him or her what a fabulous teacher they have!'

JB was nodding in agreement, although feeling slightly insecure and vulnerable, as he didn't want any potential accusations of racism endeavouring to taint his role model image. He couldn't quite understand how she could contact the school to sing his praises when she didn't know him and had never spoken to him.

'Tanks alot, dat's so generous n gracious of ya. Ya makin' me feel embarassed.'

'There's no need to feel embarassed, it's just an inclination I have. I've got good intuition young man.'

'I must admit, I like a bit o spiritualism too.'

'Nooo, I don't mean black magic. That's dark, ugly and dangerous. Just like your sort in powerful sports cars.'

'Are ya bein' racist again?'

'You've got quite a bit of humour. It's just a shame my daughter's married, you'd make a fabulous partner. Her husband's nice, but I don't trust him. He's always going back home to Africa and saying it's a business trip. D'ya think he has another wife?'

'Ooooo love, I don't know. It seems a l'il strange, but maybe e as good reason.'

'He works in pharmaceutical industry as a chemist. A really well paid job.'

JB smiled to himself and had an inclination that he was masquerading as a chemist, but was really a drug dealer. Why the regular visits to Africa?

'Ow often does e travel to Africa n where abouts?' asked JB.

'He goes to Gambia and Somalia for a couple of weeks at a time. I'm really concerned.'

'Maybe it could be a wise idea to ask ya daughter to pay for a Private Investigator. It could be quite expensive, but maybe worth di investment?'

'I'll speak to her about it, because she's a little suspicious too.'

'Yes JB, what's happenin'?' shouted Rocca.

He jogged to the driver side window and stood next to the elderly lady, but made sure he stood upwind, so not to inhale the smoke from her cigarette.

'I'm good tanks Rocca, jus chattin' to ya neighbour ere.'

'How ya doin' Mildred?'

'I'm great thanks Rocca, just chatting to this handsome young man. He was playing his riff raff music a bit too loud, so I had to come out and ask him to turn it down. Matilda's sleeping inside, so I was concerned she'd be woken up.'

'I'm sorry about that Mildred. Jammin', how many times do I ask ya to turn down the music?!'

'Ya right man, ya know I jus get inspired n wrapped up in it. It makes mi feel more alive.'

'I know, but there are young children who live here n young ladies who need rest, aint that right Mildred.'

'It is Rocca. Go on then you two, you seem like you're in a rush. Go and enjoy yourselves. What was you're name again, I didn't quite catch it?'

'Ya need to be like Jumpin' Jack Flash to catch me Mildred. Ha haaaaaa. It's JB love.'

'That's a strange name? Two initials only.'

'Because I'm special Mildred. It stands fa…Jovial and Beautiful!'

'It's quite accurate young man. Take care and keep that riff raff down! Enjoy the weekend,' said Mildred.

She walked away puffing the remainder of her cigarette. They both said bye to her, Rocca opening the boot, throwing his bag in. He slammed it shut, walked around to the passenger side door, opened it, climbed in and then closed it.

'Yes brother, give me a squeeze.' said Rocca.

They both hugged it out, JB struggling as he had to wrestle with the seatbelt over his shoulder and waist. 'Let's go n ave some fun n savour some therapeutic heaven.'

JB moved the gearstick into first, indicated, looked over his shoulder, took the handbrake off and slowly drove away.

'She as some umour fa an old bird.'

'Yeah, she's a lively old girl. Her daughter's absolutely stunning. She's with a low life. He's never there n they're married. She always tells me he's over in Somalia or Gambia on business. Quite strange considering he goes for a few weeks to a month at a time n he has a young daughter.'

'It does seem strange man, but we ave to earn a crust when we can. It ain't always easy to make ends meet, dat's why second n tird jobs are priceless. E could be bonafide, just eadin' to Africa to make an onest buck, but it does seem suspicious.'

'He doesn't deserve her. She's always telling me she's unhappy n confides in me.'

'She probably fancies ya Rocca? Maybe di man's a bigamist n leadin' a seperate life as a doppleganger?'

'It wouldn't surprise me. He's friendly enough, but always appears to be really coy n secretive.'

'Ya mate, di old dear Mildred was sayin' I'd be ideal for er daughter. Weird considerin' she's di Mother-in-law, but I suppose it emphasises she don't like di man or tinks e's no good!'

'Damn right. I'd like a piece, but she never gives me that kind of attention.'

'Rocca, di woman's got a ring on er finger, so it means she's off limits man. You can't be tryin' to seduce n snare a married woman, dat's sacrilege.'

'I wouldn't do that, but just hope she splits from the dodgy geezer to give me a chance.'

Conversation was flowing as their appetites were growing in preparation for Friday evening yoga. They didn't normally have to book, because the class was never normally full. It usually attracted about fifteen gym goers, so there was room for another ten in the main Studio which was a good fifteen by twenty metres square.

'What's di gal's name?'

'She's called Candy.'

'Candy man! She must ave a damn mighty fine sweet taste!'

'Candy Man's that scary n evil creature in the movie released in 1992. He had a hook for a hand n prayed upon vulnerable unsuspecting victims. D'ya remember, he became a well known artist n was attacked by that lynch mob who cut off his hand. He decided to replace it with a hook as opposed to a prosthetic hand.'

'Yeah man, I remember im! Why's ya neiiiiiiiighbour called Candy? Is she a pedigree filly orse?'

'Believe me, she's well groomed n I'd love to take her out past the finishing post! If you know what I mean.'

'I'd like to meet dis woman. D'ya tink she's called Candice or Canderel?'

'I doubt Canderel, because that's an artificial sweetener n there's nothing false about her. That's just her husband!'

They had just reached the gym car park and were pulling into a space under a bright street light just a few rows from the main entrance. JB managed to drive it in first time, without having to square up his Audi between the white parking lines. He pulled the handbrake up, turned off the lights, left it in first gear and turned off the ignition. The space was on a slight incline, so he left it in gear so it wouldn't roll backwards into another stationary car or one that was driving by. The lively house anthems stopped with the ignition. Both JB and Rocca opened their doors like clockwork, synchronised like Olympic choreographed swimmers. JB pulled his driver front seat forward by lifting up the lever at the outside, bowed his head and took his complimentary Virgin bag from the back seat and then pushed the seat back to its upright position. They both closed their respective doors shut, Rocca walking round to the boot, so he could take his bag out. He opened the boot, leant forward and took out his complimentary bag. You could have mistaken them for twins apart from their skin complexion, hair, dress sense and height. In fact everything was so dissimilar apart from they had the same bags, a padlock and their entrance card. Rocca shut the boot with a deafening slam as if he was clinically disposing of a basketball from point blank range while momentarily hanging above the rim. The difference was that he was less graceful. JB pressed his car key twice to activate central locking and the immobiliser. They walked to the entrance, through the automatic sliding doors, acknowledged the receptionist, swiped their cards in the electronical reader and glided through the aluminium turnstyles. It was five minutes to six, giving them both time to dress down to their yoga attire, locking away their possessions in a shared locker. There had been a few locker break ins in recent months, so they made sure the bluetooth feature was switched off and phones switched to silent.

Chapter 36

Bubble-Icious

'Breathe in through your nose and out through your mouth. Nice deep exaggerated breaths...Goooood. Close your eyes and imagine relaxing on a desert island, hearing the ocean water gently splashing against the sandy shore, birds tweeting and whistling with the aromatic scent of a scorching Barbecue. Relaaaaaax! Let your minds drift away into a soothing state, gooooood, and puff your cheeks out and allow all your limbs to slowly release all the tension.'

The yoga teacher/guru had been taking classes for a good thirty years. She was in her early fifties and looked absolutely stunning. Her skin radiated beauty, glowing and glimmering under the lights, cheeks a beautiful tinge of rosey pink, her hair a shiny mass of ebony, tied up in a green bobble. She wore a figure hugging black lycra vest top that accentuated her pert bust, lime green silky skin tight leggings that clung to her ass, also highlighting her streamlined toned legs. Her feet were naked, decorated with dark green sparkling nail varnish that matched the ones on her fingers.

'Aaaaaaaargh, aaaaaaaargh!'

'What's wrong now man? Jus chill out n savour dat splish splashin'!' whispered JB.

'I've got cramp in my calf. Aaaaaargh.' Rocca yelped again.

'Just pull your toes towards your legs and breathe nice and slowly. Is that better?'

'Oooooo! Yeaaaah, that's much better Gloria.'

'Goooood. Just allow your legs, bottom, back, shoulders, arms, fingers and head to sink into your mat. Clear your mind, cleanse your soul and think of nothing. All your thoughts will gradually disappear.'

Rocca's salt deprived calf muscle was beginning to relax, the spasm had come and gone as quickly as the night had turned into day. He had been yelping out in pain a minute or so earlier, until Gloria's calming and soothing influence had magically helped to alleviate the muscle twitching frenzy.

'Rocca, I can't wait for a jacuzzi. I feel so relaxed now, I could go to sleep.'

'Mi calf's thankfully eventually decided to chill out. That was agony man.' whispered Rocca.

'You need to ave someting salty before you come to di gym. Maybe try some o dem salt tablets, or munch some beans or egg on toast about two hours before. Put a l'il salt on n dat should elp to minimise di cramp, you lightweight.'

'I'll give you lightweight when I box ya nose.'

'Maaaaan, you punch like a feather. A duster causes more pain. I mean, look at ya. Crampin' out tru a yoga class! Ha haaaaaa.'

'When I catch you, you'll know about it. JB, you're as soft as ya fro.'

'Mi eart's soft, but mi mind, body n soul are as strong as dey come.'

'We'll see about that when you're on the receiving end of a stiff Rocca one, two, three.'

'How are you all feeling?' asked Gloria.

'Energised.'

'Released!'

'On another planet!'

'Out of this world.'

'On a magic carpet.'

'I feel like a new man n like I'm floatin' on air, eadin' to paradise island. Ya sessions rock Gloria.'

'Well thank you JB, that's most kind.'

'Just a few minutes left, so keep falling deeper, deeper and even deeper into your unconscious state of mind. Feel your body gradually begin to lift, float and drift serenely away, as if moving to another galaxy!'

Gloria's voice was so hypnotic and soothing. Whenever she spoke, she put people at such calming ease. Everybody in the class had their eyes closed, bodies sunken into their grey workout mats, breathing softly. The music Gloria chose was also poignant for the class. Instrumentals that encompassed many animals from birds of prey to bull frogs, from elephants to wild monkeys. It was a fabulous Friday evening pleasure. JB started to have one of his lucid dreams once again. He was visualising being in a jacuzzi with a harem of heavenly honeys. All scantily clad, sensationally shapely and exuding super model beauty. He was begining to grunt like a hungry pig, but not too loudly, although Rocca could hear him. He leaned across and poked him in the ribs.

'Sssshhhh Jammin'.'

He was unflinched and continued to grunt softly. Rocca poked him again, but this time he swung his left arm which just brushed against Rocca's right elbow. JB's body shuddered a few times and then returned to a relaxed state. The grunts were increasingly now becoming a little louder.

'Welcome to animal farm, JB,' said Gloria.

He was still unmoved, as if he was thousands of miles away, relaxing on that imaginery desert island.

'He's miles away Gloria.' responded Rocca.

Rocca's eyes were also closed after opening momemtarily when JB started to grunt and flung his arms after he'd been poked in the ribs by one of his right hand men.

'Open your eyes, shake your arms and legs, lift up your head and upper body and slowly move into a kneeling position. Flex your fingers, clench your hands into a fist and then loosen, flicking out your fingers. Climb to your feet, bend over and touch your toes, come to an upright position, stretch your arms out above your head, put the palms of your hands together, take a bow and give yourselves a round of applause. Well done everybody, Take care and have a great weekend.'

'Take great care Gloria!' replied Rocca.

'Ave a fab weekend n many tanks for another extra special class. I feel so relaxed I could fall into bed now.'

'You might have a problem with that JB. One, you need to magically find a bed and two, if you don't, you're gonna bang ya head on a wooden floor and knock yourself out!' said Gloria chuckling.

'If you were dere to pick me up, I'd defo be floatin' to another land.'

'Come on JB, stop flirting!'

'Don't worry Rocca, he's tame. He'd be putty in my hands!' responded Gloria.

'Seriously? Do you want to put some money on dat?'

'To be honest JB, you couldn't afford this,' she said pouting her lips and flicking her hair flirtatiously.

'If ya prepared to take di challenge, we can see whedder or not ya can andle dis expensive jewel.'

'Hhhhmmmm... I may have to take you up on that!'

'When ya free, jus let me know. I'd love some private one to one yoga tuition!' laughed JB.

'We'll have to organise something then!' smiled Gloria.

Rocca was absolutely astounding how suggestive JB had been, and let alone the yoga teacher succumbing to it. Then again, it was hardly a surprise as he was one of Marlborough's most eligible bachelors.

'See you next week.'

'Yeah, have a marvellously action packed and enjoyable weekend.'

'I most certainly will.'

'See you Gloria. I'll make sure I look after him, without leading him astray!'

Everyone else had left the class apart from the three of them. Gloria started packing up her yoga mat and taking her CD out of the stereo system, while JB and Rocca walked through the swing studio doors and headed to the changing room.

'Lord, she's one ot chick boy.'

'Yeah, she's in phenomenal shape for her age, but you've no chance with her. She's teasing you and would eat you alive if she was interested.'

'Ooooooo, ow I'd love to be tamed by a wild, educated, mature, sophisticated n sensuous woman. It'd be explosive alright! You ave to agree, dem leggins ug er booty n legs like a Grand Prix Formula One car uggin' an air pin bend. If she was my partner, she'd be on lock down, because she'd be unted by dem ungry vultures in dat jungle out dere! Ha Haaaaaaaa.'

'You surprise me Jammin'! I didn't think you were so protective of your women?'

'She aint mi woman, but if she was, she'd be on lock down n only be paraded out when di light disappears n di night time come.'

'Stop being so suppressive man!'

'I'm only jokin' Rocca. You've known me fa long enough.'

'You know that... Far too long! Haaaaaaa!'

JB pushed open the male changing room door, almost falling through it, reminiscent of earlier today when he rugby tackled Beth. He just managed to stop himself from hugging the man that had pulled the door open at the same time. The man smiled and apologised. JB followed by Rocca walked though the door thanking the man for his courtesy. JB bent down and discreetly rotated his lock numbers until it opened. He passed Rocca his bag and took his own out. They stripped off, but weren't wanting to indulge in any changing room man to man antics. JB slipped on his swimming shorts, took his black cap out of his sports bag, so he could keep his hair dry while chilling in the jacuzzi. He normally washed it, either every week or every other. Afro hair was a lot coarser than the average white person's hair, so it shouldn't be washed too often, otherwise it wasn't healthy for it. It had to be cultivated, nourished and respected, allowing natural oils to flow, giving it a more refined and silky look. Rocca slipped on his shorts, but didn't need to emulate JB with the cap. Rocca was admiring his beautiful self in the full length mirror directly opposite, posing and pouting as usual. It was surprising, because that was normally JB's trick.

'Ave ya finished wid ya bag?'

'Yeah thanks. Just put it back in the locker please!'

'No worries.'

JB put both bags back in and locked it up.

'I still don't understand why you don't wear flip flops like any normal human being?'

'Why should I be normal? Dat's why I'm extraordinary.'

'You can say that again.'

'Dat's why I'm extraordinary!'

'Joker!'

JB was proud of his black jelly bean shoes that fitted a treat. They walked to the showering area first to clean themselves before heading downstairs to the spa area. Towels draped over their shoulders. It was ten past seven, so Virgin was busy, although not as busy as a midweek day, because a larger proportion of people tended to go out and celebrate the start of the weekend. The two swimming pool lanes were relatively quiet, however the open area was busy with an aqua aerobics class. JB and Rocca had a glance to admire the water babies, but most of them were a little on the larger side. There were a few slender ladies who opened their eyes a little larger, but no sensational honeys.

They decided to go through into the warmer zone which had a jacuzzi, a steam room, solarium and sauna. There was also a showering area which had a bucket with ice cold water in it, a shower with a hot and cold option along with another shower with icy cold water. It was a great area to go into, after coming out of the jacuzzi or one of the three sauna areas to cleanse sweaty skin. The jacuzzi bubbles were in full flow, so the boys hung their towels over the hooks at the side along the wall and sauntered in.

'Dis is beautiful man. Perfect after di cold walk down ere.'

'Uuuuuum, it certainly is a beautiful experience down here.'

Rocca nudged JB as he caught sight of Gloria relaxing with her eyes closed in the bubbles. She was wearing a black bikini, the top fastened around the back and a skimpy pair of bottoms. She looked incredible. The bikini exhibited her curves far more than the vest top and tight leggings she wore for the yoga class earlier. JB's eyes were almost popping out of their sockets, while Rocca was licking his lips. The two Romeos were in their element. The bubbles area was full, so they decided to go under the powerful jet spray showers that were opposite. What a way to relax and recuperate after a long tiring week of work.

'What are your plans this weekend Jammin'?'

'I'm gonna go ome tonight n chill, maybe munch some pasta n savour a warm glass o red. Tomorrow, I'll ave a lie in, in di mornin' n den take a friend out to shoot some pool n ave a few drinks in di avo stroke early eve. What's your script?'

'The same as you tonight and then tomorrow and Sunday, no plans. Do you want to watch a movie tonight at mine?'

'Dat's quite temptin', but I wanna chill at ome wid Felix. If ya wanna join us, ya more dan welcome.' replied JB.

'I would Jammin', but I'll need to eat my tea and then relax, so probably won't have time!'

JB opened the glass door of the steam room. A couple walked out before they entered.

'Tanks. Do I look like a door minder? At least ave a l'il respect n decency, otherwise next time I'll slam it in ya face…' said JB seething.

'Oh, I'm really sorry, my boyfriend's deaf!'

'Are ya both blind too?'

'It was genuinely unintentional.' replied the woman.

'Just a tanks wouldn't go a miss, or at di very least a head nod to acknowledge! God gave us lips n mouths to be able to speak.'

'I can only apologise once again for both.'

'OK den. Take care n don't fall over ya air!'

'I'll try not to. Bye now.'

'Jammin' man! Why don't you just leave it out, instead of creating a scene?'

'Rocca!! I couldn't give a damn man. It aint ard to ave just a tiny amount o decency n respect. Di world 'd be a much better place. I can't stand rudeness, ya should know dat!!'

'I agree, but the man was deaf and her hair was in her eyes, so she probably didn't see us!'

'So because e's deaf, does it mean e's excused from courtesy?'

There was a deadly silence.

'Weeeell… No.'

'Dere we go den, exactly. Remember dis sayin'… Manners cost us notin'!'

Eventually they managed to sit down in the steam room following the escapade that had occurred at the doorway. JB was right in principle, because it would have been so easy for the couple to have acknowledged Rocca and JB's presence, especially when they had acted with a great level of etiquette and allowed the couple to walk out of the steam room before they walked in. Rocca just felt that JB should have humoured them, but why should he. Within probably less than a minute, they were both dripping with sweat. The temperature must have been in excess of eighty Fahrenheit. You could barely see beyond your nose with the large quantities of steam. JB had managed to cool down in temperament, but was scorching in temperature, whereas Rocca had been ice cool all along. The steam room was quite full, equipped for about a dozen people with light grey, royal blue and white mosaic tiled seats three feet above floor level and platforms at about four and a half foot for the more courageous to rest on.

The door opened and in walked Gloria, although the boys couldn't see her initially. They were both sitting down at low level.

'Can I just squeeze past you please?'

'Yeah, of course ya can.'

'Is that you JB?'

'Yeah, who's dat?'

'It's your favourite yoga mentor.'

'Gloria, ow ya doin'?'

'Great thanks. I thought I'd drop in here after enjoying a soothing bubbles session.'

JB's heart skipped a beat.

'You made di right choice. It's tropical in ere.'

'I bet whereever you are, it's tropical,' Gloria said.

'What d'ya mean?'

'Sunshiiiiine on a rainy day, makes my soul, makes my soul, drift, drift, drift away-aaaay.'

'Wouch! You ave a beautiful voice Gloria. If I'd ave closed mi eyes, I'd ave tought di person dat sang dat song was beside me!'

'You'd be right. She is beside you.'

'Noooo... noooo... I meeeaaaan, di original artist.'

'Oooh sorry, aren't I good enough for you?'

'Of course you are. Ya worth more dan a million dollars, especially wi ya yoga DVD sales, expert tuition, elegance, sophistication n beauty,' said JB flatteringly.

'Oooooooh... I think I'm going to faint. What beautiful glowing comments JB. You chivalrous Romeo.'

'Uuuuuurgh! Dat's so sickly. He says it to all the ladies.' said Rocca enviously.

'I jus speak mi mind n di truth, dat's all Rocca. No need fa di sarcasm.'

'You're so enchanting JB! I think you and I should go out some time. As I said earlier, I think you'd be putty in my hands.'

'We'll soon see about dat.'

They relaxed for a further few minutes, after the conversation had slowly diminished. They must have been in there for a good fifteen minutes.

'I'm feeling a bit dizzy now. Shall we get out JB?'

'Jammin', did you hear me?'

'Ey?'

'I said, did you here meeee!'

'Sorry Rocca, I tink I must've dozed off. Let's get out, it's sizzlin' in ere.'

'You can say that again.'

'Take care boys, and have a fab weekend,' said Gloria.

They both said farewell, opened the steam room door, walked out without any awkward moments, apart from JB having to adjust his swimming shorts, as a foreign body had appeared in them. He had to walk quite briskly to pick up his towel, with his back to the jacuzzi, as he didn't want anyone to see his sizeable manhood poking out of the top of his shorts. Rocca closed the door behind them.

'Why are you walking like you wanna go to the toilet.?'

'I'm not I jus feel a bit faint man.'

'Ya not standing to attention are ya?'

'Don't be daft man. Do I look like a soldier?'

'Maybe not, but you look like ya holding a sizeable weapon. Ha haaaaaaa.'

'I can see you've ad a ceasefire.'

'You're disgusting. Are you coming outta the closet or what?'

'Not yet, but if I came out, I tink I'd don some eels, micro mini n boob tube.'

'I better take you to the Rocky Horror Show then.'

'Ooooooo, please darlin'. Don't mind if ya do.'

They picked up their towels and made their way upstairs after a Friday evening of therapeutic bliss to remember.

Chapter 37

Beth Be Going Then

A gloriously warm Saturday morning, with more weekend shenanigans on the horizon. Felix was snuggled under the quilt, resting on JB's naked legs. A tiny gap in the dark blue curtains let in the day's natural light. JB's eyes slowly began to open, before being suddenly closed by the penetrating glare and stare of the sunshine. He had to roll over, so he could wake up slowly without any starry eyed bright solar powered face offs. JB lifted up the quilt and looked down to see how comfortable Felix was. He opened his glistening green eyes and looked up at JB, miaowing happily. JB turned off the socket which his iPhone was connected to, as it had fully charged, and checked the time. It was ten thirty three.

JB's phone flashed and vibrated as it was in silent mode. He unplugged it from the charger, picked it up and read it. It was from Beth. She was just wanting to confirm their meeting place and time and said she was excited about their date, and the feeling was very mutual. Felix had moved himself up to the top of the bed and was resting against JB's right shoulder. He was becoming a little restless though, as he knew it was past his usual early morning feeding time.

'Let mi just ave a stretch n den go downstairs n feed ya. Mi belly's also rumblin' too.'

JB stretched every sinew of his body, which was slightly more supple after last night's yoga class. He pulled back the covers. Felix stretched himself too and jumped off the bed, ready and raring to snaffle his weekend breakfast of chicken and liver Whiskas mixed in with a crunchy portion of lamb biscuits. JB climbed out of bed. his meat and two veg swinging handsomely in the air. He slid open the wardrobe and took out his blue jogging bottoms and plain white t-shirt and put them both on. He trotted downstairs, pursued by Felix hot on his heels. He went into the kitchen, opened the blinds to let daylight in, turned around and opened the fridge door and took out Felix's cat food. He placed them on the work surface next to the sink and took out the stainless steel cat food fork from its solitary holder, removing the pet food tin cover. He turned round and walked over to the twin bowls, one for food and the other for liquids, picked it up and carried it to the sink. He turned on the hot water tap and ran it at the side of the bowl until it started to increase in temperature. The hot steam began to ascend from the tap tip to the base of the sink, so he pushed it to the side and over and into the bowl. He flicked the the top of the washing up liquid, lifted it up and squirted a portion into the bowl, simultaneously turning off the hot water tap and turning on the cold to cool the bowl enabling him to wash the cat bowls thoroughly. He moved the tap to the side and rinsed the cat bowls. He pulled off about half a dozen pieces of kitchen towel, so he could wash the remnants of last night's cat food. He picked the washing up bowl up with one hand, just about managing to steady it with the weight. With the other hand he put the cat bowl into the empty sink. He then held the washing up bowl with both hands as he was struggling with the weight, pouring about a quarter of the foamy contents into the cat bowl, it proceeding to splash back at him with a few droplets catching him in the eye.

'Maaaan, ya a damn nuisance cat. I wish ya could elp me wi dis sometimes. I don't expect dis daily struggle n fight wid ot water.'

'MIAOOOOOOOOOOOOOW!'

Felix was evidently annoyed and agitated and couldn't understand why his owner was criticising him for his own errors.

'Sorry Flixy, it ain't your fault. I'm jus gettin' a l'il nervous about mi date today wi Beth. Probably exactly di same as you were when ya first met Petra.'

JB bent down and picked up Felix, rubbing his belly and kissing him on the top of the head. Felix began to purr, accepting the apology from JB who had acted rather hastily momentarily. He adored Felix whole heartedly, he was his pride and joy. He hugged him for a few minutes and then put him down, but Felix as usual wouldn't leave him alone, bobbing and weaving in between his legs and feet. JB turned on the hot water tap to rinse and clean his hands as they were covered in ginger fur. He then dipped them in the bowl of hot foamy water on the side to clean. Mission complete! He used the remaining pieces of kitchen roll to dry out the dish as he didn't want to cross contaminate the tea towel. Humans can eat animal food, but it probably wouldn't be a mouthwatering proposition. JB threw the sodden and damp pieces of kitchen towel into his bin, flipping up the lid first and then closing it. He moved back to the side of the sink, placed the washing up bowl back in there, dipped the fork into the tin of chicken and liver Whiskas and gouged out the remainder of the contents placing the sumptuous amount into the revitalised gleaming dish. He turned on the cold water tap and ran it into the empty bowl, so Felix had a drink. He was frantically trying to climb up JB's jogging bottoms, digging his claws into the material.

'OUCH! Cat, jus relax n wait will ya. I ain't a piece o prey ya know. D'ya tink I'm in di jungle n ya only piece o meat?'

JB flicked his leg, forcing Felix off. He carried the bowl over towards the customary spot close to the kitchen table and placed it down on the floor. It was a feeding frenzy, no time to waste for an empty bellied feline. JB returned to the sink, turned on the hot water and rinsed out the cat food tin. He poured in an amount of washing up liquid to agitate and remove remaining remnants of conjealed food and then left it to soak on the side.

'What shall I ave fa mi brekkie? I'm so damn ungry. Uuuuuuuum, full English on di orizon me tinks. I'll rinse it down wid a cup o erbal too. Yum yummy, all dat flavoursome goodness ideal fa mi tummy.'

He was so excited about the realisation of savouring a rendezvous with Bethany. They were going to head to a pool hall called Eight Ball which was popular in Marlborough and hosted about a dozen or so lilac and blue felt clothed pool tables. It was decked out in an American theme. He opened the fridge to see what concoction he could rustle together for his later than usual breakfast. There were half a dozen fresh eggs, an open packet of bacon with three rashers in it, some pork, sage and leek sausages, several ripe plum vine tomatoes and half a punnet of mushrooms.

'Yeah man, ppprrrrrrrrrrrrrfect, don't ya tink Flixy?' asked JB.

'MIAAOOOW,' responded Felix.

Whether or not Felix understood JB's conversation, he appeared to have an immeasurable telepathy. He bowed his head and continued to thrash it from side to side as if in pain. It was his peculiar eating style. He was very content and was in his element with no distractions. JB was distracted by the tingling tongue tantalising terrific taste of his Saturday treat. Bethany preceded by a fried food filling. He took out all the ingredients for his breakfast, mushrooms, plum vine tomatoes, eggs, bacon and sausages before closing the door. JB bent down and opened the cupboard that stored saucepans, blender, wok, slow cooker and other utensils. He took out two saucepans, one small and the other medium sized, along with a griddle pan and the wok. He took a plate from the drainer and started to slice the mushrooms and then halved the tomatoes. He had to take out milk and margarine from the fridge as he was going to scramble the eggs, so wanted them to be a little creamier. He poured a sparse amount of olive oil into the griddle pan, turned the heat on low and placed the three rashers of bacon in it. He poured a small amount of oil into the wok too for the sausages. He was feeling greedy, so decided to put all five in. He wanted to stay as sober as possible, so didn't want to be embarrassing himself in front of Bethany and also wanted to ensure that he could get an erection if the rendezvous eventually became a raunchy and scintillating sexual encounter. A substantial satiating breakfast was of course a must. He turned the heat up for the wok and placed the glass lid on. He moved to the sink, crouched down, opened the cupboard door and took out the packet of kitchen foil. This was to be placed on the baking tray so he could grill the mushrooms and tomatoes in the oven. He was going to wait to prepare the scrambled egg as this would take the least amount of time. He tore off a sheet of kitchen foil which was about a foot square. He opened the cupboard under the sink and put the cardboard packet back. He kicked the door gently shut and checked on the sausages and bacon on the hob.

He opened the oven door fully so it lay down horizontally like a canvas sprawling boxer. He slid out the top shelf halfway and placed the piece of kitchen foil on top. He picked up the plate that held the mushrooms and tomatoes, one by one putting them on the foil sheet. He slid the tray back in, closed the door, twisted the knob to the grill setting and twisted the temperature knob to just below maximum. The sausages and bacon were browning nicely, Felix miaowing profusely as the aroma of the meat circulated in the atmosphere activating his and JB's naval cavities. JB opened the kitchen door, picked up Felix and carried him into the living room, dropping him down on the floor. He came back into the kitchen and closed the door as he didn't want Felix jumping up on to the hob, stealing meat or burning his paws. Naturally he was going frantic and pawing at the kitchen door and jumping into it. JB took out a stainless steel spatula with thin rectangular holes in it along with a hard plastic big spoon, so he could flip over the bacon and roll over the sausages, but not with the same financial exultation that a huge jackpot lottery win would provide, simply just a feeling of contentment that the mouthwatering meat was sizzling with sublime satisfaction.

'FELIIIIIX… Just relax cat. I'll give you a piece o meat if you behave yaself. It'll be ready in about ten minutes.'

'MIAOOOOOOOOOOOOW!'

JB couldn't remember whether he was meeting Bethany at two, two thirty or three pm, so he decided to fly her a text. He was enjoying the peace and tranquility of Saturday morning, which was a rare treat as he usually had music blaring out quite loudly or the TV on. The noise of sizzling sausages and bacon was therapeutic but drowned out by Felix's constant yelping.

'Boy, I've lost mi tread, where am I again n what am I doin'? Dat's it, I need to text Beth to confirm what time we're hookin' up.'

He spun around twice then moonwalked towards the kitchen table where his phone sat. It wasn't resting respectfully at the table on a chair, more of a disrespectful lazy lounge down on the table top. It was an electronical gadget, so it could be excused for lying down on the oval shaped pine wooden masterpiece. JB pulled one of the chairs out and sat down with his legs sprawling out to both sides, like Hugh Hefner chilling out pool side at his Playboy Mansion in Hollywood. He typed in the pin code to unlock it, selected the message app, scrolled down to Bethany's name and started to type.

'Yes Beth, ow ya doin' lady? What time did we agree to meet 2day, mi minds goin' all doolally, it mus b di effects o di week catchin' up on mi. I'm sure it was two ish? Jus cunjurin' up a special Sat full English brekkie n mi belly's rumblin' n palate tinglin'… Uuuuum uuuuuum. Lookin' 4ward to seein' you later. X'

He jumped up from the chair and jogged over to the hob, took the lid off the wok and rolled the sausages over a bit more to brown the pale bits. They were almost done. The bacon was done in the griddle pan, so he turned the heat off.

'Stupid damn Fool! I can't believe I've forgotten about di beans n di chopped tomatoes. I tink I'll leave di tomatoes because I'm avin' vine ones, but I better tro a few slices o toast in.'

JB opened the cupboard door above and to the left of the hob and took out a tin of Heinz baked beans, peeled the top off with the ring pull, moved to the sink, turned on the cold water tap and rinsed it, before throwing in a plastic bag on the floor he used for re-cycling. He turned the tap off, closed the cupboard door, as he didn't want to have a collision, a black eye and be knocked out before his later shenanigans. Then again, Bethany might be aroused and attracted to a bruised and battered man? The sausages were now done, so he turned the heat off, lifted the wok lid, gave them a spin with the spatula, put the lid back on, emptied the beans into the smaller sized saucepan, placed it on the spare front hob and rotated the knob to number four. He pulled open the oven door to check on the mushrooms and tomatoes. They were just about ready, the mushrooms a light shade of brown and the tomatoes looking a medium soft texture, so he closed the door and let them grill for a couple of minutes longer.

'Am I goin' senile man? Flixy, jus relaaax now please. It's almost done, so ya can come tru in a sec. Jus need to put di toast in, scramble di eggs n we're finished.'

He eventually opened the fridge and took out low fat margarine-Vitalite and a two pint container of green top semi skimmed milk, closed the door and lifted the lid off the margarine. In went a teaspoon, delving its way into the yellow soft textured margarine, a second or two later it was flying through the air heading towards the saucepan. With a few taps of the handle on the side of the pan, in it dropped. He put it on the spare left hand rear hob and cranked the heat up to the maximum. He glided like a ballet dancer towards the cutlery drawer, opened it and took out two knives, a fork and a teaspoon. He shut the drawer, placed one knife and the teaspoon on the work surface next to the hob and took the spare knife and fork to the table. He returned to the hob, stretched to the side, lifted up the sliding flap of the bread bin and took out the bag containing half a dozen slices of seedy granary bread. He closed the horizontal sliding shutter of the Brabantia stainless steel bread bin. JB pulled open the crockery cupboard and took out a dinner plate. The door was pushed shut with his head. He took three slices of bread out of the bag and placed them on the plate. The medium sized saucepan's contents were now bubbling, so JB cracked each of the three large sized free range eggs that were on the side and poured them into the pan. He used the same spoon that had been used for the sausages and stirred the eggs in with the margarine. He unscrewed the top off the milk and poured some into the now bubbling eggs. The bright sunshine yoke of the yellow was now being tamed with the moon white of the milk which resulted in a beautiful spring lemon shade. Two of the slices of granary bread were dropped into the toaster, the button was pressed down and the toasting process had started. He stirred the beans again to make sure they weren't going to stick to the pan.

JB took the rashers of bacon out of the griddle pan and placed them on the same plate as the now remaining solitary slice of bread, at least now it had some food accompaniment. He turned the oven off, crouched down and opened the door.

'OUCH, dats ot man! I better get an oven glove n protect mi and.'

Everything was just about ready, apart from the toast. The toaster popped up the two slices, which JB took out and put next to the rashers of bacon. He dropped the remaining slice in. The lid was still off the Vitalite, so he used the spare knife he'd taken out of the drawer earlier to spread an even portion over both toasted slices. He then cut them in to quarters, as if feeding them to a young toddler. It was just his preference. His navy blue oven gloves were hanging up on a hook near to the hob, so on they went, hugging his hands, allowing him to pull out the plum vine tomatoes and mushrooms. It was going to be another balancing act like the one earlier with the washing up bowl and the twin cat bowl. This time he mastered it perfectly, tray in one hand and fork in the other, he picked them up one by one and put them on the plate. The tray was then returned to its home, the beans were spooned out to the side of the plate. The scrambled eggs were ready, so the heat was turned off and using the same spoon he'd used for the beans, it was scooped into the fluffy eggs and scraped every last drop from saucepan to plate and over the toast. There were just a few items missing: Felix, sausages and the last slice of toast.

'Flixy, you wanna come in now?'

Felix scraped, scratched and attacked the door, appearing to slam into it with a heavy thud. Probably with his side, as a collision with a door of that stature would definitely have head and neck complications for a small species. JB pushed the door open, Felix dashed in attempting to jump up on to the work surface.

'Oh no you don't! I'm gonna give you some o dis bacon n a sausage.'

'MIAAOOOOOOW… MIAAOOOOOOW!'

JB took the lid off the sausages, took the spatula and managed to lift them all out of the wok and onto the plate with skillful prowess. He dropped a little oil on to the hob. PPPSSSSSSSSSSS!

Felix jumped, shocked by the noise.

'It's alright cat, just a small amount of oil on di ob. Let mi cut one o dese sausages up n give ya some bacon.'

He walked over to the cutlery drawer, opened it and took a pair of scissors out. He picked up one sausage and went over to the cat bowl, bent down and cut the tasty meaty morcel into thin slices which would be easier for Felix to digest. SWISH… SWISH.

JB's phone flashed and sounded. It was probably a response text from Bethany, to confirm what time she wanted to meet. Felix was virtually pushing JB out of the way, so he could tuck into his late morning treat. Considering he'd only recently finished his own breakfast, chicken and liver jellied delight, it was amazing that he had room for extras. The final piece of toast popped up, so JB took it out, put it on the plate, coated it with a layer of margarine and quartered it. Following this he returned the tub of Vitalite to its original resting place, the fridge. There was just enough room, although now the grey and blue plate was virtually overflowing. He squirted a splodge of citrus Fairy into the small and medium saucepans and placed them in the bowl in the sink, turned on the hot water and moved the tap so the water flowed into the bowl. He put all the other crockery and cutlery in there apart from the wok and lid, filled the bowl up so the items could soak. He picked up the salt and silver stainless steel electronic pepper grinder and seasoned the hearty full English breakfast. He returned them to their position and took the full plate to the table and rested it on one of the cork mats. He returned to the hob to ensure that every one had been turned off, it had, so he could rest easy and enjoy his scrumptious food. One thing was missing… A drink, but obviously a non alcoholic one.

'I need a drink Flixy, what should I ave d'ya tink! Sometin' soft or sometin' a l'il stronger. Gladiator proportions!'

'MIAOOOOOW.'

'Dat doesn't make mi decision. Was dat one miaow fa soft n maybe two fa stronger?'

'MIAOOOOW… MIAOOOOW!'

'Ya one clever kitty kat. Ow blessed I am to ave you by mi side.'

JB thought it might be a little too early to open a bottle of wine or maybe mix a spirit up. He was meeting Bethany mid afternoon, so wanted to wait till then, albeit Dutch courage would be an advantage for the average Joe, not Fluffy Donkey though, or for that matter JB. He was incredibly extrovert and never had problems with inhibitions. He still hadn't checked his phone to see if the text was a response from Bethany. Surely she couldn't be cancelling? Maybe she was ill? Maybe she was experiencing stage fright? Maybe she was having second thoughts and realised that she wasn't really that attracted to him? Was JB just experiencing momentary paranoia? He was going to leave the suspense for a while longer, well… Just a minute or two until after he had made or poured a drink.

'I'm not gonna bother wid any ting strong Flix. I only want a soft one fa now. I tink water'll be di perfect tonic, to keep mi hydrated.'

He opened the glass cupboard. It wasn't made of glass, but contained all the glasses any household needed from brandy to wine, water to QC sherry divine, shots slightly bigger than the average shallot, you name it, it was in there. Out came a transparent one, very basic, a conventional pint glass. It was clasped in JB's right hand, ready to be filled with water. He opened a two litre bottle of sparkling water. PSSSSSSSSSS… Slowly and methodically so it didn't start spraying all over the place. The dioxide was released into the atmosphere. He poured the water into the glass, about two centimetres below the rim. The bubbles were fizzing away and tingling JB's nose.

'Now I can see oo dis text is from. Probably Beth jus wantin' to confirm arrangements I ope.'

He sat down at the table, pulled his chair in, and checked his iPhone,. It was from Bethany. 'Lovely to hear from you. I think we said 2ish, but let's make it three, bkoz, I've got a few things to do 1st, besides looking half decent for you. See you outside Eight Ball @ 3pm. Xx'

'Yeah man. Pheeeeew! I almost tought she was gonna cancel. I still ave di Midas touch. Yup, yup, yup. Ya know what I'm sayin' Flixy.'

He picked up his cutlery and began to work through his gigantic portion of full English breakfast. It wasn't traditionally the total package as there was no black pudding or tinned tomatoes, but it was as good as. The steam ascending from the plated ingredients entwined with the captivating aroma of the pork, sage and leek sausages. Felix's tail was wagging, seemingly happy at being given an extra helping of breakfast this morning, a change from his usually predictable weekly staple food. You could tell he was rejuventated, chomping away at the sliced sausage, licking the salt off the bacon and slurping the water in the neighbouring bowl to wash down the treat. The twin cat bowl was an animal consumption version of a semi detached bungalow, with nothing upstairs, just food and liquid on the ground floor. Occasional sleeping quarters for any leftovers.

JB gazed at the adjacent main feature wall and thought it looked bare and was in need of a more attractive look. Should he paint it pastel colour or opt for a bolder primary one? Maybe it would look more asthetically pleasing with a photo or canvas painting on it, just like the Manhattan skyline canvas in the living room on the entrance wall. That could be left for another day, however, it was good that he was thinking about refurbishments. A woman's touch wouldn't go a miss in this instance, so chatting to Mum, Tyresia Marianna, his Nana Joanie or one of his female friends would be advantageous.

'I know what…I'll chat wi Beth about dis later today. She's very vogue, arty n creative. I'm sure she'll ave a few bright n inventive ideas,' he said loudly.

Shanghai noon was fastly approaching, so after finishing his breakfast, he would revitalise, replenish and resurrect his thick mass of jungle afro. It was in need of a transformation as it had passed the customary two week window. It was gradually becoming a little matted and shaggy. It was silent outside, apart from the occasional singing of the birds. The sun was almost at its height, JB was relishing his morning breakfast bite, the sky was bright, accentuated by the fluffy clouds of light white, ooooo, how he longed for Bethany's sweet scent of perfume and natural fresh body odour and touching her slim yet curvaceous body, so pert, juicy, ripe and tight…

BANG… BANG!

Felix's ears pricked up and he jumped a few centimetres off the floor, fur suddenly looking puffy like a fluffy rug. JB's heart skipped a beat, pupils almost popping out of their sockets, mouth suddenly becoming as dry as the desert, frozen momentarily as the sound reverberated through his body. He almost choked on the piece of sausage that was in his mouth. He suddenly shot up and dashed to the window.

'What di ell was dat?'

'MIAAOOOOOOOOOW MIAAOOOOOOOOOW,' Felix shrieked.

JB opened the cutlery drawer and took out the house keys frantically, unlocked the door and opened it hurriedly, which inadvertently banged into the drawer, closing it. He ran outside to the gate to see what had gone on. There were joggers and pedestrians on the pavement, some with headphones in, some walking dogs, others reading the morning papers, all engrossed in their own world, cars passing. The only person appearing worried was JB.

'Excuse me, did you ear dat?'

'Yeah. It was a car back firing!' replied the old gentleman reading his broadsheet as he walked.

'Tank you. Geez, I almost tought someone had been shot.'

'That wouldn't happen around here son.'

'I know, ya right.'

JB turned round and slowly walked back to the house, relieved that a serious crime hadn't occurred. He could now resume and enjoy his most scrumptious meal. Felix was waiting at the door for him, perched on the outside step, raising his head and staring at JB with affectionate starry eyes. His fur had returned to its normal soft, smooth and refined texture, a transformation from the wild image of a minute or so ago. JB closed the door and marched back to the table with relief in his mind.

'We're lucky dere Flixy. I almost tought someone ad been shot down! I would never ave imagined anyting like dat to appen ere dough. Pheeeeeeew! Bon apetit.'

He sat back down, pulled his chair in and remembered where he was. The plate was still at least half full with a mosaic of colour. He slurped his sparkling water and continued feeding. All the ingredients had been cooked to perfection, just like baby bear's porridge in the Goldilocks story. The sausages firm and crispy, the bacon juicy and succulent, the beans piping hot and not mushy, the egg scrambled, light and fluffy, the mushrooms a darkened tan and the plum vine tomatoes rich and toasted on the outside, juicy and squelchy in the centre.

For some reason it seemed like a Sunday, pure peace and tranquility apart from the earlier noisy al fresco surprise. It had been a typically slow paced start to the day until the incident with a car backfiring on Mysterious Street. The temperature appeared to be increasing as the sun wasn't obstructed today by any mass cloud cover. An extremely exciting day lay ahead for JB and possibly for Felix for that matter, if Petra was in an entertaining mood later. JB wanted to improve the mood, not that he was subdued or anything, but background music would liven up proceedings and prepare him for the pleasures of the mid afternoon to early evening. His docking port was on the large rectangular central work surface, so he got up from his chair, taking his phone to it and sitting it on the charging unit, selected the music application and scrolled down through the artists. 'Shall I play some Bobby Marley or Aretha Franklin? I tink on a day like today, Bob's ya Uncle n Aretha's ya Aunt. Yeah man, dat's di one. Stiiiir it up, ba-bomb-bomb-bomb, little darliiin', stiiir it up, ba-bomb-bomb-bomb, liiittle darliiiin'! Bobby it is, decision made.'

He scrolled down to Bob Marley and The Wailers-The album Legend, selected it, then pressed play. *Is This Love* was the first track to play which got him in the mood for some potential evening loving, he could wish for it anyway, without any guarantees. It was time to continue with his full English as he didn't want it going cold. Felix would adore that, because he could then finish the leftovers, but JB wouldn't let that happen. Felix had eaten more than his fair share of food this morning.

'Don't worry, about a ting, cause every little ting, is gonna be alright...'

JB thought *Is This Love* had been re-mixed.

'Dat ain't di version I downloaded to mi playlist.' he said rather puzzled.

He eventually realised it was his mobile phone ring tone and Ash was calling him.

'Am I damn stupid or what?'

He swiped the arrow to accept the call.

'Yeah man, what's appenin' Ashilito?'

'I'm all good n you?'

'Fabulous ya know. What's ya script today den, you busy or jus chillin'?'

'I'm meeting up with Bella, we're gonna head for some food n drinks in town.'

'Yeeees... Who da man. Are ya goin' to Marlborough?'

'No, we're gonna head to the city n live it up. Do you want to join us with Jen?'

'I would, but I'm jus gonna chill tonight n ave a quiet one. I'm still exhausted from a hectic one las weekend. Ya better be careful boy, n protect ya back after di car crash, ya don't wanna be aggravatin' it. Ow's it feelin' at mo?'

'It's much better thanks. That witness I told you about, Mushy Pea, I called him the other day and he's preparing a statement for me. I'm delighted.'

'Dat's all good. Ya bound to get a decent compensation for it, you, Fluffy n Stace.'

'Yeah, I sincerely hope so. I must dash, as I've got quite alot to do today. Uuuuurgh, uuuuurgh, uuuuurgh.'

'Ya better take it easy man, like I told ya. I don't want Bella splittin' you in two. Ha haaaaaa. Enjoy yaself n savour di big City life ce soir. Take care brudder.'

'Don't you worry, we'll have a sensational time, just a shame you can't come with Jen. She's desperate to get her hands on you tonight.'

'Nooo man, I can't lead di girl on. It's too dangerous. She's wantin' to get er claws into me n dat defo ain't gonna appen. Di girl's obsessed, I'm sure she's got a compulsive disorder!'

'Ha haaaaaa. You funghí.'

'Are you tryin' to say dat I'm bacterial?'

'I said you're a funny guy, you joker!'

'I'll let you off dis time. *Puto madre*! Take dat… Baaaaaaaam! Ave a great weekend brudder n don't injure yaself, if ya know what I mean. Peace n love.'

'Yeah, take care Jammin' and see you next week hopefully.'

JB ended the call.

'Jen's dangerous. I wish she'd take a back seat n cut mi some rough ass slack, I'm ardly gonna let er ave mi babies.'

He cut part of the granary toast off with beans and scrambled egg on and shovelled it into his mouth. It was going down nicely. The plate was becoming visible again, as the portion gradually became less and less with every mouthful. There was still a shallow river of beans flowing on the grey and blue elegant piece of crockery, lit up by yellow scrambled egg fields, a few sausage logs and some red tomato combine harvesters. It could have been used as a piece of conceptual art. JB could hear a noise that appeared to be coming from the kitchen door. Felix's ears pricked up once more.

'MIAAOOOOOOOOOW.' A long strained cry.

Felix licked the bowl clean, the side that had had food in it, before lapping up a few tonguefuls of water to cleanse his palate and then turned and walked to the door. JB wanted to be able to relax without having to jump up every ten or so minutes. After the week he'd had, he thought he deserved some quiet time, but then again, it hadn't exactly been stressful. He was fortunate enough to have several free periods throughout the weekly timetable. Most of his fellow teachers didn't have the luxury of any free periods, so JB was a very lucky man. Finally the plate was looking like a barren land with virtually every piece of food consumed, apart from a quarter of toast with some fluffy egg on top and half a rasher of bacon. Down came the fork, plunging itself into the remnants, reminiscent of a Golden Eagle swooping in on its prey. Up it was delivered into an open cavity. It was chewed with joy, leaving JB in a state of satiety. The chair was slid backwards, the cutlery presentably positioned side by side. Up he popped, walking to the sink, dropping in the remaining piece of bacon into Felix's bowl, before placing his items at the side of the sink. He flicked up the catch on the kitchen entrance door, pulled down the handle and opened it. In walked Petra as proud and sophisticated as could be. What a sublime pedigree she was. She made her way towards Felix and began to wrestle the last piece of bacon out of his mouth. He was resigned to give her half of it, because she wouldn't forgive him that easily. Could this be pre-requisite of the frolics JB and Bethany would experience later in the day? It was Saturday twenty fifth of June, four days after the summer solstice, so hopefully they were in for a scorching hot season. While Felix and Petra were enjoying their moments of flirtation, JB had to hurry, as the pots needed to be washed, his jungle haired afro had to be nourished, skin to be showered and revitalised, teeth to be brushed, wardrobe to be chosen, although that wouldn't take long for the spontaneous dresser.

After washing up breakfast, He jogged upstairs to the bedroom and stripped his clothes off, because now was grooming time. His afro comb with aluminium tongs was in the bathroom along with the African shampoo and conditioner. For once Felix didn't follow him as he was accompanied and being entertained by Petra, engaging in some feline frivolity. JB made his way to the bathroom after throwing his clothes on the bed, as it was time to get wet.

The bathroom door was already open, so through he walked, but before stepping into the shower he opened the window to let some air flow through, to prevent the window and mirror from steaming up too much. One pull of the chord for the extractor fan, in he stepped, closing the sliding doors behind him. Off came the hair bobble, which was placed over the cold water lever, a twist of the hot lever and jeronimo…

'We ave lift off. Seriouuus, uuuum, uuuum, serious profession, seriouuus, uuum, uuum, seriouuus profession. Dat's what I'm talkin' about… Yeeeeeaaaaaah,' he half spoke and sang.

The water ran for about thirty seconds, directed into the corner of the basin, as he didn't want to pick up any respiratory disorders that could be caught from limescale build up and othe bacteria from the shower head. It was always the same strategic method. He opened the sliding doors, stepped out and stretched for his afro comb that was resting on the window sill, picked it up, stepped back in, closing the doors behind him. He put the comb on the large surface area that seperated the cold from the hot water levers. At least a minute had passed, so he moved the cold water tap fractionally to cool the temperature as it was now becoming quite steamy. He centralised the shower head so it was dropping a deluge on to his afro, initially just bouncing off as if it was like a piece of velcro. After a short while it did start to get wet as he massaged the water into his scalp beneath the depths of soft yet gradually matted hair. There was a container of vanilla and ylang ylang Foamburst in the rack hanging down from stainless steel ítem, which he picked up with his left hand, squirted a splodge into his right, proceeding to massage it into his body.It built up into a thick, rich and creamy lather very quickly. One container was enough to last at least forty or so washes, if used sensibly. The smell was divine, inevitably it would entice Bethany to want to get closer to him. He remembered the text conversation they'd had on Thursday evening about him being a sponge in the bath, massaging her body. This had an instantaneous effect as his middle legged friend started to stand to attention like a soldier on parade. He continued to clean his dirty pores from head to toe, saving the best till last, which was the afro. When every part of him was clean and rinsed, the top of the African shampoo and conditioner was flicked open, poured into right hand and massaged in deeply and penetratively. It usually needed two applications, as it had to be cleaned thoroughly, otherwise it would emit an unpleasant stale stench from the areas near to the scalp that hadn't been reached.

Two applications complete, a final rinse with the shower head, massaging his fingers through to ensure every last drop of foamy shampoo and conditioner had been removed. The water became transparent once again as it flowed from his head. He picked up the afro comb, turned the water off and dragged it through to remove any split ends and large clumps of entangled hair. This didn't take too long, as the dirty work had been done. He only used his left hand because he was left hended, so had to rotate the comb around skillfully, ensuring there weren't any neglected bits. He opened the sliding doors, having to reach out, making sure he didn't slip, to take the long charcoal grey fluffy towel hanging over the heated stainless steel radiator. He dried his feet and the rest of his body, before stepping out onto the white ceramic floor tiles. Even though his feet were now dry, you could see the outline of his footprints with all the moisture, a result of the steam circulating before escaping out of the extractor fan and window. His hair could self dry, but it was missing one important final piece of the sacred afro cleansing process...The Vidal Sasoon hair dryer. He dried the final bits that were his bottom, dogs balearics and now flacicd penis, hung the towel over the radiator, hop, skipped and jumped to the bedroom, opened the wardrobe, took out the hair dryer and returned to the bathroom to finally cultivate and groom his hair.

Chapter 38

Having A Ball

Felix and Petra had been out for their fitness session, JB called them in and without hesitation back they trotted, Felix nibbling at her side playfully. Petra had been given permission to stay tonight, the time being quarter to three, fifteen minutes before JB and Bethany's rendezvous time. JB closed the door behind them, double checking to make sure he had everything.

'You two behave yaselves! I don't wanna come back dis evenin' or tomorrow mornin' to see you've wrecked di place. Enjoy yaselves, but be sensible, otherwise Petra won't stay again fa a while! You ear me?'

Comically, they both responded, 'MIAAOOOOOW!'

There was plenty of cat food in the bowl, mixed with lamb biscuits and water. They had enough to satify their needs, most importantly each other. JB's afro was big and ultra cool, smelling of the sweet scent of hair mayonnaise. He was wearing a beige DKNY t-shirt, a plain dark blue cardigan, white Armani boxer shorts, light blue 501 skinny jeans and a pair of white ankle Converse boots with a blue star on the side. He was definitely dressed to impress, probably a knock out, but would have to wait and see if Bethany was inclined to agree. After their recent text conversation, she'd certainly be upfront and tell him. He checked his pockets.

'Bank card, andkerchief in back pocket, strawberry Lipsyl, black wallet, condoms, I tink dat's all I need!'

The Lucky Star taxi had just arrived and pipped outside. DIIIIIIIIIIIIIIIIIIIR! JB had flossed and brushed his teeth, sprayed on some Armani eau de toilette, creamed his body with coco butter, dewaxed his ears with cotton wool buds, had a shave, leaving a well manicured goatee, dressed and was ready to party.

'It mus be dat driver from di weekend, because, no one else as a crazy assed orn like dat!'

JB had closed all the doors apart from his bedroom and the kitchen. All the essential appliances had been turned off, the smoke alarm's were in full working order, so hopefully a fire wouldn't break out. The light switch timer had been set, so he just had to key in the alarm code, pull the kitchen blinds closed and be ready to go. He dashed to the door, took the keys out, undid the Yale lock, pulled the handle and opened the door.

'Take care kitty cats n enjoy yaselves n don't do anyting I wouldn't!'

He locked the door, waited for the alarm to activate... Done. Away he walked with swagger to the waiting silver taxi. He opened the gate, walked through, closing it behind him.

'Well, well, well, if it isn't my friend from last weekend. Pleased to meet you, how you doing?'

'I'm great tank you. Jus eadin' into Marlborough to di pool all. Ya know di one don't ya?'

'Is that the one called Eight Ball or the other one?'

'It's Eight Ball. What's ya name again?'

'I can not believe it! You don't remember?'

'Nooo... I'm really sorry. I know it starts wid di letter J dough.'

'Noooo, Its not play dough, that's what children play with!'

'Nooo, not play dough, it's J isn't it, it begins wid J?'

'Ha haaaaa. I was joking about the play dough. You're correct! It is J for Jaleem.'

'Yeeeeaah, dat's right, now I remember!'

'How's the gorgeous girl with the red hair? She was a sight for sore eyes n a real livewire!'

'She's all good. Di girl's almost uncontrollable. Ya quite right about di livewire bit, because, she certainly as a spark n can be quite explosive. You'd need to be a strong man to ave any control n old over er!'

'I bet she'd be great in the more intimate of surroundings, if you know what I mean!'

'No doubt. One o di guy's dat came out las Saturday ad is way wid er. Apparently e's still strugglin' to walk a week later!'

'Seriously?!'

'Noooo... I'm jus kiddin', but she'd be an experience alright.'

'You mean a Sexperience!'

'Dat's probably more like it.'

'Who ya meeting today then?'

'Ooooh, jus a friend from school.'

'Is she female?'

'I'd be a l'il concerned if she was male, don't ya tink?'

'Ha haaaaaaaa! You got me there. So am right yeah! She's definitely female!'

'Yeeeaaah. We're jus friends dough. We're gonna shoot some pool, grab a bite to eat n den go our separate ways!'

'You're funny. You mean, she'll go in the front door n you'll go via the back?'

'Weeell... I don't do dat on di first night!'

'Noooooo... I mean, you'll keep a low profile!' Jaleem said in his soft Indian lilt.

JB showed Jaleem his left knuckles, in turn he took his left hand off the steering wheel momentarily and touched knuckles with a closed fist, ensuring to keep his right securely on it. Jaleem winked at JB, approving of his Romeo ways. They drove through Saturday traffic to Marlborough. It was a pleasant journey, JB and Jaleem engaging in conversation, happy at being re-united one week later, inadvertently.

'Ow come you came to pick me up today Jaleem?'

'I heard there was a job on the radio for 33 Mysterious Street, so how could I refuse to take it? I told the telephone operator I was reasonably close by, so offered my services, knowing it would be appropriate and thought it would be you or a fine young lady.'

'I'm delighted Jaleem, because one, you're a beautiful genuine man n two, ya make me laugh out loud ya know.' said JB chuckling.

'Is that what the young people abbreviate to lol these days?'

'Yeah man. Dat's di young peeps speak by text n e-mail. I jus prefer to... Haaaaaa haaaaaaaaa out loud.'

'For me, I just do a smiley with its tongue out!' sniggered Jaleem.

'Like dat.' JB stuck his tongue out, screwing his face up and closing his eyes.

'Perfect.'

They pulled up at the traffic lights just around the corner, as they were on red. There were a few cars in front of them. In a minute or two, they'd be there. The pavements were dry, the markings on the road shining brightly, reflected by the sun's powerful gaze, the newly smooth black tarmacked road. In the distance you could see a haze ascending, heat radiated from it, a sign that summer was officially here. Freshly cut grass verges sent their sweet scent into the air.

NAA NA-NA, NA NAA, NA-NA, NA-NAA, NA, NA-NA NA, NAA NAA, ERE COMES DI HOTSTEPPER, MURDEREEER.

Music blared from a passing convertible car's stereo system. It appeared the neighbourhood was jumping, houses rocking and people swaying from side to side as the bass reverberated and ricocheted off acoustic building materials.

'Looooord, dat's loud ya know. I guess it's summer time n people dem wanna play di music out loud wi di top down, so we can all get into di spirit! What a great summer time classic dough. Di otstepper, murderer, lyrical gangster, murderer, excuse me Mister Officer, murderer....'

'I've seen the car in your driveway and I bet you like playing music quite loudly with your roof down!'

'Ow did ya guess? Not dat loud dough. Dat was deafenin' maaan!'

JB was being slightly economical with the truth, especially when Rocca's neighbour's mum Mildred had asked him to turn down his car stereo, because it was threatening to wake up her granddaughter Matilda. He was exactly the same, a poser of the highest order. The scenery was rather breathtaking and the scantily clad ladies weren't bad either. The temperature was twenty five degrees, which encouraged most of the pedestrians and motorists to dress down considerably. The odd African and West Indian person from a previous generation still wore trousers, jackets or coats, because for them it wasn't a scorcher.

'I forgot to ask you, did you enjoy your partying exploits last weekend? You had a good crowd with you!'

'It was sensational, Jaleem. A birthday party to remember. It ad everyting from food to fashion, good conversation to gorgeous girls, music to mojitos n comedy to craziness! Everybody ad an unbelievable time tanks.'

'I wish I could have joined you, but I had to work and earn some money.'

They pulled into a car parking space outside Eight Ball, just after three pm, Bethany was standing there looking incredible, talking on her mobile phone. She had brown two inch strapless cork heeled shoes with a toe peep hole, a light blue denim mini skirt, red figure hugging vest top with a bra underneath, brown and gold bangles on her left wrist, a wooden beaded loosely dangling necklace and two inch diameter hooped dark wooden earrings. Her hair was blow dried and straight bob combed and to finish the look she had a contemporary light brown leather bag with a golden linked strap and golden ringed clasp to fasten. JB's jaw dropped, eyes bulging out of their sockets. She looked far more attractive than at school, but that wasn't a criticism as she was eye catching, however very subtle, without the need to create a fuss. Plus at Oatmill she was in a professional environment. Less was definitely more, her features glistening in the light, with just a small amount of red blusher on her cheeks, bright red lipstick, some mascara and eye liner with matching scarlet nail varnish on fingers and toes.

'I'm guessing that's your friend? She looks more than a friend with the way she's dressed,' said Jaleem curiously.

'We're jus friends dat's all. We're gonna shoot some pool n live it up.'

'That'll be just seven pounds JB.'

'I tought ya normally charged ten fa dat journey?'

'You're a good guy and I like you, so you receive the usual discount.'

'Joe, I'm gonna pay ya an Ayrton Senna, because ya a legend boss. Ya always so generous.'

'Just doing my job. Also, I'm impressed you remembered my name. Joe being the same as Jaleem in the Punjaab region. If you like though, you can call me Jalla for short.'

'Jalla, put dat in ya sky rocket n ave a safe night. Many tanks n take it easy n stay real smooth, yeah.'

'Thank you. You take great care and look after the beautiful lady, she's pukka.'

JB undid his seatbelt, shook Jaleem's hand and then gave him a knuckle touch of approval, before pulling the handle and opening the passenger's side door of the silver people carrier. He climbed out, winked at Jaleem and shut the door behind him. Jaleem winked back, indicated and pulled away.

'Yes Beth, what's appenin' lady?'

'I'm good thanks, and you?'

JB walked towards her, his heart absolutely racing, although he disguised it with his usual cool, composed and relaxed demeanour. He lifted up his right hand, fist clenched, showing Beth his knuckles, in which she reciprocated and touched.

'I'm greee-aaaaat… tanks. Ya lookin' more dan good n smelliiin'… Ooo la laaaaaa.'

'I'm pleased to hear it and thank you. I'm not too happy about this knuckle touching lark though. We're not in the staff room now, so are you gonna do it properly?' she said sternly.

'Sorry, I tought we were doin' di formal ting? If ya like den!'

She smacked him quite firmly on the bottom, an evident gesture that she fancied the 501s off him.

'OUCH! Ya don't wanna lose ya and d'ya?' JB teased.

'Lose my hand on that tough sexy assed nut! Reaaally!'

She wrapped her arms round him, encouraging him to do the same, although he was trying to appear overtly cool. He sunk his nose slowly into the side of her neck. The odour was hypnotic, just like it was when they collided at the staff entrance doorway yesterday..

'What perfume ya wearin', it's luscious man.'

'You should know after yesterday's escapade!'

'Oh yeah, don't tell mi. Is it dat one by Gucci?'

'Yeees, that's right, but what's it called?'

'Because I'm guilty, guiiiilty, of love in di first degree!'

'Well done! I'll get the first drinks in then, my treat. Was that a song by Bananarama in the eighties?'

'You know it.'

'Shall we then?' she asked.

'Let's do it.'

They walked through the push door entrancee and up the staircase to the first floor where the bar and pool tables were. He noticed how shapely her legs were, as she normally wore trousers to cover up her sightly figure.

'Wouch! Dere ot property,' he muttered under his breath.

'What was that? Did you say something?'

'Nooo, noooo, I'm just in a trance at di mo.'

They reached the first floor, walked through the double door and into the hall. The music was on at just the right volume, so you could hear yourself think and speak. It was soft jazz music.

'I'm just gonna dash to the toilet Jammin', I won't be a min.'

'What would ya like to drink?'

'I don't mind. Surprise me.'

With the weather being quite hot, he thought a nice bottle of rose would do the trick, plonked in an ice bucket.

'Excuse me, can I ave a bottle o rosé please?'

'Yeah, sure. Which one would ya like? Do you want to check the list first?' asked the bar girl.

She handed him the booklet for food and drink.

'Tanks. It's probably a good idea I check first.'

There were four different rosés, all looking rather palatable.

After perusing the menu and attempting to portray he was the archetypal wine connoisseur, he opted for the cheapest bottle, a light and crispy fruity wine that would wet their pool playing appetite.

'Have you made your mind up yet?'

'Yeah, I'm gonna plump fa di first one. Three Choirs please. Outta di four tenors, dis was di best one!'

'I like your humour. You could also call it a string quartet,' said the bar girl.

JB felt a pinch on his left bum cheek and a sharp fist to his kidneys.

'I can't leave you for a minute can I? Back I come and you're chatting up the bar girl!'

'No, don't worry, we were just discussin' the comedy aspect of the Three Choirs in an orchestra.'

'It's OK, I was only joking. We're just good friends.'

The bar girl smiled and could tell by intuition that they were possibly a little closer than friends. It was a moderately accurate assumption, as Beth was dressed down and their banter seemed slightly more than just friendly. The bar girl picked up a silver wine bucket, threw in plenty of ice cubes, opened the fridge with the wines in, took it out, closed the door and put the bottle of Three Choirs on the bar.

'You'll probably need a couple of glasses too.'

She turned back round, took two from the shelf in front of her, swilled them under the automatic glass washer and cleaner and placed them next to the bottle.

'Ow much fa a game o pool please?'

'It's a tenner deposit and then five pounds per hour.'

'Boy, dat's cheap ya know. A set o balls too please.'

This made Beth chuckle.

'How many d'you want?'

'A few more dan a couple'll do,' said JB with a smile.

'That'll be a straight twenty and pay the rest when you've finished.'

She took out a hard black plastic container full of balls and handed them to Beth, as JB would have his hands full with the bottle of wine and glasses. JB took his wallet out of his pocket, opened it and took out a crisp twenty pound note.

'Dere ya go. Tanks fa dat.'

He closed his wallet and placed it back in his pocket.

'You're on table number eight. Enjoy your game.'

'We will.' responded Bethany.

They made their way over to table eight. The cues were hung up on wooden rectangular racks with thick holes for them to stand in and the chalk for the cues were attached to the side of the tables by a dangling rope, on the end in a clip. It looked a little bit like soap on a rope, the kind of Christmas stocking filler millions of parents bought for their children way back in the eighties. It came in handy when players wanted to have a better grip of the cue ball for screwing back and securing a good table position. There were still half a dozen tables spare. It was relatively quiet for a Saturday afternoon, probably because the majority of people were al fresco working on improving their tans. No doubt it would be hectic as evening came though. Table eight was next to one of the large windows in the far left corner, so they had an amount of privacy. Clink clonk was the sound of the wine glasses as they touched and came apart as JB put them down on a small four foot high dark wooden round table. Bethany placed the rack of balls on the lilac table cloth.

'D'you know how to set them up?'

'No, do you?'

'I wouldn't be asking you if I knew would I?' she remarked firmly with a smirked look.

'Of course I do. I'm gonna show ya. Let mi pour di wine first.'

He took a few ice cubes out of the bucket and put some in each glass, unscrewed the top off the bottle of rose and poured half a glass in each and then put the top back on. He walked over to the table and gently moved Bethany to the side placing both hands on her hips sensuously.

'Are we gonna dance?'

'Not yet, but maybe later!'

He took all the balls out of the rack and put them on the smooth cloth, took the triangle from the end of the table, hanging on a holder and organised the balls into the correct formation. To ensure fairness while playing, at the break all balls should be tightly packed. The only must is that the number eight black ball is positioned in the centre of the rack and one spot and one stripe ball are placed at each end of the foot of the rack. JB explained this to Bethany, so she would know for future reference. They both had a cue in hand and were ready to play.

'Shall I break or do you want to?' asked Bethany.

'I don't mind, I ain't parsh. If ya like, we can toss a coin?'

Bethany opened her bag, took out her purse, flicked it open and pulled out a pound coin.

'I'll go heads.'

'Tails never fails fa me den.'

She flicked the coin up, caught it in her right hand and put it on the table.

'You're right, it's tails.'

'You break den.'

Beth took her bag over to the lilac velvet covered long bench and put it down next to the table of drinks. She handled the cue as if she'd played before. The cue ball went crashing into the pack, four balls hitting the cushions. It was a legitimate break, one stripe and one spot dropping into a pocket.

'The table's all mine,' she said with a big grin on her face.

'What ya gonna choose den, stripe or spotty dotty?'

'Hot spots for me.'

The balls were nicely spread out for her, if indeed she had played before, to possibly wrap the game up at her first visit. She potted three balls with aplomb, consecutively, which meant she only had three more plus the black to win the opening game.

'Rubbiiiiiish. You hustler!'

'I never said I hadn't played before! You should've taken my text message seriously, as opposed to thinking I'm a push over,' said Bethany.

'I jus tink I was probably a l'il too complacent. Shall I pass you ya drink over?'

'Oooooo, yeeees please, I could do with a mouth wet!' she answered licking her lips.

That really turned JB on, as she looked so damn hot and sexy. Her legs were amazing, accentuated by the two inch heels. JB picked up both glasses and carried them to the table. He passed Bethany hers.

'Dere ya go.'

'Thank you kind sir. Shall we propose a toast?'

'Yeaaah, why not.'

'OK then. To a fabulously fulfilling freaking weekend, compliments to Oatmill for bringing us together today, compliments to Eight Ball for hosting us, to the glorious summer weather....Respect!'

'Ha haaaaaaa. Respec to you too.' chuckled JB.

They clinked glasses and sipped the mouthwatering flavoursome wine.

'Ooooh yeah. That's so refreshing. The company's not bad either!' she said, winking.

'The company's ultra hot n you're not bad either!'

'Uuuuum!'

She pulled him by the neck of his beige DKNY t-shirt towards her with her spare left hand, gazed into his eyes and planted a soft and sensuous brief two second kiss on his lips, before pushing him away. JB almost stumbled over as he moved backwards towards the bench.

'OMG.' he muttered under his breath.

'Sooorry… Did you say somethin'?' she responded softly and flirtatiously.

'Noo, noo, nooo! I was jus a l'il…'

'Speechless by any chance?'

'Nooo, I jus almost lost mi balance.'

'How come?'

'I jus tripped over someting on di floor as I was walkin' backwards!'

'Hmmmmm,' she replied, knowing he was being economical with the truth.

'Are ya ungry Beth?'

'Yeeaaah, ravenous. Especially when I've schooled your butt too. Grab us a menu from the bar.'

'What did ya las servant die of?'

'Being hustled and out muscled. Come on, Jammin', I've got some more balls to drop!' she answered sexily.

'OK, because it's you, I'll look after ya.'

He went to the bar and picked up a menu, taking it to the table. He sat down on the lilac bench and browsed through it.

'D'ya see anything you fancy?' she said as she bent over the table to take her next shot.

'Oh my lord, please elp mi, dis is ridiculous,' he mumbled.

This was reminiscent of Jasmine's antics last weekend, although Bethany wasn't blatant like her and exuded more refinement and sophistication. Because he was sitting down on a lower level looking at the appetising dishes, he couldn't help noticing Beth's red racy lacy knickers under her mini skirt. Thankfully she had decided not to wear a thong, as that would've probably made him faint. She was stood on her tip toes just about, calves slender and toned, the upside down heart shape of muscle protruding outwards, the hamstring and thigh contours a pleasurable sight, concluding with a glimpse of the bass of the buttocks.

'Oops, sorry. You can't see anything can you?'

'Lots of appetisers. Di one I like most is di succulent legs, thighs n rump. I can imagine dat wi some ot pepper sauce to give it more flavourin'. In fact, forget di sauce, it don't need it, it looks cooked to virtual perfection!' he laughed.

'Are you lookin' up my skirt Mister Herbert?'

'No Miss!'

'You better not be, otherwise you'll be facing detention in my office. You bad, baaaad boy!'

She took her shot, sinking yet another ball, leaving just two more and the black. She pulled her skirt down a little as it had ridden up and she didn't want to be showing her adorable ass to all and sundry. JB had just one more visit to the table, managing to pot three stripes, to spare his blushes from being eight balled by Bethany. The afternoon had disappeared in the blink of an eye. One more bottle of wine and three hours later and some quality American diner cuisine, they were ready to move on. It was six thirty and decision time.

'D'ya wanna stay ere n' ave a few more drinks, or go to another bar?'

'I'm feeling quite tipsy, but having a fantastic time!' she said giggling.

'We could ead to di cinema possibly?' Proposed JB.

'Or go back to mine?'

'I don't mind to be onest. Ow far d'ya live?'

'It's only ten minutes in a cab to the other side of Oatmill. You know where I live anyway!'

'It's Mangoville isn't it?'

'You see, I knew you did,' she said, slurring a little.

'Let's ead to to yours den, because we don't wanna get caught by any kids or teachers. Ya know what dere like fa spreadin' gossip around.'

'I'll phone a cab then and you pay for the pool. I'll give you some money towards it.'

Bethany phoned for a taxi and then went to the toilet to freshen up. JB went to the bar, taking the balls back and to pay.

'Hi dere, can I pay fa di pool please.'

The same bar girl served him.

'Yeah. Did you enjoy yourselves?'

'Yeah tanks. We ad a lot o fun.'

'It seemed like it. Next time you're probably better off getting a room.'

'Were we dat bad?'

'Noo. I've seen couples slightly worse and trying to get it on on the tables after dark when the lights are dimmed.'

'SERIOUSLY?'

'Yeah. But you two were just kissing and caressing. Tame! No doubt she'll be wild tonight though? She's a real catch.'

'Ha haaaaaa. I doubt it. We're jus good friends.'

'I don't often see good friends with tongues down each other's throats.'

'She ad someting stuck in er tonsils.'

'Your tooth de-scaler, in other words, that long object that enables you to talk,' laughed the Bar girl.

'Is anyone special playin' ere tonight, or is it jus di usual resident DJ?'

'Just the resident tonight. He's fab though. Just pay me fifteen pounds for the table, so another fiver'll do.'

'Tanks fa dat.'

'It's nearly half past six, but I'll give you a special Saturday rate. When ya girl comes back too, I'll give ya both a shot of whatever you like!'

'I'm bullet proof, so ya can't penetrate me!'

'You're something extra, I like it! Here she comes.'

Bethany returned as JB took his wallet out and pulled a crisp five pound note out from the zipped section.

'Ya ready to make a move den?'

'Yeah. Revitalised and ready for even more fun,' she said, pulling herself in close to him and kissing and nibbling his right ear lobe.

He handed the five pounds to the bar girl.

'D'you want Jaeger, vodka, rum or tequila?'

'What's this for?'

'I just told ya boyfriend that you could have a free shot on the house!'

'Ooh, thanks. Tequila for me please.'

'Make it two.'

'I'll make it three. I can't leave myself out can I!' replied the bar girl.

She picked up three clean shot glasses, a bottle of Tequila Gold, unscrewed the top and filled them up. She took a piece of lime each from the tray below the bar, slid across a salt pot. They sprinkled some salt onto the spot between the base left knuckle and index finger.

'Ready?'

'Yeah, let's do this,' said Beth.

'Let's get it on!' replied JB.

'I'm sure you will,' said the Bar girl.

'One, two, tree.'

They all slurped the salt, downed the shots and frantically nibbled at the pieces of lime, slamming their glasses down on the bar. They all high fived.

'Many tanks.'

'Thank you. That's so kind of you. Take care.'

'Take care. Bye,' said the bar girl.

They walked out of the double doors and down the staircase to the pavement outside.

'That place is fab. I love the American theme with all those famous actor framed portraits.'

'Yeah, it definitely gives ya di impression ya shootin' pool in a small town down in Tennessee.'

'I'd say it had more of a majestic mid thirties movies magic to it, a Manhattan feel.'

'I like ow it provokes dat kinda sentiment, when people use a bit o empathy n get immersed in di moment.'

'Good point well made Jammin'. Now where's this taxi I booked?'

At about the very same time, up pulled a taxi, outside of Eight Ball. The driver's passenger side window came down.

'Hello there, what's your name?' asked the driver.

'Is it for Beth?'

'It sure is, jump in.'

JB opened the rear passenger near side door, Beth climbed in, followed by himself.

'Can you take us to The Waterfront in Mangoville please.'

'Of course I will, let's go.'

They both put their seatbelts on, sitting side by side with Beth cosying into JB's right arm. The journey took about five minutes as it was one of the neighbouring suburbs to Marlborough. They'd had a lot of fun, shooting pool, drinking wine and relishing the tasty delights of typical American diner cuisine, burgers, fries and salad. They were full up after the generous customary portions and ready to relax at Beth's. The temperature was still warm, dropping down to the late teens, enough to not have to wear a jacket, with a light breeze blowing. There were still dozens of people on the streets, heading back from shopping in the town, playing ball games, sunbathing or barbecueing at the park. The traffic was becoming busier with out of towners coming into Lillyford and Marlborough to party for the weekend, by coach, train and car. Lillyford was a very lively and popular city for entertainment in the North, attracting thousands from far a field. Tonight though, for Bethany and JB it would be relaxing in front of the TV or maybe some bedroom Olympics? Who knew..

They arrived at Beth's attractive and modern appartment complex. It was an eight storey block consisting of eighty odd appartments, built of traditional brick construction with a mansard slate roof, two protected internal fire escape staircases, internal dry riser firefighting main, twenty four seven security and CCTV surveillance, two lifts, an upper and lower basement for car parking and a convenience store on the ground floor. The appartment complex was about ten years old and Bethany had lived there for half of that time.

Chapter 39

Waterfront Bathing

The taxi pulled up outside the complex, the time approaching six forty five, the sun starting its descent, ready to set for the night in the west.

'How much is that, please?' asked Bethany.

'Six pounds, please.'

Bethany took her purse out of her bag, pulling out a ten pound note. She undid her seatbelt, leaned over and handed it to the driver. He took four pound coins out of his holder and returned the compliment. JB undid his seatbelt and pushed the door open, climbing out and almost stumbling as he did.

'Was that another stumble there Jammin'? I think I'm going to have to put you to bed!' laughed Bethany, just catching him out of the corner of her eye.

'Is dat a promise?' replied JB.

'Thanks driver, take care.'

'Thank you lovely.'

She followed him out of the car and closed the door behind her, pushing it forcefully to ensure it shut properly.

'Sooorry JB, what were saying again?'

'I just asked if dat was a promise.'

'Hmmmmmm… Please enlighten me!'

'You said ya were gonna ave to put mi to bed?' JB stated enquiringly.

'In that state, I might have to. I've got two bedrooms, so it's perfect, one each!'

'I can crash on di sofa, I don't need a bed.'

'Ooooooo, you're easily pleased aren't ya!'

'I'm jus like di Martini gal, anytime, any place, anywhere!'

'Uuuuuuum, d'you look hot in a skirt too? I bet you can't roller skate though?'

'Dat'd be a challenge. Can you?'

'I used to ice skate when I was younger and bladed frequently, but it's been several years. We'll have to go skating some time!'

'I'd like dat. Someting fresh, random n different.'

They walked to the entrance, Beth taking her fob out of her handbag and holding it up to the automatic sensor. The door unlocked, so in they walked to the foyer area. It was very spacious with a reception desk to the right and a seated section to the left with three comfortable looking black three seater leather sofas, a few small rectangular solid dark brown tables, a few tropical plants and flowers strategically positioned to provide a horticultural feel.

'Enter my palace.'

'Tanks fa dat. You've been a great host so far, so I look forward to an eve at ya casa.'

'You will!' She smiled, puckering her lips together and then blowing him a kiss.

'Are dem plants n flowers di real McCoy or jus artificial ast... asthe... aesthetics?' he stuttered, a result of the wine he'd drank.

'Nothing's fake around here.' She looked down at her toes, up her body to her breasts.

They walked to the lifts, she pressed the button and the right side door opened as it was at the ground floor. They entered the lift and she pressed the seventh floor. The doors closed behind them. The interior walls were stainless steel and on the entrance facing wall a full length mirror with an aluminium hand rail halfway up. Bethany homed in on JB, wrapped her left arm around his waist, gently pulling his head forwards and downwards so that his face was opposite hers. He had to bend down as she was five foot five inches with her heels on, shorter than him. She closed her eyes, opened her mouth and began to kiss him sensually. The lift pinged, the doors opened. Bethany stopped momentarily and pressed the LB button, the doors closing instantaneously, allowing them to continue their sensual interlude. JB's hands started wandering down to her firm and toned buttocks, where they massaged the cheeks over the denim mini skirt masterfully, exciting Bethany immensely. Their kissing became even more passionate, the thrill of the lift doors opening and being caught in the act by visitors or residents. The lift eventually reached the lower basement, the doors opened, but stood there in the entrance to the well lit up car park was tranquil empty space. Until, spoiling the peace, a car immobiliser squeaked and two voices could be heard in tandem with footsteps that sounded as though they were heading towards the lifts.

'Dat voice sounds ever so familiar!'

'Hmmmm... it does, doesn't it.'

They both gazed out of the doors, catching a distant glance of one of those voices heading towards them. Their pulses racing, breathing quickened already by the steamy encounter.

'OMG, it's Mister Robertson, our ead of year.'

Bethany pressed the number seven button, as the doors began to close, the footsteps speeded up, as if they were trying to catch the lift.

'Pheeeeew!' said Bethany.

The doors closed and then pinged again, re-opening. Their hearts were beating even faster now, afraid that Mr Robertson was going to see them together. Bethany closed her eyes. JB's were wide open like a rabbit caught in dazzling car headlights. Both of them feared the worst. The doors were now fully opened, but fortunately the vision in front of them was once again silent empty space. Mr Robertson and presumably his wife- had got into the neighbouring lift, as miraculously it had also come down to the lower basement level. Talk about pure horse shoe luck. The mirror in the lift was totally steamed up, a result of the heavy breathing, sensuously motivated and heightened by a near-miss with a fellow Oatmill High professional.

'Put ya and on mi eart. Can ya feel it beatin'? It's like a bongo drum.'

She put her hand on his heart, feeling it pulsate. The lift quickly returned to the seventh floor. JB and Bethany straightened their clothes out, and she adjusted her bobbed hair. This time they stood apart in case anyone came in. Without any more interruptions and scary hair raising, heart palpitating incidents, the lift doors opened, allowing them to make a safe exit to Bethany's flat, number seventy seven. She opened her bag and took her keys out, unlocked the door turning the key twice, pulled down the handle and in they walked.

'I can't honestly believe that, what's Mister Robertson doing here?'

'I don't ave di foggiest! Di chances o dat are probably as remote as me gettin' mi afro shaved off. I'm jus so pleased im n is wife didn't see us.'

'They must have friends or family living here, because in all the time I've been here, I've never seen him. In five years.'

'We'll find out next week what dey were doin' ere!'

The door shut behind JB, Bethany locked it with the thumb lock. The apartment was laminated all the way through, from the hallway entrance to the kitchen and living room. The bedrooms were both carpeted and both had en suites. They both took their shoes off and left them next to the door.

'Let's get inside and get cosy Mr Herbert.'

'Miss Duke, it sounds like an invitation too good to resist.'

Beth opened the door to the kitchen and living room, showing her hand, pointing towards the sofa inviting JB to sit down and cosy himself. The L-shaped musky brown leather sofa hugged the long and short partition walls in the living room.

'Turn the TV on, the remote's on the table top. Make yourself comfortable. What are you drinking?'

'Anybody would tink I lived ere? I don't know what you ave. Enlighten me!'

'Weeeeeeell. Aichooo, aichoooo, aiiiiichoo,' she sneezed.

'Is dat a bit like Typhoo tea?' chuckled JB.

'Geeeeez, give me chance. I've got red wine, white wine, plenty of spirits, vodka, white rum, amaretto, dark rum, whisky, brandy etcetera.'

'Too many choices. I tink because we started on di wine, ow about crackin' open a bottle of red?'

'My thoughts entirely. You must have read my mind.'

She took the wine bottle opener out of the drawer, took out a bottle of Campo Viejo from the wine rack which was between the dishwasher and washing machine. She scored the gold paper wrapped around the top of the bottle and removed it and then inserted the spiral screwer into the cork and started to twist the head until the arms were pointing towards the ceiling, like a gymnast acknowledging the crowd after their apparatus performance. Bethany then pulled the cork out, heaving slightly… POP… and out it came. She took two glasses out of the cupboard, rinsed them under the cold water and then poured the fruity oaky wine in. She took them both to the sofa putting them on two coasters on the glass coffee table.

'Tanks Beth. What wine is it?'

'Campo Viejo, a delicious Spanish one.'

'Uuuuum, dat's delicious n one o mi favourites. I adore riojas, dey taste so plummy, oaky, rich n fruity.' he said.

They picked up their respective glasses, moved them towards each other and clinked.

'Cheers Beth.'

'Cheers JB. Shall we propose a toast?'

'Great idea! I tink towards a successful afternoon of pool and a congrats to my resounding victory?'

'Your resounding victory?? Hmmmmmm. Considering I won about five games and you two, how does that compute?' she queried.

'I tink di winner was defo di game of pool. I must ave conveniently missed an andful of games?'

'Yeeeees, that appears to be the case and all the games I won. I blame the bottles of mid afternoon wine.'

'Yeah, I felt a l'il tipsy before we ad di food, so I'm usin' dat same excuse too. Ha haaaaaa.'

'To be honest, I did warn you I could play.'

'You didn't say ya were dat good dough. Oops, I mean damn ot.'

'I thought you'd have taken the hint and realised I could play moderately well. The scary thing is, I'm worse right handed too.'

'Noooooooooo... Now I know ya jokin'!'

'Maybe I just think so when I'm drunk, like you thought you took a handful of games off me earlier, eh?'

'I tink jus to finalise who's di superior one, we need a rematch.'

'Deal!'

They both shook with their free hands. JB swirled the rich fruity dark red wine around in his glass, making sure he didn't spill any on the laminate flooring. If he had, it would wipe off easily, however, he wanted to exhibit his alleged wine prowess. The wine flirted with the summit of his glass, before the rouge bloody ocean became a calmer water.. Legs were present on the side of the glass. 'Dere almost as shapely as yours!'

'Thankfully mine are not as red as that, apart from when I get sunburnt!'

JB raised the glass to his nostrils, covering the right with his thumb and inhaling deeply with the exposed left. Following this he reduced the size of his lips to a centimetre diameter and slurped the wine, swilling it around in his mouth, before swallowing.

'Aaaaah, very interesting Jammin'. I never knew you were quite the Connoisseur of Cabernets, Regal of Riojas and Saint of Shirazs. I'm mightily impressed. Verdict?'

'A very rich, ruby, oaky wine, accentuated wi di sweet soft fragrant n palatable vanilla essence. If it were a movie, it'd be a lip smackin' five.'

'I say, I say you country gent, what a prudent and most articulate definition of ye olde rioja. I'm so impressed. Spiffing, raaather spiffing!' joked Bethany.

'Oooooo, tank you kind luscious n decorous lady. D'ya wanna put on some music, maybe TV or jus converse wid charismatic cuthness?'

'I know what I'd luuuurve to do right now...'

She was desperate to strip him stark naked, stroking, poking, kissing and caressing from his fro to his baby toe. She decided to play it as cool and as reserved as she had all afternoon, although they had engaged in a few gentle kisses at the pool hall, concluding in a steamy intimate interlude in the lift, almost being caught in the act by Mr Robertson.

'Tell me den!'

'It's about time you returned the compliment and massaged my neck. It's feeling a little sore n tight.'

'Yeah, dat's no problem. Ya deserve di best treatment. After destroyin' mi ego at pool, you can resurrect it again by complimentin' me on one o mi trademark soothin' massages.'

'You'll have to wait first. I'll tell you whether or not it's a yay or nay! But then again, if Jen enjoyed it, I'm one hundred and one percent certain, I will too.' she said, slurring slightly.

They had one more sip of their wine, put the glasses on the coasters on the glass coffee table. JB stood up and moved over to the corner of the L of the sofa, sitting right back against the comfortable leather. Bethany stood up and walked to the state of the art stereo system to play some music.

'Wouch! I noticed dat when we came in, it's very sleek n innovative. What make is it?'

'It's Bang and Olufsen. When I first moved in, I wanted to invest in a state of the art stereo system. It was expensive, but fortunately I managed to get sixty percent off in the sale. It still cost just under a grand, but well worth it.'

'It's a real gem lady. It's so petite and gives ya room far more space, as opposed to one o dem massive intrusive older systems. It's di dogs!' said JB.

She put on some Barry White, appropriate for the mood, location and ambience. She turned up the bass to give it some more oomph and sat back down between JB's legs. JB could see a distinct pink tinge on her neck, before she turned round to sit down. This was evident that she fancied him, even though it wouldn't take an Einstein to calculate that and square root it. JB's fingers started to work their magic as Bethany oooed and cooed with every stroke. From behind he could see her toned thighs, this really aroused him. He was trying hard not to rub his crotch up against her cocyx, as she would have known immediately he was erect and excited.

'D'ya wanna get some cream, because it'll make it easier to massage n break down dem knots as big as mi fist.'

'Surely they're not that big?'

'Big enough, so run along n bring di cream, so I can ave some strawberries wid it!' laughed JB.

'You joker. Incidentally, I have some in the fridge.'

She stood up, pulled her skirt down a bit as it was riding up, displaying the bass of her left buttock just below her lacy knickers. JB almost fainted in shock. What an adorable taut and smooth cheeky sight. She swaggered away, stumbling slightly as she bumped into the edge of the sofa. JB thrust his fist in the air, as he thought it was definitely 'Game On.'

He had another slurp of his wine, almost spitting it out as Bethany returned with less than she left with.

'Aven't you forgotten someting?'

'Stupid me! Yeah, the cream.'

She went back to the bedroom to pick it up. Within ten seconds she was back. She passed the Johnson's baby lotion to JB and sat back down. He flipped open the top and squirted a portion into his right hand, placing it onto her shoulders.

'OUCH! You could warm it up first?'

'Sorry!'

She smacked his left foot because of his cheek. He massaged it into her shoulders softly, but firmly. Kneading it with his fingers, identifying and then breaking down the knots. She was one happy lady. JB couldn't believe she'd taken her vest top off to reveal part of her nakedness. He was extremely overwhelmed, but delighted at this, as he could see all the toned contours of her upper body. His next intention, probably in thirty minutes or so, was to unveil her ample sized chest. He was desperate to massage cream into those beauties. The music was playing in the background, goose pimples on Bethany's skin, warm cream on JB's hands, wine poured, a few clothes discarded entwined with pulses racing, the speed of a pedigree racehorse.

'Oh, oh! That's wonderful. Your touch is sooooo… Oooo la laaaaa.'

'Tank you. I always aim to please ya know.'

'You're not going to go any further than that tonight though. I'm not a first date sex lady, so don't be getting your hopes up!' she said with aplomb.

'I never ad any intention o di kind. What made ya say dat n ave dose impressions?' replied JB, shocked and disappointed.

'I'm just saying, NO shenanigans of a more intimate nature. If you play your cards right, another date might be on the cards!'

'Would tomorrow mornin' classify as another date?' he answered cheekily.

'Don't forget Monday's a teacher training day, but we're not due in until after twelve, so ya never know!'

'Isn't Stacey supposed to be back Monday?'

'Yeah, I think so. That's what somebody mentioned yesterday.'

JB continued with the massage and somehow managed to encourage Bethany into removing her denim mini skirt. She was lying down on a towel with JB straddling her from behind. He hoped to be repeating the act naked at a later date. He didn't know where to put his eyes, as her firm buttocks were directly beneath him, his manhood still standing to disciplined attention. Her bra strap was now unclipped, enabling him to slowly and powerfully use all his mastery to excite her and relieve all the aches and pains from her neck to the base of her spine. He was desperate to place his hands on her bottom, but still wanted to play it cool. He could have easily stroked her divine rear, but decided against it, as his heart was still palpitating at a frantic rate, plus the longer the wait, the more explosive the encounter.

The lights were low, Barry White playing on the stereo, baby lotion smeared in, two bodies yearning for each other, twilight setting in, pheromones off the scale, such a plethora of goodness. It was approaching ten o'clock, still early, a full moon appearing outside, music upstaging theirs booming from the floor above, what else should they do? At number seventy seven, The Waterfront, the ambience was just about perfect.

'Are you going to soothe my aching legs?'

He lifted his body up from the jockey position, glaring down at her phenomenal lower extremeties and the ass... That was just something else! After seducing Jennifer last weekend, The sight in front of his eyes was just as good, albeit the skin a lighter complexion.

'Yeah, daft question eh? Is ya booty off limits, or would ya like me to soothe dat too?' he proposed.

'D'you remember the text I sent you about washing my back and neck in the bath!'

'Yeeeeees.'

'D'you fancy doing that?'

He gave a gigantic sigh.

'Ye, ye, ye, yeeeeaaaah, why n-n-n-not,' he stuttered.

'Come on then.'

He stood up, she fastened her bra strap, rolled over on to her back, beckoning him to lift her up. He acknowledged. She led him to her ensuite bathroom. She put the stainless steel plug in and ran the hot water, throwing in a generous helping of bubble bath. It was a virginal style bathroom, with everything apart from the taps, plugs, shower hose and fittings and radiator being stainless steel. It was so spacious, you could almost live in it, apart from it being without modern domestic kitchen appliances. The bath was filling up, half full, so Bethany turned off the hot water and ran in some cold, testing it first with her finger tips.

'Are you gonna get stripped off then? I wanna see the alpha male sculptured adonis in the flesh, that is JB!' she said winking.

'I better get di glasses o wine first, mi mouth's a li'l dry!'

'Run along then.'

JB went to fetch the glasses along with the bottle of Campo Viejo. He put them down in the corner of the bath near the tap. Bethany had climbed in, still wearing her underwear.

'Aren't we gettin' naked?'

'As I said, on a first date I don't indulge in gratuitous goodness! It can wait till maybe tomorrow night or whenever that time arises, if and when,' she teased.

JB undressed, leaving his clothes piled up neatly in the corner. He left his Armani boxer shorts on, as he didn't want to put the frighteners up her so soon, member threatening to bulge out. He climbed in tentatively behind her adjacent to the tap side. The water was scorching for him, so he couldn't understand how she could tolerate it. The bubbles were fluffy and big, he cupped some in his hands and blew them out. All the particles breaking up into thin air. He splashed some water onto her back which she enjoyed and then proceded to resume the massage. He was still hoping for a repeat performance of last weekend, testing the water, literally, wondering whether Bethany would comply? 'D'ya mind if ya hair gets wet?'

'No, it's OK, just continue with your soft healing and soothing hands!'

'Whatever ya request ya majesty.'

He was wincing quietly, as the water was too hot for him. Somehow, with a lot of courage, he managed to cope with the temperature. He was breathing quickly still, a combination of being in hot water, not in a bad sense though as he was behind the beautiful buxom Bethany. What a lucky man. He was desperate not to develop a reputation for seducing half of his colleagues. This was only strike number two, but with his charisma and skilled seductive repertoire, the statistics could begin to climb towards double figures. Not to mention, he had already seen Annabelle in all her naked morning glory, albeit inadvertently at his bathroom door, when he was resting on the toilet. That was surely a great exaggeration though, as there were only about twenty teachers in the whole school, of which half were female. Plus he didn't find all of those attractive too. Consequently it would be a slur on his reputation, potentially leading to his position becoming untenable.

It was such a cosy experience, being in a bath with Bethany, the hot soapy water, the white ivory decor, music playing in the background, he slowly drifted away to sleep.

'Jammin', Jammin', I wanna jammin' wid you. We're jammin', we're jammin', we're jammin', we're jammin', I hope you like jammin' too! Are you asleep, or just resting on my shoulders?'

There was no response from him, just the noise of gentle and relaxed breathing coming from his nose and mouth. Bethany turned herself around to face him, his head dropped forward, jaw relaxed and mouth gaping open, she could have done anything to him. Soaked a sponge and stuffed it into his mouth, played tonsil tennis, stripped him naked, taken her bra off and put her breasts in his mouth?? That could be a plan, but she didn't want to do that too soon. She poked him in the chest, no response. She stroked his eyebrows, nibbled on his ear, kissed his neck... Nothing, apart from continuous relaxed breathing. She knew what would work, as long as he didn't bite it off in shock. Her little pinkie would surely do the trick. She sucked it and then ran it slowly onto his top lip, before moving down to the bottom ones. He didn't wake up, but spasmed momentarily, as if somebody was walking over his grave. Of course he was alive, well, not kicking, but sleeping in a seated position in a warm bath of soapy water. She sucked it once more and then inserted it, placing it on his tongue.

'Uuuuuuum, uuuuuuuum, gi me more. Oh yeeeees. Ya nipples are so sweet n tasty! Jus like ripe strawberries, juicy n wholesome!'

'I'm pleased you like them, it's your special Saturday night bathtime treat. Suck em softly, suck em hard. Oh yeah, feel the texture on your tongue!'

His eyes eventually began to open.

'You tease! All along I tought I was suckin' on ya pinkie n not ya nipple.'

'You were suckin' on my pinkie.'

'I know, not quite di same dough.'

'As I said earlier, if you play your cards right and avoid the joker, that Queen of Hearts may entertain her Ace of Diamonds?'

'Hmmmmm. I can't wait fa dat luxury.'

The bath was so spacious, you could fit a family of four in there. It also had a whirlpool facility too.

'Move forward a little n let me squeeze in behind ya!'

She sat down behind him, pressed the whirlpool button and hey presto, they had their very own mini jacuzzi. The jets were fabulous, projecting copious amounts of water from the bottom and the sides. In total there were six of them, ideal for a long hydrotherapy massage. Bethany enhanced that sensation by giving JB a neck, shoulder and back one too. They spent a good hour in the bath, chatting, massaging and sleeping. Eventually they both got out, dried each other and got ready for bed. Beth took off her underwear in private, away from JB's gazing starry eyes, to alleviate any possibility of some more hands on approach. She put on a white vest top with matching nylon shorts and went to join him in the room. They cuddled, drank, chilled and chatted on the sofa, occassionally staring at the moonlit sky, glistening with many star constellations. The hours rolled by, the rioja was drunk, every now and then, a clink and a clunk, Bethany being entertained in her own abode by one of Oatmill High's favourites, Mr Duane Herbert the hunk. They were dozing on the sofa, until JB suddenly woke up from a lucid dream. He felt a sticky sensation in his boxer shorts, quietly and carefully standing up, to head to the bathroom without waking Bethany. He closed and locked the door, pulled down his skinny jeans and checked the damage.

'Oh man, dis certainly ain't cream fa di strawberries. Ow dis appen? I better take em off n clean off di substance.'

He removed them, ran the water in the sink and used the towel he'd dried himself with to wipe away the sticky gunge. He tried not to wet them too much, because he had nothing else to sleep in, apart from his jeans. If Bethany asked him to, or decided to remove those herself, she'd be astounded by what lay beneath. Not an anaconda, but probably more of a spitting cobra. When he'd finished, he hung them on the heated towel rail and sat on the toilet in half of his birthday suit, his modesty hanging loose.

Once again he'd manage to doze off...

KNOCK... KNOCK... KNOCK... 'Who's dere?'

'What d'you mean, who's there? It's me Beth!'

'Sorry Bee, I must o fallen asleep in ere.'

'You've been gone for well over an hour, I thought you'd gone home without the decency of a goodnight kiss?'

'I wouldn't o done dat. Di toilet were callin' me. Give me a minute.'

'It's almost two o'clock, I'm sleepy. Are we goin' to bed?' asked Bethany.

'Dat sounds like a plan. Shall I crash on di sofa?'

'Aawww... What a gentleman! You can keep me warm if you like! But NO funny business alright!'

'Don't worry, I'll jus tickle ya!'

'Ha haaaa.'

He was hoping his boxer shorts had dried, because surely he couldn't sleep in his skinny jeans, they may be a bit too uncomfortable in bed. He checked them, they were drying but not quite right. He had to somehow use stalling tactics and persuade Bethany to stay up a little while longer.

'Beeeeeth!'

There was a silent pause. He wasn't too sure whether she'd heard him with all the commotion upstairs. The party was still in full swing and appeared to have no desire to quieten down. It was Saturday night/Sunday morning, so potentially it could go on for another few hours.

'Jammiiiin'… Did you say something?!'

'Yeah, I was just gonna suggest us finishin' di bottle o wine, n den opefully we'll be knocked out by di volume. It may be too difficult to fall asleep at di mo! What d'ya tink?'

'For me, it sounds… Boom, boom, boom, shake-shake the room… like a good idea. Anything to induce sleep. No offence, I'm here with a gorgeous guy, but feel quite sleepy, probably not enough to be able to drift away with the party crew upstairs.'

He nervously re-checked the state of his Armanis. He was just hopeful they were dry, knowing that within a couple of minutes since last checking, he was dreaming. Another forty minutes would do the trick, unless the boiler inadvertently broke in that time. Why was he panicking? Worse case scenario, he could crash on the sofa. He could sleep next to Bethany in skinny jeans only, he could go home, he could borrow a pair of her shorts? How the hell would they fit, being a size eight!

'Pull yaself together man. What's mi problem! I'm makin' crazy Himalaya Mountains outta ant ills. Dey'll be dry soon, which means I can spoon er wi clothes on,' he re-assured himself.

He pulled his jeans back up, got up off the toilet lid, unlocked the door and went back into the living room. His glass was full once more, along with Bethany's, but the bottle was empty.

'Get cosy n join me here. We'll probably fall fast asleep here on the sofa.'

'If we do, don't be wakin' up n tryin' some o dat funny business!' he said, mocking her.

They continued chatting, drinking and relishing each others' company, until incidentally, they both fell asleep on the sofa, with Bethany resting her head against JB's chest. It was a warm night, so Bethany didn't feel cold wearing only a white skimpy vest and matching shorts.

The birds started tweeting in perfect harmony and the bright light of the rising early morning sun shone through the living room window. It was approaching five thirty am. Bethany and JB were both soundly sleeping on the sofa. The party upstairs had finished. Thankfully the music was non-existent and peace had eventually been restored. After all, JB didn't have to worry about his boxer shorts, which would certainly now be dry. He was cuddling her in spoons, his crotch resting against her bottom, this making no difference to his conscience, as they were both in an unconscious state of mind.

Chapter 40

Sunshine Sunday Brekkie

Bethany opened her eyes momentarily, disorientated, with a brief smile at the comfortable position she was in. Then she closed her eyes once more and fell back to sleep.

After a soothing seven hours of shut eye, JB was the first to awake, blinking a few times and trying to become acustomed to the bright natural summer light. He stretched his arms, gently climbed over Bethany, who was still sleeping, and made his way to the bathroom to check and re-don his previously creamed boxer shorts. He turned off the radiator, checked the material. They were now fresh smelling without any gooey testosterone fuelled gunge, ready to be re-united with their owner. Off with the jeans, on with the shorts, covered up by the jeans once more. He ran the cold water, washing his face a few times to wake himself up properly. His mouth felt dry and clacky, so he squeezed some toothpaste on to his finger, massaging it into his teeth before taking a mouthful of water, gargling and then spitting it out, repeating the process a few times until his mouth felt fresh. He wiped his face and returned to the living room. He knelt down and gave Bethany a kiss on the cheek, resulting in her slowly opening her eyes, gazing at him, stretching her arms out in front of her, pulling his head towards her and planting a sensuous open mouthed kiss on his lips.

'Good morning Mister Herbert,' she said after withdrawing her lips.

'Mornin' Ms Duke, ow ya doin'?'

'I'm feeling good thanks. D'you know what time we dozed off?'

'I don't know, but I jus remember wakin' up n tinkin', tank di Lord dat pumpin', jumpin' n thumpin' music ad stopped upstairs. Mi ead was spinnin' around earlier like an outta control escapin' car wheel.'

'Yeah, it was loud wasn't it? What d'you want for breakfast?' asked Bethany.

'Someting tasty please.'

'That's so helpful and descriptive. Could you give me a clue?'

'Wouldn't it be easier if ya told me mi choices! I'm not telepathic ya know.'

'Ooooooo… are you being cheeky young man? D'you want me to throw you over my knees and spank you?'

His heart started to beat quicker than the average one hundred beats a minute again, along with his body temperture increasing slightly. 'OMG, dat's an offer I couldn't resist! D'ya want mi pants on or off Miss?'

'I wouldn't tell you, just make an impulsive decision.'

'I'd prefer to keep em on, because I don't want any red and print marks on mi bum. I don't tink mi mum would be too appy!' he said laughing hysterically.

'You Mummy's boy. In this instance, ya Mum'll have nothing to do with the treatment I'm gonna give you, if you misbehave!' replied Bethany winking and sucking her index finger sensuously.

'Miss Behave?? I tought you were Miss Duke!' Teased JB.

'I can be who ever you want me to be.'

'Dat sounds irresistible and mouthwateringly delicious, jus like dis mornin's brekkie we're gonna munch on. D'ya ave stuff fa a fried full English?'

'Whatever you want, I have.'

'Sizzling sausages, bootiful bacon, enterprisin' eggs, tantalisin' tinned tomatoes, marvellous mushrooms n baked beans please.'

'Why d'you need to dress up all the ingredients? It won't make them any more attractive and appetising!'

'OK den. I'll dress em down,' he said, fantasising about being in an compromising position with her, legs akimbo.

His imagination was so vivid. She walked towards the door that opened onto the spacious balcony. JB was transfixed at the stunning sight of her shapely ass.

'I'll make a full English for us and we can eat it on the balcony, if you like?'

It seemed like a perfect idea, as the weather outside looked absolutely glorious. There was barely a cloud in the sky, an unbroken mass of light blue with a few white trails from aeroplane jet engine smoke. 'Yeah, dat'l defo hit di spot. Ave you got any erbal tea too?'

'It's your lucky Sunday. If you look in one of the cupboards, there are several boxes of herbals, just don't take the drugs.'

'What d'ya mean?' enquired JB.

'Weeeeeell, there's a box of Bush tea.'

'Ya mean like cannabis plant?' JB responded curiously, looking astounded.

'Nooooooo… It's a healthy tea from the Caribbean. I bought it especially for you, with your roots and all that.'

'Dat's my girl! Well, not literally my girl, just a sayin' ya know! I'm so grateful n enamoured dat you tought of me.'

'I went shopping after work last night and bought some essentials for us!'

'Last night?' said JB.

'Eeeerm,' she paused. 'Noo, I meant on Friday evening after school. This sunshine's tiring me out.'

'Probably more di effects o di rioja n my wonderful company!'

'Get a move on and stop your flattery. My mouth's dry and in need of a soothing morning herbal tea. Hurry up Bush man.'

'Keep ya knickers on!' said JB chuckling.

'I'm notwearing any,' said Bethany.

His jaw dropped, mouth gaping wide open, enough space to squeeze in a mini football. She was teasing him and flirting outrageously. It reminded him of roughly this time a week ago, when Miss Luis-Cortada was using exactly the same seductive and hypnotising methods. He was hoping for a case of deja-vu, but this time with the divine, decorous and deliciously formed Miss Duke aka Bethany. He wandered over to the cupboards, opening a few until he found the one with multiple boxes of herbal teas. Chamomile and spiced apple, rooibos, lemon and ginger, echinacea and strawberry, licorice root, cardamom, fennel. JD was a fanatical consumer of herbal teas and evidently Bethany was too.

'What tea d'you want?'

'I don't mind. Surprise me, make it with some *je ne sais pas pourquoi et piece de la resistance.*'

'Does that mean, as it comes?'

'I'll leave it to your imagination. I'll make a start on the brekkie.'

JB took out the detox one along with two mugs for the drinks. It had the licorice root, cardamom and fennel. They were both feeling quite revitalised after a good sleep, albeit on the sofa. A good average seven hours sleep was just what the doctor ordered. JB put some water in the kettle and boiled it, dunking the bags into the mugs ready for an enjoyable morning beverage. Bethany took ingredients for the breakfast out of the fridge and cupboards and started preparation. The kettle had just boiled, so JB poured it into the mugs and stirred the bags round with a teaspoon.

'D'ya ave any oney Bee?'

'Yeah. There's some in one of the cupboards. I don't want any in mine though.'

JB found the honey, took it out of the cupboard, unscrewed the top, inserted a fresh teaspoon from the drainer, because the one already in one of the mugs would cause it to run straight off, as it was scorching hot. He twisted a heaped spoonful, twisting it around a few times to make sure it didn't start dripping onto the work surface. He put it into his mug, stirring it in until it disolved. JB had a plain white mug that was square in design, while Bethany had a conventional curvy black one that was covered with sunflowers. He thought it would be a romantic detail after their first date together, elevating the mood, just like the weather.

The pans were making all kinds of noises, spitting, sucking, slurping, as the eggs were scrambled, sausages fried, beans boiled and the bacon and vine ripened tomatoes being grilled in the oven. The aroma was beginning to drift through the atmosphere.

'D'ya want any elp wi di food?'

'I'll be OK thanks. Go outside and sit on the balcony and admire the panoramic view from the Waterfront. You'll be amazed. Thanks for the tea, it's good.'

JB took his mug of tea outside, making himself comfortable on the balcony. It was spacious enough to have a barbecue on there. Bethany had converted it into a horticultural haven by placing a couple of plants at either end to give a more colourful feel. There were three wicker chairs and a pure white table that looked like marble. If it were, it would be very expensive. Bethany took great pride in her possessions and was partial to a lavish item or two. That was evident with the state of the art stereo system that would be worth more than a month's salary for the average working class person. It was a very plush partment in a picturesque location, with the views being panoramic. JB was admiring the design and materials that had been used to construct the balcony. Its base was made of stainless galvanised steel along with the hand rail and vertical supports, built with rigid strong integrity ten milimetre thick glass. It was weather resistant to maximise longevity. It protruded a metre from the building face and was six metres long. JB could see the reflection of himself as the sun shone brightly on to the glass panels. He was busy grooming, making sure his hair was presentable and his skin was in good shape. Probably a better idea to use a conventional mirror, as that would be literally a true reflection of image. The detox tea was cooling quite quickly, so he could now take longer sips.

JB took his phone out of his pocket, selected the message app, scrolled down to Ash and typed.

'Yeah brudder, what's appenin'? Did u njoy ya nite wid Bella n Jen? I'm chillin' dis morn after a relaxin' nite. D'ya wanna hook up 2day, or r u savourin' some more delicious fruity goodness wi di gal dat's quite Bella? Peace n Harmony-D Boy.'

'JB, are you ready?' shouted Bethany.

JB put the phone back in his pocket and put his feet up on a neighbouring wicker chair, without footwear of course, otherwise that would have been quite disrespectful at someone elses place. He hadn't heard the shout from Bethany, as the door was only slightly ajar.

'Jammin', are you ready for brekkie?'

'Bee, did you say someting?' asked JB.

She had walked to the balcony door, opened it and poked her head round.

'Hello Mister, I was asking if you were ready to have some delicious brekkie!'

'Of course I am, mi belly's empty n needs a good fillin',' he said smiling, hoping that she would receive a good sexual filling in the next twenty four hours or so.

He stood up from his chair and followed Bethany into the kitchen. It smelt incredible. It was all neatly displayed on two flying saucer size plates, a mosaic of Sunday morning colour.

'D'you want to eat in the room on lap trays, or go al fresco and enjoy the weather?'

'Let's go outside, because di weather's absolutely bootiful. Too good to resist.'

Bethany opened a drawer and took out some cutlery, while JB pulled the salt and pepper grinders and brown sauce out of the cupboard.

'Would you like a gerbil tea top up?'

'Did you jus say gerbil?' said JB.

'Nooooo... Herbal!'

'You're a wom-animal. Lord, I can't believe ya want a pet in ya tea!' laughed JB.

'I'm not into cruelty to animals, so can I please emphasise, an H to the E to the R to the Beeee to the A to the L! Do your job, boil the kettle again and sort out the drinks please.'

'Oooooo, ya said it so lovingly n sensitively, ow could I turn dat demand down!'

'Thank you. I'll take the plates outside n waft the wasps n flies away!' chuckled Bethany.

'You jus do dat, because I don't want any dirty wings stuck in mi teeth,' he said sucking his teeth with his tongue.

The kettle boiled, the birds outside sang. JB was playing it ice cool with Bethany, hoping he could entice her to break her no sex pact. He emptied the remaining cold water into the sink and then poured hot water into the mugs. He added some more delicious honey for good measure and carried the drinks outside to the balcony. The food did smell beautiful, accentuated by the sausages that were pork, leek, apple and cinnamon.

'You're looking quite fresh faced this morning, what happened?'

'I spooned dis sexy n sassy chick fa several ours, so it mus be di G-factor effect! She was quite ot, n dat's bein' critical,' JB said, sniggering.

They sliced and shovelled the food down. JB's phone vibrated in his pocket, probably a response from Ash. He left it, as didn't want to appear to be rude when in the presence of a lady he was fond of, especially on the morning after their first date. In theory, you could classify this as a second date.

'Are you going home or do you want to stay for dinner later?'

'I tink I'm gonna go ome, because I need to get a few tings done before work tomorrow!'

'It's a teacher training day don't forget.'

'Yeah, but we still need to be in fa midday-ish don't we?'

'That's right.'

'I jus wanna get mi clothes ready, feed di cat n tidy up, but I'm keen on ookin' up later if dat's OK wid you?'

'I'd like to engage in some more of ya company. We could watch a movie after dinner, if you like?'

'Dat's a super option. Shall I bring mi toothbrush?' Joked JB.

'You managed with ya finger earlier, but it's probably a better idea, because you may need to get those fly wings out of ya teeth,' Bethany said.

'Ha haaaaa. Would six-ish be alright?'

'Prrrrrrrrrfect. I'll surprise you with a Bee style roast. I can guarantee, you won't be disappointed.'

'Why, are ya gonna serve it in ya birthday suit, or jus wid a pinafore on?'

'Don't be so cheeky. I might put a pair of heels on though!' Bethany said with a glint in her eye.

They continued relishing the morning delights of the seventh floor panorama, sweet scent of the detox herbal tea, brekkie odour and of course the enriching company. The morning passed by without any event, apart from the pair of them continuing to flirt outrageously, indulging in the ocasional kiss.

Chapter 41

Home Sweet Home

After breakfast JB called a taxi and returned home for a couple of hours. He had to feed Felix, tidy the house and organise his wardrobe for tomorrow's teacher training. The dress code was always relaxed though, a non uniform type day. Felix was in full voice, having spent the afternoon, night and morning without his loyal owner. JB couldn't keep a good pedigree feline down. He was jumping up, wanting to be fussed over. Petra was minding her own business, not literally, as the cat tray was surprisingly empty. They had been alone for almost twenty four hours and not a cat faeces in sight! Were they both constipated or just feeling lonely without the urge to want to relieve their bowels after some nourishing goodness? Speak of the proverbial devil, Petra gracefully made her way to the cat litter tray, stepped in, squatted down on her haunches, face in full concentration, eyes closed, squeezing her bottom and then... There it appeared, fresh stools. As if magically or subliminally, JB's presence had suddenly enticed the sanitary experience. No sooner had Petra flicked the cat litter on to her business, Felix was also hypnotised, in he went, making sure he avoided the area where Petra had been. He had a good old sniff, before sneezing, blowing some of the sawdust into the air, before repeating the stance she had just performed. It was like their very own artistic cat dressage, although the waste produce wasn't that attractive unless you were a conceptual artist fascinated by animal droppings.

JB jogged upstairs to his bedroom, took off the lid of the wicker linen basket and took all the clothes out. It was full to the brim. Something smelt fusty in there. He emulated Felix a minute or too earlier and had a good sniff of his clothing. It was the stale stench of sweat from the white Umbro vest he'd worn for the Yoga class on Friday night. He put the lid back on the basket and carried the big heap of clothing downstairs to the washing machine in the kitchen. He opened the door and shoved everything in. It would take approximately two hours, which gave him time to do some domesticated chores. He cleaned out the cat tray, putting it into old newspaper, wrapping it up like a fish and chip portion. If only it smelt as attractive as that. He put it into fragranced disposable double bags, went outside and dropped it in the bin. He now had to clean the bathroom and hoover upstairs and the stairs, leaving the downstairs till tomorrow or later in the week. He opened the bathroom window to ventilate, turned on the extractor fan, picked up some Jiff cleaning cream, flipped the top and squirted it into the sink, running some warm water and wiping and swiping away. He gave the bathroom a good once over, shower basin, bidet, toilet with Dettol wipes and dusted down the heated towel rail, window sill and window frame. He sprayed some air freshner to give it a sweeter scent. He moved on to the bedrooms, going into hoover mode. It took a good hour.

JB checked his phone, it was two pm. There was a message response from Ash.

'Yes Brother, I'm all good thx. What an amazing night with the ladies. We had a three some, it was phenomenal! Ha haaa, I'm only joking. Jen was pining for ya. A few glasses of wine thankfully relaxed her. We watched Hangover, absolutely hilarious. Following that, Bella and I savoured part deux....Owwwww-uuuuuuuuu. I'll tell you about it later. Unfortunately I'll be busy entertaining these two ladies for the rest of the day, so maybe a hook up this week? N.B. I phoned that nurse from Lillyford too. We're gonna hook up next week! ;-P Stay safe and njoy. Peace and Love. X'

It was probably a good idea that Ash didn't want to hook up, because JB wouldn't really have enough time, as he had to be at Bethany's for six. He wanted to relax now the upstairs cleaning had been done. He changed his clothes, putting his skinny jeans back in the wardrobe along with his navy blue cardigan, the beige t-shirt and boxer shorts in the linen bin. He put his navy blue jogging bottoms on and a plain lemon t-shirt. He was feeling a little sleepy, but wanted to give the cats a run outside, so went downstairs, opened the back door and out dashed Felix and Petra. He realised there was no cat litter in the tray after cleaning it earlier. Thankfully they were both obedient animals, so wouldn't be mischievious and squirt their urinal waste in a corner of the house leaving their scent. He closed and locked the door behind the cats, took the bag of fresh litter and poured an even amount into the tray and then shook it to push it into the corners. There were a few remnants around the side which he hadn't cleaned, so he got several pieces of kitchen roll and some Dettol and cleaned them off, then threw the soiled pieces in the bin. An afternoon siesta was definitely calling, so he made sure everything was tidy and secure downstairs, windows and doors, washed his hands in the kitchen sink to kill any unwanted germs, trotted upstairs, dived on to the bed, picked up his iPhone and set the alarm for five pm. He could now relax for a few hours, drifting away into dreamworld before getting ready for an evening with Bethany. He was hoping for big things, predominantly an intimate interlude with her.

Chapter 42

Beth-Taking

JB's iPhone alarm started to sound at five pm. He was in a deep sleep, so didn't wake up straight away. He slept for a further minute, until his eyes began to slowly open. He sighed, gazing around in a dazed state, before realising the sound was his alarm. He scrambled his hands on the quilt, eventually finding his phone and turning it off. He dragged himself up from the bed, stumbled over his own feet as if he were drunk, walked to the bathroom and washed his face to wake up. After a couple of hours' siesta, he felt worse, probably because he wasn't used to siestas, albeit occasionally falling asleep on the couch in the staff room at Oatmill High now and again on a Friday afternoon. He shuffled through his trousers, shirts and cardigans, pushing coathangers to the left and then to the right, unsure of what to throw on. He was muttering to himself.

'Shall I wear someting simple, someting smooth, someting jazzy? I tell ya what man, I'll pop on mi skinny jeans again, dis pink DKNY v necked t-shirt n mi light blue American Eagle hoodie.'

To compliment the look, he was going to also wear a pair of white Calvin Klein boxers. It was probably a sensible idea for him to have a shower to revitalise and a can of Red Bull to revive him, as he was feeling shattered. It was his second day of recovery after the working week and thankfully he could have a lie in in the morning because of the teacher training day. He placed all his clothes on the bed and then went for his shower. The jets were so therapeutic, relaxing his aching shoulders and back. The water was so soothing as it blasted into the swimming cap on the top of his head. He closed his eyes and allowed his mind to drift serenely away to another place for a few minutes. The shower hose smacked against the wall tiles as he lost his footing and banged his head, which soon woke him up. He could have done with a seat in there, at least dozing off wouldn't be a hazardous past time. He picked up the vanilla and ylang ylang foamburst, squirting it into his left hand and smearing it over his body to ensure he smelt sweet. Bethany would be consumed by his extra strong pheromones, enhanced by the foamburst and Palmer's cocoa butter.

'Tonight's di night, fa daaaancin', romaaaancin', I'm in di mood fa danciiiin', romanciiin', Oooooo I'm givin' it all tonight.' he sang while shaking his body side to side.

After rinsing himself off, cleaning the last remnants of soap from his back, sack and crack, the shower was turned off. He opened the doors, pulled his towel off the radiator and dried his clean skin. After drying himself, he put the towel over the radiator, flipped the top off the toothpaste and slowly squirted a pea sized amount onto his electric brush. He ran the cold water momentarily to wet the brush and then buzzed away allowing the bristles to clean his pristine ivory enamel. He cleaned his tongue, his teeth brushing ritual, making sure it was a smooth and soft texture as opposed to a coarse dirty carpet feel. Not that the tongue was similar in appearance or for that matter or texture of a carpet, but he wanted it to be attractive for his tonsil tennis exchanges with Bethany. He was extremely happy, hoping to fraternise with his friend and colleague later this evening. He creamed his body to emit the customary chocolate cocoa butter odour, before going downstairs to take his laundry out of the washing machine, as the cycle would have finished by now, after his siesta and shower. His meat and two veg were swinging freely in the air probably knocking out microscopic bugs.

BOOOOOOOOOM, KAPOOOOOOOOOOW, OOOOOOOOOOOOW, EEEEEEEEEE, BAAAAAAAAAM!

He pressed the off button on the washing machine, opened the door and took the large pile of clothing upstairs to the bedroom Ash and Annabelle had slept in. He took the clothes airer out from the side of the wardrobe, after putting the clothes down on the bed and then hung them all over neatly to dry. He went back to his bedroom and got ready. It was five thirty five pm, not that he had to be at Bethany's for exactly six on the dot, but he wanted to be fashionably late, just after. He slid open the wardrobe door, pondering for a moment. He had to take a change of clothing for tomorrow, as he would go straight to school from Bethany's. The skinny jeans he wore yesterday and this morning were still clean and were on the bed with the other clothes, so he put them on. He surfed, not literally, as he didn't have a mini pool with wave machine in his bedroom, the base of the wardobe which is where his footwear was stored.

'Shall I wear di navy blue All Stars, di white ones or di black slip on Vans? Too many choices man. Seen as Flix isn't ere to give me a miaow of approval, I'm gonna go fa di black baseball stylie ankle boot All Stars. Decision made!'

He sprayed on his favourite Issey Miyake in all the appropriate places. He was feeling like a Prince, ready to embark on part deux of his Beth-taking adventure. He put his mobile phone in his jean pocket, with strawberry Lipsyl and Wrigley's Extra cool breeze chewing gum.. His hair needed freshening up, so he took the mayonnaise out of the wardrobe, unscrewed the green top and dunked his right hand in. Thankfully it wasn't a jar of Hellmans, as that would have been a bizarre ingredient to put into his hair. He scooped out a sizeable amount, rubbed both hands together and massaged it rigorously into his afro. Result, ready to hit the road after letting Felix in. He styled his jungle sized mass to make sure it looked attractive and didn't have random slimy pieces of cream left unrubbed. That would look uncouth. He put the jar back in the wardrobe.

He closed the doors, made his way around the house to ensure windows were securely closed and locked, curtains and blinds left partly open or shut and electrical appliances turned off that had to be. When downstairs, he opened the fridge and took out a can of Red Bull as he wanted to revive and revitalise his body, as fatigue had set in. He pulled the ring pull and slurped it down in seconds, shook his head, roared like a lion in the Serengeti, beat his chest with his fists and then closed the fridge. Felix came in through the cat flap, miaowing rather loudly. Felix walked straight to his food bowl, which was empty, so JB put a handful of biscuits down for him and replenished the water bowl. He dashed upstairs to wash his hands as it wouldn't have been very alluring, smelling of cat snacks. He took out a plain light blue v necked t-shirt, deodorant, got his toothbrush from the bathroom, a clean pair of boxer shorts and a packet of three Durex featherlight condoms, just in case he got lucky. He didn't want to go scuba diving without flippers, so ensured he was protected. He put all his belongings into a drawstring Reebok sports bag, threw it over his shoulder, picked up his Audi car keys from the bedside chest of drawers, closed all the doors apart from his bedroom one, so Felix could sleep in there. He set the burglar alarm, left the kitchen door ajar, slipped on his baseball boots, went out of the house locking the door behind him, waiting outside until the alarm beeper to let him know it had set. He unlocked his car with the fob, walked along the drive to open the gates, got into his car and drove out, before completing his ritual, by closing the gates behind him. He arrived at The Waterfront at bang on six pm, just to give him a few minutes to get up to the seventh floor, which would make him fractionally late. He hated being punctual, apart from for work. His perception was that punctuality was for freak geeks who functioned by clockwork. He pulled into the entrance to the underground car park, put the handbrake on, took his phone out of his pocket, and phoned Bethany. It rang several times with no response. She probably had the music on, her hands full with preparing the Sunday roast and getting herself ready to look hot for JB. Maybe she was masturbating, exhilarated by the impending explicit probability, or was it solely just a possibility? It went through to voicemail, so he left a message, asking her to let him into the car park as soon as possible. He flicked through his phone apps, killing time, waiting for her to reply. After all of two minutes his phone rang, it was Fluffy Donkey. He was aghast, thinking it was so coincidental that he would phone at this precise time.

'Yes Fluffers, what appenin' boss? Eeeee-aaaaaaaaw!'

'JB, I'm good thanks, how you doing Cabbage?'

'I'll give you a few leafy shots to the stomach if ya don't watch ya mout! Yeaaaaaah, yeeeeaaaaaaah!'

'When ya big enough, we will discuss that prospect. Anyway, forget this sledging for once, let's have a normal conversation.'

'I'm all ears! Go on then, you phoned me.'

'D'ya want me to come round there n give you a stiff beating?'

'I sincerely hope ya not gonna be excited n wanna beat me wid ya rhythm stick?! Ha haaaaaaaaaaaaa.'

'I wouldn't waste it on you!'

'I should ope not. If ya plannin' on comin' outta di closet, keep dat disco stick away from me n use it wid ya udder partyin' friends wi di same sexual inclinations. You know I'm no backstreet boy! I'll hug ya n kiss you on di cheek, but noting more brudder. Ya feelin' me?'

'I feel your tongue sticky n soft!'

'Quit ya disgustin' slavva, it's such a turn off!' replied JB with disdain.

'Anyway Hedgehog, the reason I was phoning you, was to say, I stayed at Stacey's last night and uuuuuuum uuuuuuuum. We had one hell of an evening. Her back n neck pain have subsided n she'll be back at work tomorrow. The sex was, OMG... Mindblowing! Her body's absolutely sensational.'

'Weeeell, congrats man I ope you gave er di truly classified Fluffy treatment!'

'Donkey dick, I'm going, gotta go to Mum's for dinner. I'll phone you in the week. Peace n shenanigans yeah!'

Bethany was calling.

'I'm gettin' another call, so I mus go bredder. Perfect timin'. Peace, take care wid PHAT Love.' He picked up the call. 'There you are. What ya been playin' at woman? I've been parked up outside di complex fa di las five minutes, ya ready now?' JB asked.

'Yeeeaaaah... Sorry. Just been carving the holy bird, making gravy, setting the table n making myself look pretty. Walk to the front of the complex n I'll drop the keys down to ya.'

'Dat's a distance. Twenty five metres plus. I'm not an international cricketer or baseballer ya know. I'll probably injure miself!'

'You'll be fine, just don't cut ya lips, because I wanna lock my juicy ones on yours.'

'Ooooo, ello missus!' laughed JB.

'Are ya ready?'

'Geeez woman, I need to get out o mi car first n walk round di corner!'

He turned the engine off, opened the door, climbed out, pushing the door closed with the sole of his foot and wandered round to the face of The Waterfront appartments. 'Yeeep, I'm directly below now. Make sure you throw it outwards, because we don't want it landin' on someone elses balcony causin' serious injury. Three, two, one, gooooo.'

The key fob came flying down at breakneck speed. It took all of five seconds to travel from the seventh heaven to the ground floor. It was swirling round through the air, hitting the glass face of the last first floor balcony. 'You got it?' asked Bethany through the phone.

He had to put his phone in his pocket temporarily, as he didn't want to crack the screen with the fob. What a catch, right down the throat of his hands. An international cricketer would have been immensely proud of his ability. 'Got it. See you in five!'

'Bye. You still there?'

'Just, yeah.'

'You can park anywhere with a space marked V for visitors. Take ya pick, upper or lower ground. He walked back round to his car, climbed in, pointed the fob towards the car park entrance roller shutter door, pressed it, turned the ignition on and drove down the slope as it slowly opened. The car park was chocca block, with many residents deciding to relax on Sunday evening, or going out without their cars. He eventually found a space in the lower basement after driving round for a couple of minutes. He was lucky, because it appeared to be the only one available, otherwise he would've had to have parked outside.

'Damn, I forgot to bring a bottle o wine! Maybe dere's one in di boot?'

He climbed out, quite a tight squeeze as the car to his right, a beautiful sleek silver Bentley Continental was almost straddling the white line. Thankfully he was only a medium twelve stone build, so could get out. Anybody bigger, no chance. They'd of had to climb through the sun roof or out of the passengers side. The boot would've been an option worse case scenario, but thankfully it was on the other foot. He closed the door, walked around to the boot, opened it and took out his Reebok sports bag half full with his Essentials, toiletries and clothes for tomorrow's teacher training day. He slammed the boot shut, encouraging a lady close by to jump out of her skin. She turned round..

'I thought today was a day of rest?'

'It is. Mi boot jus needed a l'il corporal punishment, e's been a naughty boy today.'

'Don't be too hard on him, he may never forgive you!'

'As ya know its di Sabbath day, so if I'm repentant, I'm sure e will be!'

'OK. Good luck, see ya n Happy Sunday.'

'Appy Sunday to you too, mysterious woman.' he replied winking at her.

As she climbed into her car, she waved and winked back. He shook his head in amazement, another hot girl.

'Dis place is littered wid ot property oney's... W-Oucha! Boy, I'm gettin' distracted, I've forgotten to look fa dat bottle o wine now.'

He turned back round and went back to the car, opened the boot and had a rummage inside. There she was, under a blanket in the corner, hiding. Maybe she didn't want to be found, opened and abused. Hoping to be left for longer, enabling her to mature into an even more sophisticated wholesome red. She was certainly well bodied, probably accentuating luscious fruity and fragrant flavours. She was as potent as a pirana, but palatable at the least, with a bark worse than her bite. Berberana Rioja, a vintage female at that. Ideally left for a four year period, enabling her consumers to relish the enriching qualities she possessed. He pulled her out, opened his drawstring bag and plonked her in. He closed the boot for the second time, pressed the fob immobilising and locking the car. This time he wouldn't be in a position to engage in a passionate interlude reminiscent of the movie Disclosure, although Bethany wasn't in a position of hierarchy enabling her to exploit and ruthlessly decimate JB's profile, wellbeing and integrity by accusing him of sexually harassing her. On the contrary, she fancied him and wanted to enjoy some innocent no holds barred exhilarating sex, with possibly more on the agenda? That was definitely Jennifer's motive, whereas Bethany was more relaxed, coy and only wanting to fulfill her hormonal needs. He reached the twin lifts, pressed the button and waited for one of them to come down to lower basement level. It was eerily quiet, until... Piiiiing, the left lift door opened. JB walked in and pressed the number seven. The doors closed, up it went stopping at the upper basement.

'Please now man, don't let it be anyone I know!' he muttered to himself.

The doors opened, in walked two girls and two guys. It looked very much like they'd been on a througher, meaning all night and day partying session. The guys were dressed almost matching with black skinny jeans, white slip on pumps, same matching black hairstyles, blow dried and waxed with a left to right sweep. The only difference was one had a light tangerine tight round necked t-shirt, his pale ghost like skin exposed, the other wearing a loose fitting dark blue and white checked short sleeved shirt with tanned hairy arms showing. The girls... What weren't they wearing?? One had dark brown plaited hair stretching halfway down her back, bright red lipstick, a tight white vest top that was now seethrough revealing her erect nipples! What a sight! On her bottom half, there was a micro denim mini skirt with big royal blue buttons up the side and at least five inch heels. Her skin was olive. She wore a pair of big circular Gucci shades. The other girl had short bobbed blonde hair, pink lipstick, a flowing lilac summer dress flowing to just above her knees. On her feet were a classy pair of purple two inch heel shoes with a dainty flower on the side, toes poking through the front. She had a dark brown wooden beaded necklace, hooped earrings to match, big false eye lashes finished off with lilac eye shadow. She was also beautifully tanned. You could tell the boys were excited, getting ready to savour frivolous pleasures with the girls. JB thought it was highly likely they'd been at the party above last night, as they had pressed the eighth floor. The girls were very giggly, merry on alcohol. You could smell the odour in the lift. Both girls were astounded by JB's afro and couldn't take their eyes of it.

'Excuse me mister, d'ya mind if I touch ya hair?' asked the blonde.

'No man, of course ya can,' said JB smiling widely.

You could tell the guys were jealous and wanted the girls all to themselves.

'Ooooooooo, it's so soft n silky. It's really sexy! Do you want to come to the party with us? It's upstairs on the eighth floor, number eighty two! Bring a few friends if ya like.'

'I'd love to, but I'm goin' to dinner wid a friend. Many tanks fa di invite, maybe later?'

'We can't have you coming, you'll be too much competition for us.' laughed the pale skinned guy.

'I wouldn't wanna steal ya thunder, I'd jus wanna share dat's all!' chuckled JB.

'Oooo, we love sharing!' said the brunette.

The lift reached the seventh floor, the doors opened and JB walked out.

'Don't forget, if ya interested, number eighty two! Bye.' said the blonde.

JB returned the farewell compliment and walked to Bethany's appartment.

'OMG, I'd love to ead to dat party. Let's see where di night takes us. I tink I'll be entertained enough by Beth, so won't ave a need fa any more activities!'

He knocked on the door, after a few seconds it opened. Bethany standing there in dark brown hot pants, a yellow vest top with gold and silver bangles on each wrist, silver stud earrings and light brown leather sandals with tiny camouflaged flowers on. She looked a knockout. She threw her arms around JB and gave him a full open mouthed kiss on the lips. He was thinking he'd made the right choice for sure, plus how could he have even contemplated the invitation to number eighty two, when he had a dinner date with the beautiful Bethany. It was a no brainer! The scent from the kitchen was absolutely delicious.

'You're lookin' fabulous Jammin',' said Bethany as she withdrew her lips from his.

'I must return di compliment. Ya lookin' quite sensational yaself lady!'

He closed the door behind him, took off his baseball boots, putting his night bag on top of them and followed her into the kitchen/living room.

'I've rustled up a treat for you. Full Sunday roast with all the trimmings. I hope you like it.'

'I'm sure I will. D'ya need a hand wid anyting?'

'Just park your butt on the sofa and put ya feet up. Put the TV on and put on whatever you like.'

He made himself comfortable on the L-shaped sofa, picked up the remote and laid back. He flicked through the Sky channels and put some basketball on.

'D'ya like B-ball Beth?'

'Is that new cool street for basketball?' she asked.

'It sure is Miss Duke,' he replied cheekily.

He was in awe of the dining table and chair set.

'D'you want a glass of vino to start with?'

'Oooh, yes please.'

'Red or white?'

'I'll plump for a juicy red please.'

'Coming right up.'

'Hold on a min. Before you open dat bottle, I've got a surprise fa ya.'

He got up off the sofa and went back into the hallway to pick up the wine. He came back into the kitchen.

'Close ya eyes.'

He leant in to the side of her neck, blowing gently, before nibbling her left ear lobe. Her whole body shuddered. He then lifted up her vest top to reveal her navel and naughtily placed the cold bottle on her stomach.

'Aaaaaaargh.' she yelled, slapping him firmly on the left shoulder.

'Sorry, I didn't mean to make you jump.'

'I'll make you jump later young man,.' she replied with glee.

'Uuuuuuum, d'ya want me to be ya jockey?'

'At this rate, your pedigree filly will be unseating her rider!'

'Oooooo, sounds kinky!' he said sniggering.

'The only thing kinky'll be your mint sauce decorated roasted bird.'

'Oooooo, I can't wait. Should be a sizzling scorcher!'

'D'you like my new dining table and chairs, they came this afternoon. They were supposed to come yesterday, but there was a delay with the delivery.'

'Yeah, it's absolutely beautiful, I was in awe of it a few moments ago. Where is it from?'

'I ordered it from So Interiors on the Internet. They specialise in bespoke furniture.'

'I love di design wi di x support n di extendable clear glass top. I bet it was expensive!'

'I managed to get it in the sale at a reduced price. Just under a grand with six chairs. It's called Giomani Design.'

'You n ya charmin' ways eh.'

The table was set with circular cork place mats, salt and pepper pots and a large white candle flickering in a safe glass holder. It emitted a soothing vanilla scent. Bethany was carving the chicken and spooning out the yorkshire puddings, roast potatoes and plentiful veg. It was a meal fit for a king, that was for sure. The plates the food was being served on were as big as sombreros.

American style portions. JB's mouth was quickly becoming moist, his belly rumbling and his pupils dilating and that wasn't just because of the food. Besides the mouthwatering food prospects, he was wanting to get his teeth stuck into a far tastier and appetite quenching morsel, although it wouldn't be edible, unless you were a canníbal. His eyes were fixated on the nether regions of Miss Duke's body, from the hot pants down. Her legs were something else. Perfectly shaped and toned.

'Are you ready then Jammin'?'

'Ow could I not be ready fa dis delicious spread. It smells like an eavenly dish, I can't wait ya know.'

There was a monster sized mound on the plates, more on JB's as he inevitably had a larger appetite, although Bethany shouldn't be underestimated as she could also put food away, not just in the cupboards or fridge! JB's flickering and flashing eyes were on the ultimate prize which would hopefully be a fresh, creamy and sensuous five star dessert... Sex with the B-ster. She put both plates down on the table, giving JB half of the roast chicken, seasoned with herbs and spices, filled with stuffing, lemon and limes with garlic cloves wedged in here and there to give it more of a kick.

'I hope you like it. Let me get the gravy and mint sauce. Ooooops, I forgot to bring you the glass of red.'

'Yeah, mi mouth's a bit dry, I tought I was missin' someting'?!'

'Don't be cheeky, otherwise you will be summoned to a ceremonious beasting!' she chuckled.

'Should dat be grilled, poached, baked or jus old fashioned roastin'?'

'Hush ya mout now man,' she responded in her imitation West Indian lilt.

It made JB laugh. 'Not bad for a European lady. Ya missed out di teeth suck dough. Try it!'

She practiced sucking her teeth.

'Is that better?'

'Jus imagine ya suckin' a sweet, tryin' to take all di remainin' bits o sugar out. Like dis...' he sucked his teeth with tongue squeaking frenzy.

Bethany tried again.

'Ows dat now man? Can dis average l'il white girl suck wi di best o dem?' she asked in her accent again.

'Dat's alot better. I'll be di judge o ya suckin' sexploits!'

'Did I just hear you correctly?'

'Of course ya did. I said suckin' exploits!' he said winking.

'Don't play games with me Mister. Didn't you say sexploits?'

'Boooooooy... Ya imagination's runnin' away wid ya!'

In her mind she was curious as to how could he, would be between the sheets. She envisaged him being a real Casanova. Even though she had a high level of dignity, sexual integrity and restraint, her usual three to four date rule was probably about to be broken. It wasn't as if they'd only just met, they'd been friends for a few years. She put the silver pot of mint sauce and jug of gravy on the table and then went back to pick up the two glasses of red wine she'd poured earlier. They both sat down and started to eat.

'Shall we propose a toast Miss Duke?'

'What d'you want to toast to? Right said Fred?'

'Eh? I don't understand? Dey were a pop group in di eighties,' he responded, looking rather puzzled.

'Right said Fred rhymes with bread.'

'Dat doesn't make any sense dough?'

'Of course it does. Give us this day our daily bread. OK, OK, it's just a new rhyme I made up, you know. like apples and pears, whistle and flute in cockney rhyming slang.'

'Aaaaaaaaah, what an interestin' tought process. I tink we should propose a toast to di beautiful wedder n our virginal meal togedder! What d'ya tink?'

'That sounds just right. Thank you for providing this appetising meal for power and strength, thank you for wine for the blood, sunshine for happiness and this gorgeous man for sex appeal.'

'I second dat, but I'd only give me a six outta ten, but tanks anyway. Tanks Lord also fa allowin' mi di pleasure of spendin' di Sabbath wid one ell of an ottie. Respect! To ealth n appiness too.'

They clinked glasses together and winked at each other. Anyone would have thought JB hadn't been fed for months and he'd been plucked off the street by Bethany and this was his homeless shelter, because the plate was half empty in only a few minutes. He decided to take a breather, which was probably a good idea as he wanted to break wind. That gross act would've been so off putting and repulsive and scuppered any chance of shenanigans.

'Excuse me!'

'Why, what have you done?' asked Bethany.

'I need a quick toilet stop.'

'Run along then. We don't want you wetting your pants, do we!'

He got up from the table and walked briskly to the main bathroom. He locked the door behind him, undid his jeans, pulled them and his pants down and decided to do a she-wee. He sat down.

'OUCH! Dat's so cold man.'

He stood up, realising he'd forgotten to lift up the lid. Take two! He sat down again and let out the most ghastly fart. The toilet water became a jacuzzi momentarily, as the wind blasted into the basin. Thankfully there were a few doors between the living room and bathroom, otherwise Bethany could've heard, fortunately not. He complimented his flatulence with a loud burp. At least now he was wind free, full of sunshine and ready to return to the table. He didn't even want to go for a wee, so stood up, put the lid down and flushed. He made himself look respectable once more, washed his hands and re-joined his date.

'Are you feeling better?'

'Yeah tanks. Much!'

He sat back down and took a sip of his wine.

'Are you enjoying it?'

He puffed his cheeks out.

'Boy, I jus wanna let ya know, dat dis is sometin' quite special! Di food n wine aren't bad either!' he laughed.

'Thank you. Come again!' answered Bethany with a smile as bright as the sunshine.

He wanted to come once, never mind again. He couldn't get the vision of her naked body out of his mind. He slapped his right cheek.

'Are you OK?'

'Yeah, just a l'il ot.'

'D'ya want the balcony door opening a bit more?'

'No, it's alright. I tink I'm jus gettin' ot flushes.'

'I wonder why?' asked Bethany.

'It's probably because di suns out n summer's officially ere!'

They continued to eat their sumptuous meal. It was a colourful spectrum with crunchy white vegetable trees of cauliflower, sliced luscious and juicy carrots, butternut squash and parsnips coated in honey, roast potatoes sprinkled with rosemary spice, rounded off with the half seasoned tasty bird and small Yorkshire puddings. The chicken was so finger licking good, spicy and sweet, the effects of the roasted garlic, stuffing and citrus flavours. They both ate with etiquette and decorum. It wasn't the time for primitive prodding and picking proportions. He'd just managed to avoid blowing the food and Bethany away from the table, courteously excusing himself and fleeing to the bathroom, so his refined manner was attracting her even more.

'After the main course, I have a real treat for you.'

'What is it? Human, wom-animal or…'

'Or what?'

'Or someting sweet, juicy n creamy?'

'I can assure you, you'll be drooling at the prospect!'

'Lord, I can't wait, I wanna enjoy it now!'

'It wouldn't compliment the main course to be honest. When you've finished this, the reward will come your way.'

'Uuuuum, I'm so excited, I'm about to lose control n I tink I like it. Do-do-do-dooooooooooo!'

'What kind of face d'you pull when you lose control?' asked Bethany with intrigue all over her face.

'Wouldn't ya like to know!'

'That's exactly why I asked,' she responded abruptly, smirking.

'If ya lucky, ya may be able to visualise it wid ya very own eyes!' said JB winking.

The dessert was a creamy and crumbly traditional cheesecake with ice cream, fresh cream or strictly solo. Knowing JB he would opt for the ice cream option, as that was one of his favourite desserts, with cheescake of course. Bethany must have heard him chatting about his favourite foods before, or she was just psychic.

The plates were now empty apart from chicken carcass and the remainder of gravy. JB had earned the privilege of being able to taste the mouthwatering dessert, hoping this was the second of three courses and the best was yet to come..Bethany stood up.

'Have you finished, or d'you wanna lick the plate clean and get your teeth stuck into those bits of bird bone, like a ravenous scavenger?'

'I tink I'm all done. Ya can take di plate away now. Tanks.'

'Did you enjoy it?'

'Ya better ask mi belly, because it's rumblin' fa dessert. Don't stop till ya get enough, Keep on with the force don't stop, Don't stop till you get enough!' said JB half chatting and singing.

'I think I've almost had enough, but then again, saying that, I can probably squeeze in a little more!' responded Bethany smiling.

JB was thinking how he'd love to slip something in. There was always a chance, he'd just have to wait and see if fornication occured. Bethany took the crockery and cutlery to the side of the sink and then opened the fridge, taking out the cheesecake.

'What d'you wanna have it with?'

'Oooooooo, so many choices. Any chance of it being smeared over you n me being able to lick it off?' he said cheekily.

'I think it's a bit too early for that. After the watershed may be a different proposition all together.'

'Uuuuum, uuuuuum! Mi belly's a bit full now, so I might wait another couple of hours?'

'It's OK, you can have some now and more later. It's big enough.'

'Damn right, it's big enough. You'll see dat later on when it's in ya face,' he mumbled.

'What was that?'

'I said, I know it's plenty big enough. At least two portions worth!'

'So, take two... What d'you wanna have it with?'

'Tell me what you ave?'

'Fresh squirty cream, vanilla ice cream, chocolate sauce, raspberries, blueberries. Take your pick!'

'I'll plump fa di ice cream wid blueberries n raspberries please.'

'Five star Michelin dessert dish comin' up!'

'If dat's five star, what are you den?'

'I couldn't begin to imagine.'

'Ya defo a six n alf! At di very least.'

'I hope that's not out of ten?' Bethany said.

'Noooooo. Don't be daft girl. Outta five. You're off di scale,' said JB flirting outrageously.

'Geeeeez, you know how to flatter a lady, don't you! You smooth, slick talking silver tongued Romeo.'

'I'd say mi tongue's more golden, especially when mi mout's full o sweetcorn.'

'You crazy man.'

Bethany took a tub of vanilla ice cream out of the freezer, sliced the cheesecake up, took out two plates.

'Would you like a spoon or fork?'

'Can I ave a spoon please.'

'Yeah, of course you can,' replied Bethany.

She took two clean teaspoons from the dish drainer and put them on the medium sized plates she'd taken out of the cupboard.

'I'll sort di wine out. D'ya want anudder glass?'

'Please Romeo.'

'Comin' right up.'

He walked over to where she was standing, brushed passed her deliberately rubbing his crotch against her bottom, reaching over to pick up the bottle of red. He took it back to the table, sat down and filled the glasses half full. Moments later, Bethany came back to join him.

'Here you are. I hope you like it. It's my own recipe.'

'Not dat one ya stole from di supermarket?' he laughed.

'Don't be so damn cheeky, it's my very own recipe. Weeeeell, OK, I'm slightly exaggerating. It's been passed down through the Duke generations. Mi Dad's mum got the ball rolling, my mum stopped it, picked it up, swallowed the recipe, spat it out, but not literally, recited it, put the ball down again. It rolled to me and hey, voila.'

JB picked up his spoon disturbing the beautiful and elegantly light fluffy topping, angling it in to pick up and fly it through the air to his drooling mouth. Right on cue, Bethany was right about the effect it would have! In it went. He swirled it around his mouth and slowly swallowed it. He pouted his lips, nodded his head and screwed his face up in acknowledgement.

'Woucha, I mus say, dat is quite irresistible. Ya right about di watershed, I'll be wantin' some more later.'

'Glad you like it. I used Philly to give it a more creamier texture.'

'I can taste it. I was gonna ask ya if you'd used Philly. It tastes creamy to perfection. Oooo la proverbial laaaaa!' he said winking.

Bethany had given herself a smaller portion than him, as she was feeling quite full after the sizeable main course.

'Do you want to watch a film later, sit outside on the balcony, chat and play cards, listen to music, or go for a walk?' asked Bethany.

'I tink playin' cards on di balcony while listenin' to music sounds like a good shout.'

'Yeah, why not!'

'Are ya more of a Poker Princess or merely a Pauper?' he teased.

'I'd say, exclusively a Princess, I mean, the meal's been regal hasn't it? Unless you've just been teasing me? I sincerely hope not with all the effort I've gone to. Especially with this cheesecake. My Dad's Mum would be deeply offended, if it wasn't to your satisfaction!'

'Isn't ya Dad's Mum ya Granny?'

'For all you know, I could've been adopted?'

'Were ya?'

'Noooo. Thankfully I was fortunate enough to have been brought up by two good parents.'

'Snap, Booyacka sha, people di dance n people dey romance!' JB replied with lyrical charm and a wide smile upon his face.

The cheesecake was going down a treat, a real joy. The sunshine was still powerfully shining through the balcony windows, forcing Bethany and JB to squint every now and then. It was fastly approaching seven thirty pm and JB was quietly subconsciously willing on the watershed, not that shenanigans would occur exactly on cue, without the snooker of course, although pocket billiards was a possibility, if Bethany's hands inadvertently found their way into his trouser department!

'How is it?' asked Bethany.

'It's quite more-ish! I'm really enjoyin' it, although, I could do wid some more ice cream!'

'I'll get you some then!'

'I'm jokin'. It's a perfect portion tanks.'

'Good, I'll tell my Dad you like it.'

'Dere's no reason fa dat, it's only a first date.'

'Hmmmmmmm… I think it's day two, don't you?'

'Oooooops, yeah… sorry, I forgot! We're almost into day three,' he laughed.

'Just another four n a bit hours to go.'

'About di poker, d'ya ave a set?'

'Yeah! It's my Grandad's.'

'Goooooood, make sure you've got a bit o money, because it's gonna be comin' my way!'

'What makes you think I can't play? D'you remember your arrogance at pool, which brought you tumblin' back down to earth when you were schooled by a girl!' chuckled Bethany.

'If ya remember rightly, I wasn't arrogant n did say I tought ya may be a hustler! Was I right?'

'Indeed you were. I was only teasing!' she said before planting a wet and creamy kiss on his cheek.

'Uuuuurgh. I tought ya might've cleaned ya lips first?'

'Are you tryin' to imply I'm a dirty girl, or is it just the way I look?'

JB thought, *'What a sexy n gratuitous sight, a dirty sleazy role play wid Beth playin' di role of a hooker!'*

'Weeeeell?'

'We'll see later won't we!' he said quite convincingly.

'I can tell you categorically, I wash when dirty and have a clean mouth, so there's your answer Mister Romeo!'

'I suppose dat's put me in mi place den,' he mumbled.

The cheesecake was so irresistible, they both had to have another portion. This course eventually turned into a food fight, Bethany being the protagonist, flicking the topping on to his face, with some of it splashing on to his pink DKNY shirt. Ice cream was then smeared on her face, enticing JB to start licking it off. Some ended up in her hair.

'I can't believe you've thrown ice cream in my hair, of all places. It's freshly washed, meaning you're going to have to make amends Mister!'

'Ow di devil am I supposed to make amends? D'ya want mi to turn di clocks back five minutes or jus massage di cream into ya scalp?'

'Much much more than that. You're going to have to wash it clean.'

'Ow can I wash it, am I supposed to lean you over di sink n shampoo n condition it?'

'That's so boring and traditional, you're going to have to use your imagination for this one!'

'Mi imagination ain't dat vivid, so gi mi alf an our to tink about it.'

'You've got plenty of time, but don't think too hard will you?' Bethany joked.

Thankfully the wine wasn't thrown around, as that would've annoyed JB as he loved his shirt and didn't want it pebble dashing. He liked art, but wasn't ready for a modern decor image that looked as if a young child had gone wild and crazy with prime colours. They embraced in a passionate kiss at the table, Beth sliding her chair out and straddling JB on his. He was once again hard and hoping this could be the moment. Her hands were frantically moving all over his afro. She pulled out the hair bobble and threw it on the table. Her yellow g-string was soaking wet, now was her time to be taken by him. She whispered in his ear,

'Let's go to the bathroom. We don't want to be in the glare of the public!'

He was slightly baffled as they were on the seventh floor, so could hardly be seen by any possible paparazzi, it wasn't as if they were famous, but if any sexual voyeur from the adjacent block was desperately panning with a telescopic lense, she didn't want to give them the audacious privilege of erotic snap shots or video footage for self-gratification. She climbed off him, he stood up from his chair, lifted her up and cradled her in his arms, carrying her to the bathroom. The excitement was about to literally explode! He opened the door, struggling as he had an arm full of woman. She wriggled a little, encouraging him to put her down. She unbuttoned his shirt, kissing him in the process, running one hand under the material stroking the sculptured contours of his skin. The shirt was now undone, being slipped off and thrown to the floor. She pulled her yellow vest top from the base and lifted it over her head.

'OMG!' he thought without blurting it out.

Her bra was perfectly cupped around her breasts, what a phemonenal sight. She unbuttoned her hotpants and slid them down to her ankles, stepping out with one foot and then flicking them with the other. JB could barely contain himself! He unfastened his jeans and took them off, so they were both virtually naked apart from a few underwear garments. He couldn't believe that the special moment had almost arrived. Christmas had come early. You definitely wouldn't receive a stocking full of those prized assests, an apple and an orange, but they weren't even half the size.

'Don't think… you can just come… to my place, wash your hands, eat my… food, drink my drink and get… what you want! You have to… earn it first!' she half stuttered as his fingers were massaging her scalp and mouth nibbling her lips.

'I'm like a spoilt child… I always get what I want!'

'We'll see about that!'

His hands eventually skillfully moved their way down to her bra clip and within seconds it was dropping to the floor. He withdrew his lips from hers and moved down to her neck, his hands for the first time stroking her sizeable, sumptuous and sensational twin peaks. Oh, the joys of sexual allure. He dribbled saliva on to her left nipple and then sensually licked, sucked and kissed it, so gently.

"Ooooooooh, ooooooooooh. Oooooooooooooh yeeeeeeeeeeees, don't stooooooop!' she moaned.

The temperature was off the scale. Bethany's body was beginning to perspire a little. Her eyes closed and she was virtually breathless. JB was seducing her with magical maverick mastery, Don Juan-esque. He didn't want to slide her knickers off just yet, as he'd prefer her to take the initiative, because he didn't want to force her against her will. There hands moved in all directions, tugging on hair, massaging upper extremities, squeezing bottoms, stroking loins, you could've probably predicted it with American dollars, South African rand or Great British pound coins. Bethany lifted her hands to JB's chin, held it firmly, continued to kiss him passionately and then withdrew her lips, pushed him playfully in the chest, walked to the bath and turned the tap on. She pressed the button to push down the plug hole and then hit the jacuzzi jets button. The water was gushing out like there was no tomorrow. Beth removed her yellow g-string and JB almost fainted. The view was totally Beth-taking, out of this world. His middle man stood to attention immediately. After all the insistance that nothing was going to happen, this was only date two and already she was naked.

'Are you getting in then?'

He wanted to get in alright, but he wasn't too bothered about the bath, just hot.

'Yeah, comin'!' he said, wondering how she'd interpret that, not meaning to be smutty.

'Get a move on then, don't keep me waiting!'

He slipped off his boxer shorts, thankfully there was enough space behind her, as he didn't want to climb in in front, as she might be slapped in the face by his sizeable member. This time the water wasn't quite as hot as yesterday, so he didn't have to dangle a leg, delicately dip it in, pull it out until he grew in confidence and was ready to tolerate the steaming heat. It was bearable, so he eased his body in, sliding his legs to the outside of hers. He picked up the bar of soap from the dish on the side, plonked it in the water, took it out, rubbing it in his hands to create a foamy soapy lather. He massaged it into Bethany's back with a gigantic smile on his face. She moaned and groaned, her nipples protruding like mini bullets, splishing and splashing her hands in the water as the jets fired against her skin. The water rose to just above waist height, so JB pushed the button to halt the flow. JB couldn't see, but Bethany's face was a picture, she was screwing it up, contours everywhere, in a state of pure ecstacy. The temperature continued to increase, with body heat alone it was scorching in there, so it was exacerbated. Eventually she turned round to face him, this astounding him as it was the first time he'd really seen her stark naked in front of his very eyes. It was actually the second time, as she had undressed a few minutes earlier, but the visual hadn't quite sunk in then. Her skin glistened as the water ran off it, soap suds gathered sporadically over her body. She straddled him, his middle man sliding off her private region inadvertently. A good job as he wasn't willing to have unprotected sex with her, as he had no idea about her sexual history. They'd been friends for quite a few years, but he strongly objected to going scuba diving without his flippers and facemask on.. The intensity continued to increase, frivolously fornicating in an extremely passionate and intimate way, lips juicy, tongues wet, hearts frantically beating, bodies tight, what an interlude. A couple of JB's fingers were stroking her labia and then gently and gradually being inserted into her vagina. The screams became even louder now, pleasing him no end. Deeper and deeper, stroking the front wall of the cavity, her moist juices flowing rapidly until her body shuddered into an orgasmic frenzy several times in the space of about a dozen seconds. Her breasts stood on end, encouraging him to lick and kiss every single ounce. It was as if he'd been let loose in a grocery store. As they were unable to contain themselves, the water was aggressively reaching towards the rim of the bath, tidal wave proportions, their own mini tsunami developing. JB was intent on teasing her for as long as possible, a challenge to find out how much restraint she actually had, in relation to the three to four date rule. After the slow and meticulous foreplay, he was now inserting and withdrawing his fingers at a pulsating pace in and out of her, her orgasms intensified even more, she was clenching her fists and lashing them down into the water. The taste of her body was divine, as sweet as a ripe strawberry, even though he wasn't plunging his enamel in and extracting chunkfuls of her skin, he was savouring the saltiness of it. He couldn't get enough. She was unable to take any more, so she pushed him away and at the same time banged her elbow against the side of the bath, as her vagina once more exploded with incredible joy.

'Oooooh, ooooh, ooooooh, ooooh! OUCH!' she said.

'Ya pussy's delicious.'

'You haven't tasted it yet. It's so sweet, you'll want to suckle it all night!'

'If it taste's alf as good as ya skin, I'll faint no doubt, later.'

'I want you to suck it, nibble it, kiss it and make love to it! Treat it like your bitch!'

'Oooooooo, ya bein' so naughty now. I couldn't contemplate treatin' it like dat!'

'Just do it!' she whispered in a saucy and sexy voice, smiling.

She climbed off him, turned around so her ass was in his face, resting on her knees and hands. The view was phenomenal, he thought he was dreaming. Never in his wildest dreams had he ever visualised this sight, after all the years they'd worked together, the closest he'd ever come to seeing her naked, was without make up, wearing a short sleeved blouse, skirt and exposing her bare legs, besides earlier wearing underwear in the bath. By no stretch of the imagination was she his dream woman, very attractive all the same, but hardly a Cindy Crawford, Karen Mulder, Shakira or J-Lo. She oozed sex appeal without really even knowing it, a very humble and demure woman. He pulled her ass closer towards his face, rubbed his nose over her vaginal lips, feeling the texture, soft and wet with a fresh distinct smell. He extended his tongue and began to stroke it along the lips, backwards and forwards, sucking and nibbling it every now and then. He was in wonderland without Alice, but with the B-ster. The more he pleasured, the wetter she became. As they were in the bath, this was obvious, however, his sensuous touch had a magnetic and mindblowing effect. Her ass began to shudder now, her waist jolting from time to time. He retracted momentarily,

'Don't dip ya ead in di water, I don't want ya drownin'!'

'Just keep on doing what you're doin'.'

It was as if she was his dick-tator! Like most women, she had that magical aura of emitting pheromones that enticed the male species. The water was becoming a little cool, so JB hit the jet button again, Bethany wriggled with excitement as two of them projected into the side of her breasts.

'Ooooh, ooooh, oooh my god, this is out of this world!' she muttered.

After several minutes of stroking, caressing, licking, sucking and nibbling, he plunged his tongue deeply into her passage, pure bliss. The sensation made her shudder and judder once more, bringing her to an earth shattering climax. She turned around and hugged him tightly, a show of appreciation for his linguistic performance. He returned the compliment, although didn't want to display too much affection, as it was only date number two and he didn't want her falling for him. How would that work, Bethany and Jennifer?

'Oh, oh, oh, oh, oh, oh!' he thought.

She stood up, took his hand and led him out of the bath, making sure she turned the jacuzzi jets off, otherwise the bathroom would eventually have been flooded. She took a towel off the radiator and wrapped it around her, hinting for JB to dry her. He massaged her skin over the towel which helped to absorb all the water's moisture. He did the same for every part of her body, apart from her hair which only had a few droplets of water in, not soaking wet as she hadn't washed it, although JB had ran his wet hands through it. He took the towel from her and dried himself, which didn't take long as he had drip dried while focusing his attentions on beautiful buxom Bethany. She picked up a bottle of Dove indulgent nourishment body lotion that contained shea butter and nourishing cream, flipped open the cap and squirted it on to her breasts. It was yet another sexual gesture as she was now wanting to be taken by him, cunnilingus again definitely, but this time craving his powerful, large and sculptured milk chocolate member. He massaged the cream sensuously into her torso, shoulders and stomach, paying the most attention to her breasts. He couldn't leave them alone, totally transfixed by their shape, texture and size. He led her to the bedroom. She lifted the corner of the duvet and threw it to the other side of the bed, climbed in pulling him with her. He squirted some more cream on to her legs and feet, ensuring no part of her was neglected. He was at the bottom of the bed, so couldn't resist glancing up at her vaginal lips every now and then. Her pubic hair was elegantly cultivated into a thin Hollywood strip... Bethany was very attractive, her labia protruding a little and her lips tight reminiscent of a young twenty year old virgin. He creamed her feet softly, which made her giggle as she was quite ticklish. He was extremely attentive when it came to the female species, especially his lovers. He meticulously stroked each toe allowing the skin to naturally absorb the cream's moisture.

'Oh my God, you're a professional. You take so much care, TLC to the max,.' she murmured.

'I don't like to rush tings. My guests are always kept appy by dis jungle afro chappy.'

'You're the guest, not me.'

'I know dat, but you're mi student who I'm caterin' fa!'

'You make me sound like a piece of cake! Catering, you crazy MoFo.'

'Damn right ya a piece of cake. A creamy, scrumptious n moreish gateaux. I like di taste o ya cream too, what kind is it?' he said cheekily.

'It's a special brand of home made. Freshly produced today!'

'It's fresh alright. So damn good, I tink I need some more!' he panted.

Without further ado, he finished massaging her feet, threw the manufactured cream on to the floor, slid himself up between her legs and began his second course of dessert. He closed his eyes and slopped away like a dog licking out the remnants of his food bowl, although JB exuded more class and refinement that tittilated Bethany no end. He opened his eyes sporadically, almost having to pinch himself at the sight of the human Himalayas at the top of her torso. Last week Jennifer, this week Bethany, who could it be next weekend? She was continuing to moan and groan, immersed in pure gratfifying euphoria. It was a comprehensive performance by the afro man.

At least forty five minutes later, JB had her begging for mercy, she was unable to contain herself any longer, the temptation of impending intercourse too much to resist. He slid off the bed and went towards the bathroom for his protective balloons, in other words… condoms.

'Where are you goin'?'

'To get some condoms!'

'It's OK, I've got some in the drawer down there!'

'Talk about bein' prepared eh?'

'I always get them from the sexual health teacher, or from the clinic! What were you expecting anyway?'

'Condoms in your pocket.'

'Noooo, I tought ya might've ad some in di bathroom cabinet?'

'What gave you that impression?'

'It's where di medical equipment's normally kept, so jus a long shot really.'

'Ironically, I do have some in there too!'

'Equipped fa every eventuality den! Dat's what I call, a gal wid immense strategic preparation. Like di Martini girl, any time, any place, any where!' he chuckled.

'I'm not anything of the sort. I just remember when I was younger, the scout's moto, always be prepared! I don't have sex with any Tom, Dick and Harry.'

'Ow about dis den?' he responded pointing to his large erect penis.

'That's a special specimen, attached to an extra special man!' Bethany smiled, laughed nervously, puffing her cheeks out at the prospect of being entertained by it.

JB walked nonchalantly back to the bed, dived on at the side of her, starting to nibble her right ear, moving down to her neck and breasts once more. She was purring with excitement, ready for the dream topping piece of dessert.

'Oo la laaaaa, what do we ave ere den?'

'A woman who needs a good seeing to!'

'I beg ya pardon! What does dat mean?'

'Get a condom out of that drawer and come and fulfill my dreams!' she panted.

He didn't need any invitation, it was now literally showtime! In his mind, he was visualising being in the red corner pre fight, with the Master of Ceremonies introducing him, body relaxed, focused on the task in hand, ready to go to work, but not to Oatmill, to outsmart, class, skill his opponent with some explosive, elegant exhilerating blows. He wasn't going to beat her pussy to a pulp though, but his penis might. His mind returned to the performance in hand, opening the drawer and taking out a loose packeted featherlite Durex condom. He pulled the corner using both hands and gently tore it off, easing out the latex length that was rolled into a circle. He pushed the drawer shut with his foot, climbed on to the bed and slowly slid the sheath on to his manhood. Bethany's eyes were like stars in a moonlit sky, dazzling brightly, lips quivering, neckline reddened, nipples standing to attention. He began kissing and caressing her chest once more, finding it difficult to leave alone, gradually working his way down to the money box of love. He prized the lips apart with his fingers, inserting his tongue in between and resumed. They were now laying in the Kama Sutra sixty nine position. Unbeknown to JB, the condom was flavoured, so she lifted her head up towards his member and started to lick and suck as if it was her favourite lollipop. This enabled her to divert attentions from the mindblowing act occurring below, the fellatio the perfect tonic. It was now JB's turn to wriggle around with excitement, talk about payback. What they needed to make it even more of a sensuous and erotic highly charged interlude, was some romantic soulful music. They were both producing their own music though, with oooo's and aaaaaarghs, eeeeeee's and iiiiiiii's. Vocals without any wind or percussion accompaniment. He was still intent on making her wait, to see if her three to four dates guidelines were just a figment of her imagination or the real deal.

He was making it a foreplay marathon, unlike a large proportion of men who had exclusively selfish traits and whose sole purpose was to ensure they climaxed, not giving a damn about their partner. Women require special sexual stimulation and aren't just an object for male gratification. If he treated her with sensitivity, satisfying her needs, she would unequivocally reciprocate, heightening the emotion.

Bethany was savouring the lollipop indulgence, a milk chocolate one at that, while the black forest gateaux was going down a treat, pure hedonistic pleasure. After taking him deep throat, activating her gag reflex, almost choking, she spluttered out, '

Come and take me now. Enough's enough!'

His pupils dilated with joy, inserting his tongue even deeper while frantically stroking her clitoris, until she held on to the bed sheets, clenching her fists as once more her body shuddered to yet another earth shattering orgasm.

'STOP, STOP!'

With this, he nibbled a little more, this inducing a jet stream of juice into his mouth. What an incredible, irresistible and insanely illicit encounter, phenomenal and Beth-taking! When her body started to relax again, he turned himself around to face her so they were in the conventional missionary position. He slapped his penis against her clitoris, which she was unable to handle, as that erogenous zone was now too sensitive. She slapped him around the face, quite powerfully in an erotic manner, encouraging him to slip it in, as she felt the prelude was now over and craved him uncontrollably. At last, what she'd been waiting for, as hungry as he had been for her Sunday roast, this was it! In he slid, Bethany groaning with unadulterated pleasure, forwards and backwards, rotating himself around the clock and then the other way. This is what he'd been waiting for, Waterfront Apartment number seventy seven paradise. It was as erotic and as passionate as the scenes from box office hits such as Basic Instinct and Nine and a Half Weeks, almost triple x-rated. They changed positions with her then riding him like a showjumping jockey, bent over the top of him with her breasts swinging, sliding backwards for even deeper penetration until she climaxed again. JB knew how to hit the right spot like a clinical potent assassin.

'OMG, that was gooooood.'

'Ow about di ride?'

'That was awsome!'

'I'd call dat a rivetin' porn star performance!'

'By me or you?'

'I didn't tink I was auditionin' fa a role, were you?' he joked while pulling her into his chest and planting a sensuous kiss on her lips.

'I'm an amateur, not quite up to those Adult Movie roles!'

'Let's jus say, I'm ya mentor den! Ha, ha, haaaaaaa!'

'D'you want spanking young man?'

She rolled him over so he was now on top of her and smacked his bottom as hard as she could.

'Ooooooow! Ya need to learnt to it arder dan dat. Was dat a playful smack?'

'I'll give you playful.'

This time she used her stronger right hand, it crashing down onto his left butt cheek.

'Aaaaaaaaargh! Aaaaaaaaargh! You devil child. Why d'ya need to be so cruel?' he said wincing.

'You should know the devil wears Prada and I'm playin' the role of Cruella Deville. Ha, ha, ha, haaaaaaaaaaa!'

'Prada? More like lard-er!'

'I'll give you some credit, that performance was quite R.A.D.A.!'

'So was ya dinner!'

'What does that mean?'

'Ya Sunday roast was a five star performance. Not theatrical, but practical and magical!'

'Many thanks. I'm looking forward to the away leg!' she said smiling.

'Are we goin' on oliday somewhere?'

'Ooooooo, why not this summer time?'

'Old ya orses Miss Duke, we're ardly in a relationship!'

'I mean as friends. We could go as a large group with some of the Oatmill crew. What d'ya think?'

'Dat'd be a great idea, but I promised to go away wid some o mi ome crew dis summer! I reckon we could do it in October poss?'

'Yeah, why not. Bella, Jennifer, Jasmine, Tom, Mrs Jerk, John etc. We can organise something in the next few months! If not for a week, a short three to four day break?!'

He was a little unsure as what could be worse, two fellow teachers who he'd slept with heading off on a holiday! I suppose one advantage was, they may be inclined to a *menage a trois*? It would be quite hard to orchestrate, unless it was a camping holiday, at least then he could seduce them with alcohol and fulfil another fantasy? Would it be professional though? Definitely not! Could it have disastrous consequences? Definitely so! Would it be exhilarating? Without a doubt! Could it jeopardise JB's integrity and position at Oatmill? That was a no brainer! If it was ever going to happen, it would have to be at a house party that didn't involve many of the teachers from school. Realistically, it would be advisable to quit those lucid thoughts. Bethany rolled off him and went to the bathroom, the usual post intercourse impulsion. JB was ready for round two, feeling extremely horny after a marathon debut session with the B-ster. As she wasn't as demanding as Jennifer, he wondered whether they could have a short tryst? It was potentially dangerous though, because if she found out, the Latin explosive volcanic fireworks would no doubt start. His life could then become sheer hell. The easier solution would be for him to be acquainted to that devastatingly hot Latvian lovely who he was desperate to contact. Would he ever see her again? Would he get the opportunity to speak to her face to face? Would a date ensue? The easiest way would be to do some investigatory covert sleuth detective work through the Home Economics teacher Mrs Jerk.

Bethany came back from the toilet, looking stunning. Their eyes met, a twinkle in hers.

'Are you ready for part deux then?'

'Are we gonna ave some more cheesecake?'

'You can stick your black pudding in my creamy gateau! Put another condom on!' she ordered.

He was astonished, as she was so demure, pensive and unassuming at school and now transformed into a dominatrix!

'Can ya pass me one from di drawer please?'

'My pleasure.'

He peeled off the one he'd just used and tied it in a knot, making sure that the runny gooey gunge didn't drip out on to the bed. He placed it to the side of the bed. He was still erect, exciting Bethany, who was finding it hard to contain herself. She split the wrapper, slid out the condom and inserted it into her mouth. How bizarre! That's exactily what Jennifer had done. Had she given Bethany lessons, or vice versa? Was it purely a coincidence? She crouched over his shaft placing the teat over his helmet, slowly rolling it out until it finished at the base. It gave him quite a few tremors. She knelt down on the bed, encouraging him to park himself into the bike stand, which he didn't need another invitation, not that she had written it down on an immaculately decorated piece of folded card with the letters R.S.V.P. at the bottom, excuse the pun, but if a woman was naked in that position in a bedroom, she wasn't wanting to play Monopoly, just Poke(he)r…

With that he obliged. The view was out of this world, her ass being panoramic, but more curvaceous than an undulating mountain range. He ran his fingers across it slowly, appreciating every muscle contour, texture and image.

Once again the Belinda Carlisle massive 80s classic, 'Heaven is a Place on Earth' came into his head.

JB was masterfully fingering Bethany's orifices between her perineum, with anatomical aplomb. He was tantalising her until she demanded once more that he refrained from flirting around the juicy edges and enter the fruitfulness of her fabulous femininity. He thrust himself in to the summit, Bethany squealing breathlessly, as he repeated this at a frantic pace. The sound of slopping and squelching was louder than ever as they became increasingly sexually confident with each other. This interlude lasted well over an hour as JB took her to the point of no return on several occasions, eased out of her until she was begging, before continuing the cycle. This being evident, as the wheels were securely parked, but the chain was well oiled allowing the pedals to pump in perpetual motion. At times the pace was unrelenting and pulsating, at times pedestrian . It was a marvellous majestic marathon of love making of the highest order, as if they were seasonal regulars with telepathic traits of a couple who had been together for years. Conversely, even though they were friends through work, it was the first, well second, third and fourth time they had engaged in copulation.

'Aaaaaaah, oooooooo, uuuuuuu, eeeeeeee, Ooooooooooow, OMG… I'm coming, effin' hell…!' screamed Bethany in total ecstacy.

She had multiple orgasmed once more. JB was behind her, still in the doggy position, having penetrated deeply into her. He withdrew himself slowly, this giving Bethany an incredible tingling sensation, shuddering one more time. His face was a real sight. He licked his finger and blew it, as if to say, 'I'm the Daddy Casanova!'

She couldn't see him thankfully and would've probably slapped him for his act of bravado. The sweat was dripping down from his brow, dropping on to the crack of Bethany's bottom, making her jump and tingle once again momentarily. She was still trying to get her breath back, sweating too, their skin glistening under the spotlights. JB rolled her over onto her back and was trying to arouse her again, but Bethany said she was well and truly knackered. After several minutes of recovery, Bethany implied she was in pain, as JB had given her a ceremonious couple hours of fornication, masturbation and sexual gyration that had taken her to her desirable satiated threshold.

'My word Mister Herbert…That was oh so good! I seriously can't take any more. It's been a while and my pussy's in pieces! You're a thoroughbred alright!' she said, puffing her cheeks out, amazed by the length of performance.

'It's alright ya know. Jus make sure ya ready for di twilight tantric bits o tittillation! Probably a good idea to ave some more food now n stock up on energy resources?' he suggested.

'Honestly Jammin'. You've well n truly broken me…I don't think I can take any more?!'

'Seriously?! If we lubricate ya wi some KY jelly or udder juices, ya may be able to manage?'

JB was extremely hopeful, but in reality he had given Beth a real good old fashioned seeing to. Talk about euphoria, delirium, fulfillment, ecstacy and any other word that described the experience at the Waterfront Apartments. They both fell asleep for an hour as they were knackered after the sexploits.

JB woke up with saliva dribbling down his cheek. He wiped it off with his hand, stood up from the bed and went into the kitchen, looking for a glass so he could rehydrate after a few red wines. He found one in the cupboard above the cooker, took it out and filled it up after running the water cold for ten seconds or so. He pushed the cupboard door shut, as he banged the corner of his head against it, forgetting it was there. He gulped down the water and then refilled the glass. It was still light outside, but the dusk was setting in, as the sunset started to gradually disappear. He wasn't sure what time it was and as he glanced down noticed the clock on the oven face. The digital display read ten thirty two pm. He was about to head out on to the balcony without a stitch of clothing on and then realised it might not be such a sensible idea, as he'd seen Mr Robertson the previous evening. He trotted into the bathroom, picked up his boxer shorts, slid them on and then went outside. The horizon looked stunning, wonderful colours of red, blue and light grey. It was becoming considerable cooler now, as the sun had disappeared, still warm enough though at seventeen degrees, just as traditional summer weather should be.

'Are you quite cosy there?'

JB was a little taken aback, as he didn't expect Bethany to wake up for a while.

'Yeah, jus gazin' over di balcony n seein' what kinda life's goin' on below n all around!'

'That's one hot piece of ass on my balcony! D'you want to take me over it?' she asked saucily and naughtily.

'Pardon? Did I hear ya clearly den?'

'I should hope you did.'

'Was it, sometin' about givin' me a makeover?! I could do widda facial, I aven't been pampered fa months!'

'We could definitely arrange that! I said… d'you want to take me over it!'

'What d'ya mean? Could ya be a bit more explicit?' he responded turning round to see her naked in all her evening beauty and glory.

His eyes popping out of their sockets almost. 'What the…!'

'Did you just use the word 'the'? I thought you only used it for teaching proper English!'

'I do, but you've caught me a l'il by surprise, I mean, jus standin' dere in all ya birthday suit glory. I like di joke anyway!' he retorted.

'I'm being deadly serious! When it gets a little darker, I'd love you to fuck me over the balcony!'

'Can I jus pinch mi skin, slap mi face n drown miself in a bucket of ice cold water! And did ya jus say di word dat rhymes wid cook?'

'Yes, yes and yes to all three acts!'

'OMG, I tink I'm once again in luck! I didn't tink you'd use dem explicit expletives on a Sunday?'

'Listen afro man, if ya want another piece of the cake, shut your mouth and come and get it!' she said resoundingly.

'We can't do di dirty stuff on di balcony! We're both professional individuals n what would appen if we were caught by one o di parents, a fellow teacher or a pupil? We'd be summoned, suspended n probably dismissed!'

'We're not workin' today, we're in the confines of my appartment, so we can do what the hell we like as long as it doesn't bring teaching into disrepute!'

'Meanin'?!'

'To make it easier, give me a second and I'll get changed!'

Bethany moved from the living room back to her bedroom, while JB was thinking, how exciting exhibitionistic and risque sex on the balcony could be. Unbeknown to him, the person next door was on holiday and the other apartment was empty and waiting for a deal to go through. The plants at either side of the balcony would also help to obscure any public misdemeanours.

'I need anudder glass o wine. Dis is puttin' me totally outta mi comfort zone! Lord please elp me n protect me n make sure no-one can see, apart from di birds, flies n eyes o di plants!'

He went back into the living room and poured another glass of red for them both. The bottle was now empty. This would thankfully provide him with some dutch courage. He was far from shy, very extrovert, charismatic, but having sex al fresco in his own country, let alone a neighbouring town to the school he taught at, could be fraught with danger. He would be more than inclined on holiday overseas, but in his own back yard, virtually? He slurped his wine.

'Jammin' are you ready for me?'

He turned round. Beth had walked to the door of the balcony wearing a tight seethrough body stocking and a black micro mini skirt. Most people called it a belt skirt, as it barely covered a woman's modesty. To finish off her tarty look were a pair of four inch black stiletto heels. She walked out on to the balcony with her glass of wine, placed it on the marble table, bent over to take something off her shoe. JB almost fainted. Her body stocking was crotchless and besides that, she was knickerless.

'Lord, please forgive mi for mi trespasses!' he mumbled.

JB was a Christian, but far from devout. He had been contemplating about becoming agnostic. He thought, 'What di ell, let's ave some more saucy, scintillatin' n sensual fun!'

Bethany sat herself down on one of the wicker chairs and started to satisfy herself. Her fingers stroked and caressed her moist lips, eyes opening every now and then, arousing JB with her expression. He walked over to her, stood over the chair and began to play with himself. She moved his left hand, pulled him towards her, opening her mouth, licking her lips and easing him inside. She licked, sucked and spat on his excitable soldier, taking it slowly in and slowly out, relishing every inch. She continued to pleasure herself down below too.

'I tought you were urtin' from di lovin' I gave to ya earlier?'

'I was, but I used some KY jelly to soothe my aching lips. It's done the trick alright!' she said, smiling like a Cheshire cat.

Darkness was fast approaching, as the clocked ticked towards Cinderella time. JB was frantically looking around, hoping that no-one could see their balcony sexploits. He placed his hands on her head, resting as it moved backwards and forwards. Bethany was having a fabulous time and for that matter, so was JB, fellatio at its finest. It was very quiet down below, apart from Bethany's choking occasional gag reflex, a few car horns sounded now and then. Probably taxis alerting their punters that they'd arrived, or an animal in the road and motorists not being aware that the lights had changed to green, being distracted by their mobile phones.

'Oooooo, aaaaaargh, eeeeeee, mmmmmmmm!' JB noisily relished Bethany's sensuous touch.

What a jaw dropping two day and two nights' experience. He would never have expected such an action packed weekend taking him into a second successive dalliance so soon, with a fellow colleague. It was worth every minute, but over the last few years relationships had been a nonentity, as he was holding out for the prized catch. Maybe he should take up fishing, invest some of his hard earned cash on a boat, head out to deep waters, giving him the opportunity to scoop a marine gem. Realistically though, adventuring overseas and scuba diving in the tropical Pacific, Atlantic, Caribbean Sea or the Mediterranean would maximise his chances of the treasured pearl in the oyster. He wasn't short of options in his love life, but he hadn't met anyone that made him tick. In other words, a compatible soul mate. Even though he was a raging extrovert, he'd had his fair share of interludes, but still an empty ring finger. He felt that society put a lot of pressure on his generation to walk down the aisle or run off to Gretna Green or fly out to Las Vegas for a low key civil ceremony. Men were pressurised by their partners, who wanted a ring on their finger as a status symbol, call it materialism, otherwise they felt life was passing them by because their friends were doing it and didn't want to be left on the shelf, out of reach, like an eighteen certificate magazine for a minor. Marriage isn't a fashionable concept, it's for when two people want to consummate their relationship and commit themselves for life. A special bond between two people, love and cherish, honour and obey, sickness and health, richer and poorer... Great sentiment, but what does it mean? One word... BOND, but not as in the Special Agent 007!

JB was inserting himself once more into Bethany, her legs spread eagled with bottom forced back into the chair with the back banging against the balcony door window and front legs lifting off the floor every time he thrusted. His condom was glistening as it slid partially out, the flowing juices created by pheromonal attraction. His left arm was in the air, swinging forwards and backwards as if he was a steeplechase jockey celebrating sweet victory. The view was once again Beth-taking, her fringe sticking to her forehead, her mouth gaping open, goose bumps all over her skin with a reddened tint, the hole in her crotch and the profile of alpha male dominance. He could see the moonlight reflecting in the window and street lights in the distance along with himself, the epitome of the king of her castle.

'Yeah, uuuuuurgh, uuuuuuurgh, take it deeper, yeah, feel ya drippin' pussy, uuuuuuuuum!'

'Oh yeah, give it to me big boy, give me all you've got! I love it! Fill me up with your juicy cum.'

The brief conversations were graphic to say the least. He was so shocked as he'd never envisaged her in this light, or darkness.

'Take me all di way, moooore. Dat's di way!'

'Oooooooh, oooooooooh, ooooooooh my god! It's amazing!'

She shuddered for the umpteenth time, coming to an earth shattering orgasm. Her body froze, startled and hypnotised by the electric sensation. Pure unadulterated bliss. He knew now she was definitely satiated and would probably be walking with an unusual gait in the morning. He would be moving with grace and an inimitable swagger, no doubt. The cat that got the cream. He hoped Felix was behaving himself and wasn't running amok back at the ranch in Honeyville. A strange notion after a blistering encounter. I suppose it was quite apt though, pussy on the lips and even more in the mind, a true pedigree at that.

JB massaged her head which sent even more tingling sensations through her body. He admired himself in the window reflection and the stunning view of Bethany's rear profile. He winked at himself, almost expecting a wink back. Was he confused? Was he dreaming? He was just overcome by his own testosterone, pheromones and the incredible experience throughout one scorching hot exhilarating weekend in more ways than one. Time passed by as they drank more wine on the balcony, laughing and joking, stroking, kissing and caressing intermittently. Bethany's bed was the eventual resting sanctuary shortly after midnight. Teeth brushed and faces washed, their birthday suited bodies snuggled cosily side by side with the quilt pulled backwards as it was a very humid night.

Chapter 43

Training Day

Today was the day that Stacey returned to Oatmill after her car accident involving Joe and Ash. Hopefully she was totally recovered after her whiplash and bruising. They had all been extremely lucky, as the consequences could have been fatal, but thankfully that precious day, a God was shining down on them.

The sun was shining through the curtains in Bethany's bedroom. JB's eyes began to slowly open. It was six thirty am and they didn't have to attend the training day until twelve pm, so they still had the morning to relax. His eyes were fluttering, he rubbed them and then shuffled his legs, twitched his toes, clenched his fists, before flicking out his fingers, rolling on to his back and stretching out his arms and yawning. He turned to his left and gazed at Bethany's nakedness again. He was feeling very wanton. If it was the last time they had sex, or just the start of something more than just that, he wanted to make sure he seized on the initiative, as didn't want to let the opportunity slip away through his fingers and dog's balearics. She was still asleep, as he could hear her light breaths blowing on to the bed sheet. He picked his phone up from the bedside table, then surfed the news to find out what had been going on around the World. He smiled as he browsed various stories.

'I'm so damn appy to be alive. What a precious gift dis is. Dad was so right. I love ya so much. Always tink yaself lucky n realise people are in a far worse position dan yaself. Tank you fa everyting n Mum too!' he whispered.

Bethany twitched and then rolled over, so her pert beautiful breasts were in full view.

'OMG, she's freakin' ridiculously ot. I so wanna bump into dat Latvian gal dough, because she was off di scale man!' he thought.

He pinched himself to make sure he was alive and kicking, although he didn't want to give Bethany a rude awakening with his middle man poking into her stomach besides his feet hurting and bruising her shins. Just a figure of speech or thought. He was alive alright, heart pulsing slowly at about forty eight beats a minute. He was relaxed, extremely comfortable and preparing for the morning after the night before with more of the same, if of course she was game on and not just wanting a post performance bath. He lifted his eyes and looked round the bedroom. He hadn't really had time to admire the decor, feng shui effects and other finer details, because he'd been busy fulfilling his fantasies by circumnavigating her body, around the anatomical globe. Thoughts began to distort his conscience about the shenanigans of last night, predominantly having sex on the balcony in the buff. Had anyone seen them? Had anyone heard them? Would the interlude be the talk of the Waterfront Apartments or was he worrying unnecessarily? Hopefully the latter, although residents or passers by would have some super footage on video or just fabulous action stills for their perusal. Realistically though, being so high up on the seventh floor, the only people who could've seen them were people on balconies above or to the side. Thankfully the appartments to both sides were vacant, due to a couple moving out and another guy being on holiday. Naturally he was nervous just in case any scandal started to circulate. One consolation was that his hair was tied up in a pony tail and not a tight, gigantic mass of afro hair, so if any allegations occured, he would vehemently refute them. There was no reason to be worried anyway as they were in the confines of Bethany's apartment enjoying themselves al fresco, so it couldn't be construed as a public place. She wasn't unduly worried, so neither should he be.

He checked his phone, a way of occupying his time while Bethany was still sleeping. He'd missed two texts last night while he was prior engaged, one from his sister Tyresia and the other from his cousin Jay Mie. People who didn't know him well thought his cousin was called Jamie. He was named Jay, but acquired the nickname Jay Mie as it made an alternative full name. Quite comical, but that's how children's minds work, forever creative and inventive. JB hadn't seen his cousin for a while, so was happy to see he'd been in touch. He was about as reliable as a young child holding an edible gift in its hands and being told by the parent not to eat it. He was a beautiful person, but had a tendency to go AWOL on many occasions like an Alzheimers sufferer lost in a bus station. Both texts were asking how he was and wanting to organise a meet. With the summer holidays fastly approaching on the horizon, a month away, JB would have plenty of opportunity to spend time with friends and family.

'Hhhhhhmmmmmm… Morning gorgeous, how you doiiiiing?'

'Oh, you've woken up! I tought ya were still snoozin'?'

'I was, but I think my mind and body were craving a tall, dark n handsome stranger!' said Bethany flirting.

'I'd say small, wid a spark jungle fro'd ranger! If I were to score miself, I'd probably say I was an average six n certainly no stranger!'

'Uuuuuuuuum… That gives me an idea! Shall we role play? We can meet at a nudist camp and get it on, maybe video it too?!'

'I'm down wi di first option, but filmin' it won't be necessary! I don't wanna find footage of miself grindin' on one o dem social networkin' sites or YouTube!'

'Don't worry, I wouldn't do that. Just keep it for my own personal pleasure!' she laughed.

'We're ardly in a relationship, so dat won't be necessary!'

'I'm only teasin' Mister Herbert, I wouldn't do that to ya!'

JB was a little concerned about the ideas she had. He was hoping she didn't have the same monopolising and obsessive traits as Jennifer. He wondered what he'd got himself into. Two teachers being strongly attracted to him, not that he was going to become involved in a Fatal Attraction scenario, but problems could occur. The easiest solution would be a Mills and Boon love affair with the mysterious minx from the East.

'If I find any videos on YouTube, I wouldn't be very appy n also I don't tink di Educational Authorities would take to it too kindly!'

'Relax Jammin', you don't think I'd seriously contemplate doing that do you?' she replied disconsolately.

'Nooooo, of course not! I'm jus teasin' too.'

'I've got a good reason to tie you up sir and to give you some no holds barred S and M treatment!'

'Ooooooooo, ow I'd love dat. Will you keep di memories strictly photographic dough?'

'No chance. I'll go straight to the papers and taint your image, get a quick healthy buck and emigrate!'

'I'm visualisin' tabloid eadlines now. Tantric Teacher's Tornado Torment! English Teacher's Eloping Encounter! Corporal Punishment! S-Exams!'

'Aren't we being sidetracked? You're supposed to be chatting me up at this nudist camp!'

'Come on den, let's chat wid more action!'

JB stood up, went to the bathroom, squirted some toothpaste onto his finger, massaged it into his teeth, turned the cold water on, cupped his hands filling them up and slurped it from them. He leant backwards and gargled it for twenty seconds or so and then swilled it around his mouth before spitting it out. He bent over and put his mouth under the tap took a mouthful, swilled it round again and then spat it out. He looked in the mirror and said,

'She's gonna get di good stuff again! I'll make sure she walks wid swagger today. Let's get it ooooon.'

He returned to the bedroom. Bethany was sitting on the edge of the bed reading a book, wearing an elegant pair of designer glasses.

'Hi dere, ow ya doin'?'

There was no response from her. 'Excuse me, ya alright lady?'

Still no response. He tried for a third time. 'Excuse me miss, what book ya readin'?'

She raised her head from the book momentarily, turned towards JB and replied, 'It's a raunchy novel about two people who meet at a naturist reserve! It's getting to a really exciting part now. The guy begins to massage her from behind while she's in a seated position on a wooden bench under an apple blossom tree. The art of seduction begins. Care to re-enact it?'

He was rather taken aback by the proposal. He coughed nervously.

'What did ya say again, I tink I miseard ya.'

'I said, do you want to re-enact that scenario?' she said, licking her lips sexily while twitching the stems of the glasses and then pouted seductively.

'If ya game, I'll defo bring mi A game wid me Fancy a game o tennis?'

'Mmmmmmmm, that sounds too good to resist. I'll serve first. New balls please.'

She put the novel down and beckoned him over to stand between her legs, before gently touching his scrotum. She held them in her hands, running her fingers in all directions, which gave him a tingle of joy. His body shuddered, eyes closing, he then felt them becoming very wet and warm as they were eased into her salivating mouth. She sucked on them, occasionally spitting on them, licking and stroking them. JB bent forward and started to nibble on her left ear. Her head shook a little as she relished the warm, wet and arousing touch on her lobe. His middle man started to change from being loose and limp to being hard, pointing due north and being ready for sexercise. Ooooo's and Aaaaaaarghs were softly and loudly ringing out every time that magical spot was titillated. It was a role play of two absolute strangers, talk about almost wham, bam, thankyou Mam. No introductions and Play… Astonishing!

Another encounter was complete, concluding with a highly erotically charged naturalist stranger role play. They'd fallen asleep once more after the pulsating experience. Today was going to be a more relaxing one than normal, as everyone was on pre-holiday wind down. GCSEs and A Levels were being taken, but that only involved three year groups. The itinary would be all geared towards best teaching practices, teacher and pupil empowerment and achieving Success.

The traning day would comprise of role playing and initiation tests. It was going to be an action packed, fulfilling and rewarding day, which everyone was looking forward to. The weather was another summer scorcher, inspiring to most. JB woke up first once more, while Bethany was still sleeping. This time as his eyes opened, it was a shock to the system, as his head was resting on her chest with his lips touching the right nipple. This was erect subconsciously, a sign of happiness and contentment. JB rolled over towards the bedside table and picked up his phone. He checked the time, it was nine thirty am. A combination of intercourse and advanced sleep had accelerated the hours. He got up and went to the bathroom to wash his face and take a shower. He was feeling quite fuzzy after the alcohol they'd consumed last night, so wanted to wake himself, revitalise and rehydrate. He closed the door quietly so he didn't wake Bethany. He looked in the mirror, pulled all kinds of faces, grimacing, smiling, gurning, laughing, pouting and then gave a mean stare while flexing his muscles.

'I feel good, good, good, I feel wonderful, wonderful good, I'm rockin' n poppin' n droppin' some hot n phat musical beats in dis neighbourhood! Yeah man! Oh what a night, late June Summer back in 2010, oh Jammin' oh what a night!' he sang his own medley of musical tracks.

He stepped into the shower and hoped he could manage to enjoy it in peace without Bethany wanting to gatecrash. He'd had his fun and wanted some lonesome time now, without any eye candy distraction. He shut the sliding doors and realised he didn't have his swimming cap, but thankfully hanging up on the toiletries rack was a transparent shower cap. He turned the water on and adjusted it to the right temperature, as it came flowing out at a scorching heat.

'Ooooooooooow! Freakin' ell, what appened dere man?' he screamed out.

He stepped to the side to take evasive action, banged into the side door, fell over, crashing his left elbow into the ivory tiles below the shower basket.

'Aaaaaaaaaargh! Man alive, can someone save me from dis ludicrous eat.' he yelled out while managing to scramble to his feet miraculously without burning himself any more.

He was back on his feet and ready to fight against the burning element. Now, at last the temperature was perfect, cooooooool. He stood underneath the shower head and let the water bounce off the shower cap, deflecting off the glass doors. He felt relaxed now, enjoying the experience. He took a step backwards, moving his body so his shoulder could be cooled, as it was burning after being scalded by the initial water gush.

'Ooooooooooo, ooooooooo-oooooo, oooo-oooo-who, oooooo-ooooo-who, don't worry be appy, don't worry be appy!' he sang in full voice.

He spent a good twenty minutes in the shower, soaping, scrubbing and replenishing his skin. He drank some of the water, as it was cold enough, but checked to make sure there wasn't any limescale on the shower head before hand. That felt much better, even though it wasn't a more invigorating sparkling bottled version, Honeyville's hard water was enriching enough with its mineral content. He breathed a huge sigh of relief that his showering experience was over without sustaining any serious injury, as he could've been whisked down to Lillyford Park Hospitals A and E unit with concussion, first degree burns and a dented ego. He couldn't believe he'd fallen over in the cubicle after scalding himself, he wasn't wanting to self harm, as he didn't need to cry for help with his life swimming smoothly, armbands off, speedos on, goggles tight. He turned off the water, shook his skin reminiscent of a dog self drying after a plunge in a waterway, slid open the doors and stepped out, took the towel off the radiador and rubbed away. Hopefully he wasn't going to be hung out to dry by the Education Services for being caught with his pants down and penis out by a prying photographic potent lense. It was still on his mind, especially now in the cold light of the day, the morning after with a clearer more rationally thinking head.

The bathroom door opened,

'Good morning loverboy. What a beautiful wake up vision. Mister Herbert in all his morning glory!' she said greeting him, smiling as she lifted up the towel for a closer look.

'Well, ello dere Ms Duke, ow ya doin' n feelin' after an action packed weekend?'

'I'm great thanks. Just need to take a shower to freshen myself up.'

She was stark naked also, a most attractive aesthetic addition to the ivory bathroom.

'Dat shower's bootiful, di prrrrrfect tonic after a swelterin' ot night. Many tanks fa di ospitality, it's been a sexperience n tree quarters... Di company's been decent too!' he said laughing.

'Watch your mouth you. I think you should scrub my back and make amends for that disrespectful comment!'

'I was biggin' you up, I'd never be insultin' n ungrateful! I forgot to compliment you on di food too. Dat was off di richter scale!'

'You're forgiven. Help yourself to breakfast and make me some too.'

'Lord, talk about bein' dominant n trowin' down di gauntlet!'

'Whose roof is it? Whose sofa is it? Whose food is it? Whose bed is it and whose body is it?'

'What ya tryin' to say?'

'I'm not trying, I'm just telling YOUUUUU! Thanks for being so understanding sir!'

'My pleasure ya ighness!'

She hugged him, kissed him on the lips, and smacked his bottom.

'OUCH! What was dat for?'

'You know full well why!' she replied chuckling.

He had a small red handprint on his left buttock. An artist would've been proud of the conceptualism of the piece. A red hand print, the image of Bethany's disdain and JB's pained expression, but ultimately the thought provoking idea behind it, excusing the pun!

'Because I deserved it!'

'At last, for once, you've acknowledged your bad behaviour. Naughty boy!'

He nodded, smiled and walked to the bedroom to get dressed. He checked his overnight bag and realised he hadn't brought any cocoa butter, so had to use Bethany's Dove nourishing body lotion instead. It was on the side still, so he flipped the cap and squirted away. On his chest, stomach, arms and legs and massaged away, allowing his skin to absorb the sweet smelling moisture. He put some on his face too, as it was quite dry, rubbed the remainder over his hands, finito. He got dressed and went into the kitchen to prepare breakfast for them both. He browsed through the cupboards looking for a whole hearty breakfast.

'What should we eat? Sometin' rich in protein, fibre wid a l'il carbohydrate!'

He found half a loaf of seedy wholemeal bread that was pre sliced, half a dozen eggs, a tin of baked beans, fresh ripened tomatoes and mushrooms that were chilling in the fridge. It was just what the doctor ordered.

Cooking breakfast was in full swing when Bethany put her head round the door.

'Hello there Mister Herbert, how you doing?' asked Bethany.

'I'm good tanks. Just makin' sure di brekkie's comin' along smoothly.'

'It smells goooooood, just like your body, good enough to eat!' she said and then purred like a feline.

'Ya not gonna go into carnivore mode again are ya?'

'Noooo, not yet, but maybe before we have to leave for school!'

'Ha haaaaaaa. Jus make sure ya don't draw blood! I don't want any questions bein' asked.' he said hoping to discourage her from any more shenanigans.

He had forgotten something. The vine ripened tomatoes and mushrooms were still at the side of the hob in their plastic containers. He picked up both and ran them under the cold tap to wash away any posible pesticides still present. He took the chopping board from behind the dish drainer and a sharp knife from the drainer. The tomatoes were sliced in half along with the mushrooms. He removed some dirty residue on the mushrooms by hand and then re-washed them.

'Where's di kitchen foil Ms Duke?'

She walked behind him, hugged his waist before blowing and then nibbling his left ear. It sent a shiver down his spine.

'I'll get it for you.'

She opened the cupboard next to the washing machine and took out the foil.

'Can you pull me some off please?'

'I could pull something else off if you like lover boy? Miaaaaaaaooooooooow!'

'Jus foil tank you.'

'Ooooooo, someone's moody!'

'I'm not moody, I jus wanna provide ya wid a top quality Monday mornin' brekkie of ya dreams!'

'That's more like it.'

She tore a piece large enough to place over the grill tray in the oven.

'Tanks!'

He opened the oven and pulled the tray out quickly without burning his hands. He drizzled a small amount of olive oil onto the foil, before putting the foil on top, stood up, picked up the chopping board and carefully put the tomatoes and mushrooms on the grill tray. He pushed it in and closed the door.

'Could you sort out di toast please.'

'Of course I will. What do you want to drink? A Bloody Mary, glass of red, herbal tea, water, juice…'

'Just a glass o water please.'

Bethany took some ice cubes out of the freezer, putting a handful into two large glasses and then filled them up with sparkling water. She took the glasses to the dining table along with cutlery and condiments. Breakfast was just about ready to be served.

'Did you sleep well?'

'Yeah, like Goldilocks wi di tree bears. Dat beds so comfy.'

'Yeah, I know. I love it! I better sort out the holy ghost.'

'What's dat? Ave you a few spirits livin' in ere or is it di vodka n rum?'

'Very funny! Ha haaaa haaaaaa. It's the toast!' she replied sternly.

'Please excuse me. I feel quite delicate dis morn. Must've been di night of mind blowin' proportions!' he said winking.

'I'd say it was quite a special one.'

He checked on the tomatoes and mushrooms. They were just about done. The beans were bubbling away, so he turned the heat off and put them on the spare back hob next to the scrambled egg.

'Showtime! Let's get ready to rumble!'

'I'll rumble with you any day Mister, as long as you don't blow me away!'

'I'll try not to. I'll jus eat up ya body, mind n soul wid a volcanic eruption!' he said laughing.

'Uuuuuuuuum… I love the sound of that! I thought I was the canníbal though?'

'You are. I said eat up n not eat up!'

'That's the same thing!'

'No, ya need to listen to di pronunciation, it's different! Listen…'

'I'm doin' that. You haven't said anything'?'

'I'm gonna eat it all up. I'm feelin' a l'il cold ya know, I need eatin' up! Get it?'

'Aaaaaaaah, now you're makin' sense!' Teased Bethany.

He continued with breakfast preparation, stirring the baked beans to make sure they didn't stick to the pan. Bethany passed him two plates for the food. He opened the oven door once more. The tomatoes and mushrooms were done, so he put on an oven glove, turned the heat off, pulled the tray out and carefully spooned each item on to the plates and then returned the tray to its rightful place. Smearing olive oil onto the foil ensured the vegetables wouldn't stick to it. The toast was also ready, so JB smeared margarine on each slice, spooned on beans and scrambled egg. The sunshine breakfast was now ready to EAT as in consume. It had been H-EAT-ED up, but the lack of meat meant it wasn't attractive to a carnivore. To the relief of JB and Bethany, there weren't any real cannibals in the vicinity of number seventy seven the Waterfront. PHEEEEEEW! JB took the delights to the table, he and Bethany tucked in.

'This is just what I need first thing on a Monday morning! I could do with something else too though.' she said licking her lips and the tomato sauce that was lying on her upper lip.

'What's dat Ms Duke?'

'Some hearty wholesome morning sausage. A bratwurst, just like the one I had last night!'

'I didn't tink about dat. D'ya ave any in di freezer?' he replied pretending not to hear the anecdote.

She put her right hand on his crotch and gave it a squeeze.

'That's the one I was talking about!'

He grimaced, although she couldn't see as he'd turned his head to the right. He was concerned that despite an innocent, highly charged sexually gratifying and explicit weekend rendez-vous, the hallmarks of Jennifer were beginning to become apparent. He had to continue to play it super cool, hoping that this would cool down without blatantly spurning their advances. They chatted at the table about their interests, their ambitions and other general chit chat. They drank orange juice and sparkling water with ice, as the time passed by. Bethany was being flirtatious again, trying to coax JB into one last hoorah.

'Oooo, I'd love to B-ster, but it's ten past eleven n we need to be at school in fifty mins!'

'Oh my Bloody Marys, I didn't even realise the time. At least someone's switched on! Next time, eh?'

'Sounds like a plan.' he answered, sounding convincing.

'Leave the pots, I'll do them later. I'll load the dishwasher. That's what I call a breathtaking breakfast, thanks!'

'I tink ya bein' a l'il dramatic.'

'I do teach performing arts, Jammin'!'

'I'd say it was quite mouthwateringly Beth-takin'!'

'Ha haaaaaaa. Good use of English language Mister Herbert. Lovely play on words.'

They both got up from the table, taking pots, cutlery and condiments to the kitchen. JB went into the bedroom to pick up his night bag, carried it to the bathroom and took out his toothbrush to customary morning clean. Bethany cleaned up the mess at the table and sprayed detergent all over the work tops after loading the dishwasher.

JB's phone vibrated in his pocket. He took it out and checked it. It was a message from Ash. He opened it.

'Yes my brother, just a quick one. Happy not so manic Monday. You know the hot nurse from Lillyford Park Hospital whose digits I got last week, we're gonna get it oooooooooon. I have a date this Friday! ;-) Woooooohoooooo.X'

JB smiled. Apparently she was damn hot. A foxy petite bobbed French nurse, oo la laaaaaaaaa! JB put the phone back in his pocket and turned on the vibrating oscillating tooth cleaner after splodging a pea sized amount on. Bethany, dressed in a pair of skimpy blue hot pants and tight white vest top was singing as she came into the bathroom to join him. She brushed her teeth, they were side by side, both looking in the mirror, a moment of true original Vanity Fair. Foamy paste mixed with water dribbling down their chins, such an unattractive sight. Bethany kept bumping her waist into JB which was beginning to annoy him. She didn't say anything, apart from gargling speech and body language that was rather transparent. He wasn't inclined to indulge in a passionate quickie, as he'd savoured his weekend fill. He finished brushing his teeth and then washed the fluoride gunge off his face and then cleaned it on the towel hanging over the radiator.

'I'm gonna ave to ead off Beth, because I need to check on mi cat before di trainin' day starts.'

'Oooooh, that's a real shame, I thought we could have driven in together and then come back here for some early evening frivolity?'

'If I wasn't so busy tonight, I'd ave accepted ya invitation, so I'm sorry about dat!' he replied, relieved in his mind, as he was concerned about her eagerness.

She finished brushing her teeth, washed her face too and then gracefully moved towards him, pulling herself into his body, thrusting her pelvis forward, planning a sensuous kiss on his lips. He was quite taken a back, his loins becoming warm again as a strong rush of blood filled up his penis. He had to pull himself away, as it was time to vanish.

'Jammin', I thought we could…'

'We could what? Dance di foxtrot ot maybe a pasa doble?'

'Mmmmmmm… That'd be a start. I was thinking more of some more bedroom gymnastics.'

'Unfortunately Ms Duke, di clock's run out n Mister Erbert as to get a wriggle on.'

'Hhhhhmmm, I suppose Ms Duke should too,' she responded in a resigned manner.

He kissed her on both cheeks, continental style, forever the gentleman, then hugged her tightly and moved backwards.

'See you in forty odd minutes. Many tanks for a truly irresistible weekend. It was worth every penny.'

'Oh, charming! You make me sound like a hooker!'

'I'd say more of a scrum arf or stand off!'

'What are they?'

'Dey're Rugby League positions!'

He picked up his overnight bag, moved into the hallway and put his light blue American Eagle hoodie and black Allstars boots on.

'See ya Jammin'.'

'Take care Beth. See ya soon.'

He shut the door and went down to the car park to collect his car and drove home.

Chapter 44

Latvian Lust

JB arrived at Oatmill High at a minute to noon. He was so relieved that Felix hadn't left a trail of destruction back at 33 Mysterious Street in Honeyville. The house had been left spotless, apart from a few balls of fur that he'd vomited out. As the outside world had been out of reach for a night, he'd had to be content with cleaning his stomach out by chewing and swallowing particles of his fur. Cats regularly clean out their stomachs by eating grass, which acts as a dental floss, also helping to produce bile to empty their gut.

Back at Oatmill, JB walked in through the main reception and headed for the staff room. He pulled the handle and pushed open the door, without any awkwardness, as nobody was coming out at the same time.

'Good avo all, ow ya doin'?'

'Great thanks Jammin'!' said Jasmine.

'*Fabulosa gracias*,' replied Jennifer.

'Fantastic thanks Mister Herbert. I had such a super weekend over at my sister's. Isn't that where you live Ms Duke?'

'Where's that Mister Robertson?'

'At the Waterfront Apartments in Mangoville.'

'Yeah, that's where I live, how did you know?'

'I heard you talkin' about it a while ago. What a coincidence. It's a shame we didn't bump into you, we could've had a drink!'

'I was really busy this weekend and didn't spend too much time at home.'

'Thaaat's really strange, because I thought I saw you?'

Bethany's heart started to beat frantically and her face began to turn a light shade of red. In other words, she was blushing.

'Did you?' she answered a little dumbfounded.

'Noooo, I'm just pullin' your leg.'

She put her head in her hands momentarily, mighty relieved that she hadn't been seen with JB in the lift. JB was totally oblivious and found the whole escapade amusing.

'Where's Stacey?' said JB, trying to change the subject.

'She's definitely coming. I spoke to her yesterday,' said Annabelle.

'Mister Herbert!'

'Yes Mister Robertson.

'As you can see, we're a few teachers short at the moment, one being Mrs Jerk. Can you go and see her in my office please!'

'Of course I can!' he answered.

JB was perplexed, wondering exactly what Mrs Jerk wanted to see him about. Why wasn't she in the Home Economics room? Why couldn't she speak to him in the staff room? He was certainly about to find out. He left the staff room and walked down the corridor to Mister Robertson's room. He was curious, wondering if she had some West Indian recipes for him. Was Miss Latvia there, having travelled over from Riga? Had he offended her unintentionally recently? Was it a setup and Mr Robertson had seen him and Bethany having sex on the balcony last night? What in the world could it be? He reached the door and knocked.

'Come in!'

He opened the door.

He was in total shock.

'Mister Herbert, are you OK?'

'Huh?'

He'd fainted and fallen on the floor. Thankfully the Latvian lady had just about managed to break his fall, preventing him from breaking any bones. He would most probably have cracked his head open and suffered other cuts and bruises, if it weren't for her swift response.

'Mister Robertson, Mister Robertson?' called out Mrs Jerk softly.

The Latvian lady had taken an ice pack out of the first aid box. It was one of those that froze when you crack a small sack inside it. A superb invention. They had lifted him up into a seated position. Mrs Jerk was kneeling behind him, propping him up, while the Latvian lady was holding the ice pack to his forehead. The door opened.

'What's happened here?'

'Mister Herbert just fainted Mister Robertson.'

'Deary, deary me. Who could've Adam and Eved it!'

'Sorry?' replied the Latvian lady.

'My apologies, what's your name?'

'Kiki.'

'Sorry Kiki. It's cockney rhyming slang for, who would've believed it!'

'Cockney rhyming slang? Huuuh!' answered Kiki, slightly puzzled.

'It's a dialect from London.'

'Ooooh. Interesting!'

'I'll leave you ladies with this handsome gentleman. Please don't take advantage of him though. He's a wee bit weak and in need of some TLC. We'll get started in twenty minutes, we're just having a few drinks in the staff room. Try not to be too long!'

'We won't,' said Mrs Jerk.

Before he left, Mr Robertson and the two ladies helped Mr Herbert on to a chair, to make him more comfortable, loosened his clothing and gave him a cup of water from the ice cold dispenser in his room.

'How many fingers?' asked Kiki, holding up three in front of his eyes.

'Two.'

She was wearing a white blouse with the top two buttons open, so he could see the top of her cleavage. That was distracting, so he wasn't really paying any attention to her fingers.

'I think you need a few more minutes to cool down. You're still disorientated.'

'Pleased to meet ya Kiki.' he said, giving his hand to her.

She responded,

'Pleased to meet you too.'

'What appened?'

'You walked through the door, stood looking weird for a few seconds, andthen fell into my arms! Can you imagine, FYI, SYN, seriously.' she said laughing.

'Geeeeez! Ow embarassin'!'

'Are you gonna ask him, Kiki?'

'Ask him what?'

'Weeeeell… Use your imagination!' hinted Mrs Jerk.

'Ooooh yes, sorry. Would you like to go out for dinner? My treat!'

'I'd love to!' replied JB.

THE END